Conversations with My Ancestors

Conversations
with My Ancestors

The Story of a Jewish Family in Hungary

Andrew Sanders

gefen
publishing house
JERUSALEM ◆ NEW YORK
Est. 1981

Cover Design and Typesetting by S. Kim Glassman

ISBN: 978-965-229-501-9

1 3 5 7 9 8 6 4 2

Gefen Publishing House, Ltd.
6 Hatzvi Street
Jerusalem 94386, Israel
972-2-538-0247
orders@gefenpublishing.com

Gefen Books
600 Broadway
Lynbrook, NY 11563, USA
1-800-477-5257
orders@gefenpublishing.com

www.gefenpublishing.com

Printed in Israel   *Send for our free catalogue*

For Zsuzsi

Two men who live in different places,
   or even in different generations,
      may still converse.
For one may raise a question,
   and the other,
      who is far away
      in time or in space,
   may make a comment
      or ask a question
      that answers it.

So they converse
   but no one knows it
      save the Lord,
   who hears and records
   and brings together
      all the words of men,
   as it is written:
      "They who fear the Lord
         speak to one another,
         and the Lord hears them
         and records their words in His book."
      (Malachi 3:16)

                    –Rabbi Nachman of Bratslav

Contents

Preface

This is the story of how a small tribe of Jews in Moravia found the best place in the world. How they were encouraged to move to Hungary, how they were given increasing opportunities to grow, prosper and be free; and how in turn they made a primitive and backward country into a beautiful, modern, successful, thriving land.

And how they were then murdered.

Three hundred thirty years ago there were practically no Jews left in Hungary. The few who lived there before 1680 either escaped with the retreating Turks or were massacred by the victorious Austrians. Yet by 1910 there lived nearly one million Jews in the country. Almost all of these were the descendants of several thousand families, who immigrated to Hungary in the eighteenth and nineteenth centuries from Bohemia and Moravia, western and eastern parts of today's Czech Republic, and from Silesia and Galicia, western and eastern parts of southern Poland.

In 1726, the emperor Charles VI of Austria brought an evil decree against the Jews of Bohemia, Moravia and Silesia. When his daughter, the infamous Maria Theresa, enforced the decree, most of the younger Jews had no choice but to leave those lands where they had lived peacefully for hundreds of years and find a safe haven in neighboring Hungary. This book is the story of the families, and particularly of one family, who made the exodus from Moravia to Hungary.

A Note about Spelling Names:

In the eighteenth century, Jews of the Austro-Hungarian Empire were forced to adopt German surnames. Many were not familiar with writing in Latin characters, so those surnames, if written down at all, were written in Yiddish. When the Jews needed to transliterate their names for official German documents, not much importance was attached to consistency. Perusing old documents, a genealogist is used to seeing the same name spelled three, four, or five different ways – thus we have Tausek, Taussek, Tausig, Tauszig, etc. Given names tended to take an even larger variety of forms: Rosalia, Rozália, Rosi, Rozi, Sali, Szali, etc. With the rise of Hungarian national consciousness in the eighteenth and nineteenth centuries, names were increasingly adapted to Hungarian spelling on official documents, thus producing further variants.

A *Very Important* Note about the Diminutives Attached to Hungarian Names:

The names of children and loved ones are usually referred to with diminutives, sometimes multiple ones. Thus Rózsa (meaning Rose) would be called Rózsi, then Rózsika (the most common diminutives are *ka* and *ke*, and vowels at the end of a name were often changed to *i*). The possessive suffix *m*, meaning "my," can vary these names still further. Rózsikám would therefore mean "my little Rose," or "Rosie." Likewise, Andriskám, Lacikám, Erzsikém, and Zsuzsikám mean "my little" András (Andrew, Andy), László (Leslie, Les), Erzsébet (Elizabeth, Liz), and Zsuzsa (Susan, Sue). Ilona (Helene, Helen) could become Ilonka, Ilonkám, or perhaps even Ilka.

And Still Another Note, about Place Names:

To alleviate the problem of practically unpronounceable place names, at least for the English-speaking reader, I have found English equivalents for several key towns in the book. Thus, Nyitrazsámbokrét (in Slovak Žabokreky nad Nitrou) became Zestmeadow-on-Nyitra, since the Hungarian term is very zesty. Aranyosmaróth (Zlaté Moravce) became Golden Morava, which is a fairly literal translation. And Rimaszombat (Rimavska Sobota) was slightly changed, to Rima-Sobota. Other town names, such as Zólyom (Zvolen) and Losonc (Lučenec), were thought sufficiently manageable so as not to require translation.

Acknowledgments

Appreciation is due to several people who have provided invaluable assistance in gathering, sometimes with great difficulty, all the diffuse facts that I just had to have for this book. I thank my friends, Dr. Peter Hidas and Dr. György Haraszti, highly qualified experts on the times and places covered in this book, and Sam Schleman, who has provided highly valuable advice to me. In addition, I want to thank the three researchers, one in Slovakia and two in Hungary, who worked with me diligently, visiting libraries, national archives and old cemeteries – as I have – in an effort to discover secrets long hidden. Further, I would also like to express my deepest appreciation to several friends who read the earlier versions of this book and provided most valuable advice about improvements toward its comprehensibility, style and indeed, the approach to the historical content and its presentation – particularly, to Bill Glied and Giora Leshem – and to my wife, my most severe critic. I thank Mr. Lee Glassman, who has found the quote from Rabbi Nachman of Bratslav, so apt, so moving. And I am grateful for the many, many details provided by my late sister, Susan Timar – Zsuzsi in the book – who remembered everything from the age of six months.

Maps of Europe and Slovakia

Map of Central Europe
Political map of central Europe, showing Moravian Jewish migration.

Map of Western Slovakia
Partial Map of the Nitra-Zlate Moravce Area

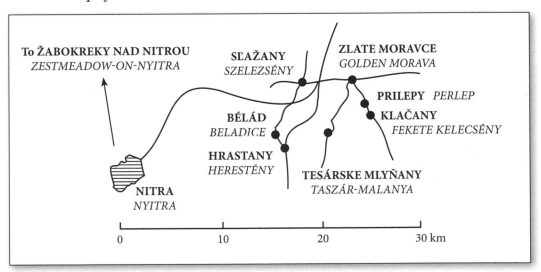

Prologue

A small town in Moravia, around 1765, probably Ungarische Brod. Narrow, cobblestoned, curving street, the houses reaching the sidewalk, entrance by one step up. This house is very typical, with a front room, a kitchen, and a shed at the back. The man and the woman talk while the children run around them, tugging the woman's skirt; she does not notice them.

Man: Yes, we have discussed it after service at the *shul*. There is just nothing that we can do.

Woman: What do you mean, nothing? It's ridiculous, you cannot just accept it!

Man: No, of course not, but what do you want to do? Go up to Vienna and tell the empress that she is an idiot?

Woman: Shh! Don't talk like that in front of the children. They might repeat it somewhere.

Man: Well, anyway, the decree is there, we cannot change it.

Woman: But we must do something! There is Yossel, and Yankele, and Moishe, there may be others yet…

Man: *B'ezras Hashem.*

Woman: Yes, and don't tell me that they will all grow old and won't be able to marry!

Man: No, of course not. They will marry, every child will marry. They will find a way.

Woman: What way? If it is illegal? And also, what about the girls? What about Sali and Sarele and…and all of them?

Man: Why, there is no decree against them. They are allowed to marry.

Woman: And who will marry them? In each family, only one son can marry, the oldest one – well, there will not be enough boys for all the girls!

Man: Yes, well, as I said, they will just have to find a way. Maybe they will marry in secret.

Woman: And have the authorities find out and put them in jail?

Man: They don't need to find out. But you are right, that's not the best way. You know what?

Woman: What?

Man: Shmuel ben Avram came up with a good idea at the *shul*. He said that the children might go over the border to Hungary. They could marry there.

Woman: Hungary? Why, is it not under the empress?

Man: Yes, but it is now empty. There are very few Hungarians left there, after the Turks were chased out, there are Slovaks and other people. The Magyars would probably like us Jews to come there, and the emperor would not mind it.

Woman: That's what Shmuel thinks. Did he ask anybody?

Man: Did he ask the empress? No, Shmuel has many friends, but the empress is not among them. But he heard it from somebody who heard it from somebody. I think it's true.

Woman: So what are you saying? That we should pack up and move to some dirty village in Hungary?

Man: No need to pack up yet, the children are small. But when they grow up, say when the older boys are about eighteen, nineteen, then yes, maybe then we should move there, at least for a while, if things don't change by then. And why do you say a dirty little village? They have towns!

Woman: I can imagine. Towns, with animals all over, no sidewalk, no street cleaning, no entertainment, no music, no stores…

Man: You know what? We still have quite a few years. We could take a trip, or several trips, visit there, see what kind of towns they have, meet with some of the local Jews, ask them about schools and everything…

Woman: How could we afford to travel that far? Just to see?!

Man: Why far? The border is less than thirty miles from here, and then we would find the first large town in another ten miles. We could get there in a day, sleep there somewhere and get back the next day.

Woman: And if we moved there, what about the rest of our family? Are we just going to leave my parents here? My brothers and sisters? And yours?

Man: Your brothers and sisters, and mine, too, have children of their own. They have the same problem, we shall all go together. I am not sure about our parents, they could come with us, if they liked, or stay here, we could always come back to visit.

Woman: I don't like that. I don't like this whole idea. I don't want to move to Hungary.

Man: So you have a better idea?

Woman: I don't want to talk about it. Leave me alone with the whole thing. *(Crying, she runs to the shed.)*

STEINER

Bernát Steiner

Meeting Grandfather

"Rózsikám, do we have any coffee left?"

"There is a little still, Apuska."

"And perhaps a little bread, to dunk in the coffee?"

"We have a little dry bread, it will get soft in the coffee. I'll get it for you in a minute."

"And then, you can tell me again about where the children are. Andriska and Zsuzsika."

"Yes, Apuska. Wait a moment, the coffee is almost ready... Here, and I'll put in some saccharin."

"No sugar?"

"We have not had sugar for a long time, you know that. Here is the bread. No, it's better if I break it up into smaller pieces. Here is your spoon."

"Let me taste it. Hmm, it does not really taste like coffee at all."

"That's all we have, Apuska. For a long time, we've had nothing but chicory. It tastes a little like real coffee, no?"

"Not at all. And what kind of milk is this?"

"Powdered milk, Apuska. Please understand that there is almost nothing left. We are lucky with this powdered milk, there is at least some nutrition in it."

"I am always hungry. So are you, Rózsikám. You never eat anything."

"Soon we shall be liberated, and then there will be lots to eat."

"You keep saying that. When will that 'soon' happen?"

"Really soon. Just a few days. Why, we can already hear the Russian guns, can't you hear it? Listen... Wait a moment... There, did you hear it? Boom! Did you hear it?"

"I heard nothing at all. But I believe you."

"Yes, they are getting closer every day. Next week at the latest, they'll be here. Let me now tell you about Andriska and Zsuzsika."

"Andriska and Zsuzsika. Yes, have you heard from them?"

"No, I have not heard anything new, but I know that they are all right. They are at the Red Cross children's home, they are well protected there."

"The Red Cross...and who looks after them?"

"Mimi is with them, she managed to escape from the Nazis. They are safe."

"Safe. Good. Good... And where is Laci? Is he safe?"

Quiet.

"Is Lacikám safe? Tell me!"

"Let us not talk about him, Apuska. Not now."

"And why not, may I ask? Because you don't want to tell me the truth."

"Leave it now, please. We'll talk about it tomorrow."

"Why tomorrow? Always tomorrow. Do you think that I am stupid? I am old, but that does not make me stupid. Do you think that I don't know?"

Quiet.

"What, Apuska?"

"That Lacikám is dead."

"One cannot know that. You never know what happens on the Russian front. Last we heard, he was all right, but he had to rest briefly in a hospital in Kiev."

"I don't believe it. Not a word. He is dead and you all know it. You are trying to spare me."

"Why do you say such things, Apuska? We don't know where Laci is. He will turn out well and healthy after the war."

"Zsuzsika told me that her father was dead."

"No, she did not. She knows that you are not to be…that one should not say lies."

"She did not actually say it, but when I asked her, she could not deny it fast enough."

"Anyway, she is only four years old. What does she know?"

"Oh, she knows enough. She is smart, that little girl. She is smarter than Erzsébet was, and she was a very clever little girl, too."

"Erzsébet? But she died when she was eleven months old!"

"Yes, but she was such a clever little child. And then she died. Ilonka cried and cried, for months she cried."

"Well, of course she cried, it was her first child. I cried, too, we all cried."

"Yes, you loved Erzsébet, didn't you?"

"Of course I loved her. Such a sweet little baby. She should not have died."

"You mean Ilonka should not have taken her to Losonc."

"Yes, I mean that. There were good doctors right in Rima-Sobota. Why take a little baby twenty kilometers away, when she was so ill?"

"You know that Ilonka wanted to take her back to her parents. And they had a very good doctor there. Only it was too late…"

"Right, she shouldn't have done it. That's why I told you, when Laci was born, that I would look after him."

"I remember. And you certainly looked after him well. Yet you were a little girl yourself then."

"Not so little. I was already nine years old when Laci was born. Nine and a half."

"Yes, yes. You were a little mother to him."

"And Ilona knew nothing about raising children."

"Ilonka. My dear Ilonka… So many years. And where is Ilonka now?"

"You know where, Apuska. She died four years ago."

"She died. My Ilonka died. My Fanni died. My Erzsébet died. And here I am, at age eighty-two, still alive. What for?"

"What for? Because you are wanted. You are needed by your family, Apuska."

"Wanted? Needed? By whom? Who is this family? There's you, Rózsikám, and that's it. Where are the others?"

"They will all come back. Andriska will come back, and Zsuzsika, and Mimi. And then Gyurikám will come back from Russia, and of course Laci. Even Lenke, your step-granddaughter, wants you. She will come home from France. With her husband."

"Have you heard from Gyurika?"

"No, it is the same way as with Laci… Oh, not the same way, God forbid. He will come back."

"While Laci never will."

Quiet. Crying.

"I saw that wall plaque under the main gate."

"What plaque? What main gate?"

"The brass plate under the gate of the house, on Hollán Street. Where Laci and Mimi live. Where we lived before they took us here, to the ghetto."

"You did not. What did it say? You did not see anything."

"I know; you had somebody cover it with his back. But later on I saw it. I was not looking at it at the time, but somehow I saw it. It said 'The widow of Dr. Something'…"

"So what, who cares about Dr. Something?"

"I care. Because I think the Dr. Something was Dr. László Székely. Lacikám."

"Nonsense, Apuska. It was somebody else."

"Dr. László Székely. How proud we were, Ilonka and I, when he got his doctorate. Our son, the lawyer."

"And how handsome he was at his graduation."

"My son, the lawyer. I always wanted to be a lawyer, but of course we could not afford the money for the university."

"You did not do badly, Apuska. You were the director of the law court in Rima-Sobota. That is a big job, an important job."

"Yes, I know, but I could have been a lawyer myself. Those were different times. It was very difficult for a Jewish boy to raise himself to a high professional level."

"While today, of course, a Jewish boy has an easy life, he can have everything he wants."

"Don't be sarcastic, Rózsikám. Is there any more coffee?"

"Not much, Apuska. Should I make you another?"

"No, let us wait a little. Tell me about Andriska and Zsuzsika. Where are they now?"

"But I just told you about them. They are at the Red Cross children's home, with Mimi."

"Yes, I know you just told me. I am checking up on you. I cannot believe everything you tell me. You are trying to protect me from the cold truth."

"No, Apuska, I tell you everything. Why don't *you* talk to me about things? Tell me about my mother."

"Ilonka? But we were just talking about her."

"No, about my real mother."

"Yes, Fanni. Sweet little Fanni."

"Talk to me about her, Apuska."

"I loved Fanni more than anything. I also loved Ilonka, later, but that was different. Fanni was so young, and so sweet. She was everything to me. And I was everything to her."

"How old was she when you married her?"

"Only seventeen. And she was so young and so sweet and so beautiful. I asked her parents for her hand, and they were also happy for her, and for me. They loved me very much, and I loved them. They were like parents to me, real parents. You know that my own father died when I was only sixteen. And then my older sisters married and moved to Vienna, and my mother went after them with all the other children. And I lived with my uncle then, Uncle Samuel. Until he died. You know that by that time we no longer lived in Perlep. We lived in Golden Morava. That was much better, it was a larger town."

"Yes, I know, Apuska. Should I make some more coffee?"

"It would be nice, Rózsikám. I am hungry."

"There is nothing else to eat, but I'll put lots of milk powder in the coffee, and then we'll dunk more bread into it."

"You are so good to me."

"To whom should I be good to, Apuska? Nobody is left, not here. Andor died many years ago, Gyurika is on the Russian front, Lenke is in France. The children and Mimi are in the Red Cross center. There is nobody here but you and me."

"Nobody. And we had such a large family."

"Large? It was never so large. You never had more than one wife and two children, at least at the same time."

"I don't mean that. In Golden Morava. In Perlep before that. There were always many children there. I had brothers and sisters, lots of them. And cousins. Especially after we moved to Golden Morava from Perlep. I remember the move so well, yet I was only five at the time. Father had a new cart, a large cart with two wheels. And he had a horse. I liked that horse so much. I gave it sugar when we had some. It was a large cart, or at least I thought it was large. It was large enough for one piece of furniture, a table or a cabinet. So that every piece had to be moved separately, on a trip by itself. But it did not take long: Golden Morava was only three kilometers from Perlep. I walked into town often, with my mother, before the move. Rózsika, is there any more coffee?

"We moved into such a different house in Golden Morava. In Perlep we had a small house, right on the main street – there was only a main street, no other. Not even a lane. We were about twenty houses away from the tavern, my father's tavern. I ran there often, bringing him things from Mother. Or Herman took me. He was my big brother, you know, Rózsika?"

"But when we moved to Golden Morava, that was so different. It was a large town, not really that large, but it seemed a metropolis to me. There were hundreds and hundreds of houses. There were dozens of streets, some going this way and some the other way, I mean perpendicular to the others. And our house was not a very large one, but we had stables at the back. And the well was not far. I was often sent for water, especially as I got older.

"In Rima-Sobota we had running water in the kitchen. But that was much later, I was married by then. I got married for the second time in Rima-Sobota. Fanni, we were married in Zólyom, where her parents lived. But Ilonka and I got married in Rima-Sobota – no, that's not right. We lived in Rima-Sobota, but we married in Losonc. That's where she came from, at least that's where they lived at the time.

"And then Erzsébet was born. But she died. And Ilonka cried and cried. But then, later, Lacika was born. And he grew up a healthy boy. Not that healthy, I suppose, he was never robust. But he was a nice, well-behaved boy. Until 1919, of course, when he got into trouble with his politics. That was horrible. Poor Ilonka was so upset, and so was I. But I understood – he wanted something better, he wanted to change the world. Young people often want to change the world. He was not really a Communist, he did not even understand what Communism was all about. And then they kicked him out of all the high schools. Ilonka hadn't cried so much since Erzsébet died. But I told her that I had connections, I would have him in university soon enough. I did not like to say that. Even if one has connections, one should not use them for private gain. It is just not right. But Ilonka cried so much, and it was really unfair to kick Laci out of all the high schools. We wanted him to be a lawyer, and a lawyer he did become. A handsome, elegant young man, intelligent and sensitive. I was always so proud of him. And then he married Mimi, who was just the right wife for him, and from a well-to-do family, too – that is important, Ilonka was right in that. And two lovely children. Andriska is so clever, and so is Zsuzsika. Maybe Andriska will become an engineer."

"No, Grandfather, I did not become an engineer in the end. I had a different career and now, I am writing books."

"Grandfather?"

"Andriska?"

"Yes, Grandfather, it is me. Andris."

"Grandfather?"

"But…but how old are you, Andriska?"

"I am now sixty-seven years old, Grandfather."

"Sixty-seven? Then how old am I? That could not be!"

"Well, you cannot just count the years that way."

"What do you mean, you cannot count the years that way? How can you count it? I don't understand. I am confused. Rózsika? Where are you, Rózsika?"

"Grandfather, let me be blunt. This is the year 2002. Rózsika is long gone, she died some thirty-seven years ago.

"Grandfather?"

"And I?"

"Yes, I am afraid, you, too. You were born in 1862, so you could not expect to be alive today. You would be 140 years old now. It couldn't be."

"Grandfather?"

"So this is the future, I am dead and you are somehow calling up my spirit, evoking me from the dead?"

"I don't know if I would put it that way. This is not a séance. I am not conjuring your spirits from the beyond. No, I would rather say that I want to write a book about you, and I need to talk with you."

"And you think that you can talk with the dead, if that's what I am?"

"I hope so. I need to talk with you, and with my grandmother. I also need to talk with your parents, yours and Grandmother's, all four of them. But I don't know anything about them. You will have to tell me about them, and then I'll be able to talk with them."

"And why do you want to write a book about me, about us?"

"Good question. I have written about times long gone by, about the first and the second centuries, and about the twelfth. And then I realized that I know so little about the nineteenth century, that of my own grandparents, and the eighteenth, when their own grandparents lived."

"Watch it, boy. Your grandmother and I, we were twentieth-century people, modern people, even if we were born in the nineteenth century. Your grandmother was born in 1867, a full two-thirds of the way through the century, and she died in 1940, so she lived the larger part of her life in the twentieth century. And so have I. At least – when exactly did I die?"

"In 1945, Grandfather. Just after the end of the war."

"When we were so hungry. That does not surprise me. So I lived forty-five years in the twentieth century and only thirty-eight in the nineteenth. Surely that makes me a twentieth-century man."

"Yes, of course it does, Grandfather. And come to think of it, your own grandparents must have lived almost all their lives in the nineteenth century, not the eighteenth."

"That's right. Father was born in 1832, and so was Mother. I don't know exactly when my four grandparents were born, but it must have been around the turn of the century. So forget about the eighteenth century, unless you want to write about my great-grandparents, too. I know nothing about them."

"No, I don't need to know much about them, only where they came from and about when and why."

"Well, I can only tell you that they came to Golden Morava, at least to the neighborhood of Golden Morava, to Perlep, from Zestmeadow-on-Nyitra."

"Yes, but wasn't that town close to the Moravian border?"

"I suppose it was. So you think that they came from Moravia?"

"Yes, I am almost certain that they did."

"Could be. I have never heard that mentioned in the family. But my parents spoke German among themselves. All adults spoke German. So did we, until we started going to the Hungarian schools. Then we learned Hungarian and stopped speaking German completely, except when talking to our parents and especially our grandparents."

"So Grandfather, you do remember your own grandparents?"

"Of course I do. My father's parents lived right with us, first in Perlep and later in Golden Morava, of course in a different house. I did not really know my mother's parents. They lived nearby in Szelezsény, but died before I was born. Anyway, that's where most of the Wassermans lived."

"You see, Grandfather, this is the sort of information that I need to find out for my book. I expect to turn to you often for help, if you don't mind."

"No, Andriska, I don't mind at all. By remembering me, you are helping me to stay almost alive. Talk to your grandmother also, she will appreciate that you think of her. She was a good woman."

"Yes, I shall. Goodbye, Grandfather, we shall be talking again soon."

Rima-Sobota Records – 2000

To tell you the truth, I knew next to nothing about my paternal grandfather's family. I knew him well, of course. I loved him, more so than my other grandfather. We visited him and Grandmother every Sunday. Rózsám, my aunt, lived there, too, and we used to have lunch with them. During the Holocaust, for a while, Grandfather and Rózsám moved in with us – Grandmother died in 1940 – because our apartment house was declared a Jewish building, while theirs was not, so they had to leave it. I knew them and loved them, but I knew nothing *about* them. It's frustrating, in retrospect, to think how much I could have asked my grandfather – about his past, his siblings, his parents, about the place he lived as a child and as a young man, and more. He would have been so happy to talk to me, but of course, as a child of ten, I could not care less about those things.

Still, I did know a few things. I knew that Rózsám was his daughter, but not my grandmother's; Rózsám's own mother had died when Rózsám was little. I once noticed that in their living room, in a glass cabinet, there was a pair of small, bronzed shoes. When I asked about them, Rózsám took me out of the room and whispered that I was not to mention them again. They were the shoes of a child, born before my father, a child who had died after only a year. I knew that before coming up to Budapest, the family had lived in Rima-Sobota – that's where my father was born. Rima-Sobota was then in Hungary but later became part of Czechoslovakia. My grandfather was director of the law court there, I knew that. But he had since retired.

And I knew a lot about Rózsám. Her name was really Rózsa, or Rózsi, but I called her Rózsám, "my Rose," and the name stuck; everybody called her that afterwards. She had a son, Gyuri, whom I don't remember ever having met; he was a graphic artist and decorator. But he was away much of the time, visiting his older sister Lenke in France. Lenke was Rózsám's stepdaughter, her own mother having died when she was maybe ten or twelve. Rózsám's husband, Andor, died before I was born; that's why she lived with her parents. I seem to recall somebody telling me that Andor died of a nosebleed.

Grandfather's name was Bernát Székely. He was a rather short, slim man, with a nice, square forehead. He wore a mustache, he had nice, well-kept hair, if somewhat thinning by then. His clothes were always immaculate, he wore a bow tie, he had lots of dignity, and yet he was never pompous, never put on airs of self-importance. His main occupation in those days was reading the newspapers, at least as I recall. Grandmother, on the other hand, read novels, always novels. Always foreign novels, always in the original language. We knew that she had a rather low opinion of people who would read important literature in translation. She was immobile, set in an armchair by the window. She got up with great difficulty and used crutches to go to the toilet. She did not always read; she spent much of her time looking out from her ground-floor window on Garay Street and watching the pulleys move back and forth in the small plant across the street. I was dimly aware even then that it was a poor street, that of the lower middle class, at best, and that my grandparents did not belong there. Yet there they lived, in one of the two apartments in that building that actually had an indoor toilet and bathroom. Rózsám showed me where the public toilets were on the other three floors of the building – in the middle of the outside hallways, near the courtyard. People had to wait for other residents to finish; there was one toilet for about eight apartments on each floor.

Later, my mother told me about her in-laws and why they lived in such a nasty place. She said that Grandfather had had an important pensioned position, but after the First World War, due to the inflation, his pension became worthless and they ended up with very little. Rózsám also was quite poor as she did not work by then – few women did in those days – and of course Grandmother never worked a day in her life. Fortunately, they managed to put their son László, my father, through university and he eventually became a lawyer. They were very proud of him. Later the Nazis took him…but that's another story.

And there matters stood for many decades. I knew an awful lot about the other side of my family, my mother's parents and brothers and sisters. I lived among them, had many cousins – thank God still do – heard the stories of their lives and those of their ancestors. I could draw a family tree with most branches complete for five generations back. In our apartment in Haifa, where we spend nearly half the year, two large portraits look down on us in the dining room: my maternal grandfather's and grandmother's. The reason I did not like my mother's grandfather so much was that he wanted me to become religious and I had no interest in doing so. I was the oldest of ten grandchildren. On Friday evenings and on holidays he would take me to the synagogue, a small Orthodox place where I had to *daven*, to read the prayer book, like everyone else. I could not read Hebrew well enough so I had to pretend while I mumbled, and that annoyed me very much. Also, we depended on him for financial handouts. After my father's death, we did not have much to live on. Mother would drop hints to Grandfather about my need for a new winter coat and such. He ignored the hints, or appeared to, but when business was good, when he made a deal – he had the largest real estate brokerage in Budapest – then he would take me to the most expensive children's clothier in downtown and buy me the coat or whatever I needed. Yet he hardly ever said a word to me. He did not know how to talk to children and neither do I now. He was good to us and I should have loved him, but I did not; nor did I love my mother's mother, who disapproved of us and scolded us children all the time.

But the Székely grandmother just smiled benignly; I think she patted my head and as I recall, never said a word. Her husband loved us, never demanded anything, never took us to the synagogue – for a while I thought that he never went himself. Later I remembered the Bethlen Square synagogue – Rózsám pointed it out to me a few times, as we rode by on a streetcar – as the one that Grandfather attended.

And so I was quite content with my limited store of knowledge until an acquaintance introduced me to a Hungarian Jewish genealogical group on the Internet. Its members were looking for their ancestors and exchanged many messages. One message gave the addresses of the Slovakian government authorities in various areas, including Rima-Sobota, specializing in genealogical information. So I wrote to them, asked for some data about my father. They replied, asking me for some money, which I sent, and in due course I received the photocopies of two birth certificates, that of my father and of his older sister Erzsébet. I was a little surprised; somehow I had thought that the older sibling was a boy.

Those birth certificates gave me additional information. The dates of the two births were given: my father's as I knew it, November 13, 1901; his sister was born on May 1, 1898. The name of my grandfather was given as Bernát Székely on my father's birth certificate, but as Bernát Steiner on that of his daughter's, three years earlier. I had known that at some point he had "Hungaricized" his name, as most Hungarian Jews did, but I had not known what his original name had been. Later I found out that my sister had always known it. The document also gave the Hebrew names of my father and his older sister, as well as those of their parents. My father's name was Yehoshua Zelig, which of course I knew, except that a third word was inserted between those two names, something like *hei, mem, nun* (or *chaf*), *yud*. (Hameni? Hamechi? There is no such name.) The girl, Erzsébet, was called Yehudit in Hebrew. Their mother's name was Leah; I had known that already because my sister, who was born shortly after her death, received that name. Grandfather's Hebrew name was Yissachar Dov, which I had not know known. And the documents gave us the birthplaces of both grandparents: Perlep, in Bars County, for Grandfather, and Békés, which is in Békés County, for Grandmother. Grandfather's occupation was given as clerk or office functionary.

Clerk? Was he not supposed to be the director of the law court? That puzzled me. But then, of course, I realized that if he was the director, that must have been near the end of the First World War, in 1918, at least fifteen years after these events. Pending what I was to find later, there was no inconsistency.

My appetite for information was whetted. I had to find out more.

Erzsébet – 1898

"Grandfather, it is I again, Andris."

"Andris. Yes, my little grandson."

"Well, yes, not so little anymore: sixty-eight years old now."

"Yes, yes. And I am dead and buried for many years."

"Yes, I am afraid so. Grandfather, could you talk to me about Erzsébet?"

"Erzsébet? My little Erzsébet."

"Yes, I know, she was really little. She died quite young."

"Yes, she died. She was not yet one year old."

"Tell me about her."

"What is to tell? She was sweet and lovely. She smiled a lot, she hardly ever cried, except at the end, when she was so sick."

"I suppose you all loved her? Grandmother, too? Rózsám, too?"

"Of course we all loved her. How could one not love such a sweet little baby? Even the maid loved her. Now what was her name?…"

"That doesn't matter, Grandfather. But Rózsám wasn't jealous of the new child?"

"Jealous? How could you say such a thing? Of course not. She loved her very much, as much as Ilonka and I loved her."

"Did she play with her a lot?"

"No, she did not. Ilonka did not want Rózsika to play with her. She thought that she was too rough, that she might hurt the little girl."

"Why, older sisters play with newborn babies everywhere, they never hurt them."

"Yes, I know. I tried to explain that to Ilonka, but she got this idea into her head, I don't know where, maybe from a book. I thought it did not matter, soon enough the little girl would grow and then the problem would disappear."

"I understand. But then she became sick."

"Yes, and then she died. Rózsika was heartbroken. So was Ilonka, of course, and I. Even the maid. Now what was her name…?"

"Yes, and I suppose the little girl's grandparents were desolate too."

"Grandparents. Yes, Ilonka's parents. Her father was still alive, and of course her mother. My parents were both dead by then."

"And Grandmother said right away that she wanted another child?"

"No, on the contrary, she said that she never wanted another. She could not go through that suffering again, losing a child."

"But you wanted another."

"Yes, I did. And Rózsika wanted another sister or brother."

"And the two of you eventually convinced Grandmother?"

"Yes, eventually. Rózsika and Ilonka were very close at that time. For a few years they were good friends, almost."

"But not later?"

"No, not later. Later things got more complicated…"

"So what did the two of you tell Grand— Ilonka, to convince her?"

"It was mainly Rózsika. She said that she could really look after the little baby, she knew how, she would do nothing else but be with her or him all the time, she would make sure that this baby would remain healthy and happy."

"And Ilonka believed her?"

"Eventually, yes. Slowly, she came to believe that she was not so good with babies, that Rózsika had this talent to care for little ones."

"She believed her? It is difficult to picture Grandmother as talking to a girl of eight or nine, and being, as you said, almost friends with her. She was such a formal, intimidating lady."

"Intimidating?"

"Well, she seemed that way to me. Of course, I was a very little boy when I knew her. She died when I was six."

"Yes, I suppose one could look at her that way. She was certainly very respectable, not like my Fanni."

"Fanni was not respectable?"

"Oh, of course she was, a very proper young lady. But she was so young, just a little girl, almost, when I married her. Ilonka was already thirty when we married."

"And Rózsám took after her mother?"

"Yes, she did. That's why they could not get along at first, Ilonka and Rózsika. When Rózsika came back, a few months after I married Ilonka, there was some trouble between them. Ilonka tried to be a good stepmother, but Rózsika was so temperamental. And Ilonka had to pretend…"

"Pretend? Pretend what?"

"Did you not know? She had to pretend that she was Rózsika's real mother."

"Actually, now that you mention it, Grandfather, I seem to have heard about that. My sister Zsuzsi told me once. And did that work? Did Rózsám believe it?"

"Yes, she believed it. She was too little to remember her real mother. So they got along well for a little while, but then they began fighting. There was so much shouting in the house, I did not like it."

"And then, when Erzsébet was born…?"

"When Erzsébet was born, it got worse. But later they became friends."

"When Erzsébet died?"

"Yes, after she died."

"Somehow I had this impression that Rózsám blamed her stepmother for Erzsébet's death."

"Blamed her? I don't think so. Well, there were a few words, we were all bitter about it at first, but then we all cried and hugged each other, and after that they became friends."

"If you say so, Grandfather."

"Of course I say so."

"Yes, Grandfather. I must go now. We shall talk again, soon."

Golden Morava – 2000

Once I received the birth certificates of my father and Erzsébet, I rushed to the atlas to look up the places they listed. Perlep was a suburb of Golden Morava, in northern Hungary (now Slovakia), a good distance away from Rima-Sobota. Békés was easier to find, a sizable town in Békés County, southern Hungary.

Well, the next steps were obvious: to write to the local authorities of those two towns and ask for further information. I knew that in the case of Bars County, I had to write to the regional Slovak genealogical branch of the government. And so, without making a conscious decision, I was deep into genealogy, searching for my ancestors.

While waiting for the reply, I speculated. How did Grandmother and Grandfather meet? I knew that his first wife had died young, leaving him with a small girl. But Rima-Sobota – if he already lived there – and Békés, were very far from each other, a different part of the world in those days. The journey from one to the other must have taken many days. Yes, he needed a new wife, but why one from so far away? Who brought them together? I asked people for suggestions and everybody assured me that the *shadchanim*, marriage brokers, had lots of people from all over the place in their portfolios. Still, I doubted the practicality of that. Perhaps, I thought, the two towns had rabbis who attended the same yeshiva and one wrote to the other about the problem of one of his flock? Or they happened to have a common friend somewhere, perhaps in the capital? This suddenly became an important question for me, for now I needed their marriage certificate and I had no idea where to look for it. In Rima-Sobota? In Békés? In Budapest? Well, as it turned out, the resolution of that question was still a long time away.

In a few weeks, the Slovak authorities – this time in Nyitra, the area's regional capital – responded with news of my grandfather. They wrote a long letter, which confused me a little, but this early confusion was nothing compared to that which developed later. Here is what they wrote:

> Between 1856 and 1876, the following children were born to Markus Steiner and his wife, Rosalia Wasserman, in Perlep:

Pepi, in 1856;	Berman, in 1862;	Matilda, in 1873;
Herman, in 1858;	Juda, in 1866;	Ignác, in 1876.
	Hermina, in 1870;	

The exact day and month of each birth were recorded. In the case of Berman Steiner, the birthdate given was December 8. I remembered that as my grandfather's birthday. Berman was, presumably, the German version of the name Bernát that he used later.

But the Slovak authorities also informed me that they had checked the 1870 census of Golden Morava, the larger town of that area. There, they found the record of a house at 170 Long Street. The residents included:

- Markus Steiner, born 1829 in Zestmeadow-on-Nyitra, Tapolcsány district
- Rozália Wasserman, born 1829 in Bélád, Nyitra district
- Ilona Steiner, born 1856 in Perlep
- Herman Steiner, born 1858 in Perlep
- Jozefina Steiner, born 1861 in Perlep
- Bernát Steiner, born 1862 in Perlep
- Rozália Steiner, born 1864 in Perlep
- József Steiner, born 1867, not in Perlep, but in Fekete Kelecsény, a nearby town.

So now I knew where my great-grandparents were born. But József and Jozefina? Perhaps Jozefina died by the time her brother was born. (Incidentally, in German *Pepi* is usually a diminutive for *Jozefina*.) And Rozália? It is not customary in Jewish families to name a child after a living parent. I was puzzled.

And in any case, how to reconcile the two lists? I tried:

Pepi was not listed in the census – presumably he died.

Herman was in order.

Berman was there as Bernát. Good.

Juda was missing. Must have died.

Hermina, Mathilde and Ignácz were born in and after 1870, so they could not be listed in the census. Fine.

But what about Ilona? Born in 1856, the same year as Pepi?

And Jozefina? She was not among those listed in the Perlep birth register. Neither were Rozália and József! So where did these siblings of my grandfather came from?

After turning it over in my mind I finally decided that the problem lay with my not having access to the details of the birth registers. I wrote to the Slovak authorities again and asked for photocopies of some of the registers. Specifically, I asked for those of Pepi (to find out his or her gender – perhaps

Pepi was a girl who could somehow be identified with Ilona), Juda (to ascertain that his mother's name was Rozália, for he was born in 1866; if his mother was a different woman, then the name of his older sister Rozália could be explained), and of course Bernát – I wanted to have the full birth record of my grandfather.

In due time, they sent me what I ordered; well, not exactly that, but close. They did not make photocopies of the birth registers, but they prepared full-page extracts. Those were revealing documents.

The Slovak authorities hastened to explain that Pepi's name had been corrected to Leni, not by them, but right in the Jewish birth register. And they confirmed that Leni was the same as Ilona.

Juda's mother was listed as Wasserman.

And Berman's record included the notation that on November 14, 1899, he changed his name to Székely, by ministerial order no. 12006.

But still another puzzle. Berman's mother was listed as Roza Wasserman; Juda's mother was listed simply as Wasserman. But Pepi's mother was listed as Regi!

What Regi? Who was this Regi? Regi can be Regina, but not Rozália! Little did I know then that still more confusion was yet to come.

On the advice of one of the Toronto participants in my genealogical group, I got in touch with a researcher in Slovakia, a man named Vladimir, who specialized in helping foreigners find their ancestors. I asked him if he would be willing to accompany my wife and myself on a visit to some of those towns – Golden Morava, Bélád and Zestmeadow-on-Nyitra. We agreed as to terms, time and so on. I then wrote letters to the mayors of those towns, explaining the reason for our visit and asking for their help. I also mentioned in the letters that I would be willing to make a small contribution to some worthy project each town might have. I also wrote to the mayor of Rima-Sobota, inviting ourselves to his town, my father's birthplace. For that visit we would not need Vladimir – the town was close enough to the Hungarian border that if they could not speak English, we would manage with our Hungarian.

And with that we prepared for our trip.

Journey to Hungary and Slovakia – 2000

After visiting some relatives, my wife, Judith, and I rented a car in Budapest and set out for Slovakia. The trip to Rima-Sobota took less than three hours. We crossed the border past Salgótarjan and were surprised by the change in our surroundings. While in Hungary the roads were all busy with trucks and cars, but once we were in Slovakia the roads cleared. There were fewer trucks and hardly any personal autos. On the other hand, we did encounter a few horse-drawn carriages and quite a few people – young and old men, and many old women – on bicycles.

Rima-Sobota turned out to be a pretty little town. Despite the fact that it was a weekday morning, the main street was full of people walking along, animatedly conversing with their friends. We parked in the main square and asked the parking attendant about the city hall. It was to be found one block away, on the other side of the square.

Most people in the town spoke Hungarian. We walked around the square, a very attractive place. There is a bust of the great actress, Lujza Blaha, who was apparently born there. The mayor was not there, but Eva Murarikova, who I believe was the head of the vital records department, knew about our coming, and she had prepared some material for us. We met several city employees, all of whom treated us with great hospitality.

The most important document the department had found was my father's birth register. We had one already, the rabbinical record, but this was the civil registration. It too gave the occupation of my grandfather as law court clerk. It also gave my grandparents' address – 20 Jánosi Street; the ages of my grandparents in 1901 – my grandfather was thirty-eight, my grandmother, thirty-four; and it had my grandfather's signature.

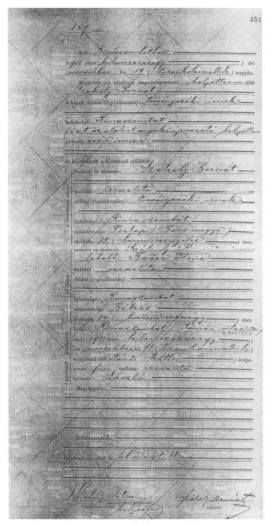

We were told that Jánosi Street was originally named for the village János nearby, and was later renamed Leningrad Street; now it is called Béla Bartók Street. We went to see the building. The nearby houses were single residences, but number 20 was a three-story unattractive apartment building. It is quite possible that in 1901 they could afford no better. Yet some doubt remains about the identity of the street, as there was actually a Jánosi Street nearby. The city employees claimed it was not named so in the past, but they may have been wrong. In any case, all old houses on that street have long since been demolished.

I made a donation toward some worthy city project, in memory of my father.

Next we visited the cemetery. The Jewish section was relatively small, fenced and locked; a local lad opened the lock. It was in relatively good condition; most of the stones were standing and their inscriptions were still legible. I could not find any Székely or Steiner, although I would have expected Erzsébet to have been buried there. Probably a tiny stone in the corner, long obliterated.

We had arranged to meet with our guide Vladimir the next morning in Golden Morava, which was some 160 kilometers away. We could have easily driven there in the afternoon, but since we were not sure about the road conditions we had made arrangements to sleep at a town named Zólyom (now Zvolen), which was about two-thirds of the way there. As it turned out, the roads were in excellent condition, and of course the fact that they were so lightly used made driving much easier. Still, we drove west to Zólyom, passing through another town called Losonc (now Lucenec) on the way. It was relatively flat country, with only small hills in the distance. All around us were freshly ploughed fields, sometimes stretching for kilometers. When I asked about this later, they explained that the land was still held by the *kolkhoze*s, large collective farms forced onto the population by the Communist government and apparently still in existence through inertia.

I had no idea then that both Lucenec and Zvolen would play important parts in the story of the Steiners. If I had taken the trouble to look up the Hungarian translation of these Slovak names, the names Losonc and Zólyom might have rung bells. But then, there were so many Slovak towns; I could hardly have looked them all up. Still, these were the important ones on our way.

Since we arrived in Zólyom early, we had time to visit the nearby town of Banska Bystrica that day. It is a very attractive old town, with many churches. Attached to one of the churches stood a palace built for King Matthias of Hungary. Later we drove back to our hotel, the Poľana, in Zólyom. Our room faced an interesting-looking fortress, but though we drove around the area we did not have time to visit it.

The next morning we left Zólyom early for our nine o'clock appointment. After driving further west on an excellent road which wound through flat farmlands, we reached Golden Morava, a medium-sized town in western Slovakia. Our guide, Vladimir, was waiting for us in his car. As he explained later, he was originally from Slovenia, but had married a Slovakian girl and was now living in Nyitra, one of Slovakia's largest cities. He was proficient in many languages, including English, though he did not speak Hungarian. Vladimir had a surprise for us. At the request of the Golden Morava mayor, he had brought with him Mr. Richard Lamm, head of the Nyitra Jewish community (comprised of about fifteen families, or forty people). Mr. Lamm spoke Hungarian; he had lived in Golden Morava as a boy. He was an older man, short and wiry, very pleasant. Vladimir, on the other hand, turned out to be much younger than I had thought – about forty years old. He was a big, friendly man with a ready smile, anxious to please.

As the mayor of Golden Morava, Mr. Peter Orban, had indicated in his letter, he was unable to be in town that day, but we were very hospitably received by the assistant mayor, Ing. Lysy, as well as by the woman in charge of records. They presented us with gifts, including a pair of engraved champagne glasses and numerous books about the city.

The assistant mayor took us to the site of the old synagogue. The building still stands, and it is recognizable as a synagogue by its shape, but it is used for some other purpose now. We were not allowed to enter (presumably they did not want us to be disappointed by what we would have found inside).

Taking our leave of the assistant mayor, we drove to Perlep, two or three kilometers away – the village where my grandfather and his numerous siblings were born. It is truly nothing more than a small village; it has only one street. We visited an old lady of extremely unkempt appearance, living in a similarly disorganized house, who turned out to be the local historian. She had researched the history of the town and had recently visited Israel. She took pictures and videos of us with her expensive-looking equipment and insisted that we accept several samples from her own handmade tablecloths and laces. Very reluctantly, she accepted a gift of two thousand korunas from us. Unfortunately, she had no information about the Steiner family. But she claimed that there had been a synagogue there, in the building that was currently used as a gym. (When, later, I learned more about the place, I had to conclude that this was highly unlikely: in the nineteenth century, there were never more than two Jews living in the village at any time, and I could see no reason why many more would have moved there in the twentieth century.)

From Perlep we returned to Golden Morava, to visit the Jewish cemetery. It was fenced and locked; the local people did not have the key. They called city hall, who told them that the key was with the Jewish community in Nyitra. But the head of that community, Mr. Lamm, was with us and immediately denied that statement. I borrowed a chair from some construction workers and, with the help of Vladimir, and despite the desperate protestation from my wife, climbed into the cemetery (there was a drop of about two meters inside the wall). The cemetery was in very bad shape. There may have been as many as a thousand graves there at one time. At least 95 percent of the gravestones were overturned or missing entirely. Of the remaining few, the inscriptions on at least half were illegible. Still, I managed to find two adjacent markers of Wassermans, who may be related to us, as well as one of a married woman whose maiden name was Steiner.

Before leaving city hall I made a donation toward some worthy city project, in memory of my grandfather.

It was now nearly lunchtime, but we had to hurry on to Bélád (now Beladice), about ten kilometers to the west. Fortunately they had a few snacks waiting for us there at city hall (or should I say town hall, as the place is too small to be considered a city – even the town designation is questionable). There we met the mayor, Ing. Maria Časarová. She had brought in an old lady who remembered Wassermans; several of them – Imre, Laci and Dodo – had rented land there. They had been from Szelezsény (now Slazany), a small town located between Golden Morava and Bélád. The woman told us that Dodo had died during the war (presumably World War Two). Mr. Lamm then mentioned that as a child, he had had a friend named Wasserman, also from Szelezsény.

We asked the mayor about the Jewish cemetery. She had a glint in her eye as she explained that up to the day before, she had never known that there was one near her town. In preparation for our arrival she had asked around, and one of the older people had remembered something, way out in the fields. So she had gone there, the day before, to investigate, had found the place and was ready to take us there.

We drove for about eight minutes, on a narrow road which became ever narrower. Finally, we had to leave the car and walk on the path another kilometer or so; then we turned onto a ploughed field and walked across it, following the plough mark, for a good two more kilometers. Our apparent aim was a clump of far-off trees. When we got there, under a dozen or so trees we found as many old graves, all in very bad condition. At least one grave had been dug up and emptied. Few stones still stood, with old Hebrew characters which were very difficult to decipher due to their condition. We found no familiar names.

Nevertheless, we were impressed by the mayor's kindness and effort in making that long trip twice. Subsequently she pointed out another Jewish cemetery situated closer to the town, also in a field. It was almost impossible to approach, however, due to the recent ploughing of the field. Upon questioning, she admitted that this cemetery would have been more relevant to our quest, as it was close to the old town of Bélád destroyed by fire some time in the twentieth century.

I have sketched the relative locations of the town and cemeteries:

Beladice and environs

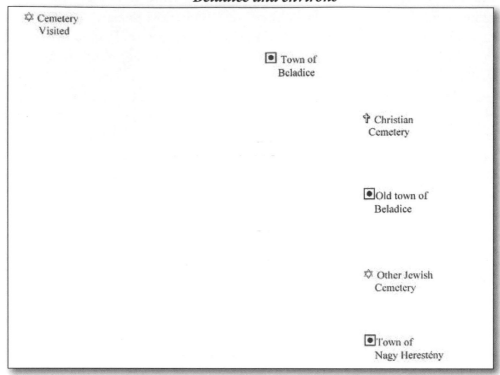

From Bélád, we drove further west, through the city of Nyitra, where Vladimir left his car and joined ours. We said goodbye to Mr. Lamm (after insisting that he accept a small donation for the Jewish community of Nyitra which sadly lacked the means for many important projects). We turned northbound to Tapolcsány and past that major town, to Zestmeadow-on-Nyitra. Now that we were some forty kilometers further north I had expected to see mountains, but there were only some small hills dotting the horizon. The landscape was more pleasant than in Golden Morava, but there wasn't really much that you would call natural beauty. Of course, my ancestors might have considered the land itself beautiful, who knows…

We parked at city hall; our car was the only one in front of the handsome building. A soon as we got out of the car, the mayor, Dipl. Ing. Otakar Sneženka, ran out to us with his daughter Jana. With the help of Jana, who could speak English, they greeted us warmly. Inside, they introduced us to the mayor's wife and the staff of four women. They treated us royally, providing ample food and drink. They showed us an old handwritten chronicle of the town, including a letter written by the Turkish lord Kücsük Pasha in 1644, threatening the

Hungarian population for not paying their taxes ("You dirty dogs, if you don't pay your taxes by the time I get there, every one of you will hang...").

Among the town records, some references to Steiners were found, including one Herman Steiner, baker, but this clearly was not the Herman Steiner who was my grandfather's brother. After showing us the town records they brought in an elderly lady, "Bubka" Loviškova, age eighty-nine. She told us that as a young girl, age fifteen, she knew (I think she worked for) old Mr. Steiner, then age ninety. When I showed her family photos (which, as it turned out later, were incorrect), she picked out one man who I, at the time, thought was my grandfather, as resembling this Mr. Steiner. But then she considered the photo of another unrelated woman in the picture, and stated that Mr. Steiner's mother looked like that. Apart from the fact that there was no blood relation between those two people, we asked how she could possibly have known the mother of the ninety-year-old Mr. Steiner. She mumbled that well, he might have actually been less than ninety. All in all, I considered her testimony at least in this regard to be less than reliable.

But we also received a copy of a written testimony by "Bubka" Loviškova of the fate of the town's Jewish population during the Nazi era. I will include some of her notes a little later.

The mayor presented us with gifts, including a very nice ceramic wine jug and six cups, as well as various books about the town. We were taken on a city tour, during which we were shown Uzka Street, presumed home of the Steiners. We were also shown the old synagogue from the outside – it did not look much like a synagogue – and the adjacent "rabbi's home," a palatial building with Greek columns, quite unlikely to have served that purpose.

We were then taken to the Jewish cemetery. Fifteen Jews had been executed there during the Nazi era, the bullet holes still clearly perceptible in the wall. Of the markers, only about 20 percent were still standing, many of whose inscriptions were illegible; we found no familiar names.

In memory of my great-grandfather, I gave a donation toward the building of a new Christian cemetery(!), as this was the project closest to the mayor's heart.

Having said goodbye to the kind mayor and his family, we drove back to Nyitra, where Vladimir reclaimed his car; we agreed that I would send him details about my ancestors and he would try to help in discovering further facts.

*   *   *

All in all, was the trip worthwhile?

We certainly did not discover any dramatic new facts about my ancestors. Yet I considered it a necessary step in the research – at the least, I had to see where they lived, get an idea of the lay of the land, to be able to form a mental picture of their lives some 150 years earlier. But more than that, we did come back with important information:

- I had a new birth certificate of my father, providing details of my grandfather's position at the time and the family's residence. It also bore Grandfather's signature, which I had never seen before.

- I guessed (and later confirmed) that the great actress and singer Lujza Blaha was born in Rima-Sobota; this fact had significance that I shall reveal later.

- I met Vladimir, our guide and genealogical researcher. Our subsequent correspondence over e-mail was made much easier by our having met in person.

- I visited the Jewish cemetery in Golden Morava, there finding two gravestones of Wassermans. Later I did find out who they were.

- At Bélád, I learned from two different sources that the Wassermans lived mainly in Szelezsény.

- Discovering that little cemetery in Bélád in the middle of a ploughed field – even though we found no known names there and it was probably not even the cemetery used by the Jewish residents of Bélád at the time in question – was a very moving experience. It made me realize what miserable lives our ancestors lived, to the extent that they had to negotiate with some farmer to sell them a remote corner of his field for a cemetery, much like our father Abraham once negotiated for the cave of Machpeila.

- I found that wall at the cemetery in Zestmeadow-on-Nyitra, where the Jews were lined up and shot, where the bullet holes were still in the wall.

- But then there was that monk in Nyitra; I'll tell you about him soon.

- And we also drove down to Békés, in southern Hungary – but I'll relate that visit later.

Miserable Life in Small Villages – 1862

"Markus Steiner?"

"Yes, that's me."

"I would like to talk with you. Let me introduce myself."

"Who are you? Where am I?"

"That is difficult to explain. You see, I am here from the future. I am talking with you a long, long time after you died, even after your sons and grandsons are long dead. Does that bother you?"

  Quiet.

"If you were alive, you would be close to 200 years old. Well, not quite that, but over 170."

"So where am I now?"

"Well, you are nowhere, really, except in my mind. But that does bring your spirit back, in a sense. I am thinking of you, so for me, you are now alive. Can we talk?"

"So who are you?"

"I am your great-grandson."

"Great-grandson? Which? Whose…?"

"Your son Bernát's grandson. I think you called him Berman."

"Berman. Yes. There was Herman and then there was Berman. We thought it was funny. Rozália thought so."

"So, Great-Grandfather, if I may call you that, would you talk to me about Rozália? And about the children and about your life in Perlep?"

  Quiet.

"Will you tell me things? About your life there?"

"Well, I can tell you things, sure. What would you like to know?"

"I am not asking you about how you got to Perlep, not yet. That will come later. But once you got there, what did you do?"

"All right, I'll tell you. We got a house in the little village. It was the estate of the count Migazzi. We had to pay rent for the house, of course, and also for the inn."

"What inn?"

"It was not much of an inn, more like a tavern. That was part of the deal. I got to be the tavern keeper. The count Migazzi wanted to build up that village. He had some plans for industry there, he owned a lot of forests in the area. He decided to build a paper mill in Perlep."

"And he needed a tavern for that?"

"Yes, because he wanted many of his serfs to live there – maybe I should not say serfs, they were just peasants by that time. So he had these houses built for them and also for us. Everybody had to pay rent. And he built the tavern and was looking for a tavern keeper. He found me. I said that I could do it, and I did, even though I had hardly stepped into a tavern ever before."

"So how did you know what to do?"

"Of course, then I did visit some taverns. On the way there, we stopped at a couple of places where I spent time with some tavern keepers. They were Jewish, and they were happy to teach me, give me pointers."

"Pointers for buying and selling?"

"Yes, of course. How to get good wine and some other things, too. How much to pay and how much to ask from the customers."

"And about music? Did you have music?"

"Yes, sometimes we did, when I could get a gypsy band to stay there. It was difficult, for people liked the music, they liked to sing and even dance, but they did not want the gypsies staying in the village. In the summer they camped on some fields until they were chased away, but in the winter they wanted to stay in a house or a shed, something that protected them from the weather. I had to negotiate with the peasants, sometimes with a few small landowners, for not everything was owned by the count. Only most of the land."

"Did you have any other troubles? Like, for instance, with rowdy people, drunks?"

"Sure I did. Every tavern keeper does. And those Slovak peasants could get very rough once they had a liter or two."

"So how did you deal with them? Were you a very strong man?"

"Not at all. The way to do it is to have a few friends among them. Good, reliable people, who liked to sit at the back of the tavern, drink a little, not too much, get some food – we always had a thing or two cooked, they did not have to pay for the food – and then, when trouble came, they just stood up, walked over to the loudmouthed ones and told them to shut up, or they'd get what was coming to them. Sometimes they had to take a few out and rough them up a little. Not too much, I made sure that nobody would suffer real damages. On the whole, it worked out well."

"Tell me, what language did you use then, how did you talk with your customers? Did you know Slovak?"

"Now you're talking. That was the real problem. No, I did not know much Slovak, not at first. I knew German: that was the language we spoke at home."

"Not even Yiddish?"

"Yiddish? No, nobody spoke Yiddish there, not at that time. I was told that my grandfather knew Yiddish, but we never used it, nobody in our family. It was always German. So I had to learn a little Slovak, to talk to my customers. But I also had to learn Hungarian."

"Were there Hungarian customers?"

"There were a few, from time to time, yes. The soldiers came often – they spoke Hungarian – and the county officers. Even the count, when he came by, insisted on speaking Hungarian, yet he knew German as well as I did."

"Was he not Italian?"

"No, only his name. I suppose his ancestors must have come from Italy."

"Now, you said that there was some food served there. Who cooked? Surely not yourself?"

"Ha, ha. Me, no. I could not cook a slice of bread with butter. No, it was a local woman at first, sometimes my mother. Later, when I got married, then Rozália often cooked. The way it worked, she cooked for us at home, for the family, and she cooked enough so that I could take some of it over to the tavern. Not many customers wanted food."

"What kind of food would that be?"

"Oh, simple food. Some potato soup, cabbage with meat, maybe a little noodles with fruit jam, farfel, such things…"

"What about overnight customers? You said it was an inn. Did you have guest rooms?"

"We had two rooms, but they were seldom used. When we had visitors, personal visitors, family or even traveling Jews, they usually stayed at our house. Sometimes county officers needed a room for the night. Then they ate at the tavern. I asked one of the local women to make the bed for them and to cook some breakfast the next morning."

"And you found all this, the tavern, with drinks and all, profitable?"

"Profitable? Well, I would not call it that. There were so many taxes to be paid, for the rent and to the count, especially the rent to the count, it was called *árenda*, and to the county and to the emperor and everybody else, there was not that much left. But we managed. We had enough left for food and clothes, and also for wood in the winter, and later coal."

"Were the winters very cold?"

"Bitterly cold. We were on the plain, no mountains anywhere near. The wind blew very hard. Yes, it was cold, but we did not mind that so much. The spring was worse. The spring and the fall."

"Why?"

"Because of the mud. Whenever it rained a lot, there was mud everywhere. Getting to the tavern in the snow was not so bad, but slogging through all that mud, I hated it. It took me a quarter of an hour to clean the mud off my boots and trousers. And going home, the same thing. Everybody hated the mud."

"There were no sidewalks?"

"No, nobody bothered to build sidewalks. This was not a town. It was a village. There are no sidewalks in villages."

"Tell me, what about the children? What did they do? Did they go to school?"

"Yes, the government insisted that every child go to school. A good thing, too, if you ask me. Of course, they learned a lot at home – reading and writing, and arithmetic – but that was not enough. And what they learned at home, it was all in German."

"While at school, they learned Hungarian?"

"Later, yes. First, they went to an elementary school, right there in Perlep. There, all the children were Slovak, so they learned Slovak, but we thought, Rozália and I, that it would be more important for them to learn German, so they had to go to school in Golden Morava. They opened a German-speaking Jewish school there just when my children were small."

"They learned only German? Not Hungarian?"

"Later, the government forced the school to teach Hungarian, too. Good idea, if you ask me – that was the language of the land, if they wanted to move down to Pest or the other larger towns…"

"And the children walked to Golden Morava every day? How far was that?"

"That was three kilometers away. They often got a ride from a man who had a cart, especially in the winter. But when the weather was nice, yes, they walked. Rozália always worried about their catching cold."

"Did they often catch colds?"

"Not that often. A little walking was good for them, I thought. But she was the worrying kind. Every little cough frightened her. Why, when I started coughing, I could not put her mind at ease, I tried to explain that this was nothing, just a little wind on the road, but she would not believe me. Well, as it happens, she may have been right, I think that I did catch tuberculosis… When did you say that I died?"

"I did not, but… Great-Grandfather, let's talk about something else. Tell me, what did you do when you wanted to go to a synagogue?"

"That was difficult. We had no synagogue in Perlep. Do you know how many Jewish families there lived in Perlep?"

"No, I don't yet know."

"Two. Just two families. Me and my father."

"So you just did not go to a synagogue at all?"

"I did not say that. There was a *shul* in a village not too far away. Later on, there was a house in Golden Morava with a larger room, sometimes they had a minyan there. We went there on some Sabbaths and on all the important holidays."

"Did they have a rabbi there?"

"Are you joking? Why would they have a rabbi? We did get to see a rabbi from time to time, when there was something important. He lived very far from us. There was a *mohel* a little closer; when a boy was born, we sent for him. We went to the rabbi's house when we wanted to get married, or sometimes he came to our place."

"And when someone died?"

"When someone died, we buried him. Or her. Usually they were children. We buried the child and said an *El moleh rachamim* at the graveside. Then we went to town a few times, so we could say *Kaddish* with a minyan. That was it."

"But surely there was a proper synagogue in Golden Morava?"

"No, there was not. At least, not in my lifetime. They talked about building one, but it was just that, idle talk."

"Would that have been an Orthodox synagogue, or a Reform one?"

"We did not have Reform there."

"Sorry, not Reform. Neolog?"

"Neolog. No, we were not Neolog. We remained 'status quo ante.' But only after that stupid conference in Pest, when was it, 1869?"

"Yes, I believe so. Why, what were you before?"

"Before, we did not talk of such things. There were those who were more strictly religious, and those who thought that making a living was more important than spending all their days *davening*. Our family was not that religious. If we were, we could never have come to the Golden Morava area, we could never have lived in small villages, just one or two families in a place. You could not properly *daven* that way. We did not mind. But we were good Jews: we respected the law, we did not eat *treif* food, we did not behave the way *goyim* sometimes behaved. We remained nice, decent people, just as Jews everywhere. Only not so much *davening*."

"Tell me, why did you stay at that small village? Why not just move in to Golden Morava?"

"Why, I had my livelihood there."

"But could you not have done something else, in town? Like other people did?"

"Has my wife asked you to talk to me like that?"

"Your wife?"

"Yes, Rozália. Why, she was your great-grandmother, was she not? She used to talk to me like that all the time. When do we finally move to town? Why can she not wear proper clothes, like the other Jewish woman, why does she have to spend her whole life in this mudhole, why can the children not grow up like decent city people, why, why, why…"

"But you did agree with her, did you not? You did move to Golden Morava?"

"That was later. But it was difficult. I could not get a tavern there. That would have cost too much money."

"No, you became a merchant, did you not?"

"Merchant. Yes, but there are merchants and there are merchants. What do you mean by merchant?"

"What do *I* mean? Well, somebody who has a store and sells something there."

"Ah, yes, that would be a merchant. A store. Why not a wholesaler? But when we Jews moved to Hungary, when we decided to leave Nyitra and go to Bars County, to Golden Morava, then those who were merchants carried their merchandise on their backs! All their things in a bundle, they walked from village to village, offering their wares. My father was that kind of merchant. Sorry, that was not for me."

"I understand. And I suppose that Count Migazzi invited you to become an innkeeper, not a merchant. He did not need merchants."

"Well, I don't know about that. There were plenty of merchants that he supported. He and the other big landowners, the Paluškas and the Forgách families. You see, they encouraged the Jews to take their local products and sell them wherever they could, and also on their way back to bring them things they needed, things they could not easily buy locally. Luxury things."

"But they did not offer you that alternative?"

"They offered it to my father. He had a small general store in Perlep. I was happy to be an innkeeper. It worked out all right, it was not a bad decision. Now if I could have afforded a store in town, let alone a wholesale establishment… But these were dreams."

"Yet some people, some Jews, did achieve that, did they not?"

"Don't rub it in, as Rozália did. Yes, some managed, though not at first. Golden Morava was a forbidden town for the Jews when we moved to the area, though the count promised that it would soon change. It did, too, but that took many years. The local merchants did not want to let the Jews in."

"Were they afraid of the competition?"

"I suppose that was the real reason. But they created some ugly scenes. They used to meet in the main square and inside the town hall, shouting things about the Jews. All in German, too."

"Why, did they not speak Hungarian or Slovak?"

"No, not a word. All the merchants were German, and they spent years trying to keep the Jews out. But in the end, the mood of the town turned against them, what with the 1848 revolution and the worry about foreigners taking over the country."

"But people were not worried about the Jews?"

"Worried? Why? We were not taking over anything. We became good Hungarians, too, all of us learned the language. Some people, some Jews, worried that their grandchildren might not know German at all. How about you? Surely you know German?"

"Well, Great-Grandfather, I have to admit that I know very little German. I learned it as a small boy, but then I made an effort to forget that language."

"I don't understand. What effort? To forget? Why?"

"Let's not talk about that, that's another story. Certain things happened in the middle of the twentieth century that you don't want to hear about. Tell me, how much did you earn as a tavern keeper?

"At first, only about 50 forints. But later, when things got better, in some years I made 100 forints, even 150. But that was before all the taxes and dues. We seldom had 100 left over."

"But that was enough for all you needed, food and clothes and wood and coal…"

"Yes, but it was not enough for one thing I really wanted."

"What was that?"

"A good horse. It took me a long time to save enough for a good horse, so that I could move to the town and be a merchant, without hauling all my stuff in a bundle on my back. I told Rozália that the only way I would give up the tavern and move to town was if I had a horse and a little cart."

"There was no talk of opening a store?"

"No, that was out of the question. We did not have that kind of money."

"Yet others did."

"I don't know where they got the money for that. Maybe a loan. I did not want a loan. I did not want to be beholden to anybody. I was not the sort of person who would ever be indebted. Maybe it was stupid of me, but that was not for me."

"Tell me, could you not do something else? Could you not be a craftsman of some kind?"

"Maybe. Most of the crafts were controlled by the guilds, you could not get in. All luxury items were made by them, such things as playing cards and umbrellas and ribbons and gloves…"

"So how about carpentry? How about a smithy?"

"No, those things were also in the guild world."

"Yet I heard that many Jews worked as tailors, glaziers, tanners, furriers, bookbinders, goldsmiths…"

"No, I did not have the training for those things."

"A barber?"

"When I was young, I thought that I might become a barber, maybe, not the wigmaker type, rather like a surgeon, you know, the man who does the bloodletting, handles leeches and such things. But then I found out that most of those people were quacks, they were not good for anything. In an emergency all they did, they tried to sell you things you did not need."

"A dentist?"

"There were no dentists then, except those who traveled from fair to fair. Bath surgeons, they sometimes called themselves. They would sell you some potion against toothache, but in the end you had to pull the tooth out anyway."

"You pulled it out yourself?"

"Who else? We had good tools, pliers, you just grabbed the tooth and moved it this way, that way, turned it a little left, right, until it became loose, and then you pulled it out."

"You should have been a trained dentist yourself. Or maybe a teacher, perhaps? A notary? A rabbi, even?"

"Yes, perhaps I could have. But my parents never had enough money to send me to schools. My children… I hope they became learned adults, especially Berman. He did, did he not?"

"Yes, Great-Grandfather. Berman became the director of the law court in Rima-Sobota."

"I thank the Lord for that."

The Good Slovaks – 2000

After the day spent visiting Golden Morava and its surrounding towns, we felt that we had done what we could in Slovakia for the time being. But the next morning we had some time before heading back to Hungary and, as Nyitra was a very beautiful city, we decided to use the opportunity for some sightseeing.

There is a lovely old town in the middle of the modern city. One ascends a hill and eventually reaches, near the top, a baroque church – quite nice, but not unusual. However, attached to that church is a very old chapel, from the eleventh century. Attached it may be, but, we were told, it is not usually open to visitors.

We walked around the church, looking at seventeenth- and eighteenth-century paintings, sculptures and the usual paraphernalia, and at one point a young monk approached us. He said a few words in Slovak and quickly switched to German. When we shook our heads to that as well, he tried French, and we told him that English was our preferred language. He was a little embarrassed by that, as his English was not fluent, but it was certainly passable. He asked us if we would allow him to show us the treasures of the church, which we certainly welcomed.

The monk showed us two or three items of some interest. As we were walking, he turned to us and asked, "Actually, what are you? Catholics or Protestants?"

"Neither," I answered. "We are Jewish."

That puzzled him – his English vocabulary did not extend that far. I helped him out. "That means *žido*," I explained. I already knew that much Slovak.

His face lit up. "Really? *Žido?* I love *žido* people."

That surprised us a little. He hastened to explain. I won't try to reproduce his way of pronouncing the words.

"I visited Israel earlier this year with the pope. I was among his retinue. We went everywhere in the country. What a beautiful country! What lovely people! I loved every moment of it." And he went on, praising Israel and its inhabitants. He seemed really happy to see us.

"I'll tell you what." He seemed to make an important decision. "I shall show you our chapel. We have a very old chapel here. Come, I'll open it for you."

He led us to the other end of the entry hall. We went a few steps down and he opened an iron gate. We entered.

The chapel was quite small and round, perhaps six meters in diameter. Its ceiling was vaulted. The walls were white, without any decoration. There were four niches in the wall on the left side and a few more, I think, on the right.

"That's where the singers were sitting. It is designed for the best possible acoustics."

"They performed masses here?"

"Yes, beautiful masses. I will show you."

We were wondering, *What will he show? A mass?*

He walked over to the left wall and sat in the first niche. "Listen," he said.

And he started singing. He had a lovely baritone voice. Here is what he sang: "*Shema Yisrael, Adonai Eloheinu, Adonai echad.*" And the walls of the chapel reverberated. That whole chapel, the eleventh-century Christian chapel, had sung *Shema Yisrael...*

We must have sung the *Shema* tens of thousands of times. It had never sounded so beautiful. We looked at each other in astonishment and could not keep our eyes dry.

We tried to ask the monk more questions – where had he learned those words, that pronunciation, that tune – but his lack of English proficiency got in the way of a satisfactory explanation. Afterwards, I tried to make an appropriate donation. With great difficulty, we located a small metal box that may have been used for collection and deposited some money there; clearly, the monk was not looking for such an act on our part. We wanted to buy some memorabilia, perhaps a picture book or at least postcards about the cathedral, but none were being sold there. Later, in the town, we did locate a store where souvenirs and religious objects were sold, but the two women working there were taking a coffee break when we arrived and they refused to open the doors. Pressed for time, we left the town and drove back to Hungary.

* * *

The monk in Nyitra may have left us with the warmest memory of our visit to Slovakia, but it must be stated that everyone who helped us over the course of our stay in Slovakia behaved kindly to us – if I didn't know better, I would almost call their attitude loving. The mayor of Bélád, who took so much time and effort to visit the remote cemetery with us; the lady in Perlep who invited us to her modest home and pressed gifts upon us; the mayor of Zestmeadow-on-Nyitra, who happily introduced his family and took us to see his house – all treated us as long-lost relatives or friends. Just now I wrote, "if I didn't know better." Why? What did I know better? Was it all a show? A ploy to take advantage of foreigners? It is true that we left money at every spot, but they gave no impression of eagerly awaiting our contribution. On the contrary, at every place it took some efforts on our part to press a donation on the town coffers or, in a few cases, on individuals. They appeared happy to make our acquaintance, without seeking any financial gain.

Well then, what about anti-Semitism? Did we find evidence of such feeling in Slovakia? I am sure that there is plenty of anti-Semitism in the country – what European nation lacks it? But nobody whom we met ever expressed any such sentiments or even indicated it, unwittingly – no, we felt that their welcome was truly warm.

And yet…

The Bad Slovaks – 1944

Once I returned to Canada after the trip, I began to correspond with our researcher, Vladimir, through e-mail. He wrote to me about a book he'd just read concerning the Topolcsány Jewish community and its extinction. It was written by Robert Y. Buechler. Vladimir thought that it explained why people were so friendly; he said that he knew it was not genuine. It was, in his view, a guilty conscience. I got hold of the book. It described in great detail the origin of the community of Topolcsány, which had had a large and thriving Jewish population that grew to some fifteen hundred people by the end of the nineteenth century. Well, in the Holocaust the local Slovaks were instrumental in getting rid of all the Jews of Topolcsány. It seems likely that their motivation was simply envy and greed, for once the Jews were safely deported from the town, the Slovaks invaded the synagogues and stole everything of value. Afterwards, to cover up their deed (why bother? I assume that the Germans wanted everything for themselves), they burned the buildings. Thus all vital records of Topolcsány's Jewish community were destroyed.

Then there was the old lady, "Bubka" Loviškova, of Zestmeadow. Apparently she was interviewed, or invited to write up her recollections, for a regional newspaper. The mayor of the town gave us a copy of the article (unfortunately, the title of the publication is not shown and I have not been able to locate the original author, or the publication, in an effort to obtain their permission to include my translation of the article herein). The article, written by Anna Dobiašova, includes Mrs. Loviškova's recollections and an account of the situation of the Jews before the war, as well as the brief comments of another witness, Ladislav Hoďu. Apart from the description of the brutality against the Jews by the Slovaks, it is worth noting that even where trying to be objective or sympathetic, a vein of anti-Semitism runs through both the town's chronicle and Mrs. Loviškova's comments (though certainly not those of Ms. Dobiašova's).

REMEMBERING THE JEWS OF ZESTMEADOW-ON-NYITRA

A Memento to the Future Generations

On November 15, 1998, a plaque was unveiled at the Novaky station with the following text:

> Not far from the village of Kos, in 1941–1944, the military Slovak government set up a concentration camp. On August 19, 250 Jews participated in a revolt; of them, 38 had fallen. At this station the inhabitants of the camp were piled into cattle wagons and deported to the gas chambers of Auschwitz.

It may have been this, it may have been the stories of my grandparents, or my having read the story of the great Tapolcsány Jewish community, or perhaps my visit to the destroyed and forgotten Jewish cemetery in Zestmeadow-on-Nyitra among the ploughed fields, that gave me the urge to investigate the story of the local Jews more thoroughly…

From the Town Monograph

The Jewish community of Zestmeadow-on-Nyitra numbered two hundred, thus forming one-fifth of the population. The tragedy of the Jews, when fifty-seven thousand of them were deported from Slovakia, bore directly on the Zestmeadow-on-Nyitra community. Most of them were carried away, some were taken to the Novakov work camp and only a few managed to escape. In the Zestmeadow-on-Nyitra register almost all land, until the creation of the Slovak state, was recorded as the property of three Jews: Polak, Lang and Waelder. Similarly with the stores: there were, in those days, six taverns, four butchers, six general and dry goods stores, two liquor wholesalers, etc. – all in Jewish hands. There was in the town a vinegar plant, that of M. E. Schlesinger, and a liqueur and rum plant, that of A. H. Ulman – both Jews. Of national significance was Jenő Lang's office equipment plant (carbon and indigo papers, typewriter ribbons, ink and pencils). Jenő Lang also owned a milk market and a milk-products processing plant. The Jews, who probably settled in Zestmeadow-on-Nyitra at the beginning of the eighteenth century, transformed the village into a town well developed in every respect.

Perhaps only a few are aware that Zestmeadow-on-Nyitra was a district town from 1872 to 1927, when it was the center for thirty-seven communities, including Bosna, Chinorany, Dolne, Vestenice, Nitrianske, and Suciany. In 1934 the Jews were still in the town council and were active in the management of the town. After the war none of them returned....

Recollections of Valeria Loviškova

The coexistence of the Jewish and Catholic communities between the two wars has a living "chronicle" in the person of the seventy-nine-year-old Valeria Loviškova. She grew up here, from the age of three months, in a poor Catholic family whose head worked as leaseholder at the largest Jewish landowner. In the larger courtyards they lived peacefully with the poorer Jewish families and as a child, she played with their children. She remembers each of the Jewish families: Lang, Polak, Grün, Waelder, Weiss, Wamberger, Schwartz, Rosenbaum, Getler, Rosenfeld, Wertheimer, Rabbi Brody and others. "The coexistence with the Jews in those days was much better than how Catholics live among each other today," says the sorely tried woman. The Jews here had their own community, synagogue, school, cemetery and religion with a strong tradition. For example, Catholics were not permitted to participate in Jewish funerals. Only Loviškova and the gravediggers could be present; she carried their bags. In the town, the Jews maintained a dominant position. Loviškova testifies to this: "People had no money, only the Jews had it. But they knew how to help. When I was still a little girl and wanted to have candies, I plucked a few flowers and took the bouquet to the miss, or went to pile firewood into the oven. Actually, everybody here served the Jews. I served in Jewish houses, too, in my younger years. I shall never forget how Mrs. Binenstok ordered a coat from Pest as a gift, even if it was not new, and Czech garnets. That was a big thing in those days. Or when the head of the distillery, Wamberger, gave me a sample, when I served in the tavern…"

Loviskova's recollections are endless. They would fill a large book. But her face darkened when the topic of the deportation was raised.

The Witness of the Brutality against the Jews

"One after the other, each one of them was taken," she remembers sadly. "I stood by the roadside and cried. They piled them into hog freight cars, little children too. One of the servants rudely kicked the backside of one child as he climbed up…. And when I was at my father's at Vitkovice, close to Nemesice, I saw with my own eyes how they shot Jews. In the middle of the fields. They threw clay over them, but so poorly that after a little while legs and arms showed through, and bloated bodies. At the end they covered them with a cartful of dung…." The truth of this bestial deed can also be found in the book about the Tapolcsány Jews. Near the town Nemesice, on September 10, 1944, the Germans and the Hlinka guardsmen murdered nineteen men, twenty-four women and ten children between the ages of four months and fourteen years. "We were all afraid, we did not want to hide Jewish assets at home, when they asked us. Here some managed to escape by converting…." To the memories of Loviskova we can also add the testimony of Ladislav Hoďu, apprentice in Zestmeadow-on-Nyitra, now seventy-two years old, who saw how the Jews were crammed into the wagons at the Tapolcsány station. How Getler, the grocer from the town, was taken to the wagon. In the end, he states sadly, "There were people in the town who were pleased by this, others cried. There were Jews who succeeded in hiding or escaping. But after the war no Jew remained alive in Zestmeadow-on-Nyitra…."

* * *

But great fortunes remained that the state distributed afterwards. To this day there stand, in the middle of the town, beautiful buildings, prospering plants. Far in the middle of the field remains the cemetery. Today it is overgrown, defiled, with overturned gravestones. Even after their death, they found no peace.

By Anna Dobiašova

And then, there was that cemetery wall in Zestmeadow-on-Nyitra. The wall where the local Slovaks lined up fifteen Jews of the town and shot them dead…

The Steiner Family, from Moravia to Zestmeadow-on-Nyitra – 1820

"*Herr Moses Steiner, sprechen Sie Ungarisch?*"

"*Ja, ja, Ich spreche. Ein wenig. Warum? Sie sprechen nicht Deutsch?*"

"Not really, not very well. I am somebody who is talking to you from the distant future. This is the year 2002. I am invoking your spirit. Please talk to me, I am a distant descendant of yours. Actually, I am your great-great-grandson."

"*Gott sei Dank.*"

"Yes, you remember your grandson Berman?"

"What a question! Of course I remember Berman. He was with me till the end."

"Well, I am his grandson."

"*Gut! Sehr gut!* I was afraid that he might have trouble finding a wife, he was too educated, too refined; there was nobody suitable here in Golden Morava."

"Actually, he was twenty-nine years old by the time he married. He found a lovely girl in Zólyom."

"Good. What was he doing in Zólyom?"

"I think he found a good job at the district court there. But listen, I would like to ask you questions."

"Go ahead, ask. I have nothing better to do."

"Yes, of course. Tell me, I know that you came over to Golden Morava from Zestmeadow-on-Nyitra. But were you actually born there?"

"Yes, I was."

"And you wife, too?"

"Mari? Yes, she was born there, too. Why, where else would we have been born?"

"I just wondered if you might not have been born in Hungary at all. But surely the family came from—"

"My grandfather came over from Moravia, yes. All the families came from Moravia."

"Tell me what happened, what made them come over to Hungary."

"Well, when we were young, our grandfather told us many stories. He and his friends talked a lot about the old country, how nice it was, how civilized. They always said that Moravia, yes, that was their real home, they were just spending time here, waiting for the day when they could go home. I never thought of it that way. I never visited there. Those were just meaningless names for me: Nikolsburg, Olumouc, Ungarische Brod, Boskowitz. I think that they were small towns, but bigger than Zestmeadow-on-Nyitra. Probably they were more advanced, better developed. And they talked a lot about Brünn. Apparently, that was the center of the world. But I don't think they actually lived there. Jews were not allowed to live in Brünn."

"So you think that when they moved over to Hungary, to Nyitra County, they considered it a step down, going to more primitive surroundings?"

"Yes, that's how it sounded from the complaints of my grandparents. But my parents were, I think, born in Nyitra already, or at least my mother. No, both of them, I am sure."

"So when did your grandparents move, do you know?"

"I cannot tell you exactly. My parents were born around 1770, my father a little earlier, I think. So their parents probably moved just before that, maybe in the 1760s. I know that they were part of the last group of Jewish people from Moravia. Of course they had to move to Hungary."

"Had to? Why, what happened?"

"You mean you have not heard of the Familiantengesetze, the Familiants Law?"

"Well, yes, I have heard, kind of, but what was it exactly?"

"I must say that you young people forget fast. Do you still remember the story of Esther and Mordechai?"

"Of course we do. What a question. That's what Purim is all about. What does that have to do with the Familiantengesetze?"

"Nothing. At least not much. But listening to you makes me think that the rulers can bring any new law against the Jews, and in two or three generations it will all be forgotten. That was an evil decree against us."

"Who brought it, the empress Maria Theresa?"

"No, it was her father, the emperor Charles VI, may his name be blotted out. In 1726 he thought up a new law to keep the number of Jewish families in Moravia and Bohemia down. So he decided that in each family, only the oldest son may marry."

"What?!"

"You see, you don't know anything. Only the oldest son could marry. The others should remain single. Of course, he could not stop all the other boys from marrying outside the country. He did not care, they could go anywhere in the world, but not in his kingdom. And that's what they all had to do, go somewhere else. Not only the boys, of course, but the girls, too, for there was nobody to marry them if they stayed."

"And so most Jewish youngsters moved to Hungary. But why Hungary? Was that not also part of the emperor's kingdom?"

"Ah, but it was an empty part. There were very few people living there, after they chased away the Turks. It was just like Moravia some thirty years earlier, when the Swedes were chased out. The country was devastated, but there was a new opportunity for the brave, those willing to start a new life. The emperor and particularly his daughter, rotten to the core though she was, wanted to repopulate Hungary, so that's where we had to go."

"And what kind of welcome did you – well, your grandfathers – get from the remaining Hungarians?"

"Oh, they welcomed us with open arms. They needed us. They begged us to come. They needed our brains, our initiative, our energy."

"Like Béla the Fourth, after the Mongol invasion? Or Gábor Bethlen, much later, in Transylvania?"

"Who?"

"Oh, just some major players in Hungarian history. Don't worry about them. They needed Jews to start the country going again."

"Yes, that's what happened. They were in some kind of stupor. Their leaders knew nothing about commerce, about industry, the big landowners had all those serfs…"

"Serfs? In the eighteenth century?"

"Yes, indeed, until Josef II came they were nothing but serfs. They had to work for the big landowners, they couldn't move anywhere or start a business of their own. But the Jews could. They knew how to sell the produce of the land, how to bring in money for the lords, the aristocrats. They were certainly wanted."

"So for once, they did not hate the Jews?"

"Well, I don't know if they actually loved us. But there was another thing. There still is. Well, at least there was in my lifetime. The needed us against the Slovaks."

"How do you mean against the Slovaks? You didn't go to war against them, did you?"

"No, but we became Hungarians. They were afraid that the Slovaks and Ruthenians and Serbs and Croats and Romanians would take over the country, there were so few Magyars left. So they needed more Hungarians. We were the new ones."

"But how did you become Hungarians?"

"By learning the language. Funny, our grandparents were told to stop using Yiddish and all kinds of other languages and learn German. So they did and they became good Germans. Now suddenly, we had to learn Hungarian and become good Hungarians. Well, I was not young enough for that, but my son tried, and now his children, it seems, speak Hungarian better than German."

"And another question: why did your grandparents move to Nyitra, rather than to Pressburg? I understand that there was a very large Jewish community in Pressburg. The Hungarians called it Pozsony; the Slovaks, Bratislava. The Chasam Sofer was chief rabbi there. Some say he ruled there."

"There you have it. Our parents did not want the Chasam Sofer to rule over them."

"They preferred the rule of a big landowner?"

"You cannot put it that way. There were big landowners in Pozsony, the counts Pálfy, and there were big landowners in Zestmeadow, the Simonyi family. They invited us in. They had a right to keep Jews, and they did not have to ask anybody in Vienna."

"But I don't understand. Your parents, your grandparents had something against the great rabbis? So many Jews came to Hungary, to the Pozsony area in the early part of the eighteenth century, and they were good, law-abiding Jews. They were happy to have great rabbis…"

"Where did those people come from?"

"Where? I think they came mainly from Austria, perhaps Germany…"

"Yes, you see, but not from Moravia. I was told that our people did not want so many rabbis telling them what to do from morning to evening, every minute, every step. We wanted modernization, we wanted freedom. We saw it coming; we wanted to be free like any other people. We had been oppressed for seventeen hundred years. Listen, I know my history. Did we not deserve to be free like everyone else? Have you heard of the Haskalah?"

"Yes, of course. The movement of the Enlightenment."

"The *Jewish* movement of the Enlightenment. They told us that we *could* be like everyone else. We didn't need to wear special clothes. We didn't need to speak in a different language. We could be Germans or French or…or Hungarians, if that's what we wanted to be. We could go to schools and study regular subjects, not only Torah—"

"You did not like Torah study?"

"Now wait a minute, young man, don't you put words in my mouth. We did not reject religion. We remained good Jews. We studied Torah, but not *only* Torah. We also studied German language and literature. And mathematics – that is very important – and geography."

"You went to school in Zestmeadow-on-Nyitra?"

"Yes, I did. We had a good Jewish school, a German-speaking school."

"There was then a teacher there?"

"Of course there was. And a rabbi and a *chazan* and a *shochet* and a *mohel* and everything else that a Jewish community needed."

"It was a good life, then?"

"Did I say that? It was not easy. We had to work very hard and most of what we earned was taken away. We had to pay to the emperor. There was this *taxa tolerantialis*, they kept increasing it all the time, in my time they changed it to *kameralis taksa*. When we crossed the border to Moravia, we had to pay import and export duties. And what Simonyi demanded, that was more than all of it put together."

"What did you do?"

"I? I sold things. Went from town to town and sold the Slovaks whatever they needed. There was not that much more a Jew could do, unless he was learned enough to be a rabbi or a teacher or something like that. Yes, he could be a musician."

"Musician? Why, did you have so many musical events there?"

"We did, when I was young. Weddings, mainly. There were musicians and jesters – they were great fun. But there were fewer and fewer such events; people could not afford them."

"So earlier on, they had more money?"

"Perhaps they did, I don't know. But earlier, before my time, there were so many big weddings held in Nyitra, because everybody came over from Moravia. Later, when Josef the Second became emperor, that was no longer necessary. People stopped coming over, even though he did not eliminate the Familiantengesetze, only made it a little less restrictive."

"Tell me about Josef II. I know he was a little before your time, but people must have talked a lot about him. He was an important ruler, was he not?"

"Josef the Second? He was not a bad sort, nothing like his mother. Forgive me for my words, we are between men – she was a rotten whore, may her bones rot. No, he was a decent man, he tried to do good, but he was allowed to rule only for ten years. He permitted us to live almost anywhere, in most cities and towns. Then he insisted that we study in schools, our own schools or theirs, he did not care. And he said that we could do anything, almost no occupation should be closed to us. Of course he could not force the guilds to accept us, but we could be craftsmen or landowners, or doctors even. Yes, he was all right. Except for the beards."

"Except for what?"

"He brought a law forbidding beards. Can you imagine Jews without beards?!"

"Er, actually I can, but I see your point. Many people were quite upset, I suppose."

"More than upset, there was almost a revolt. He had to reverse that law."

"Good. Another thing. You said something before, something about him being *allowed* to rule only for ten years…?"

"Yes, have you not heard?"

"Heard what?"

"The Vienna establishment did not like Josef's innovations. He was too liberal for them. So they put him away."

"You mean they killed him?"

"No, nothing so crude. They kidnapped him and locked him in a cellar. They put a dummy in the coffin."

"You're pulling my leg! Who was supposed to have done this? Who are these 'they'?"

"I think it was the church. They were very powerful – they still are. He tried to curtail their power. I heard that a number of priests marched in there, pretending to pray or say mass or something, and they suddenly grabbed him and stuffed cloth in his mouth, so he could not scream. They bound him up and took him away as if he were one of theirs. And some others had a dummy prepared and put it in a coffin."

"You know, somehow I doubt that story. If it did not manage to come down to us 150, 200 years later, surely it has been found baseless."

"Maybe. Or the church has managed to suppress it. In any case, after Josef disappeared from the scene, all of his laws were cancelled."

"Was he not supposed to have them reversed on his deathbed?"

"You can believe what you want."

"All right. But as I recall, he emancipated the Jews, more or less, and that law was not repelled after his death."

"No, not completely. It was better than under Maria Theresa. But that's because of the situation in France."

"Yes, that revolution must have had a major effect on the freedom of the Jews."

"You can call it freedom or emancipation or whatever you want, but we still had to fight for every step of advancement."

"Were you, then, the fighting type?"

"Me, no. I was a peddler, then later I worked in the synagogue. I had no opportunity to fight. But I always thought that my grandson Berman would stand up for the rights of the Jews. Well, did he? You said you were *his* grandson. Did he fight?"

"Yes, sir. He did and so did his own son, my father."

"That's what I expected."

"So tell me, overall, do you think that your family did the right thing in moving to Hungary from Moravia? I mean, apart from the fact that they had to?"

"In my mind, there is no question. In Moravia we were well-behaving, careful little Jews, waiting for something to happen, waiting for freedom, emancipation. In Hungary we were invited to become Hungarians, free men, and look at what we created here. In my view it was a lovely experience, and it will be even lovelier in the future. Well, you *are* from the future, so you can tell me. It will have turned out beautifully, is that not so?"

"Sir, I think the time has come to end this discussion. Thank you very much for your patience. Goodbye."

Gothic Record – 2001

Actually, I did not learn about the names of Moses and Mari Steiner until later, much later. Vladimir found that information on March 15, a good few months after our trip. But he found many other things before that, important things.

First, he visited Banska Bystrica, the regional administrative center, and looked up the vital records there. He found the record of my grandfather's first marriage – but let me relate that piece of information a little later.

At Banska Bystrica, Vladimir also found information on my grandfather's children. His first daughter, Rózsika Steiner (my father's stepsister), was born on May 7, 1892, in Zólyom – the town where we spent a pleasant night, never considering that it was significant to my search. I had known of the date, but not the town – or rather, Rózsám must have mentioned Zólyom to me when I was a small child, but what did I care? And I had not known that she had two younger brothers, both of whom died as infants. Jenő (Eugene) was born in Rima-Sobota a year after Rózsám, on June 11, and died on March 3 of the following year, 1894, in Zólyom. And then another little boy, Gyula (Julius), was born in Rima-Sobota on March 13, 1896, and died on August 20 of the same year.

Incidentally, my grandfather's occupation was noted on these records as district court clerk in Zólyom and law court clerk in Rima-Sobota. Their address was also given: they lived at 10 Szíjjártó Street. Rabbi Leo Singer performed the circumcision for both Steiner boys. And Rózsika's birth register also states that later, on November 14, 1899, her father changed his surname from Steiner to Székely, by order no. 12006 of the Minister of the Interior.

After finding out what he could at Banska Bystrica, Vladimir went to the Nyitra governmental genealogical center in Ivanka. There he looked at the records that the center had sent me months earlier. He also found the birth registers of Pepi, who became Leni; Herman; Peppi (in 1861, the same year as Jozefina in the earlier census record – they missed this one); Berman; and Sali, all in Perlep. So the four younger children – Juda, Hermina, Mathilde and Ignácz – must all have been born in Golden Morava, not Perlep. This meant that the family moved to Golden Morava between the birth of Sali, in August 1864, and Juda, in June 1866.

And Peppi was Jozefina.

But…

While the first three boys, Herman, Berman and Juda, were all born to Markus (sometimes Mark) Steiner and Rozália (sometimes Rosa, Roza) Wasserman, the first three girls, Pepi/Leni, Peppi/Jozefina and Rozália/Sali each had their mothers registered as Regi. Just Regi, no surname mentioned. Rozália could be spelled a variety of ways, even Rozi or Rosi, but certainly not Regi, which is Regina. Were there two women involved? The father was consistently noted as Markus Steiner, in various spellings.

And to make matters worse, the fourth boy has not yet been mentioned. His name was József, in itself strange with a Jozefina already in the family. But he was born neither in Perlep, nor in Golden Morava, but in Fekete Kelecsény, the village a few kilometers past Perlep, further away from Golden Morava. And his mother was registered as Karolina Wasserman!

So what was going on here? Was Markus Steiner also married to Rozália's sister Karolina, in the next village? And to Regi? A trigamist? Apart from the unlikelihood of Rozália being called Regi, there was the fact that one of Regi's daughter was called Rozália (according to the Slovak authorities) or Sali (according to Vladimir's findings). It is almost unheard of in Jewish families to name a child after a living parent. But if her mother was Regi and not Rozália, then she could be given that name.

I did not seriously consider my great-grandfather a trigamist. But a possibility occurred to me, or rather to my sister: What if the custom developed among Jewish families originally from Moravia to cheat the system, the Familiantengesetze, by giving to several boys the same German name and distinguishing them by different Hebrew names? It is true that the law in question was not applicable in Hungary, but you could never tell when the emperor would change his mind...

I asked several experts in the field, but nobody welcomed my suggestion with enthusiasm. They had never heard of such a thing and thought it unlikely to have occurred. So did I, but then how to explain the discrepancy?

For the time being, there was no explanation, so I had to continue with the research. Vladimir noted several other possibly relevant facts relating to the Wasserman family. It seems that they indeed lived mainly in Szelezsény. Rozália probably had three brothers, Samuel, Mózes and David. (Much later I learned that she may have had a sister, too, named Julia.) Samuel was married to Katti Jellinek and had at least six children. Mózes married a Chaja (Ratta) and had a daughter, Éva. David had a wife Rebeka and one child, Mathilde (later I was to find that he was previously married to a Jozefa and had two children by her, Leni and Johanna). The parents of the Wasserman siblings were Herman and Pepi. Later, we also found data connecting these individuals in a variety of ways: we learned, for instance, that David Wasserman was one of the witnesses at Rozália's wedding to Markus Steiner; the other witness was Moses Steiner, Markus's father. Also, David was godfather to one of Samuel's children, Wilhelm, born in 1856. Nothing connects Mózes Wasserman to the other assumed siblings, except that he, too, was born in Szelezsény.

Vladimir also found a Moritz Leopold Steiner, merchant, who died in Golden Morava at the age of seventy-four on December 16, 1881. This man was born in Zestmeadow-on-Nyitra, so Vladimir thought that perhaps he was the father of Markus Steiner. We found out later that this was not so; he might have been Markus's uncle.

For the next two months Vladimir and I continued exchanging messages, but nothing of importance was discovered. He tried to find the death record of my father's sister Erzsébet Steiner in Rima-Sobota, but no such record came to light.

But in the middle of February I received an e-mail from Vladimir. He had called the county hall in Losonc and found out that Erzsébet Steiner had died there, not in Rima-Sobota. She died on April 10, 1899. The cause of her death was "convulsions." And strangest of all was the location of her death: a steam mill in Losonc!

What was an eleven-month-old child doing in a steam mill, thirty kilometers away from her home?

If there is such a thing as beautiful frustration, I found it in genealogy.

Meanwhile, I kept sending messages to Vladimir about all the missing data. How could we find out more about Markus, Rozália, their marriage, their parents, siblings and so on? He proposed to go to the Léva governmental genealogical center; I authorized him and he went. In the middle of March I received a very excited e-mail from him. "I found the marriage of Markus Steiner and Rosa Wassermann. With lots of info. Very difficult to read. I have never been so happy. Have a copy of the record. Will try to decipher as much as possible tomorrow."

He sent me the record and I was incredulous at first. It seemed to be about strangers, people with different names. I can read Gothic print, but this was Gothic script, a totally different way of writing. The *r* looks like a small *m*, the *e* looks like an *a*, the *a* looks like a *u* with a wing and so on. Superficially, all *a*, *e*, *n*, *o*, *u*, and *v* letters looked the same. What looked like *Rainam* turned out to be Steiner. Wasserman looked like *Mmuppmmmvw*. I looked up the script on the Internet and it helped me to decipher the document; later, Vladimir sent me his very accurate interpretation. Here is what the register looked like:

I also attach the key to interpreting Gothic script.

Apparently, they were married at a place called Taszár-Malanya, not far from Golden Morava. Markus Steiner's occupation was innkeeper. Born in Zestmeadow-on-Nyitra, at twenty-four he was a resident of Perlep. His parents: Moses and Mari Steiner. Moses worked as a merchant in Perlep.

Rosi Wasserman was born in Bélád. Her parents: Herman and Pepi Wasserman, both deceased; they died in Szelezsény. Rosi resided in Taszár-Malanya. She was also twenty-four years old.

The register was dated December 28, 1853, which would put their year of birth at 1829. There had been some doubt as to when Markus was born due to his death register, which stated that he died in 1878 at the age of forty-four. That would have established his birth year as 1834, yet the 1870 census stated that he was born in 1829. Now this third record reinforced the earlier date. Of course, we should not rule out the possibility that he was indeed five years younger than his bride and he, or perhaps both of them, would prefer to hide this fact. But marrying at nineteen? Possible, but not likely.

The witnesses were Moses Steiner, the groom's father, and David Wasserman, almost certainly the bride's brother. The rabbi was Simon Fuerst.

In addition to finding Markus and Rozália's marriage certificate, Vladimir also found a few other things in Léva. Apparently, in 1872, Moses Steiner was employed by the local Jewish community as a *Gemeindediener*, which was something like a *shamash*, or community servant. That information was recorded on the death register of Moses's wife, Mari Steiner, who died on September 22 of that year at the age of sixty-six. Moses himself died thirteen years later, on June 15, 1885, at the age of seventy-six.

Moritz Leopold Steiner, whom I took to be Moses's brother simply because both were born in the same town of Zestmeadow-on-Nyitra, died a widower at age seventy-four, on December 16, 1881.

From Zestmeadow-on-Nyitra to Perlep – 1848

"Sir, Mr. Moses Steiner. Great-Great-Grandfather. Let us talk again."

"*Ja, ja, sprechen.* Well, as I said the last time you called me, I have nothing better to do at the moment."

"Right. So I would like to find out when you moved from Zestmeadow to the Golden Morava region, to Perlep. When, and also, why. What were the circumstances, how the whole move came about."

"So I should just tell you that."

"Yes, if you would. Please."

"Just like that."

"Just like that? What do you mean?"

"What do I mean? It is not a small thing that you are asking. Why, it was the biggest decision that I ever made in my life."

"Yes. I know. I mean, I guessed that. That's why it would be important for me to find out about it."

"But it was such a long and complicated story. It was not that one day, we said, let's move to Perlep, so we put everything on a cart and moved there and lived happily every after."

"No, I suppose not. In fact, I assumed that you *had* to move."

"Had to? Well, that, too, it was part of it. But not everybody moved from Zestmeadow. Not every Jewish family. It was a decision, and a difficult one. It depended on the circumstances. Have you ever heard of the 1848 Hungarian Revolution?"

"Have I? What a silly question! I'm sorry, I take that back. Yes, of course I have. I am very familiar with it. A glorious time it was indeed."

"Glorious. Yes, I suppose it was that, too. I used to think so. But there were some ugly things in those days. You want me to tell you about them?"

"Yes, please."

"All right, I'll tell you. But not yet. I told you this was a long and complicated story. It started with the new emperor, Josef the Second. I told you about him. He brought a law saying that the Jews would be permitted to live anywhere they wanted, any town, any city. Not that it made a difference. Most cities still would not allow Jews to move there."

"How could that be, when the emperor ordered it?"

"There are always exceptions to any rule. Many cities had a royal patent that specifically permitted them to keep the Jews out. And in many others the Germans just would not allow it, period."

"Germans? I thought that we were talking about Hungary."

"Yes, we are. But in every town there were many German merchants. Germans, Greeks, Armenians. Well, the Germans knew that they could not stay in business if the Jews came to town and opened up shops. So they sabotaged the emperor's order, and nobody complained. Nobody but we, the Jews. And who cared about that?"

"Jews had no friends."

"No friends, none at all. Mind you, we did have some allies."

"Allies? Like who?"

"You would be surprised. Like the Hungarian aristocrats. Like the great landowners. Not all, but many of them. They liked to keep Jews."

"*Keep* them?"

"Yes, that's what they called it. They figured that this would start the business life going on their estates, which of course it did. They became much richer. They invited us to come to their oppidium–"

"What's an *oppidium*?"

"An agricultural town. They held fairs there and wanted us to come to those fairs, even to build a house and ply our trade. And when the town merchants would not let us move in there, often we settled on the estate of the nobleman, in little villages. Eventually he convinced the town council to let us in."

"So as to make sure that you would remain close to his estate?"

"Well, I don't know about that. Some Jews did certainly remain there and built it up. They established large businesses and factories and banks and everything. But others did not want to stay. They wanted to move on."

"Move on where?"

"Oh…to the middle of the country. To larger and larger places. There is always more opportunity in a larger town or city. Once we tasted the flavor of this country, once we understood that finally, here we can live like real people, not like oppressed little Jews, after hundreds of years here was a place where we were needed, well, we were eager to take advantage, to move where they wanted us, where they needed us…"

"So they did want you? They were happy to receive the Jews?"

"They? Who is this 'they'? The whole country needed us, that's for sure. But not everybody realized this, not everyone would admit it. But Mr. Simonyi did, the owner of most of the lands around Zestmeadow. And so did the count Migazzi."

"Migazzi. He was the big landowner around Golden Morava, wasn't he?"

"Yes, and he wanted us badly. By the time he realized this, in the early 1840s, it was no longer so easy to get Jews from Moravia. The Familiantengesetze was no longer such an important factor; people stopped coming over. But he knew that Nyitra County was full of Jews, so he figured that it might not be so difficult to get them to move over to the neighboring Bars County."

"No, come to think of it, why did you not move there earlier, on your own?"

"Well, that is difficult to say. You see, Nyitra bordered Moravia. To us Jews, or at least to our parents and grandparents, Moravia was always home. We thought, or they thought, that we were in Hungary only by necessity, only temporarily, until the situation improved. They kept going "home" whenever they could. Over the border, that was just a place to get married and find some way of making a living for the time being. But gradually, the younger generation came to like this country. I had never been in Moravia myself and neither had most of my friends."

"I understand. So you were happy to live in Nyitra for a while, but then, slowly, you came to realize that there was a whole country to the east and to the south?"

"Yes, that's about right. But I don't know if we would have moved on our own. Some may have. I was perhaps not one of the most adventurous and my son Markus certainly was not."

"So then what happened?"

"I am coming to that, don't be impatient. But it was in the early 1840s that men started to come over from Golden Morava, from the count Migazzi, and sought us out – in secret, for Mr. Simonyi would not have liked it – and suggested that we might want to move to the estate of the count."

"To Golden Morava?"

"Well, no. That was one of the problems. The town of Golden Morava would not permit Jews to settle there. You could attend the weekly market, but you could not even sleep there. What they said, though, was that we could live in a number of villages on the count's estate, not far from the town – really suburbs of the larger Golden Morava area – and eventually he would fight for our rights, so in a very few years we would end up living in the town."

"So what did you think of that?"

"Well, we thought and thought. At first, we did not take it very seriously, but the more they came and talked, the more we thought and talked. There was one big problem, of course."

"Of course. Ah…what was that?"

"What was that? Don't you see? One or two, or at most three families would settle in a little village. We would not be together, like in Zestmeadow, like in the Moravian towns. We would be on our own."

"Yes, that could be a problem. You had to rely on the community."

"More than rely. We are Jews! We need the community for our daily lives. We go to the *shul*, we *daven* there. We have our school, our rabbi, our *chazan*, our teacher. We have our *shochet*. We have our *mohel*. But in the small villages we would have none of those things. How can a Jew live that way?!"

"How indeed? Somehow, I had the impression that you, I mean, the people in your circle, were not all that religious."

"Well, now, what gave you that idea? Of course we were religious. What's a Jew without religion? But then there is religious and there is religious. As I told you last time, we were not willing to be ruled by the Chasam Sofer in Pozsony. He ruled the people living in Tapolcsány, just a few kilometers south of us, and that was not for us. Those Tapolcsány people came over from Austria, not from Moravia."

"Why, were Moravian Jews so much more independent?"

"Yes, they were. We were. There were all kinds of crazy movements in Moravia, before we came over here, but we did not want any. You must have heard of Shabbetai Zevi. The crazy messiah who became a Muslim in the end. And then the Frankists. There were also the Kabbalists. And the Freemasons. We did not care for any of them. But we talked about them. And when the reformers came from Berlin, we thought that they had something there."

"You mean, Moses Mendelssohn and his followers?"

"Ah, so you know about them? Yes, that's what I mean. They talked about religion of the mind, they said there is no other dogma but the 'dogma of the intellect.' I am not sure what that meant, but is sounded good at the time. They did not care for the Talmud, which was a pity – from what I have seen of it, it makes a lot of sense. But what appealed to us, what they said was that the dark ages were now over. They explained to us that we were just like everybody else, only our religion is Jewish, and that means we follow certain rituals. They assured us that we were all Germans, that we should all find our homeland in the country where we were, no need to dream of going back to the land of our fathers, to Palestine, because it would never happen. There was this man, a rabbi, he brought these ideas from Berlin. His name was Einhorn. I liked what he said, but not all of it. He wanted to change our Sabbath to Sunday. I thought that was wrong, we all did. He would do away with circumcision – why, then we would no longer be Jews at all! So we had mixed feelings about those things."

"Einhorn, was he not the leader of the Neolog Jews in Hungary?"

"No, that would be Rabbi Lipót Löw. At first he said the same things as Einhorn, but later he became more sensible, when he ruled in Szeged for many years. So we talked and talked about those things, just as our parents and grandparents talked about Shabbetai Zevi and Jacob Frank, and the more we thought and the more we talked, the more confused we became."

"You did not know whom to believe."

"No, we did not know what we were. Were we German Jews, or Jewish Germans? Moravians? Hebrews? Were we a people, a nation without a country, living here among other people? Or just ordinary people, who happened to have another religion? Like there were Catholics and Protestants and Greek Orthodox and Muslims? Everybody argued differently, at least those who were *chochems* enough to argue. But everybody agreed that the important thing was to move toward enlightenment. Haskala! That was our guiding light. And emancipation – no, that came a little later. Assimilation, to be like everyone else, to live like everyone else, to look like everyone else, only with our religion. We all knew that those bad old days were over, finally, finally, we were about to be freed, if not today then tomorrow."

"That was the most important thing in your lives?"

"That and livelihood, of course. We had to live, we had to sell enough to have bread on the table for the family. But once we had bread, it was to be normal life. We were yearning! I don't like to use big words, but we were all yearning for normalcy, after being thought of as a strange and funny people, a despised people, for seventeen hundred years."

"All right, and so what happened next?"

"Next? Well, don't forget that the French Revolution happened first. That was before I was born, but that gave everybody an idea, a direction. And then, then came the other revolution, everywhere but especially in Hungary."

"Eighteen forty-eight. You said it was glorious, but…"

"No, it was glorious all right. We were fighting alongside the Magyars, fighting for freedom, our freedom and theirs. For a while, it seemed as though there were no 'ours' and 'theirs' anymore. Suddenly, it came as a big shock, we were all Hungarians! Our leader, Lajos Kossuth, said that there was to be full emancipation for all Jews. *Our* leader, imagine that! There was this other leader, István Szechenyi, Count Szechenyi, he was not so sure. But everybody said that the emancipation would be made a law of the land. We Jews all joined the fight. Without exception we were on the side of the revolution, against the Habsburgs, even the *interlandisch*…"

"The who?"

"*Interlandish*. You don't speak Yiddish, either?"

"No, I am sorry, in our generation…"

"Yes, I know, we did not speak it in my generation, either, but we still understood those special words. *Interlandisch. Unterlandisch*, those who lived in the lower parts of Hungary. Because they did not let us live everywhere, earlier, we were split into two. We were the *oiberlandisch, oberlandisch* – we lived in the north and west, they lived in the south and east. We came mainly from Moravia and Austria, they came mainly from Galicia and other parts of Poland. They were more Orthodox than we – they had their miracle-making rebbes – but in 1848 they also became good Hungarians."

"So what did you do? Join the army?"

"It was not called an army, but the National Guard. I wanted to join it, and so did Markus, but in our parts of Hungary they would not let Jews in. Strangely, the Guard was controlled by Germans. Yet everywhere else in Hungary there was such a strong anti-German mood, we were all brothers, against the Germans. But not in the northwest, of course that was the part closest to Austria. We went to the National Guard and wanted to sign up. They told us, what are you doing here, you are Jews, not Magyars. I told them that we were Magyars of the Mosaic faith. They just laughed us out of the place. Later I learned that they were all Germans."

"Could there be such a thing as a 'Magyar of Mosaic faith'?"

"Sure could. There were Jewish Magyars all the way back. Many came in to the land with the original Magyars, they were called Kabars, a Jewish tribe from Asia…"

"Yes, I have heard about them. Perhaps they were Khazars."

"I don't know. And then, all the better Magyar kings begged the Jews to come into the country and become Magyars, and they always did…"

"Yes, and then they were always robbed and massacred, or at best expelled as paupers from the country."

"I suppose. But for a while, it looked like now they really wanted us, they wanted Jews to become Magyars, and we were ready and enthusiastic. But then…"

"Yes, but then? Tell me what happened."

"Well, first the parliament postponed the expected law of emancipation. Then bigger trouble started. There were pogroms, if you can believe! Pogroms in Hungary! Even in Nyitra, close to us, there were pogroms. And in Pozsony. By late April they were attacking Jews everywhere. Even in smaller towns, Jews were beaten up and robbed and many murdered. They had to escape into the forests. By early May in Vagujhely, which was north of Nyitra, they were attacking the Jews under the national flag that we supported so enthusiastically. And in Tapolcsány, just to the south of us. And then in all the smaller places around Tapolcsány. Many dead, many more injured. All this by the revolution, *our* revolution."

"In Zestmeadow, too?"

"Yes, there, too. That's what I am getting at. Our neighbors, with whom we had lived in peace, if not exactly close friendship, suddenly turned on us. After the eruption was over, they looked away. When they met us on the street, they would not dare to look us in the eye, but we knew that they would happily do it again, just waiting for the opportunity. So we started to hate the place, no longer felt at home there."

"And that's when you decided to move?"

"Yes, very soon after that. There were several places in Bars County that wanted us, but we liked the sound of Golden Morava, somehow it reminded us of the old country that we had never seen. And it was the right move, in the direction of the center of the land."

"You would not consider moving to Pozsony, for example – an important, large city that was quite close by?"

"Absolutely not. To get under the control of the sons of the Chasam Sofer? One of our problems in Zestmeadow was just the fact that we were so close to Tapolcsány that we were associated with them. It was a good idea to put some distance between ourselves and them."

"Yes, but you have not dealt with the problem you raised earlier. That you would be living in small villages, just one or two families, no *minyan*, no *shul*, no *shochet*, no *mohel*, no rabbi, no teacher, no school…"

"But you see in those few years our thinking had changed a lot. We were still Jews, and good Jews, I like to think, but we had become Magyars of the

Mosaic faith. So we now believed that we could live among other Magyars, of other faiths, and somehow we'd manage. We would come together from all the villages on the high holidays, maybe every *Shabbes*. There would be a *mohel* somewhere, when we needed one. We would send our children to the regular schools but teach them religion ourselves. We would learn how to cut the throat of a chicken or goose correctly ourselves… There would be a solution to everything."

"And that's how it turned out?"

"Well…more or less, yes. It was difficult, I admit. More difficult then we had thought. To gather at a neighborhood village for *Shabbes* service, that was unrealistic. But we did go for *Rosh Hashono* and *Yom Kippur* and some of the other *yontef*s, sometimes, and we did manage to get *matzes* for *Pesach* and there was a *mohel* not too far – we managed."

"So what happened? Did you decide one day that this was it, enough of Zestmeadow, you are heading for Golden Morava? Just packed up and went?"

"Almost, yes. Well, not quite. I'll tell you what happened. I was on the road a lot in those days, carrying my merchandise – clothes, mainly – on my back, and Markus usually came along. I wanted to teach him the tricks of the trade. He was already nineteen – he had to learn some business and selling was the only business I knew. Mari was at home, cooking, when this man I knew came to visit…"

The Decision

Mari was at home, preparing for dinner. The men would be back in a little while; Moses had promised her that they would only go to a couple of villages in the neighborhood. She did not want him to go very far in these turbulent times; you never knew what could happen. She was worried about him, worried about Markus, too, constantly worried.

She was cooking potato soup and noodles with ground walnuts. She also had to put the freshly ironed shirts away. Markus was funny that way, not like his father – he had to have nice ironed shirts all the time. He had three shirts, so that she had to wash them every second day. And bread, she had to prepare for baking the bread tomorrow morning, that was the most important thing for Moses, fresh bread. And she should go over to her sister-in-law, borrow some sugar and ask her what Moritz said about the latest proposal. And she wanted to sew a few more cockades, red-white-and-green cockades for the men to wear. Moses even sold a few; she did not know why – could not every woman sew her own?

There was a knock on the door, a strong knock. Who could that be? Surely not that bothersome Mrs. Morgenstern again! Always complaining. Moses would not knock that way. Up to the year before, he did not need to knock at all, the door was always open. But with the trouble this spring, it was no longer safe to leave the door unlocked...

She opened the door a crack. There was a man there whom she thought she had seen before. A nice, clean-shaven man, tall, well dressed. He smiled at her.

"Mrs. Steiner? Good afternoon, don't you remember me? I am Sandor Avakian. From Golden Morava. I was here before."

"Oh, yes, of course. Hello, Mr. Avakian. My husband is not at home. I suppose you wanted to see him."

"Him and yourself, and even that nice young man of yours, what was his name now?"

"Markus."

"Yes, Markus. Do you think that they'll be back soon?"

"Yes, actually I expect them back within the hour. Perhaps you would like to wait for them?"

"I would not mind sitting down a little. I have been sitting on that horse outside for hours, now, but a chair is more comfortable." Mari could see the horse tethered to a tree.

"Sure, come on in, I'll take you to the sitting room." How lucky that she had cleaned it that morning.

"Don't bother, ma'am. If it's all the same for you, I would just as soon sit here in the kitchen, watch you work and maybe talk a little."

Mari would have preferred the man out of her way, but she thought that it was not nice to pack the man away in the other room, sitting there, doing nothing; let him sit in the kitchen. Besides, it was still a cool day. This May was chillier than usual, and the sitting room might not be so pleasant. So she pulled a chair over to the table, let Mr. Avakian sit there.

He sat and looked comfortable. Mari asked him, "May I offer you something to eat? A little refreshment?"

"No, thank you, ma'am, I had lunch not that long ago. Maybe if I could have a glass of water."

"Sure you can have. Try some of these patties, I baked them today."

"Well, perhaps just one."

After a while Mari felt that she had to talk to the man about something.

"Did you ride over from Golden Morava today?" she asked him.

"Yes, ma'am, this morning. Just over three hours it took. It is a pleasant ride, and then I had lunch at the inn here, and saw some people."

"But you are not planning to ride back tonight?"

"I don't think so, I might just sleep over at the inn and ride back in the morning. Although the nights are getting longer now… We shall see. It depends on how long your husband and son will want to talk to me. Maybe they'll tell me to go away as soon as they come in." He smiled.

"No, they would not. I know that my husband liked you the last time you visited here."

"That is nice to hear. I certainly liked him very much, and the young man, too."

"They may be coming now. I hear some noise outside." Mari went over to the window. Sure enough, Moses and Markus were cleaning their boots just outside the door. She opened the door.

"We have a visitor," she warned them.

"A visitor?" Moses was surprised. "Who?"

"It is Mr. Avakian, from Golden Morava."

A special gleam came to Moses's eyes. Markus smiled at the visitor. Markus had a very friendly smile – maybe that's why everybody liked Markus.

"Oh, him. Good, I was thinking…" But Moses said no more. He came into the kitchen, Markus behind him. They all shook hands.

"Good afternoon, Mr. Avakian. Hello. Mari, why did you not seat our guest in the sitting room?"

"I wanted to…"

"No, she offered, of course, but I asked her if I might sit here in the kitchen instead."

"Whatever you want. But let us go over there now. And afterwards, surely you'll stay for dinner?"

"I was not planning…"

"I won't hear another word. Mari, there is enough for our guest, surely?"

"But of course, there is plenty. Why don't you all stay here in the kitchen, so I can hear what you discuss. After all, if it is about what I think it might be about, it might just interest me, too."

So they all sat in the kitchen. Moses preferred sitting with strangers, especially tall ones; he was rather short and stocky. It pleased him that Markus took after his mother – a thin and at least medium-sized young man, he would never be fat.

Mari continued to cook, while Moses took down a bottle of wine and poured a little for the three men.

After a while, it was Avakian who broached the subject.

"Tell me, Mr. Steiner, was there not some trouble around here these past few weeks?"

Moses nodded. "Yes, there sure was. You have heard about it. Why, was there something around Golden Morava, too?"

"No, not there. For one thing, there are no Jews yet in Golden Morava. There are a few already in the neighboring villages, but thank God, we had no trouble there at all."

"But in Nyitra, I hear, there was a real murderous pogrom."

"In Nyitra, yes. But we have nothing to do with Nyitra. Golden Morava is thirty kilometers to the east. You might say that's not too much, but it's a different world there. It is Migazzi country, I could almost say." His face broke out in a pleasant, confident smile. He was indeed a man who always seemed very confident and managed to transfer this quality to his listeners.

Moses looked at him, waiting to open up the subject.

"Well, Mr. Steiner, so have you thought more about what we discussed the last time?"

"Yes, I have. We all have. As you say, since that time there has been another argument in its favor."

"I know. So does the count Migazzi, that's why he suggested that I talk to you again."

"Only to me, to us? Not to other people?

"Of course to other people as well. I must tell you that I also saw your brother earlier today. He certainly is paying lots of attention to what I am telling him."

"Well, what did he say? Yes or no?"

"He did not say yes yet, but I think he is leaning that way. You know that it is just a little more difficult for him – with the shop and all, he would have to find a good buyer. But he does not like the way things are going here."

"Neither do I. But let's go over this thing again, let us discuss what exactly are we talking about."

"Sure thing. I'll tell you again, you might even want to write down some of it, if you like."

"No, no, I have a good memory."

"All right. Well, the count Migazzi is inviting you and your family to move over to his estate. It is around Golden Morava. Not inside the town, but all around. There are seven villages that you could choose from. He is trying to develop these villages to larger, better places where his local men can live better lives with their families. He is trying to create more work opportunities."

"About Golden Morava. It is definitely not in the town, that we are talking about?"

"No, not now. I know how you feel about that, you would prefer to live in a larger town, not a village. Right now, the town has a letter patent that says that it does not have to allow Jewish people to live inside. They can come to the fairs, but must leave by the end of the day. But that will change."

"When will it change?"

Avakian shrugged. "I cannot say for sure. The count is working on it. He has to go slowly, carefully about a thing like that, talk to the local politicians, one-by-one, put pressure on the shopkeepers, talk to the mayor, talk to the member of parliament, the county officers, you know how it is. He thinks that it might take a year or two, maybe even more, but not much more. Anyway, what we are talking about here, his offer to you, would take care of that time. He is not offering a short-term arrangement."

"So what exactly is he offering?"

Avakian had a mischievous gleam in his eye. "You will like it, I think. Since the town is so important for you, he suggests the place closest to the town, a place just three kilometers from Golden Morava, practically inside the town. It is a village called Perlep."

"Perlep? Never heard of it."

"No, not many people have. It is a small place, but growing rapidly. You see, the count is building a paper mill there, to take advantage of all the wood in his forests nearby. So the population is going to double quite soon. Where to house all of those workers and their families? He is getting a whole street built up, close to a hundred houses, small ones, bigger ones. His workers will choose where they want to live, pay him rent for the house, everybody wins."

Moses appeared impressed. "So the count is quite a practical man, it seems."

"Yes… Or at least he has very practical men on his payroll." Avakian smiled.

"Such as yourself?"

"Well, anyway, in that town, the workers will have certain needs. There are already a couple of stores, but there is a need for a general store, and a tavern. After a hard day's work, the men may want to spend an hour or two with a glass of wine. Sometimes even a little music. So he is building a general store and a tavern. He needs men like you to run them."

Moses and Markus looked at each other; the younger man was a little puzzled. "One of us should run the store, and the other the tavern?"

"Yes, that is the proposition."

"Which of us…?" Markus spoke for the first time that evening.

"I don't know, that's up to you. Have either of you ever run a tavern?"

They both shook their heads.

"Well, it can be learned. Just by spending a little time in one or two, talking to the owners, you can learn all the tricks. Perhaps, if I may make a suggestion…"

"Sure, what?"

"The young man, Markus, might be better suited to run the store, for he seems a quiet young man. Perhaps for a tavern keeper it might be better to be more voluble, more experienced in the ways of the world. But that would be up to you, I would not want to say either way."

Father and son said nothing. Clearly possibilities were going through their minds. Avakian waited for a few seconds and then added, "But a decision will have to be made very soon now. The buildings are already going up, the tavern will have to open in a few months' time. The store, too."

Moses took control of the situation.

"That's no problem, we can decide fast. But surely not today, not here, you can give us a few days?"

"Yes, of course. You can write me an answer, yes or no, in a few days. But don't you want to hear the specifics? The financials?"

"Of course, we've been waiting for you to tell us."

"Well, here is what the count offers. He will rent you a house in Perlep, much like this one, a house with a kitchen, a sitting room, a shed at the back, centrally located, close to the store and the tavern. He will lease you the tavern and the store. He does not tell you what to sell at the store, so long as it is not meat, because there is a butcher – he would not like you to compete with him. He does not tell you what kind of wine to sell at the tavern, or anything else, he is not a tavern keeper himself and does not want to be. Of course you'll have to pay him for the tavern lease and for the store lease. That is the *árenda*."

"And how much for the house, how much for the *árenda*?"

Avakian too out some papers.

"You will have to pay, for the house, a rent of ten forints a year." He stopped, looked at them, and knew that they were paying more than that for their current house. "For the store, eighteen forints a year."

"And the tavern?"

"The *árenda* for the tavern will have to be twenty-five forints. All of these will be payable only at the end of the year, except the house, which will have to be paid quarterly, two and a half forints every quarter. In advance. You might say as a sign of goodwill."

Nobody said anything, everybody was calculating incomes and expenses and *árenda*s and taxes. After a minute, Mari stood up and said, "Let's have dinner. Mr. Avakian, you will join us." The question mark was only in her eyes.

The man looked at her husband. Moses nodded.

"Yes, of course he will join us. Won't you, Mr. Avakian?"

"Well, if you insist, I would be honored."

Mari set the table for four. She served them the soup, then the noodles. Moses poured some more red wine for the men and a little for Mari, too. They ate and talked about the weather, carefully avoiding any further mention of the recent disturbances, or any possible move to Bars County. But near the end of the dinner, Avakian spoke again. "You know, if you were to run that tavern, it might be an idea to have some food available for the hungry men, at least from time to time. Noodles like this would be a great success, not to mention such a tasty soup."

"Yes, I admit that the thought has already occurred to me," agreed Moses. "Mari is an excellent cook."

"She sure is, I can attest to that. And the tavern guests would feel more at home that way. They need to feel good, to relax, eat something, have a drink and talk to their friends."

Mari interposed, "If I may ask a question, in what language will they be talking?"

"Good question. Mainly Slovak, I would think, but there will be Magyars there, more and more. Official people, financial people, the odd soldier or government officer, teacher and so on. Yes, there will be lots of Hungarian talk."

"And German?"

"That, too, I suppose, but I would not like to encourage it. That raises another subject that I wanted to touch upon. The question of languages and national identity."

Moses, Markus and Mari all looked at each other, puzzled.

"Yes, national identity. The count has specially asked me to convey his wish that if you accept his offer, that you undertake to become real Hungarians." He looked at all of their faces and saw neither agreement nor opposition, only incomprehension. He continued.

"It is very important to have as many Hungarians in this country as possible. There are too few of us and too many Slovaks. Slovaks here, Romanians in the south, and Serbs and Ruthenians and Germans. There are too few Hungarians. Slav countries, there are enough of them in this part of the world. Many of the leaders of this country are concerned that they will be run over by the Slavs. So they want more Magyars. Could you see yourself becoming Magyars?"

After a few seconds of quiet, it was Markus who spoke.

"Well, we are already Magyars. Did we not fight in the revolution against the Germans, at least when they let us? We all wanted to join the National Guard, but it turns out that it was packed with Germans."

"Yes, but what language do you speak? Can you speak Hungarian?"

"Yes, I can. Father can, too. Not so well, but he can."

"I see. I suppose not you, Mrs. Steiner?" The conversation was conducted entirely in German.

"No, I cannot, really. I know a few words in Slovak."

"That does not matter, as you will probably not be meeting so many people as the men. But in the store, in the tavern, you should try to speak Hungarian, whenever possible."

"Yes, but will the customers not be mainly Slovaks?"

"That is true, and you must know at least a little of that language, too… I suppose you do?"

They both nodded.

"But if we could encourage the Slovaks to speak Hungarian, more and more, then one day they may become Magyars, too."

He must have seen some disbelief on their faces, for he hastened to add, "Look, my ancestors were not from this country, they were all from Armenia. But I am a good Magyar, and so is my father. And I have an even better example for you, the count Migazzi himself. His family came here from Italy, some five, six generations ago. There are no better Magyars in this country than the count Migazzi and his family."

He waited.

"And I am not asking you to swear loyalty to Hungary, or anything like that. I am sure that you will be loyal subjects of the nation. I just mentioned this, so you'd understand how the count is thinking about these things. Now, are there any other questions?"

Mari stood up and started to clean away the dinner dishes.

"Yes, one or two," said Moses. "Back to those figures, the *árenda*s. You mentioned how much we'd have to pay, but how do we know that there will be enough income to cover all that, and the rent for the house, too, and you know that there are taxes to Vienna, or perhaps those will be to Pest now, and so many other things to pay. How do we know that there will be enough left over to eat and to clothe the family?"

"Now on that, sir, I cannot give you a guaranty. Look, the *árenda* has been established based on the experience of other taverns and stores. I myself did some study on my own in that. But that is what you'll have to do, talk to tavern keepers in this area, or wherever, there must be some that you know or that your friends know. Regarding the store, you could talk to your own brother, of course it would not be the same type of store, but he knows something about customers and spending and paying. And credit, too, because in a store, I suppose that sometimes you have to give credit to the customer, he will pay you when he gets his own pay from the estate. That's why the count will not ask for the *árenda* until the end of the year."

"The count seems to know a lot about these things," said Moses. "Or, I suppose, it is his friends like yourself who know about them."

"Well, I do have some Armenian blood in me," Avakian laughed.

"All right, we shall ask around. I have one more question. I suppose that there will be no other Jewish families at this Pre…"

"Perlep. No, just yourself, but there are already a few Jewish families in the neighboring villages. There is one at Fekete Kelecsény, the next village, just two kilometers from Perlep – the Pollak family from Vagujhely. Now in Knezics, there have been three Jewish families living there for quite a few years already – the Munks, the Ehrenfields and the Spitzers. And just ten kilometers to the west of Perlep, there are three villages, lots of Jewish people there. The Wassermans in Kis Herestény, the Jellineks and the Streichers in Nagy Herestény, and in Bélád, there are the other Jellineks, the other Streichers, the Spitzers and the Weisses. In Taszár-Malanya, the Schlesingers and the Stangels came from Nyitra County, but Mor Seidler's family may have been born there. That is a larger community, with five Jewish families just in Taszár, more in Malanya."

"But, look, Mr. Avakian," said Moscs. "Why could we not move then to one of those places? It would be an awful lot better for us."

"Yes, I knew you would ask that. But that is not what the count is trying to achieve. You see, he has noticed that those areas where Jews settle, before long, come to life. Commerce starts, industry starts, trade starts, and to be frank, everybody pays their dues to the count. Let us be realistic. He likes that and he wants to see more of his estate become rich. And he wants the peasants on his estate to become better fed, better educated, happier. So he is inviting smart Jewish people with a good sense of commerce to come to other villages, start something there, too. At Bélád, there are already four Jewish families, while in Perlep there are none. He needs you in Perlep, not in Bélád. You do understand that, do you not?"

Moses sighed. "Yes, I understand. That is the only difficulty, but I understand."

"So you can see, there are already quite a number of Jewish people living around Golden Morava, you won't have a problem getting a good, large group together for your holidays. And there will be many more, I bet you. I myself have been talking to many people, many families. Even here in Zestmeadow. I don't mind telling you. "

"Oh, I know," said Moses, "You have talked to the Wertheims and the Fleischners and the Singers, there are no secrets here."

"So you see, you will not be alone – these villages are all very close to each other. Well, how does it sound to you, Mr. Steiner? Mrs. Steiner? Young Mr. Steiner?" He looked at each of them with his wide, confident smile.

After a few moments, it had to be Moses who spoke.

"I must say, Mr. Avakian, that it sounds quite reasonable. But we have to discuss it among ourselves. And, as you said, I'll have to make some inquiries, with tavern keepers, storekeepers and so on. But if the figures work out, my guess is, we might just say yes to you. It depends, of course, on my wife," he took a step closer to her, "and my son – he is an adult now, he must have his say. But I hope that we'll all agree."

"Good. I thought you would say that. Listen, when you know, send me a letter. You have my address? Sandor Avakian, The Estate of Count Vilmos Migazzi, Golden Morava, Bars County. Let me know when we may expect your arrival. And then, when you come, you get the man to drive the cart right up to the front of the estate, there is a big gate there, send in word to me, I'll come out and take you right over to your new house. The house will be ready. The tavern and the store will require a few weeks work. You will have a say in how it is to be done – it's better that way. All right?"

He looked around, smiled at everybody and stood up. They all stood. He shook their hands, all but Mari's – he knew that Jews don't encourage physical touching of women. They said their good-byes and Avakian left.

Afterwards, they sat in silence for a while. It was Mari who spoke first.

"Well, what do you think?"

Markus stood, nodding his head repeatedly. "Yes, I think so."

They looked at Moses. He started pacing back and forth across the kitchen floor. He walked and walked, turning ever fifth step, for that was the length of the kitchen. Finally, he spoke. "There are lots of argument in its favor. There are a few against."

"Father, I think most arguments are for the move."

"Maybe. Let's discuss it. Not as if this were the first time we talked about it, but let us go through the whole thing again. So why should we stay here?"

Mari spoke: "It is comfortable here, we know everybody, have a reasonably good life…"

"Not that good!" said both Moses and Markus.

"No, not that good. And we have relatives here."

"Yes, but the closest ones left are my brother and his family. I want to talk to him, find out what he thinks. Maybe they want to move, too."

"I think they do," said Mari.

"Any other reasons for staying? No? Well, I'll give you one. The religious argument. Here I go to the *shul* every morning, we both go. *Erev Shabbes* we are there, all day *Shabbes*. There is the *shochet*. And if God forbid we need something, say somebody is ill, a *Mishebeirach* should be said, well, that will be difficult there."

"All right, talking about the religious argument," responded Mari, "listen to this. That bothersome Mrs. Morgenstern came over again today. I've had enough of her kind."

"What did she want this time?"

"She complained that she saw you, both of you come home Friday night when it was already getting dark, and you with your bundles on your back. I explained that you got held up, but she insisted that this was the second Friday in a row that this happened. Then she commented that she saw me outside without a kerchief on my *sheitel*."

"Damn that woman! I should go over and give a piece of my mind to her husband."

"And what would that achieve?"

Moses was quiet. Then he shrugged. "Nothing. All this in the last few years, as if we had nothing more important to worry about. Since they came up here from Tapolcsány."

"So we have the first reason for getting out of here," countered Mari. "Any other?"

Markus replied: "Yes, quite a few. The fact that it is further in the country, closer to the center. That's where we wanted to move."

"Not that much closer. Seventy kilometers."

"Well, that's a first step. We cannot move to Pest, can we? Maybe we could."

"No, son, don't even dream of it. All right, so that's an argument. Next?"

"Next, the riots, the pogroms. This has become a horrible place to live in."

"Yes, but there could be pogroms there, too."

"There could be, but so far there have not been any. The place is not so full of Germans."

"Talking about which," said Moses, "what do you think about this national identity thing? Are we not Germans ourselves? What are we? Are we going to be Magyars?"

Markus argued heatedly, "Well, why not? We are not really Germans, we never have been, that was a lie. We have always been Jews. Now we can be Hungarian Jews, Magyar Jews. Perhaps, for the first time, we can really be something other than just Jews. Some people whose religion happens to be Jewish."

"Just wait a minute, young man! What do you mean, 'just Jews'? It is important to be a Jew, a distinction. We have been selected. We are special. Don't give it up too fast."

"Who's talking about giving it up? But it seems that we have been selected for persecution and ridicule. So maybe it is time to find a country where they don't make fun of you, don't hit you and kill you because of your religion. I think that Hungary is that country, not here on the Moravian border, but deeper inside."

Moses did not disagree, for he had been thinking very much the same thoughts. "It's funny to think of moving further from Moravia," Mari commented. "Our parents wouldn't have dreamed of moving away from the border. To them, Moravia was still home. Or, at least, to our grandparents."

"You know, Mari, they would have been pleased with this particular move. To a place called 'Golden Morava.' They would have thought it was almost like going home." They all laughed.

"And the life there? The difficulties?" asked Moses.

"We shall manage," Mari assured them both. "Have you thought of the actual move there? Hiring a cart, a driver? All the furniture?"

"Yes, that is a great disadvantage, you should have mentioned it among the arguments against. But you know, somehow I don't fear it at all. I think that moving from one place to the next is already in our blood, the Jewish blood. That's what we have been doing for centuries, for thousands of years."

"Father, about that store, and the tavern."

"Yes, what about them?"

"Have you thought about it? Are you sure that it should be the way that man said?"

Moses was quiet for a while.

"You know, I am not sure. I like selling things and I have always dreamed of having my own store. But a tavern, now, would I like to run a tavern? On the other hand, how could *you* run a tavern?"

"I could learn. I think that it would be a good thing for me to learn it, it would be like a new trade. I have never really liked selling things."

"And in a tavern, you don't have to sell?"

"I think they just ask for what they want. I don't have to talk them into it. I have never really been in a tavern, other than where we stopped for some water on our way, but I don't think the tavern keeper goes over to the customer and tries to talk him into drinking more wine."

"Neither does a real shopkeeper. People come in and tell you what they want to buy. But I see your point, you might be right. Mari, what do you think?"

Mari thought and finally nodded. "Yes, I can see Markus as a tavern keeper. You should remain a merchant, with your own store."

"Well, then, that's settled. We shall have to do a lot of investigation. Talk to tavern keepers about their business volume, income and expenses and such. Storekeepers, I don't need to talk to them, I know enough about that business. But do we know any tavern keepers?"

"Uncle Moritz must know a few."

"Yes, and I wanted to talk to him anyway. I'll go over now."

"I'll come, too," said both Mari and Markus in unison.

"No, not now. There are aspects of this that he will not talk about to anybody but myself. It's better that I should go alone. I'll tell you everything he said." Moses took his coat and hat and went to see his brother.

Moritz's house was a little larger than the one Moses lived in. He had been more successful in business. He had his own store and sold dry goods in the lower town. His wife was a quiet woman; she never said very much. They had three children, with a fourth on the way. But they did not like to talk about the children to anybody but Moses, and even to him only reluctantly. Adolf, the first boy, was twelve now and healthy; but Sigmund, five years old, and Flora, two, both had the same problem: they were deaf-mute, and nothing could be done about it. This made things more difficult, and who knew about the new one that they expected in another two months?

Moses knocked. They let him in. He greeted his sister-in-law, patted the heads of the children who surrounded him. They exchanged a few words, and then Moses came to the point.

"We had a visitor today. A Mr. Avakian."

"Yes, he came here, too."

"I know. I would very much like to talk to you, Moritz, about this. Could we go for a walk?"

"Why walk? Come on over to the sitting room." His wife was used to her husband making all the decisions; it never occurred to her to insist on being included.

So they sat in the other room (they also had a guestroom with a bed, though all members of the family slept in the kitchen) and Moses opened the conversation. "Moritz, we're seriously considering the move. If everything works out, I think we're going to move there."

Moritz did not answer.

"So what do you think?"

Moritz rubbed his face. "Look, I think you're right. This is no longer the place to live. Bars County sounds much better. What does Mari think? And Markus?"

"They both want to go. So do I. I'll tell you the details. But what about you? Will you not come, too?"

"We discussed the matter yesterday, and again today. Yes, we would like to go, but as you know, there are difficulties. I built up this store, it won't be easy to sell it. Who would buy it? Should I start again from nothing? And then, there are the children."

"Yes, I know."

"Now Adolf is already twelve, he should be no problem. There will be schools, even in the villages, and after a while, in Golden Morava. Avakian claims that Migazzi is concerned about the education of all children in the area, and so he is hiring a teacher and there will be houses where they will live and teach."

"In what language?"

"Now, that is difficult to say. He says that these will be Hungarian teachers, so they will teach in the Magyar language. But most of the children will be Slovaks. Well, it could be that their parents will also want them to learn Hungarian, but it might not be easy at first. So the teachers will have to know Slovak and some of the lessons might have to be in that language."

"But not in German?"

"No, they are trying to discourage the use of the German language in public schools. But we'll have no trouble maintaining the children's proficiency in German, talking to them at home. So that will be all right. Who knows, once they let us into Golden Morava, we may build a school of our own, a Jewish school."

"That would be nice."

"Yes, but what should we do about the other children? Sigmund and Flora cannot speak, cannot hear. Who knows about the new one, let it please God, he should be healthy. Here we already have found a good local woman who looks after them. She has patience, she has some experience with problem children."

"So you'll find another one in Bars."

"Maybe yes, maybe no. I don't know. Look, I do want to move. It's really the store. I can't just give it up. If I could find a buyer…"

Moses nodded several times, sadly. "Yes, I understand. But a pity, great pity. We will almost never see each other."

"Why not? It's not that far. We could visit each other frequently. It's not more than four hours on a cart. Why, I could ride over myself on a fast horse, in less than three hours. So could you."

"You know that I am not much of a rider."

"No, so take a more comfortable horse, a little slower. Or take the whole family on a cart. We shall certainly come over to see you, all of us. Quite often. When did you think of moving?"

"Well, we have not talked about firm dates yet, but if everything works out all right, I think we might be thinking of moving in about a month, a month and a half. The main thing is to talk to people in taverns, tavern keepers. You see, here is the deal."

Moses described Avakian's offer to his brother. Moritz nodded and said, "Well, in the general store you can look forward to a yearly turnover of maybe four hundred forints and a net income of something like seventy, eighty forints. If you pay an *árenda* of eighteen forints, you may have close to sixty forints left over."

"Yes, but there are all the other taxes to pay."

"I know, but you will still have a net of something like forty-five forints left over. You can live reasonably well from that, especially in a small village where you can buy your food from the peasants for next to nothing. Correct?"

"Yes, you are probably right. Most food, not everything."

"So the question really is, what kind of turnover you can expect in the tavern. That I don't know, but you can talk to Rozenzweig, two blocks from here, you know the place. Then you should also see Sinnreich – his tavern is on the road to Tapolcsány, about five kilometers. They know me well, they will tell you what to expect. You will also have to ask them for advice. They will be very helpful."

"Actually, we thought it a better idea if I were to run the store and Markus, the tavern."

Moritz seemed a little surprised at that. "Why?"

Moses shrugged. "Hard to say. The lad does not like selling so much. And he always hoped to learn a trade. Well, the trade of a tavern keeper is not a bad one. I don't need a new trade, I know I can sell. Let him run the tavern. Don't forget, the most difficult times might be in the evenings. By that time I will have the store closed, so I can go over and help Markus."

"Yes, that's true. Yes. You may be right, let the lad learn something useful. It will all work out. Look, it's late, go get some sleep. We shall talk a lot yet, before you go. I am glad for you."

They shook hands – they were not in the habit of embracing – and each went home.

* * *

"And so you see, young man, it turned out even better than I had hoped for. Moritz found a buyer for his store, and he managed Avakian to arrange for him, somehow, I don't know who paid how much money to whom, that they allow him to open a store in Golden Morava. He could also rent a house right in town, the same house that he bought some years later. His son Samuel was already born there, in Golden Morava. We saw them all the time. For, of course, we moved, too. We both moved that year, in 1848. We had found out everything we needed to know about the tavern, there was to be enough money to be made, or so we thought. We wrote to Avakian and in early July we hired a cart and driver. He helped Markus and me with the furniture and we were on our way. We started in the morning, stopped at a Jewish tavern along the way, spent an hour there. The owner, Mr. Diamant, was very helpful, gave us many tips. We got to Golden Morava by about four in the afternoon. Before entering the town, we asked for directions to the estate. We found it easily. Beautiful wrought-iron gate, the guard stopped us. We explained that we were there to see Mr. Avakian. He knew all about it, sent a boy to fetch the man. Avakian came, he was still quite friendly. He told us to follow him, he rode his horse. In another hour, we were in Perlep."

"How did you like the place?"

"Well, to tell you the truth, it was quite disappointing at first. Zestmeadow was a real town, fairly decent streets, houses. Trees. Here, there was nothing but a dusty street, I would not even call it a street, but there were houses on either side. Poor, ugly little houses. Ours was just like all the others, the man was right, it was not smaller than what we had in Zestmeadow, only plainer, more unfinished. Mari started to cry. But I patted her arm, told her it was all right, I should pretty the house up in no time at all."

"And the tavern? The store?"

"There was not much there, just two empty houses. But next day Avakian came with a carpenter, he was willing to do everything the way we wanted, so in the end that tavern turned out to be nicer than Diamant's on the road. We could even talk them into building in two small guestrooms, so it was really more than a tavern, it became an inn of sorts. The store turned out nice, too. Well, a store does not have to be nice, but it was well planned, lots of shelves and drawers, yet enough room for the customers to stand and look. It was all right. Yes, it worked out all right. And Markus became a very good tavern keeper. I helped him often, Mari cooked some meals, it was good. While it lasted."

Markus and Rozália – 1853–1855

"Markus Steiner, Great-Grandfather. Here I am again, your great-grandson. I would like to talk with you again."

"Oh, yes. My great-grandson from the future, Berman's grandson. Well, what can I tell you?"

"Now I'd like to know more about your life in Perlep, the early days. Especially about how you got to know Rozália, how you married her, the first years of your marriage."

"Yes, I can talk about that. Those were good years, good memories. At least for me, they were the best years of my life."

"Tell me."

"Well it all started with David."

"David?"

"David Wasserman. Rozália's brother. Such a sweet man he was. He came into the tavern one day, about a month after we opened it. Short man, chubby, about thirty-five, with a big smile on his face. He did not have a beard, I did not know too many Jews in those days without beards, but this man was obviously Jewish. He put out his arm, shook my hand and hugged me in a big welcome, as if we were old friends. I had never seen him before, but right away I felt that he was my friend, so I smiled too, and we sat down to talk. There were no guests yet in the tavern. He told me how happy he was to find another Jewish family in the area. He had heard about us from Avakian, and he wanted to meet the whole family."

"So you took him over to the house?"

"I did. First I took him to my father's store. He had not yet opened it up. He didn't have enough merchandise yet, so he went to Golden Morava and other places looking for many, many things to add to his stock. He felt that he needed a well-stocked store, so word-of-mouth would then generate lots of business. He still lacked some agricultural equipment, tools and such. Anyway, David welcomed him as warmly as myself, and then we went over to the house to see Mother. He wanted to know everything about us, our life before, in Zestmeadow, our family, other people, our trip, everything. It took us an hour before we could ask him about himself and his family."

"So what kind of family did he have?"

"Well, at that time they lived in Bélád. There were five of them: three brothers, a sister and their mother. The father had died a few years earlier. His brother Mózes had just married a girl, Chaya, no children yet. His other brother, Samuel, was not yet married, although he saw a lot of Katti Jellinek. David thought that something would come of that. His sister Rozália was unmarried – she was nineteen. There was another sister, Julia, but she had gotten married and moved away from the area some years before. David was the oldest, but he had not found the right girl yet. There were not that many Jewish people in the area. He might have to travel farther, perhaps to Nyitra. We told him about a few girls that we knew about in Zestmeadow and he actually made notes. What a pity, he told us, that we did not bring a nice girl with us, of the right age. When he heard of our arrival, that was the first question he had asked Avakian. But he said that he sure wanted me to meet his sister – who knows, we might like each other, we were about the same age."

"Good idea. So he brought her over, and you fell in love and married right away?"

"Well, not quite. They invited us over for a *Shabbes* the next month, we spent the day there. Then David and Rozália came over to our place, then I visited again, and so on. There were several visits, a year went by. We talked, I liked her, it seemed that she liked me. After a few visits, after a few months, somehow we knew, everybody knew, that we would marry one day. But those were the times when I was trying to do something with the tavern, make a success of it. My father could not help much, he was working hard in his own store. In the evenings he was often too tired to come and help. So after a while, when David dropped a strong hint about it being time to make a move, I hesitated. You see, in our family it was a strong tradition that a young man should get married only once he had already established a good living for himself and his new family."

"So she got angry and told you to look elsewhere."

"No, not really. I must admit that we did talk to each other about the future, even before David brought up the matter. I asked her to wait for maybe two years and she said that she would."

"But was it not five years after your move…?"

"Yes, because of what happened. Just when I thought that things were looking up at the tavern – people came regularly, many customers, and I even got the count's man to agree to adding an extension at the back, so I was ready to take the big step – well, as I say, just then her mother's health took a turn for the worse. For about a year, they worried about her and were not in the mood for marriage. Then, early in 1851, the mother died, peace on her soul. Well, after the mourning period was over, I thought that we could get married. So did Samuel and Katti – they had been waiting for a while – and in the previous year David had gotten to know Jozefa. Well, all three weddings were scheduled for that year, for 1851. Well, both Samuel and later, David did actually marry. But not Rozi, not myself. You see, in that year *my* mother got sick."

"Really? What happened to her?"

"She got a very bad influenza. It took her months to recover, then it got worse again, and then somehow it affected her another way, something unusual. It damaged her inner parts, some feminine illness developed. For several months we did not know if she was going to live or die. That's when we had to get other people to go to the *shul* in Taszár-Malanya and say a *Mishebeirach* for her every week. We could not go ourselves. We had to look after her and also run the tavern and the store. Those were difficult times. Rozi came over to help her quite often. It took a year and a half before she was more or less healthy again. Even then, she was weak. David suggested that a cousin of theirs, a girl called Anna, who lived with relatives in Szelezsény, come live with us. She was an orphan, about nine at the time, old enough to help out around the house."

"And then…?"

"And then we could get married. Meanwhile, Rozi had collected a very nice trousseau, she had all the bedding and other linen that we needed, she also inherited a few pieces of the furniture from their house. They sold the house – David was moving to Szelepcsény. He was opening a tavern there, large enough to live at the back of the building. Mózes and Chaya and little Éva were moving to Szelezsény, very close. They had other relatives living there. Samuel and Katti actually moved to Golden Morava. I never knew how they managed to get permission. Their baby Herman was already born there. Anyway, we could finally schedule the wedding for December of 1853. There were many people there, quite a large wedding, mainly the Wassermans and their friends. We did not have so many, although by then most of those people were our friends, too."

"Did you have music and dancing at the wedding?"

"Music, yes. Dancing, no. There were not so many men to dance together to make it worthwhile."

"Men and woman would not dance with each other?"

"No, we were not that modern."

"And the music – what kind of music would that be?"

"Why, gypsy music. There was no elegant music available, this was not Vienna."

"But what about Klezmer?"

"What's that?"

"Oh, some Jewish music from the east."

"Never heard of it."

"Oh, of course. May I ask a somewhat personal question?"

"Personal? I don't know. What do you mean?"

"Would you say that you and Rozi were deeply in love? Madly? Before and also after you married her?"

"Excuse me???"

"Was it an affair of passion? If you'd rather not tell me, that's all right."

"No, it's not that. But I am not even sure what you are talking about. I know there were such things in the novels that Rozi read later, but in real life, people, a young man and a young woman, they were introduced, they liked each other. If they did, well, so they were available, they were in marriageable age, the circumstances were appropriate, so they got married. They had children and everything worked out fine, usually. We certainly liked each other and we had a good marriage."

"And you were always faithful to each other."

"What a strange thing to ask. Why, what else? Of course we were faithful, everybody was. At least everybody among the Jews. Why, did you think we were rogues and wh— No, I shall not say it. What do you take us for?"

"Sorry, I meant no offense. Let us talk about something else. Where was the wedding held, in Perlep or in Bélád?"

"Neither. In Taszár-Malanya, which is halfway between the two places. There were ten Jewish families living there, five in Taszár and five in Malanya – they were almost the same village. All those people were our friends. Several of them came from Zestmeadow-on-Nyitra: Mrs. Perl and Mrs. Schlesinger were both born there. And young Jákob Feldman, too, he was the local teacher. Yes, the ten Jewish families could afford to run a little school for all the Jewish children that lived in those two towns. Well, there were lots more than ten, if you include the neighboring places. They were all young families, with lots of small children. And they had a synagogue! Well, not a real synagogue, more like a little *shul*, in Mr. Veisz's house – that's where we held the wedding. Rabbi Fuerst came over, he was from Komárom originally, but now he lived in Léva. Rabbi Simon Fuerst, very nice man. My cousin Adolf married his daughter, that was some years later. They lived in Golden Morava. Adolf had a store there from the beginning. Well, his father did, but then he took over. He was very successful."

"So it all worked out well in the end."

"Yes, thank God."

"And the brothers of Rozália? They were all happily married, children and all?"

"Well, Mózes and Chaya had just the one daughter, Éva. She was born a year before we married. Samuel and Katti had many children. Herman was born just before we married, a few months before. He was the first of six or seven. David now, he and Jozefa had two children, Leni and Johanna. They came a little later, just about when our children started to appear in this world, but then poor Jozefa died, peace on her soul. Later, David married again, married Rebeka. They had one more child."

"And as for your own children…?"

"Yes, thank God, we had quite a few, although, unfortunately, not all lived. The first one, Leni, was born in 1856…"

A Day at the *Shul*

From Perlep to Taszár-Malanya it was only an hour's walk – well, maybe an hour and a half, when Markus's father walked with them. Markus's mother seldom went to the *Shabbes* service, only when they could seat her on some local man's cart. So about once a month Rozi and Markus walked there on the Friday evening. When Moses went with them, they closed up the tavern early; some local people grumbled about that. In the winter, Moses usually stayed behind, closed his own shop and minded the tavern until just before dark. But it was summer now, almost summer – it was the middle of May in 1855. So on this Friday evening Moses walked with Markus and Rozi; Mari was left behind in the care of little Anna.

They arrived in Taszár-Malanya in good time to wash and to change their clothes; they had brought their *Shabbes* best with them in a little bundle, along with some gifts for their hosts. Mr. Perl welcomed them. He had a little room where they could sleep, the three of them and little Samu Perl. The new baby still slept with the parents.

Soon it was time for the *Kabbalas Shabbes* service. Rozi helped the women with preparing the dinner. They would eat at the Engels, Ignátz and Helen; they too had a small child and were expecting their second. Markus enjoyed the *shul* service. He was always touched when they stood facing the entry door to welcome the Queen, the *Shabbes*. He and Rozi and his parents tried to do that at home, but it was not the same thing.

After a lovely dinner they sang a lot of songs and eventually returned to the Perls' house to sleep. The young couple would have preferred not to share their room with Moses and the child, but that could not be helped. The spare bed, made of crates, was reasonably comfortable; they had nothing to complain about.

Next morning, after washing and breakfast, they all went over to the Veisz house for the *Shacharis* service. Jákob Feldman acted as *chazan* that morning. There were more than twenty men in the *shul* and, behind the makeshift *mechitza*, about fifteen women. Lots of children were constantly running around the adults. Most of them were very small, two or three years old; quite a few babies were held by their mothers. The oldest child was nine – that was Dani Buchinger who came with his parents and little sister from Szelepcsény.

But, at least for Rozi, the most important thing was to meet with family, her brothers and their wives. All three of them came over: David from Szelepcsény, Mózes from Szelezsény, and Samuel from Golden Morava. On Friday they were all put up in different houses and had their dinner with different families, but now they were all together at the *shul*. Rozi, Chaya, Katti and Jozefa sat together and talked quietly through most of the service – well, at times not so quietly, so a few hisses were in order. Markus also exchanged more than one word with his brothers-in-law. Samuel and Mózes were both called up to the Torah – the small *shul* always liked to make their guests feel welcome.

During the *Kedusha* there was a small argument – well, not really an argument, more like a debate. When they were reading "When will you rein in Zion? Soon, in our days," Markus's father sighed deeply. The man sitting behind him, Mor Spitzer from Bélád, asked him, "Why the sigh?" Moses turned back and said, "Why not? Are we no longer waiting for the better times, for the days of the Lord?" And Mr. Spitzer assured him, in a rather loud voice, that those days have already arrived; the better times were here, now there was nothing to complain about. Most people heard the talk and there were several loud hisses.

Later, when Mr. Feldman was asked to deliver a *drasha*, he discarded his prepared topic and said he had heard the discussion earlier and he wanted to address the subject of the argument. That certainly caused some embarrassment for both Moses Steiner and Mor Spitzer; they both waved and tried to tell the teacher that it was not really an argument, he need not worry about it, but there was no deterring the young man.

"We have all been waiting for the days of the Lord," he led them on. "Yet now there are many people who would say that the wait is over, the days of the Messiah are upon us. It is not just Mr. Spitzer who says that the good times have arrived. I was talking with Rabbi Fuerst, and he says that they attended some conference in Vienna a while ago, where many of the rabbis in this country made the same point. They said that we have finally found a land where we are at home, we are appreciated, so this must be the Zion that has been promised to us so long ago. Is this true? Could it be true? Now we have been told that if we speak the language of this land, we shall be accepted as equal citizens. Are we, then, to give up our hopes for a better future, in a land of our own?"

The rabbi's words caused some pandemonium in the little *shul*. Everyone there had been waiting for the days of the Messiah, but few expected to live in those days, themselves or their children. In any case, there was no Messiah in sight, not for some hundred years now, and the last pretender had brought only more misery to the Jews. Jákob Feldman quickly assured them that no such a personage had yet been sighted, but that some claimed, at least, that the good times could arrive without an obvious heavenly emissary. It was clear, from his tone, that he believed neither in the arrival of such a person, nor of the promised times with or without him.

"But what about the enticement, the invitation we all have received, to become good citizens of this country and speak its language and then we should be equal citizens, free to do any business, study any profession, live in any town and city? Should we give credit to that promise?"

Here the majority of the attendees seemed to nod, and some voiced their opinions. "Yes, let's give it a try," said Mor Seidel, while József Dukesz shouted in Hungarian, "I am willing to be Hungarian." They all laughed, for up to this moment not one word had been spoken other than in German (with the exception, of course, of the prayer service itself).

Feldman clearly had an axe to grind. He taught the children in German, and recently he had encountered increasing pressure to switch to the Hungarian language in his little school. He was reluctant, not the least because his proficiency in that language was remarkably poor. More than that, he had a great love for German culture and literature; he did not see anything even approaching that level of sophistication among the Hungarian writers (of which significant group he knew next to nothing), and strongly believed that that barbaric language was not capable of expressing the higher, loftier thoughts and emotions of the writers, philosophers, and poets of the German lands.

Nevertheless, he was careful not to conclude his drasha with any firm pronouncements, any authoritative judgment on the issue. He left it as something to ponder over. And they proceeded with the *Mussaf*, the additional service, upon the conclusion of which all the men shook hands and drank a tiny cup of *pálinka*. The women, meanwhile, went home to prepare lunch for the families.

The guests ate the noon meal in a different house from the previous evening. Markus and his wife and father were invited to the Stangels, and indeed they had a lovely time there. After expressing their thanks, they all went for a walk in town. That was the event that most visitors waited for. It was an opportunity to meet everybody – all the local Jewish families, as well as those from Bélád, Nagy Herestény, Szelepcsény, Szelezsény, and even occasionally from Golden Morava and the more distant towns. Rozi continued her chats – or gossips, as her husband thought – with her sisters-in-law. Markus himself had long discussions with the Wasserman brothers and the other men there. He talked for a bit with the Jellinek brothers, Mózes from Nagy Herestény and Bernát from Bélád. Mózes had a two-year-old son, Jakab, while Bernát was not yet married. He was seeing a young woman, though, Mária, whom he was planning on marrying soon. The two brothers argued whether it would be appropriate for Bernát's first son, when he was blessed with one, also to be named Jakab, in honor of their father who had passed away some years earlier, may his memory be blessed. Markus wisely did not express an opinion on the issue.

David's wife Jozefa did not walk with the women: she was expecting her first child soon and had been told to be careful. Samuel's wife, Katti, the sister of the Jellinek brothers, was also expecting by the end of the year; it was to be a good year, with the help of the Lord. Rozi and Markus were subjected to a little good-natured kidding about their not doing their share ("You should perhaps stay home on more Friday evenings, ha ha…").

Soon it would be time to start walking home. But there was so much yet to discuss. Children, neighbors, menus. *Árenda*s, the landowners, the soldiers marching through their towns, taxes. And international politics – what about the king of Prussia, would he become emperor of all Germany? What about Queen Victoria, was she really in charge of England, or was it her German husband, Albert? How about the Crimean War?

It was getting a little darker. Just then, Jozef Perl and his wife Julia came up to offer the Steiners to stay over one more night. David and Jozefa thought it would be a good idea.

"But won't Mother be worried, if we don't come home tonight?" Markus asked his father.

"No, I told her that we might come back only Sunday morning."

"And what about the tavern? It should be opened Saturday evening."

"In the summer, you open it up so late, it's hardly worth your while," insisted Moses. "How many customers do you have that late in the evening?"

"Well, four or five, sometimes more…"

"And sometimes less. You won't suffer much from the loss."

"But they may complain to the count."

"I don't think they would. Let it be, Markus."

Rozi also argued for staying the night, so they finally decided – not for the first time on such *Shabbes* evenings – that they would stay.

The men gathered again in the *shul* for *Mincha* prayers. Then they made *havdala* in the Perls' house. They ate a very light meal and went to bed soon after that, so they could be on their way quite early in the morning.

All in all, it turned out to be a lovely *Shabbes*.

Visits to the Tavern

About two months after their *Shabbes* in Taszár-Malanya Markus had some unexpected visitors at the inn – some welcome, some less so.

On that particular summer day, July of 1855, he opened the tavern at ten in the morning. There were no customers at that time, so he had plenty of time to wash the floor, wipe down all the chairs and tables, polish the copper countertop, rearrange his bottles, go down to the cellar for more wine and beer, a bottle of *pálinka* or two – in short, to fulfill the duties of a tavern keeper. At around 11:30 a few men started to come, first only visitors to the area. Few locals could get away from work at lunchtime, and in any case, they seldom wanted to eat. Visitors did not want food, either, as they often brought their own; they just wanted a pitcher of wine or beer. Markus did not mind – he did not have much food to serve, just some cheese and a couple of sausages. Later, Rozi would come over and bring some soup, maybe a bowl of meat paprikash, some potatoes, or just dumplings or noodles. That was their fare, why should the guests eat better?

THE COUNT
AND COUNTESS MIGAZZI

So he was serving some drinks to five or six men sitting at two separate tables – no, three, there were two locals at one table, three men from a neighboring village, and there was that city man sitting alone – when a fancy landau drawn by four horses stopped by. The coachman opened the door, bowing, and sure enough, Count Migazzi walked in, together with his wife. They were both very young. The count was a handsome man, with a big mustache. He wasn't the man who had invited the Steiners to his estate – that was Count Kristof, who had died in 1850. This was Count Vilmos, but he was already the *ispán* of Bars County. The countess was the former Antónia Marczibányi – a good-looking woman, if not beautiful, about twenty-two years old.

When the couple came into the tavern, all conversation suddenly stopped and the men stood up, all except the city visitor who presumably was not familiar with the identity of the newcomers. The count smiled, told the men to sit. They had just come in for a glass of water, maybe wine; they were thirsty after a long ride. Markus got busy, wiped a perfectly clean table and covered it with a laced tablecloth that was seldom, if ever, used. Then he brought out a tray with two glasses of water and two glasses of the best wine he had, really a rarity. The count raised his glass and said in a loud voice, in Hungarian, "To your health, my friends!" The countess smiled and she also tasted her wine. The count commented on the excellence of the drink, stood up and walked over to the counter.

"And how is business, Mr. Steiner?"

Markus was pleased that the aristocrat knew his name.

"Not bad, sir, not bad at all. Noontime is slow, but most evenings we have twenty men or so."

"What do they drink?"

"Wine, mostly, some drink *pálinka*. They don't drink much, though."

"That's just as well. You don't want drunks around the place, they would wreck the tavern." He looked around. "I see that you keep it in very good repair."

"Well, sir, I try to do my best."

"Good. Good. Do you keep long hours here?"

"Yes, sir, I open around ten in the morning and close at midnight."

"How many days a week?"

"Six days, or so. Friday night, I close before sunset. You know that our Sabbath starts on Friday night and lasts until it's dark on Saturday. Then I usually open again, just after dark on Saturday."

"Yes, I heard that. But you know, some people complained to me about that. They would like to have a drink on Friday evening."

Markus's face turned red. He lifted his shoulders, but only a little, trying not to appear disrespectful.

"What can I do, sir? That is the most basic commandment we have, that we must not work on the Sabbath."

"Could you not hire somebody to do the work for you?"

"It is not permitted, sir. Even if I could afford it, it is forbidden, for any man or woman, even for animals to work."

"And what about opening up Saturday nights?"

"I open then. In the winter, it is easy, but in the summer, sometimes it is quite late."

"But I have heard it said that there are Saturdays when you don't open at all."

"Once or twice. It happens that we travel to another town, visit my wife's relatives. Then we would leave earlier on Friday and they won't let us ride back very late Saturday, or sometimes we don't even have a horse, we would have to walk back. They insist that we stay the night and come back in the morning."

"So my complainers have been right."

"Only two or three times a year, sir."

"I am sorry, Mr. Steiner, but it is our agreement that you run this tavern. That means keeping it open at all reasonable times. I may agree to that Friday night closing, reluctantly, if people don't complain more. But Saturday night you must open! You have to find some other way of doing that. Talk to your priest or rabbi or whatever it is that tells you what to do. I am sorry." The count ignored the misery he saw on Markus's face. He went back to his table to finish his wine.

Markus stayed behind the counter, pretending to be busy with the glasses. One of the local men came up to pay, or rather, to have his purchase jotted down on his account. He and Markus talked in Slovak. After the man left, taking his hat off to the count and countess, Markus was called over to their table.

"Tell me, Mr. Steiner, what school did you go to?" the count asked him.

"There was a German-speaking Jewish public school in Zestmeadow-on-Nyitra, sir. Every child had to attend it. It was the law."

"You see, my dear," he turned to his wife, "what a great man the emperor Josef the Second was? It was his law that everybody should attend school, and look what a great difference it makes? The Moravian Jews all became educated men and now they are changing the face of this country, all for the better. But that language has to change," he added, turning back to Markus.

"To Hungarian, sir?"

"Of course to Hungarian! I heard you talk to that man in Slovak just now. I don't want to hear that. Talk to him in Hungarian!"

"I'll try, sir. But what if he cannot speak the language?"

"Even then, talk with him in Hungarian. He will learn fast. Watch me."

He stood up and walked over to the table where now four men were still sitting with their beers or wine. He talked to each man in turn, just a few words. They answered him back, two in Hungarian, one in broken Hungarian, and one in Slovak. He had a longer conversation with that man – the count talking in Hungarian, the man answering in Slovak, but apparently understanding the count.

The count came back with a satisfied smile on his face.

"You see, Mr. Steiner, that's how you do it."

Markus would have liked to add, "when you are a count," but he kept quiet.

The couple collected their things and got up to leave. Markus opened the door for them and was happy to see them go; so were all the other customers. The solitary city man asked him later who those respected visitors were; Markus explained that he was the *ispán* of the county and the owner of the tavern and everything else around here. The man shrugged his shoulders and told him, "Mr. Steiner (for I heard him calling you that), to me you are a much more important man than that windbag."

Markus was genuinely surprised; he had never heard anybody talk that way. He assumed that this visitor must be a man of some importance himself.

Unfortunately, though, the city man's sentiments were not going to help Markus in his predicament. Later that day, when Moses came over to help his son, Markus told his father about the count's visit. "Did you promise him that you would open up every Saturday night?" Moses asked.

"No, I did not promise anything. But the way it came out, it was not a question of agreeing or disagreeing. It was assumed that I would agree. I must, or else."

"Yes, I know. He could just kick you out, you and me, all of us."

"So no more *Shabbes* in Taszár-Malanya for me. Or in Bélád."

"We shall figure it out, my son. After all, when you go, I can stay and open up for you. Then you can come back by a cart, it doesn't cost much to hire one."

"Maybe. We shall see."

They sat quietly for some time. Then Moses asked: "I assume that he did not pay for his wine?"

"You can assume that, Father. And it was the best wine that I have. But who cares, so long as he lets us stay here and does not raise the *árenda*."

"True, the *árenda*. So it was smart not to ask for the price of the wine. I always knew that you have what it takes to be a businessman, Markus."

"I am not much of a businessman. Look at Moritz. He is a businessman. Look at Adolf. He is nineteen and he is already in that store all the time. They're talking about enlarging it, hiring a sales assistant. Theirs is the only Jewish store in Golden Morava and the best, the busiest. Now *they* are businessmen."

Moses sighed. "Yes, that's something that I could never have. I was so happy that I should have my own store, finally, and it's all right, I'm making a living out of it. But it's in this little, dusty corner of the world, with a hundred families. Nobody comes here from outside the village. Now in Golden Morava, everybody comes to town from time to time, buys something."

"Well, yes, because they have the fairs every Monday, and the big fairs, four or five times a year. The place is full of people."

"And Moritz has sense enough to sell in a booth, as well as in the store."

"Father, could you not set up a booth at the fair?"

Moses thought about that. Markus kept pressing him. "You could take some or all your wares, sell during the day, and sleep at Moritz's house."

"Well, for one thing, it would not be legal to sleep in town."

"Nobody would care."

"I am not sure. There are those nasty German merchants, they could just report me. But there are other things against it."

"What things?"

"If I were to take in enough merchandise to make it worth while, I would have to hire a cart and horse. That would make it too expensive. And then, to cart everything in the morning and have the man with the cart come back in the evening, or the next morning, that would already make it a losing proposition, because I would be also competing with other merchants, I would have to lower my prices. And what if a local man, from here, comes there and visits my booth and sees that I charge less for a rake or a shovel, or even a lamp, than what I charge here in Perlep? He would complain, tell everybody here and next thing I know, I would have to lower my prices here, too. Then I would not have enough left over to pay the count and everybody."

Markus had no arguments to these. After a while, he changed the subject, and eventually they closed up for the night.

*　*　*

Soon after, Markus had two other unexpected visitors. The first was Rabbi Simon Fuerst, who arrived early one afternoon of the following week. Markus was happy to see the rabbi, and the two men greeted each other warmly. Markus offered wine, but the rabbi only wanted water; he was very thirsty after his long ride. He explained that he was visiting some people in Golden Morava and that he must be back in Léva by the evening.

"May I offer you some food? Rozália just brought over bean soup and prune dumplings. I have special dishes for you."

"Thank you, Markus, I will have a little food, not too much."

After serving his honored guest, Markus sat down with him. There were no other customers at the tavern; early afternoon was not usually a time for thirsty visitors.

"So tell me, what's new with you and the family?" the rabbi asked him.

"Not very much. Mother is perhaps a little better – that girl Anna is a great help to her."

"I will say an extra *Mishebeirach* for her. And Rozi?"

"I do have news for you. She is pregnant. Our first child, with God's help."

"*Mazel tov*! That is great news. When do you expect it?"

"Next spring. February or March."

"Great. How does she feel?"

"Not so good, right now. She gets very sick in the mornings."

"That is quite normal. It will soon pass. Have you thought about where to deliver the baby? Maybe in Golden Morava?"

"I don't think that would be necessary. I am told that there is an excellent midwife right here, in Perlep."

"Good, so long as you are sure. I will certainly be here for the *bris mila*, if it's a boy."

"But come, even if it's a girl. We shall have to name her, too."

"Of course, I am always happy to be with you."

"You know about Samuel's wife Katti, that she is also expecting…"

"Oh, yes, I knew about that. January, isn't it?"

"Yes, God willing. And David's little Leni is doing quite nicely."

The rabbi nodded. He was in frequent contact with all the Jewish people in the area. Markus asked him, "Have you heard anything new, Rabbi?"

"Well, let me see. Mrs. Perl in Taszár-Malanya had her baby."

"Yes, I have heard that. A girl."

"Yes, she will be called Julis."

"Julis. Is Mrs. Perl not called Julia?"

"Yes, but she says Julis is not the same name. I can accept that, if she insists."

"Any other news, Rabbi?"

Fuerst thought a minute. "Well, yes, in Léva, Mrs. Schlesinger died last week, she was very old. Peace on her. Did you know her at all?"

"No, I did not."

"Of course not. Then you would not know the Heimans, either. They had a new baby. Healthy boy."

"*Mazel tov*! How was your trip to Vienna?"

"Oh, that was two months ago. Interesting trip. Very interesting. There was quite an argument going on there."

"Who argued, with whom? About what?"

"Well, I argued, for one. This was the first time that I argued with my mentor, the great Rabbi Adolf Jellinek."

"I have heard of him. What was it all about?"

"About the German language, German culture. We were quite pleased with the progress we have been making here, promoting Hungarian culture among the Jews. But he was dead set against anything Hungarian. He said that German culture was far superior, the German language was the best language in the world. He insisted that we keep the German language, that we educate all Jews in German literature and thinking."

"Well, I suppose that he is at least partly right. About the German culture?"

"Sure, of course, the Germans have developed a sophisticated culture, while Hungarian culture has hardly existed here, it is just starting now, the last thirty or forty years. But it is growing fast, it will be great, and the Jews of Hungary will be among the best writers and philosophers and artists and musicians, you will see."

"I hope so. Was it just yourself, arguing with Rabbi Jellinek?"

"Oh, no. Most Hungarian rabbis were on my side. The strongest arguments were made by Lipót Löw."

"Löw. I heard that name. Is he in Szeged?"

"Yes, now he is in Szeged. Before, he was in Pápa. I know him well. We studied together, under Jellinek. Now he is the strongest promoter of everything Hungarian. Yet he was born in Moravia."

"So you all agreed that we must be Magyars."

"Yes, indeed. Speak Hungarian without an accent." Up to now, they were talking German, but now the rabbi switched to Hungarian.

"I think I can speak without an accent," said Markus, "but my father never will. He speaks the language, quite well, but he will never lose his German accent."

"Of course, it is more difficult at his age. And your mother?"

"She hardly speaks any Hungarian. More Slovak – she needs that, talking to the neighbors, when she buys milk from them, or fruit, vegetables."

"Sure, I understand that. But make sure that the little one, when he is born, will be taught Hungarian, from the beginning."

"We shall try. Rozi speaks the language quite well. We shall send him, or her, to a local school. He will learn Hungarian there, but more Slovak, I am afraid."

The rabbi thought. "You know, there is some talk about establishing a Jewish school in Golden Morava. I have been talking to some people about it – that's why I am riding there today. With God's help, by the time your child goes to school. He can go to Golden Morava. It is quite close. You won't have a problem getting him there."

"And will that be a Hungarian-speaking school?"

"Well, that is exactly what we are discussing right now. I would like that, but the local leaders, your relatives included, insist on a German school. They say that the children will have plenty of opportunity to learn Hungarian outside the school."

"Hmm. I am not so sure."

"Neither am I. But they claim that it would be very difficult to find a Hungarian-speaking teacher, one who is very knowledgeable about all Jewish subjects, Talmud Torah and everything."

"So will it be mainly a religious school?"

The rabbi considered the question.

"I wouldn't say 'religious.' They will learn everything – arithmetic and history and geography, literature, everything. But they must learn what it means to be Jewish. And that means, at the least, learning Torah. And learning about all of our customs."

"And Talmud?" Markus asked with a twinkle in his eye; he knew that learning Talmud was a sensitive subject.

"Yes, Talmud. There, we don't always see eye to eye. There is a Rabbi Einhorn – he considers the Talmud totally irrelevant, obsolete. But I disagree. I think it is full of wisdom for this age. And Löw also thinks so. He used to be against the Talmud, like Einhorn, but he has changed his views. Not only about the Talmud, about many things. He does not hold with these new thoughts any more. Neither do I."

"Do you mean that you are no longer Neolog?"

"Oh, no, I don't mean that at all. We are all Neolog. But Neolog is not Reform. That Berlin style now, that is not for us. Keeping the Sabbath on the Sunday! Not wearing a hat in the *shul*. Sitting together with women. No, I want none of that. And neither does Löw now, not anymore."

They discussed other people in the neighborhood, and the rabbi asked Markus about his brother-in-law David.

"I don't see him that often," Markus explained. "He drops by once a while, maybe every second month or so."

"Make sure to give him my regards," said the rabbi as Markus escorted him to his horse. "He is a very good man, very generous."

"I shall mention you to him," Markus promised. As the rabbi drove off, Markus stayed outside waving him good-bye until he had driven out of sight.

As luck would have it, Markus had the opportunity to fulfill his promise not much later, as David himself turned out to be his second visitor that afternoon.

He was walking from Szelezsény, bypassing Golden Morava by narrow paths that only he knew. He said it took him less than two hours, a pleasant walk in such a nice weather.

Markus brought over water, not wine; he knew that David was not very keen on wine. This was around five in the afternoon. There were by then a few customers in the tavern, so Markus had to stand up and serve them quite often.

They talked about family – about David's little Leni, about Samuel's Herman, a year and a half now; they were expecting their second next January. Éva, Mózes Wasserman's daughter, was already three, a very beautiful little girl.

David asked Markus about his parents, his mother who was not very strong.

"She is a little better this week, thank God," Markus sighed. "Anna helps a lot."

"Markus, it is Anna that I wanted to talk to you about. You know, I am a little concerned about her future."

"Why? Because of her looks? She may grow out of it, she is really a very nice girl. Not beautiful, perhaps, but in some ways, quite attractive."

"No, let us not kid ourselves. You know that she will never marry."

"Well, maybe not."

"And so, what will happen to her after your parents – let the Lord keep them for many years, but sooner or later, you know…"

"Of course, none of us lives forever."

"Now she has inherited some money from her parents. I have it. When the time comes, I meant to give it to her."

"That's very good. I didn't know that."

"Yes, but what if something were to happen to me?"

"To you? Why would anything happen to you?"

"Something can happen to anybody. I could give the money now to Jozefa, but God forbid, something could happen to her, too. Or I could give it to you."

"Yes, but something could happen to me, too. So who is absolutely protected from all eventualities?"

"I do have an idea. I thought that I would give it to your parents."

"And they will then live forever?"

"No, they won't. But I would suggest to them that they adopt Anna."

Markus was very surprised. "Adopt?" People did not usually adopt other people's children.

"Yes, why not? I think that they like her very much. And she likes them like her own parents. When one day, I hope very far in the future, they die, Anna will inherit this money and anything else they might have. Unless they decided to leave everything to you. They would have the right. Or to anybody else they wanted to, even to the Queen of England. But why would they? I am sure that they would want Anna well cared for."

Markus still had difficulty getting used to the idea. He went over to the counter, where a man was waiting for a glass of wine. After helping him and checking if any of his other customers were in need of a refill, he came back and continued the conversation. "I suppose you're right. It could work. But it's very unusual. How does one go about adopting somebody?"

"I know of a good Jewish lawyer, he could arrange it. I will take care of all expenses. Of course, this is assuming that your parents agree. They may not want to do this."

"Oh, I think they will agree, in the end. They will be very surprised, just as I was. But I will talk to them."

"Will, you? That's great, I was hoping that you would do that. It is so much easier for you than for me."

"Sure, I'll discuss it with them. With my father, first. He usually comes in here in the evenings – probably tonight he'll be here. Then he can talk to Mother."

"Thanks, Markus. I knew that I could count on you." They shook hands and David left, continuing his walk toward Fekete Kelecsény.

And so, that evening, when Moses came to help his son out at the tavern, Markus had plenty to tell his father. After catching him up on the rabbi's visit, Markus brought up David's suggestion.

"I wanted to talk to you about something else. David also dropped in today. He is worried about Anna's future."

"Her future? Why, what about her future?"

So Markus told him about David's concerns and his idea of giving her inheritance to Moses and Mari. Then he told him about David's suggestion of adopting Anna.

Moses was speechless. Markus continued. "Yes, he thinks that would be the best idea, if you adopted her. Look, you now live alone in the house. Anna is like an ideal daughter to you, why, you said so yourself. And with her little problem, she is not likely to ever marry. So she could stay with you forever, for all your lives. And then, she will inherit directly from you, that money and whatever you have. He trusts you and he thinks this would be the best solution."

Moses shook his head in wonder. "I don't know, son. I don't know. I have never heard of such a thing. I'll have to discuss it with your mother. Yes, maybe it makes some sense, but it would surely be unusual. How would one go about doing that?"

"David says he knows a good Jewish lawyer, who could easily arrange it. If you wanted, he might ask the lawyer to come here. He will pay all expenses."

"Well, I shall ask Mari. If she agrees, perhaps we should do this thing. Maybe we should ask Anna, too. She is eleven – she might object for some reason."

"I don't think she would object, but sure, you can ask her."

* * *

Later that night, after closing up, Markus also left for home. He was anxious to be with Rozália, who was not feeling so well. She was at the beginning of her first pregnancy. Thank God everything seemed to be going well, but one never knew…

He entered the house and kissed Rozi. "How do you feel?" he asked her.

"Quite well now. The morning was very bad, but now it is all right."

"Did you eat?"

"I ate a little. I cooked dinner for you. I tasted it."

"Tasting is not enough. You have to eat for two now."

"Maybe tomorrow. I was too busy, anyway."

"What did you do? Anything special?"

"No, nothing special, why should it be special? There is enough for me to do to keep busy."

"Yes, I know, dear. I know."

"I went to the well…"

"You shouldn't have. Why didn't you ask me to go before I left?"

"It's no problem. Then I cooked, then the man came with the firewood, so I told him where to stack it. Then I mended your socks and some shirts, clothes. Then I went over to your mother and showed Anna how to cook lentils. She had never cooked them before. Then I wrote a letter to Samuel and Katti. We'll have to get it to them somehow."

"Give it to me, there are always people at the tavern who are walking or riding to all sorts of places."

"It's on the table, there. And then, it was already evening. So I did eat a little, some bread and butter, and then I was reading until you came."

"What did you read?"

"This old newspaper. I finished the book that David brought me, that Otto Ludwig story. Could we not get more books?"

"In some towns there is a lending library, but not in Golden Morava. I always check the booths at the fairs, sometimes they have a few books, but very seldom. But you know what I might just buy for you?"

"What?"

"A set of dominoes. A man had a set that he bought, he showed me what a good game it is. I asked him to look for a good set for me."

"But what are dominoes?"

"They are little wooden blocks, with dots on them, different numbers of dots, on the left side and the right. You have to match them with similar numbers... it is difficult to explain, but quite easy to play. I hope he'll get it, we could play a lot."

"And how was your day?"

"Interesting. I had two visitors. First Rabbi Fuerst, and then David."

"David came? Why did he not come here, to see me?"

"He was in a hurry, wanted to reach Fekete Kelecsény before sunset. He was walking. But he wanted to discuss something with me."

Markus told Rozi about the visits; she was especially interested in David's suggestion. Yet she was not as surprised as Markus had been; perhaps the matter had already been mentioned to her before.

"So later, Father came over. We talked of things. I told him about this idea of David's, about Anna."

"What did he say?"

"He was shocked. Never expected anything like that. But I think that he liked the thought. He will discuss it with Mother. Perhaps you would talk to her about it?"

"No, of course not. It has to come from her husband, and maybe from you. But they love each other, your mother and Anna."

"Well, I hope it works out. She needs something permanent, such a nice little girl."

"Yes, but she'll never marry, with that face."

"Probably not. Pity. I got a letter from Adolf, by the way. I had asked him to get me a certain spirit Migazzi's man Avakian was asking me about. Adolf said he would order it for me."

"We have not seen them for some weeks. When do we go to town again?"

"As soon as you feel good enough. I think that a slow walk would be better. We could sit down and rest. I don't like to take you on a cart – it might shake the baby out of you."

"Don't be silly, pregnant women travel on carts all the time. I like to go to town. I like the town. Why could we not live in Golden Morava?"

"You know why. Lots of reasons. Mainly, they would not let us. They have this letter patent from the emperor."

"But that is no longer valid!"

"No, but the German merchants can still enforce it. Uncle Moritz and his family were an exception. I think money can buy anything. Why, are you not happy here?"

"Sure I am happy. I would be happy anywhere with you. But it would be nice, living in the town. There are so many things there."

"So what would you like most, living in Golden Morava?"

"I would like to walk on the promenade, nicely dressed up, arm in arm with you. Meeting acquaintances there, nodding and smiling at them."

"And meeting Germans, who would make ugly remarks – no, never mind. What else is there in town?"

"Well, of course, there is shopping, many stores. One could find nice clothes, if one could afford them, of course. I know, I am just dreaming. And you could find newspapers. You are always looking for newspapers…"

"Even in Golden Morava, the newspapers are a week old."

"So what? What's the hurry? If you wanted today's newspapers, we should move to Pozsony, or Vienna."

"Or to Pest. Yes, that would be something."

"But there are other things in town. There are often theater groups that perform there. And music. And the circus. And of course the fairs. I don't mean the Monday affairs, but the big fairs, six times a year."

"Five."

"Doesn't matter. And you could go to a regular barber, have your hair cut properly. I don't do such a good job of it."

"Yes, you do. Very proper haircuts."

"Not really. And then, if we have a toothache, that barber can pull teeth out much better than we can. And there are doctors, real doctors, when one is ill. One does not have to hire a cart and drive into town with an ill person."

"Talking about which, Rozi, have you heard of the cholera?"

"Yes, I have. I worry about it. Has anybody around here got it yet?"

"Not yet, thank God, but I worry, too. I worry that somebody comes into the tavern, maybe he has been traveling and picked up the cholera somewhere. Next thing we know, I get it and…"

"God forbid! You must stay healthy, always stay healthy, here with me."

"I'll try to. But I especially worry about you, now that you are–"

"They say that pregnant women are more likely to resist an epidemic than others. Don't worry about that. What I worry about is when the baby is born. Who knows if I will survive the birth?"

"Silly girl, of course you'll survive it. Everybody survives it these days, almost everybody. It is a question of the midwife. And you know that there is an excellent midwife right here in Perlep."

"So they say. So far, nothing has happened to any of the women with her."

"And nothing will happen to you. Don't worry, you will be healthy and the baby will be healthy, and then you will have lots more babies. Everything will be fine."

They hugged and kissed.

The Golden Morava Census – 2001

Shortly after finding the marriage certificate of Markus and Rozália, Vladimir sent me more interesting information, this time concerning the 1870 census record for Golden Morava and its environs. Steiners were listed as inhabitants of several houses in the area. The easiest to handle was the one where Moses, "community servant," and Maria Steiner lived, along with a much younger Anna Steiner. The birth dates given were in the years 1802 for the parents and 1844 for Anna. Did Markus have a younger sister, aged twenty-six at the time of the census? Living with her parents, perhaps looking after them? There were some problems with the record. Firstly, the ages of Moses and Mari on their death records suggest that they were born in 1809 and 1806, respectively. Still, by then I had learned that in those days people attached no great importance to accuracy in documents; indeed, their approach seemed to be the vaguer, the better.

More serious was the problem about Anna: By that time, I had reasons to believe that the Steiner family did not move from Zestmeadow-on-Nyitra to the Golden Morava area until 1848. Yet the census document stated that Anna Steiner was born in 1844, in Szelezsény, in the Golden Morava area! How could that be? Upon reflection I realized that there could be many explanations. They could have visited the area earlier and had a somewhat premature birth for their daughter, perhaps due to the travel on rough roads. Or, perhaps, Anna Steiner was not their daughter, but daughter-in-law. The census only gave the married names of women, never their maiden names. Then again, she could be totally unrelated, working with the older couple as a maid; there were some Jewish maids. Or, as my wife pointed out, she could have been adopted.

Most likely, in my view, was the daughter-in-law proposition. But it raised one serious difficulty for me. To accept that idea, I had to assume that Markus had a brother who, presumably, died before 1869, or why would his wife live with his parents? But who was this brother, what was his name, when was he born and when did he die? For the purposes of recreating the era and the family, I did not feel that I should just invent a person and his vital data; much safer to assume that Anna was originally unrelated, living with Moses and Mari to help them, and eventually adopted by them. This was supported by the fact that the census did not have any record of Steiners living in Szelezsény, Anna's reputed place of birth. It may have been so, it may not have been. I had to reconcile myself to the fact that I would not know everything.

But there were more important facts available concerning the other house, 170 Hosszu utca (Long Street). Incidentally, later I found out that the address was nothing like that. All houses in the town, like in all towns, were numbered randomly, probably as they were built. House no. 170 happened to be located on Long Street, along with maybe a dozen other, quite differently numbered, houses. Meanwhile, houses nos. 171 and 168 could have been at the other end of the town.

Who lived there? The information was not essentially different from what I had earlier, except for the occupation of Markus Steiner, now given as pottery salesman. His wife was Rozália Wasserman; they were both born in 1829. The children living with them were Ilona, Herman, Jozefa, Bernát, Rozália and József. Still the same problems: József and Jozefina (or Jozefa) – strange. And Rozália, the same as her mother? This was just not done! In any case, what about Regi, the mother of Pepi/Leni/Ilona, Peppi/Jozefina/Jozefa and Rozália/Sali? And what about Karolina Wasserman, the mother of József, born in a village south of Perlep?

I was hoping that perhaps the building would turn out to be one of a number of apartments, with the three women – perhaps wives of three different Markuses – living side by side; that would have explained some of the mystery. But no, it was just one woman, Rozália, with all the children (except for Juda, born in 1866; he must have died in his first three years).

Vladimir also found information about another house, 103 Plebaniai Street (of course, the street didn't have that many houses; it was house no. 103 of Golden Morava). Some Steiners originally from Zestmeadow-on-Nyitra lived there. The house had two apartments. In one lived Adolf Steiner, thirty-four, originally from Zestmeadow; his wife Rozália (née Fuerst, as I later found out); and their four children, all born in Golden Morava, ages newborn to seven. But the neighboring apartment was more interesting. There, I found Sigmund Steiner (the German form of *Zsigmond*), age twenty-seven; Flora Steiner, twenty-four; and Samuel Steiner, twenty-two, living with a non-Jewish local maid. Sigmund and Flora were born in Zestmeadow; Samuel was already born in Golden Morava. But all three siblings were congenitally deaf-mute. Apparently, Flora was looking after her two bothers; presumably, the maid served in Adolf's apartment, too. Adolf himself had a general store. Sigmund and Samuel had lowly jobs as tailor's and shoemaker's assistants, respectively.

Vladimir and I wondered, would these people be the siblings of my great-grandfather Markus? But as time went by, it became increasingly evident that such was not the case; he did not seem to have any siblings. We found a sizable death announcement in Adolf's family (he had become rich and respectable) listing all close relatives, but the listing did not include Moses or Markus or his children. Yet they were Steiners, originally from Zestmeadow. Well, why would they not have been the children of Moritz, to whom I have already assigned the role of being Moses's brother? I have found no evidence that they were Markus's cousins, but chances are, they were.

I was grateful to Vladimir for the census data, but soon I was able to examine the census records, along with all various rabbinical and later state vital records, directly from my home base in Toronto. This was due to the efforts of the Mormons.

Yes, the Mormons – or officially, the Church of Jesus Christ of Latter-day Saints – have been doing a marvelous job of collecting old vital records. Apparently, they go around the world, convincing the keepers of old vital records on crumbling paper to allow them to photograph the entire collection. The owners receive a copy of the resulting microfilm, as does the state archives; other copies are held at the Mormon headquarters in Salt Lake City, Utah. I have not researched the mechanism for this process, or the exact terms – I am just reporting the situation as it appears to me, as a user of the facility. For a user I have become: the church makes copies of these microfilms available to anybody, at numerous family history centers around the world, including one in Toronto. Upon payment of a relatively small fee, they order the appropriate reel of microfilm from Salt Lake City and in a few weeks they notify you of its arrival. Then you book a microfilm reader at the center and spend a happy morning or afternoon, more if necessary, studying it.

The rabbinical records go back to the early part of the nineteenth century. In Hungary, state records were only kept from 1895. These are also available, surprisingly in a more spotty manner than the clerical data. And the 1869–70 census is also available.

And so, I spent some days at the Mormons, studying the 1869 census for Golden Morava and the surrounding villages. In addition to helping me piece together the Steiner family, the census also provided significant information on David Wasserman. He was listed as living at Kis Herestény in 1870, acting as tavern keeper and land leaser there. He was born in Bélád in 1814; his wife's name was Jozefa; they had two children, Leni and Hana, born in 1855 and 1858, respectively. They also had two servants and two cows.

Based on the rabbinical records, there should have been more Wassermans in the area, especially in or around Szelezsény or Szelepcsény; if so, however, I was not able to find them. They may have moved away from the area, but according to the report of the old lady who we met in Bélád, as well as that of Mr. Lamm, the head of the Nyitra Jewish community, Wassermans lived in Szelezsény well into the twentieth century. Well, new information was turning up all the time; who knows, maybe more Wassermans would turn up in a year or two. (Incidentally, some information did turn up later. I learned from Chana Mills about a Wasserman relative of ours, Julia Wasserman, who was probably the sister of Rozalia and her brothers. I shall tell you about Chana later.)

Aside from the actual names recorded in the census, the census also provided me with data that I was able to develop into statistics. I decided to count the families in the various decades and especially, to enumerate the individuals who resided in Golden Morava in 1870, with regard to their birthplace. The figures were quite revealing. In that year, there were forty-six Jewish families living in Golden Morava and about twenty-five in the other villages. The forty-six families represented 209 individuals. Of those, 64 were born in Golden Morava itself. Another 74 came from Nyitra County – all but 28 of whom were born before 1848. The surrounding villages accounted for 42 people, while the remaining 29 came from various other parts of Northern Hungary, Moravia, and Poland.

More to the point, of the young people who were born in the area (for obviously none of the older Jews were born there), only six were born in Perlep – my grandfather and his siblings. Since by 1869 only one Jewish family lived in Perlep – a young couple with no children – this information suggests that there probably never lived more than one or two Jewish families there. Before 1867 Markus and his family, perhaps with his parents, were probably the only Jews in Perlep. Therefore, I could forget about multiple Markus Steiners; also, probably, about multiple wives. Somewhat reluctantly, I had to conclude that there were no exotic marriage arrangements. Markus had but one wife, Rozália Wasserman. Her name at birth was probably Regina, or Regi, and later she decided to call herself by the then fashionable name of Rozália, or Rozi. Hence Regi in some documents, Rosalia in others. That left two questions to deal with: the birth of József at Fekete Kelecsény and the fact that Rozália Wasserman (or Rosalia, according to the document) named her daughter Sali.

I think that she must have liked the name very much and she wanted a baby girl named Sali. So she therefore registered one daughter by the name of Sali (originally I was told the name was Rozália, but that information turned out to be incorrect). True, Sali was short for Rozália, but her own name was, at least technically, Regina, so there was no real problem. And she must have been called by Rozi by most people, so she probably saw no conflict with Sali. Her name is, after all, specifically written as Regi on Sali's birth register.

As for József, he is noted as having been born at Fekete Kelecsény, the second village south of Golden Morava after Perlep. And his mother is registered as Karolina Wasserman. I suspect that Karolina was just a mistake; the rabbi writing down the information probably used his memory, which was sometimes uncertain. But I would not be surprised if Rozália really did deliver that baby there. Perhaps they were riding home to Golden Morava, hurrying as her date was getting very close, and then, maybe due to the rough road conditions or some mishaps on the road, she went into labor early before they could reach their destination.

And so, as I say, I finally gave up my ideas of strange marriage customs and accepted that my great-grandfather had just one wife and ten children by her.

* * *

Analyzing the census data – as tedious as it might appear! – gives us quite an insight into how Jewish people lived at that time and place. We have some information on the distribution of Jewish people in Bars County – particularly around Golden Morava – in and around the 1850s. Based on the 1869 census records, one can draw certain conclusions. We know that in 1869, there were forty-six Jewish families living in Golden Morava, six in Szelepcsény, five in Taszár, five more in Malanya, four in Bélád, two each in the two halves of Herestény and one each in Perlep, Fekete Kelecsény and Kis Szelezsény.

But we also have information on where the children of families living in Golden Morava were born. I counted the children under ten years of age and those between eleven and twenty-two (the latter figure would take us back to the important year of 1848) in two separate groups. The findings were certainly interesting. Between 1860 and 1869, there were sixty-five children born to Jewish families living in Golden Morava. Of those, forty-eight were actually born in that town, while of the remaining seventeen, nine were born in Bars County: two in Bélád, three in Perlep, one in Fekete Kelecsény and four in Taszár-Malanya. But in the previous twelve years, of forty-five children born in the area, only sixteen were born in Golden Morava and another fifteen in Bars County: three in Bélád, two in Perlep, four in Taszár-Malanya and one each in Zsitva-Kenéz, Szelezsény, Léva and Fekete Kelecsény. During the decade before 1848 eight children were born in Zsitva-Kenéz, two in Perlep, one in Bélád and four more in other small nearby villages.

These statistics give us a picture of the distribution of Jewish families in the Golden Morava area during the mid-1900s. It appears that before 1848 (but not before 1840, when almost no Jews lived in Bars County at all) there were only three Jewish families in the county – one each in Bélád, Zsitva-Kenéz and the nearby Szelezsény. During the following twelve years, there appeared one family in Perlep (my own), perhaps one more in Zsitva-Kenéz and four families in other nearby villages. Then, during the decade before the census, some of these families moved into town, while five new ones appeared in Taszár, five in nearby Malanya, six in Szelepcsény, three more in Bélád, two in each half of Herestény and one more in Fekete Kelecsény, Szelezsény and Perlep (not my own; they had by then moved to Golden Morava). I am excluding the family of the child born in Léva, as that was a larger town with probably a sizeable number of Jewish families; the presence of that family in Golden Morava does not reflect a move to town from the surrounding areas.

So let me list the number of families who lived in the villages around Golden Morava in the year 1860 once more, for emphasis: 6, 5, 5, 4, 2, 2, 1, 1, 1. (I should note that I have not studied every village in the area, only those that are indicated as the birthplaces of children later living in Golden Morava. In addition, there may have been couples without children who lived in villages before moving to Golden Morava; since the available information relates to birthplaces of children, these families would not show up either.)

How did these people live? I am not querying their occupations – they are listed as tavern keepers, merchants, itinerant sellers and so on. But how could a Jewish family exist in a small village alone, as it were, without the support of other Jews? True, in Taszár-Malanya – if we consider the two nearby villages as one – there were ten Jewish families and probably some kind of a *shul* and perhaps other facilities; we know that there was a teacher living there. But the other villages were not all that close to Taszár.

I should mention that this situation did not come as a great surprise to me. I have always known that, unlike in Poland or the Ukraine, Jews in Hungary typically lived in small villages, with one, two, or three families per village. Indeed, there was hardly a Hungarian village without a Jewish storekeeper – probably that of the only general store in the village. Yet the question is worth asking: How did they live, one, two or three families per village? What did they do when it was time to pray? Where did they spend the Sabbath, the holidays? How did they have access to a rabbi? To a *mohel*, when sons were born? To a *shochet*? For that matter, how did they obtain kosher food? How did they marry? How did they bury their dead?

The answer must be this: with great difficulty, but they managed. The Jews in the neighboring villages must have viewed themselves and each other as members of a larger community, despite the distances. The area involved was roughly a hundred square kilometers, with the greatest distance between any two villages not more than fifteen kilometers. They rode horses; they traveled in carts; they walked. There must have been a rabbi living nearby, or at least not too far, so that marriages could be celebrated. They did not need a rabbi for burying the dead; they could say an *El moleh rachamim* themselves. Female babies were given names and registered when an opportunity arose, sometime weeks or even months after the birth. Boys had to be circumcised on the eighth day; I suppose that several men must have had to learn the intricacies of that craft.

That still leaves the question of daily and Sabbath services, *kashrut* and the other necessities of an observant Jewish life. It is my opinion that these people got around that problem by not being very observant. They probably attended services on the high holidays, either in a larger town that did have a synagogue, even if they had to move there for a few days, or in one of the villages with the largest number of Jewish residents – in our case in Taszár-Malanya – which would put up their neighbors for the duration. They probably did not go to the synagogue on ordinary Sabbaths; they made their own short services at home, even without a *minyan*, the necessary ten men required for communal prayer. And as for *kashrut*, they probably ate non-kosher food. Not pork, I think, at least not in that generation or the next even, but they slaughtered their own poultry and perhaps cattle and they did not worry too much about the minutiae of the *halacha*, the details of the Jewish law.

As for schools, I think that most Jewish people in the small villages taught their children at home, at least before the law forced them to send the children to Hungarian schools. Until then, the teaching was in German, the language of the parents.

That would still leave the question of other necessities unanswered. Not only ritual necessities, but also those of an even semicivilized life. What did they do when they needed the services of a doctor? A dentist? What did they read? How did they get hold of books? Where did they buy all of their supplies, other than ordinary food, which I suppose they could easily grow themselves or buy from their neighbors? There must have been occasional fairs, major annual ones and minor local fairs, perhaps weekly. And they must have made occasional trips to town – in our case, to Golden Morava.

Finally, Golden Morava!

"Great-Grandfather, I wanted to talk with you about Golden Morava. About your moving there after so many years and about your life there. Will you talk to me about those things?"

"Sure, young man, why not. What would you like to know?"

"Well, how did it come about? I suppose it was Rozália who wanted to move to the town?"

"Yes, Rozália, but also my parents. You know that my father's brother, Moritz, lived there since 1848. My father always dreamed of a store in Golden Morava, like his brother's."

"Did he ever achieve that?"

"No, unfortunately not. We never had that kind of money. But even without the store, he thought life would be better there. At Perlep, we did have some difficulties."

"What kind of difficulties?"

"Well, our relation with the local Slovak people was not always the best. You see, they got it into their heads that their lives were so miserable because we Jews had managed to establish a good relationship with the landowners, by becoming Magyars, while their situation was hardly better than serfdom – that it was all our fault somehow. Silly, but how can you explain that to them? So we increasingly thought that in a larger town, we would not be surrounded by such primitive people."

"But did you not say that there were similar difficulties with the German merchants in town?"

"By 1867 that was finished. There were fewer German merchants. They felt that they were not welcome so much and moved back to Austria, at least many of them. By that time there were more and more Jews in Golden Morava."

"Yes, theoretically at least, you could have all moved there after the 1840 law."

"But I told you, they had this patent. Still, the count's man managed to get Moritz a license to open up a store and live there, and after that, there were some others opening up, so the patent gradually lost its significance. By 1860 we could have moved in anytime we wanted. There were at least ten Jewish families living there by then. But we waited until 1867."

"That year had some significance for the Jews, right?"

"Not only for the Jews. That was the year of the *Ausgleich*…"

"The what?"

"The compromise. Between Hungary and Austria. So the Magyars could be almost independent, under the rule of the emperor who was to be also king of Hungary. It was not a bad deal, and it was really good for the Jews. We were granted full equal rights. You see, they understood by then that the Jews became the business leaders of the country – a new class, they called it the middle class. They never had such a class of people before."

"And did you have to give up anything in the deal?"

"No, nothing at all. Well, we had to accept that the children would be taught in Hungarian, but that was fine by me, I preferred it that way. Actually, my children were taught in German before – even when we lived in Perlep, they studied at the new Jewish school in Golden Morava. So now they were also taught in Hungarian, mixed, sometimes this, sometimes that. It worked out fine."

"And it helped make the Jews more Magyars?"

"That, too. We were Magyars and business leaders and we made towns out of villages and cities out of towns. We made this country flourish like never before. Why, even the railways were built by us, even the banks were established by us..."

"But not by you, personally?"

"No, no. I was not that kind of person. I did not have the initiative. But my cousin Adolf did. He had that general store, and before long, he started a bank, which grew into the largest bank around here."

"He had money from the store. But you did not. That's why you could not move before 1867?"

"Right."

"You told me you had a good living, especially from the tavern."

"Reasonably good. Not so good that we had a lot of money saved, for instance so that I could open another tavern in town. Or open a store of some kind."

"Your father did not have much money saved, either?"

"No, he did not. And by the time we moved, he was already old, I think sixty-five years old. Both he and Mother. In their case, it was a question of retiring from work. She was not very healthy. They had enough money, almost, to pay the rent and eat. I had to help them a little. Anna was so good with them, but she could not work and her money could not be touched."

"So anyway, in 1867 you decided to give up the tavern?"

"Yes, the count wanted to increase the *árenda* anyway, so I figured, why bother? I told him thank you for the opportunity, and maybe someone else will now be ready to take over. He found the Vilans, Nátán and Teréz, a very young couple. They were happy to get the lease. I negotiated with a local cart maker, bought a good little two-wheeled cart and a horse – not so young, but she had plenty of life in her yet – and eventually we moved. It was not so simple. We had to find the right house. We found a little one with just one room and kitchen, smaller than what we had in Perlep, and a separate apartment in a larger house for my parents – there were three small apartments in that house. And we had a shed at the back, for the horse."

"And so you moved in that year, 1867."

"Yes. Yes and no. In a sense, we moved already a year earlier, because Juda, poor little Juda, was already born in Golden Morava that year, 1866. They had a better midwife there, and my cousin insisted that we move there for a few weeks and stay with them. That's what we did, left the children with my mother and Anna, and I walked to Perlep every day to open the tavern."

"You said 'poor little Juda.' Why, what happened to him?"

"He died when he was quite a small baby. Rozi took it very hard. So did I."

"He was the only child of yours that died young, right?"

"Well, up to that time, yes. When we moved, we had three boys and three girls, apart from Juda. There was Herman, and Berman, and József – no, József was born in that year, 1867, back in Perlep – actually at the next village, Fekete Kelecsény. We went there for the midwife. We were not all that happy with the one in town, after all. And there were the three girls, Leni and Peppi and Sali. I did not like that name, Sali. It was really Rozália, but Rozi said it's different, and besides her real name was Regi. I had lots of arguments with Rozi about that, about names. She wanted a Pepi, after her poor mother, let her rest in peace. First she told the rabbi that Leni was Pepi, but later we had to correct that, then Jozefina became Peppi, well, that was all right, it is the same name. We always argued about names. Nothing else, really, just names."

"So you had six children, apart from Juda?"

"No, after we moved to town, we had three more, thank God. Hermina, and Mathilde and Ignácz. Oh, but Hermina also died, before she was three years old. That was very sad. Very, very sad."

"I know. Well, at least you had eight children that lived."

"Yes, thank God. Eight. No, wait. I just remembered. Oh, no, my poor Herman!"

"What about Herman?"

"He died. Near the end, I was very sick. And I heard something, I am not sure what, about Herman also being sick. At first, they did not tell me anything, but I knew there was something wrong. I did not know what. Something about Herman."

"And then…?"

"And then, one day, they just told me that the poor boy had died. It was horrible. I knew that I was near the end of my road, and suddenly it was not me, but my lovely firstborn son, Herman, twenty years old. He was just no more."

"What did you do? You went to the funeral?"

"Of course I did. It was the coldest day of the winter, but what difference did that make by then? We buried him and sat *shiva*, or the others sat, I lay in my bed."

"That must have been a hard time. I want to hear more about that later, but for now let's go back to earlier days. Did you have a good life in Golden Morava? You haven't told me yet what you did there?"

"Well, I did tell you that I could not afford to open a store. So Adolf introduced me to the owner of the pottery plant in town, and we agreed that I should take consignments of pots and pans, and sell them in the neighboring villages. That was not so difficult. Every day, I would ride out with my little cart, go to a particular village and knock on the door of every house. I sold some and took orders for other things. By the end of the day I would be home. Later, I ventured farther afield. Then I would not be back for two or three days, even for five days, sometimes. But I was always back by noon on Friday."

"Did you enjoy that?"

"Enjoy? I don't think that I enjoyed it. What was there to enjoy? It was a living, that's all."

"But you did at least like the weekends? When you did not work? Did Golden Morava turn out to be everything you hoped for? You and Rozália?"

"Hmm… Yes, I suppose. It was all right, it was different. She wanted to walk on the promenade and we did walk there. I bought her a very beautiful dress. She wanted to greet acquaintances there and she did, a few. We did not have many friends. She liked to look at good stores – there were quite a number of them. We did not buy things very often. And there were the other things – there was the circus and traveling performers, sometimes theater. The fire brigade had a brass band. They performed on Sundays. Yes, things were better, at least for her."

"Not for you?"

"I was happy anywhere. I did not have extravagant demands. I liked the tavern, but this life was also good. Not bad. Sometimes it was very cold, traveling on that cart in the winter. But in the summer it was quite pleasant. One rode the cart and one had time to think."

"Well, what kind of thoughts would you have thought during those days, those years, really?"

"Thoughts? Well, many things. I cannot tell you all, there were years and years. I thought about the situation, how those bad, old days were finally over, how we were part of this country, how they invited us and now, slowly, gradually, we could have good, normal lives, like everyone else. Then I thought about my parents, about Mother who was always in such a poor health. I worried about her. I thought that maybe I should go to the synagogue more often. I was not very religious, but I did go from time to time. There was a local *shul* adjacent to one of the houses…"

"Was that an Orthodox *shul*? Or a Neolog one?"

"We had no such things in those days. I know that there was a big argument in Budapest – the new name for Pest-Buda – and they split up, but we were not interested in that in Golden Morava. We were comfortable as we were and we decided to ignore it all and remain as we were before."

"The 'status quo ante' solution."

"Yes, I have heard that expression. It did not matter to me. What mattered was the well-being of all the children. All the remaining children. That's why I went to the *shul*, to *daven* and to pray for their health and success in life. The children, and my wife, and my father. My mother, while she lived. She died about five years after we moved to Golden Morava. In 1872."

"Peace be on her soul."

"Yes. The children did all right at school, especially Berman. Bernát, he started to call himself. That was later. It sounded more Hungarian. You said he was your grandfather?"

"Yes, he was. He did really well in the legal system, I think I told you. Eventually he became the director of the law court in Rima-Sobota."

"Yes, you told me. Thank God for that. What happened to the other children?"

"I am afraid I don't know, Great-Grandfather. There are many things I don't know yet. Maybe, slowly, I shall find out."

"Good. Tell me when you do."

"Will do. Goodbye for now."

A Weekend in 1870

In the mornings, Rozália only had the oldest child with her, Leni, and the two youngest, two-year-old József and Hermina, who was just two months. Leni was a big girl by then, fourteen years old – fourteen and a half, really. She helped with the work around the house, and there was certainly enough work for her, more than enough. On this particular morning she was looking after the children while Rozália went out to milk the cow. When Rozália came back in, she instructed the girl, "Leni, I need more water. Go to the well."

"But I was just there, not an hour ago."

"I need more. It's Friday, I must cook. You know that, so just go."

Leni went and brought back a pail of water. She really wanted to sit down and read, but Rozália wouldn't let her. "I wanted to mend those socks of your father, and Herman's, too, but I see that I won't have time. You can mend, Leni, go ahead, do them."

"But Mother…"

"No 'but Mother,' just mend them. It won't take long."

Leni got out the mending box and found the socks; there were eight pairs to mend. She said nothing for a while as she sat and worked, but after about ten minutes she commented, "Why don't we have a maid?"

"Because we don't, that's why."

"But if we had a maid, she could do most of the cooking and all the cleaning and washing…"

"And I wouldn't have to cook, and you wouldn't have to mend. Well, we don't have a maid, and that's that."

"But all of my friends' mothers have maids."

"So we don't, what do you want me to do about it? Argue with your father."

"He won't take me seriously. I really don't understand why we couldn't have a maid. We could afford one."

"Ah, the great expert. So you know how much money we have."

"A Slovak maid does not cost much money. She's happy to have a place to sleep, food to eat."

"Yes, and where would she sleep? There are already seven of you sleeping here in the kitchen, and the two of us are in the clean room, but when we have a visitor, then all nine of us sleep here. So where will your maid sleep?"

Leni didn't have an answer to that. Rozália thought that her daughter's arguments were exactly what she had been saying to her husband on more than one occasion; her reply echoed Markus's words exactly. Why could they not have a maid, when everybody had a maid? Because there was nowhere for her to sleep. But why should they not move into a larger apartment? Because they could not afford it. Why not? Because his business did not bring in enough. So why does he not do something else? Because he does not have money to start a new business. How do other people do it? She did not know, but other people started all kinds of stores, businesses.

Markus was a dear man, a lovely husband. She could not wish for a better one. But he was not the world's greatest businessman, she had to admit that much.

"Leni, when you are finished with the mending, dust the clean room and sweep the floor."

"But Mother!"

"What 'but Mother,' again? Do you think that I should slave here all day, while you read your books? What book are you reading, anyway?"

"It's the new one by Jókai, that Father brought last week."

"How is it?"

"Very good."

"I'll want to read it, when you are finished. Anyway, you'll have to do the clean room, and help me wash and pit the prunes and also feed József. Stop the mending and come stir the beans while I feed the baby."

Resigned, Leni did as she was told.

After a while, her mother thought of something else. "And don't forget, you have to take the chicken and the duck to the *shochet*."

Leni didn't answer.

"You do remember, don't you?"

"Yes, I remember," she grumbled.

"Ice! Ice!" the man was shouting on the street. "Ice! Ice!"

"Take that pot off the stove and go get ice."

Leni did as she was instructed. Taking some money out of the jar, she picked up the large pail that stood by the door and went to get half a block of ice. After cutting the ice to smaller pieces and putting it in the box, Leni asked her mother if she should put the pot back on the stove.

"Let me see. No, I think that's enough. You'd better take the poultry to the *shochet* now. Leave the cleaning until after, for I have a lot of work with that duck. But first, bring in some more wood."

After Leni left, József started to cry; fortunately Hermina had gone to sleep. Rozália played for a few minutes with József, then went out to buy stone powder from the hawker. Almost immediately, the pot mender came, shouting his trade. Rozália had no pot to mend, but when the grinder rang his bell, she went out with three knives to sharpen.

Leni came back with the slaughtered poultry, put it down on the table, made a face and washed her hands. Rozália put more wood into the stove, plucked the feathers off the birds and singed them over the fire. Then she cut them up, cleaned them and salted them properly.

There was music in the street, band music. The Hussars were marching by, all the children rushed to the window – Rozália had forbidden them to run out of the house and march after the Hussars, like the other children did. Sometimes such enthusiasm resulted in tragedy.

After the dust settled, there was a knock on the door. It was not fully closed, so Mrs. Florovič came in.

"Mrs. Steiner, do you have lots of sugar? I would like to borrow a cup from you." She was talking in Slovak.

"Sure, I have sugar," Rozália answered in Slovak, then in German, "Leni, give Mrs. Florovič a cup of sugar." She wanted to add, "Do you have enough eggs now?" Earlier in the week her neighbor had borrowed two eggs which she had not yet returned. Yet she did not want to be unfriendly. Not that the relations with the neighbors could be called particularly friendly; they tolerated each other.

After the Slovak woman left, Rozália looked at the clock. "It's almost noon, the children should be coming home soon."

In a few minutes, she could hear them. They came in running and shouting, all four of them. Peppi was the first in the room.

"Mother, Herman and Samuel were fighting again."

"Why don't you leave that boy alone, Herman. His mother will come and complain to me."

"But he started the fight, he called me names."

"What names?"

Herman sulked and would not say. He was twelve now and had just entered that difficult age when boys don't want to tell things to their parents. Rozália suspected that the name calling might have had something to do with them being so much poorer than Samuel's family.

Berman seemed to be in a bad mood.

"And what's wrong with you?"

"The teacher beat me with the ruler."

"Why, what did you do?"

"He did not like the way I drew the Hebrew letters. But I saw the rabbi write them that way. I told him so."

"You told the teacher that he was wrong and you were right?"

"Yes, I did."

"So he hit your backside? He was quite right. You don't tell the teacher that he is wrong."

"Why not? If he's wrong, why shouldn't I tell him?"

Rozi suppressed a smile.

"Because he is the teacher, that's why. When you grow up and become a teacher yourself, you can tell the children that they are wrong."

"Even if they are right?"

"Yes, even then."

"I would never do that. It's not fair."

"Never mind that. Go wash your hands. You too, Sali," that was to the six-year-old girl. "All of you. It will be lunchtime soon."

During lunch, which was a fast affair – Leni, Herman and little Sali wolfed down their food, while nine-year-old Peppi and seven-year-old Berman hardly touched theirs – the discussion centered on what Father would bring from his journey. It was his habit to bring at least one thing, one present, to somebody in the family. He tried to be fair and not forget anybody; last week he had brought a rattle for baby Hermina.

"I think it's my turn now," asserted Peppi. "Maybe he'll bring me a doll."

"Ya, it's Peppi's turn," added Leni. She always protected her sister's interest.

"It is not her turn – it's mine!" Herman countered. "Anyway, she's too big for a doll. Maybe a broom, so she can help you clean the place."

Peppi stuck out her tongue. Berman commented, "I haven't had anything for a while. Maybe he'll bring me a book."

"I'm not too big for a doll," said Sali, and of course she was right.

"Let him come home safely," interjected Rozália. "I don't care what he brings."

After lunch, the children were about to run out and play. "Hey, no home-work?" Rozália asked them. They all mumbled something. "All right, you can play for one hour. After that homework for everybody. Whoever doesn't have homework will help me with the *Shabbes* dinner table."

They threw a ball around for a while, but the smaller children started to cry – they wanted to play easier games. So soon they were all standing in a circle, passing a ring around, singing, "The ring goes on a journey, from one hand to the other, if you know, do not tell, where it's wandering takes it." Then other games, in which they sang, "Chain, chain, Ester-chain, the thread of Ester-chain; thread it could be, silk it could be, still it would turn around. Money could be little disk, little disk, little Sali turn around, it's little Sali's chain." One by one, the children had to turn around, and then back again.

The game Sali liked best was when they sang, "If the child is good, obedient, lines up with his fellows and everyone does like this, lines up with his fellows and everyone does like this," and they all had to imitate the gestures of the leader. Pepi preferred the game in which they lined up behind each other in pairs and took turns running through the doubled-up line, singing, "Climb, climb, green branch, tender, little green leaf. The golden gate is fully open; let you climb through it. Open, my rose, your gate, your gate; let me circle your shoulders, your shoulders; sieve, sieve Friday, love, love Thursday, bean Wednesday." At work in the kitchen, Rozi wondered, not for the first time, what this might mean. Her Hungarian was not very strong yet, but she understood enough of the song to know that it made little sense.

The hour passed sooner than the children would have liked. "It's time for homework," Rozália called.

"Just one more game, Mother," pleaded several of them.

"Just one, then."

So they played "We are coming from America, the symbol of our famous trade." Each child had to show some pretense of work at a trade and the others had to guess. Afterwards, they came into the kitchen and sitting at the crowded table, they worked at Hebrew letters, German poetry, history, and geography – each according to his age. Leni helped her mother; she was already past her school years.

"I wonder when Father is coming home," Rozi asked, really to herself. "It is four o'clock. He said he would be here by now."

She began baking the *challa*, then realized that she did not have enough salt at home. She could have asked her neighbor, but she preferred not to.

"Herman, run over to the store. Buy a kilo of salt."

"May I go, too?" asked Sali.

"Sure, go with him."

Herman and Sali went; they were away for half an hour. "What took you so long?" their mother demanded when they returned.

"The store was full of people."

"Full of maids," added Sali. Rozi had forgotten that in the afternoons the stores were always full of maids buying food for the night's dinner, not only on Friday.

"It is nearly five o'clock. Where is your father?" Again, nobody felt the question directed at him or her.

Time went by, and Rozi started to worry. It was half past five, and then six. Everything was ready, the table was laid with white linen, the *challa* was keeping warm in the oven, but Markus was not there.

"He still needs to wash and change, and then he wants to go to the *shul*, but he is not here. Something happened. I know that something happened. God forbid, maybe they robbed him."

"No, Mother, nothing happened. He will come," Herman assured her.

"I hope so. I really hope so."

In truth, this was not the first time that Markus had come home late. Still, Rozi thought it her wifely prerogative to worry.

And Markus did show up at around seven o'clock. They heard his horse neigh, and they all ran out to welcome him. He kissed each child in turn, then went into the kitchen, hugged and kissed his wife and the baby.

"What happened? What took you so long?" she demanded.

"Bad trouble, axle trouble. The axle broke – that was yesterday – it held me up for half a day before I could get it fixed. I had to stay at an inn, not the one I planned on. Then today, I had to get the horse reshod. The smith was busy – he does not like Jews. In the end I had to find another man, out of the way. Things add up."

"Poor Markus." She kissed him again. "And apart from that, how was the trip? Did you sell everything?"

"Almost everything, and I got some good orders. Not bad at all, not bad that way." He smiled at all of them.

"But then you'll have to go back there to deliver the order."

"Yes, but not for another two weeks. Look what I found." He pulled out from his large coat pocket a book, a German translation of Charles Dickens' *David Copperfield*, and gave it to Berman. "This is for you, young man. You like books. But let the others read it, too, once you are finished with it."

Berman's face glowed with happiness and pride. The others did not complain; they knew that their turn would come.

"But first," Father said, "you boys go and look after the horse and cart. Take them across to the stables (they had a shed at the back, but it was large enough only for their cow, so they rented the stables from the Slovak men across the road). Unhitch the cart, put everything onto the shelves, feed the horse – she needs lots of water. You'll have to go to the well. Rub her down, too. By the time you're finished, it will be time for *Kiddush*, I think. Is everything ready?" he asked, turning to Rozi.

"Everything is ready. You're not going to the *shul*," she stated, rather than asked.

"I don't think so, no. By the time I'd get there *Maariv* would be over."

They had a beautiful *Kiddush*, a nice meal of soup, roast duck, potatoes and peas, even pastry afterwards. And they went to bed early that night – the children in the kitchen, the parents and the baby in the clean room.

*   *   *

The next morning, after washing and breakfast, the family went to the *shul* – more or less. Rozi said that she would come over later, with József and baby Hermina. Leni stopped by a friend's house first and then the two girls went to the *shul* together. But Herman, Peppi, Berman and Sali accompanied their father and sat with him. Later, Herman went over to a group of youngsters studying for their bar mitzvas; his own was coming up right after next *Shavuos*.

The *shul* was nothing more than a large room at the back of one of the houses. There were rough benches, enough to accommodate, with great difficulty, 250 people on the high holidays, for many came in from the neighboring villages. On an ordinary *Shabbes*, like now, there were not more than forty men and maybe twice as many children. In the women's section not even thirty showed up; most, like Rozália, came much later, with small children. It was a town of young families, at least for the Jews.

Between Markus and his children, they saved one place for the grandfather. Moses came in soon after the younger people, with a big smile on his face; he hugged each of his grandchildren in turn.

"How is Mother today?" Markus asked him.

"Not so good. She is weak. Will probably stay in bed again."

"Did the doctor see her?"

"Yes, he came yesterday morning. There is nothing to do, he says. Just rest, take it easy."

"Should she be sent somewhere perhaps? A sanitarium?" Not that they could have afforded such a luxury.

"He does not think so. Just rest. It comes with old age."

"She is not that old. Sixty-one."

"Or more. She is not sure herself exactly which year she was born. Neither am I, for that matter."

The service was well under way. They all stood, as it was time to take the Torah scroll out of the ark and carry it to the *bima* for reading. Seven men were called up, in turn – not Markus or Moses this time, but their cousin Adolf was in third place. *His* father, Moritz, was away in a sanitarium – they could afford to send him.

During the reading, a couple of people sitting behind Markus got into a discussion about the split. Adolf Drexler and Mor Wertheim always argued. Markus was usually drawn into the discussion. He knew both men well; in fact, Mor was his friend from Zestmeadow. They were the same age, but they had come over to this area only recently. Mor's wife had actually been born in Moravia.

"Have you heard that in Tapolcsány they decided to remain Orthodox?" Drexler asked his neighbor, loudly enough for six or seven men around him to hear.

"Doesn't surprise me," Wertheim countered. "You know that I'm from that area. The Austrians would not hear of Neolog. Whatever the Chasam Sofer tells them…"

Markus turned back and interrupted, "The Chasam Sofer? Mor, you forget. He died a long time ago."

"His son, then. Same thing. The Kesav Sofer. When they whistle in Pozsony, the Jews of Tapolcsány dance. By now, I suppose in Zestmeadow, too."

"Not just Zestmeadow. All of Nyitra County is now officially Orthodox," Wertheim informed them.

"And all Austrian Jews are Orthodox, wherever they live," commented Drexler. "It's only the Moravians that became Neolog, fortunately not all."

"No, there are still some sensible communities. Like us." Wertheim felt strongly about such things.

"Sure, and what about the Polish Jews? They are more Orthodox than Orthodox."

"Yes, but they are Orthodox in a different way. Like Mr. Silverbach, they won't even come to our *shul.*"

"Yet we are certainly not Neologs here."

Markus turned back again and told them: "You know, I travel a lot. Around here, all communities remained status quo ante. There are very few Neolog towns."

"Any Orthodox ones?" Drexler asked.

"Some around here. Not many. But when I travel farther east, yes, there are more and more. One town is Neolog, the next is status quo ante, the third is Orthodox. Zólyom County is Neolog. Nógrád is Orthodox."

"I am told that there is no such three-way division in any other country—" but Mor Wertheim was stopped by a loud hiss from the *bima*; their discussion had already disturbed the Torah reader. Quiet, whispered talk was tolerated, but when it became too loud, they were hissed at.

After the Torah reading, the morning service came to an end, but the additional services were to follow. Before they started, a *Mishebeirach* was said for those ill, including Markus's mother Mari. Then a sermon was generally given by a rabbi, if there was one, or by a member of the congregation. And, as was the case today, that member was very often Adolf Steiner, Markus's cousin.

Adolf was a handsome man, not very tall, with a clear, open expression and a prominent, though almost straight nose. He was quite slim. You tended to trust him, which may have been the secret of his success in business. He wore no beard – that was unusual in those days. And he wore shoes, not boots, which was even more unusual. Markus looked around to count shoes and boots: he found only two other men wearing shoes. About a third of the men were barefaced. This was a big change, for ten years earlier nobody would have dared to appear beardless. Markus himself had a full, though nicely trimmed, black beard. His father's white beard was even fuller.

Adolf spoke in German. True, they had heard of Rabbi Löw's insistence that even the sermon should be in Hungarian, but they thought that was a rather strange idea. Adolf had more information on what had taken place at the Budapest conference. More than a year had passed since the conference, but news traveled slowly. They knew that the Orthodox rabbis had walked out of the conference but they hadn't heard what had led up to the break.

So Adolf filled them in. He had heard that the congress was the brainchild of Baron József Eötvös, minister of Religious and Educational Affairs, who wanted to bring the Jews into the modern world. That the Orthodox, especially the Chassidic people from the east, disliked the idea of modernization, arguing that it would destroy Jewish values – the Neologs sneering all the while. That Rabbi Löw and other Neolog leaders promoted assimilation, Rabbi Einhorn going so far as hoping that his children would marry *goyim*. That the Orthodox became more and more incensed at such talk and, seeing the Neolog rabbis taking charge of the conference, they decided to walk out, thereby defeating Baron Eötvös's hope of a modern, unified Jewish faith. And that the entire Jewish community split not into two, but three fragments: Neolog, Orthodox and "status quo ante." Their community remained in the third category, arguing that "we were satisfied before; we see no reason to change anything here just because a number of cantankerous old men in Budapest disagreed." They simply opted to keep the status quo, despite the conference.

"So the question remains, can we maintain our religious identity and affiliation within a large group of similarly inclined congregations, or shall we be forced to choose sides one day? If the latter, I am afraid that the choice would depend on the rabbis in the area. Rabbi Fuerst, who often comes here to lead the service, is firmly Neolog. Or we could ask a rabbi from Pozsony to visit, if we wanted an Orthodox one. We don't have to decide now, and I hope that we shall never have to decide. Yet the day may come when we might be forced to make such a decision. Something for all of you to think about. Let us continue now with the *Mussaf* service."

Markus estimated that if a choice had to be made now, at least two-thirds of the congregation would choose Neolog over Orthodox; his own family had moved from Nyitra County partly for that reason, to escape the strictures imposed upon them by the Pozsony rabbis. He himself would vote Neolog. Yet, deep inside he felt uneasy about that possible choice. Here in Golden Morava, there was no question of real assimilation, of intermarriage, as Rabbi Einhorn had suggested, but if that were to happen eventually it would surely be a tragedy. Would everyone agree with him on that? He wondered and decided to ask his cousin's opinion.

So at the end of the service, he went over to Adolf. "*Gut Shabbes*, Adolf."

"*Gut Shabbes*, Markus. How are things?"

"Not too bad, thank God. Tell me, will you have some time this afternoon? We haven't talked for quite a while."

"Sure, we aren't doing anything. Why don't you and Rozi come over for coffee?"

"Yes, that would be nice. Around four, four thirty, if that's all right with you?"

"That's fine. See you then."

So Markus promised his father to come over around three thirty to see his mother. By this point Rozi had shown up with the smaller children, and the whole family walked home together for the *Shabbes* meal.

After a pleasant lunch they *bentched*, reciting the blessing over the meal just eaten, following which Markus and Rozi took a brief nap, a luxury not often afforded them. Then they collected the entire family and went to visit Grandmother.

Grandmother lay in bed, her head propped up on three pillows, with Anna in close attendance. The children lined up politely to kiss her; last came Rozi and Markus. Despite her illness, Mari seemed to be in good spirits, stroking the children's heads and asking each one about school and friends. Every few minutes she turned to Anna, requesting this or that, some water, a fresh handkerchief or a comb. Anna obliged with a big smile that, somehow, made her face almost attractive, despite a slight – well, perhaps not so slight – deformity around her mouth that made her ineligible for marriage.

Anna offered them tea but they politely declined, as they were invited for coffee later. But when it came to cakes, the children accepted happily. After a while, Rozi went over to the clean room to nurse the baby; then she and Markus rose to leave, instructing Leni and Herman to see all the children home. Then they went to see Markus's cousin.

Adolf owned a big house, with two large apartments. Adolf himself lived with his wife Rozália and their four children, aged one to seven, in the larger apartment. With them lived fourteen-year-old Lina Goldstein, a distant relative of theirs who had come to them after her parents had died in the cholera epidemic. There were two additional rooms in the apartment. In one lived three Jewish shop apprentices, while the other housed the maid and Fani Vinterstein, an older Jewish lady. She was a widow and was glad to have found a job at the Steiners' as cook. The next apartment had only two rooms; there lived Adolf's two brothers and his sister, Sigmund, Samuel and Flora. They were all deaf-mute; Flora was looking after her brothers, who worked as apprentices at a tailor's and a shoemaker's. There was also a little chamber there for a maid, whose job it was to look after both apartments, but mainly Adolf and Rozália's.

They welcomed Markus and Rozi, the women kissing, seated them in the salon and pulled a cord for the maid. She came in from the other apartment right away and was instructed to bring coffee and pastry.

They drank black coffee, without milk (for it was too soon after they had eaten meat – Adolf knew that his cousin was particular about the minutiae of the law) and *parve* pastry.

"So how are things with you?" Adolf asked once the preliminaries were over.

"Not too bad, I can't complain."

"That's good. Things are improving here, in the town, would you not say?"

"Yes, I suppose," Markus agreed, although he did not see that much improvement in his own situation. "Business is good at the store?"

"Very good, thank God. We are expanding. But the big thing is this savings-and-loan that I am planning to set up, with a couple of friends. Actually three friends, two Jewish, one a Christian."

"A Christian? Can you do business with a Christian?" Markus was truly surprised.

"Why not? Some of them are very decent, solid, trustworthy people. And that will be good for the business, if it is not run only by Jews."

"But do you know that business yourself? Is it not complicated? I hear that it is almost like a bank."

"It is a bank, really. I am hiring a banker from Vienna to look after the day-to-day operations, and also a bookkeeper from Pozsony. It will be good. That reminds me of something. Were you not talking about opening up a kitchen-ware store somewhere?"

Markus would have preferred not to touch upon that subject.

"I was toying with the idea a while ago. But it is too much of a venture for me. Too much investment – I don't have that kind of money."

"Well, that's just the point. That is what a savings-and-loan is for. I would have gladly lent you my own money, but now there will be this firm. They will be in the business of giving out loans to people like you. People who need it as an investment. Listen, I know that you don't like to accept favors, so this thing is ideal for you. It's not a favor, it's a business deal. You get money for investment, you open a store, and slowly, gradually, you pay the money back, plus a reasonable interest. Not much, maybe four or five percent. Per year. That won't kill you."

Markus had known the conversation might move in this direction. He shook his head. "I don't know, Adolf, I don't think that this is for me."

"But why not?"

"There is something in me. Some deep hate of owing money. To you, to an institution, to anybody. Then I would feel that I was no longer a free man, I was beholden to somebody, to something."

"But it is just a nameless entity. No, not nameless, but not a person. It trusts you, and if it is wrong, if you tell it to go to hell and you won't pay, then it just writes the loan off as a bad decision. Not that such a thing would ever happen in your case, I know."

"Well, that's just it. I know that I could never default on a loan, no matter that my children might starve and go without clothes. That loan would be the number-one thing in my life. That is too much for me. I cannot take on such a burden."

Adolf was clearly exasperated.

"Well, suit yourself, my friend, but it is the way business is being done these days. Even I will take out a loan, when I'll need one for my business. There is nothing derogatory about it."

"No, I know. But I just hate the idea. Thanks anyway."

Adolf just shrugged and said nothing. The atmosphere was not good. Markus glanced to the other corner of the room, where the two Rozálias were talking about babies. A good thing, he thought, for his own wife would probably support Adolf's idea. He shook his head and turned back to Adolf.

"No, there is something else that I wanted to ask you, Adolf."

"Sure, go ahead. Have a cigar."

He offered Markus a box of cigars, cut off the end of one for himself, handed the cutter to Markus, and lighted a big match for both. Then he looked expectantly at his cousin.

"What you were talking about in the *shul* this morning. I was wondering, if we have to choose eventually, if we are to become Neolog…"

"Yes?"

"Well, would that not be real bad for all of us?"

"Why do you think so?"

"From what I hear about Löw and Einhorn. How they encourage full assimilation."

"Well, surely that is a good thing. We are getting assimilated here, ourselves. Talking to our Christian neighbors as equals, doing business with them…"

"Marrying our sons and daughters to them?"

"Come now, nobody is talking about such a thing."

"Yes, they are. Rabbi Einhorn was saying that he would like his children to marry *goyim*."

"I haven't heard that. But I know that Einhorn is going too far, he is losing his followers. You know, I think that there will be some intermarriage, but it will be rare, the exception."

"You may be right. But I worry about such things. We did not survive nearly two millennia in the Diaspora to become so Hungarian now that suddenly we are no longer Jews. I don't think that that was the objective of the Enlightenment."

"No, certainly not. We wanted full emancipation, and we have it now, or almost. But of course, we must remain Jews. You are correct. I just don't think that there is a real danger of anything else happening."

"I hope you are right. But I travel a lot, and I have heard ugly things said, not only about Einhorn, but also about Löw."

"What things?"

"In the villages east of here, they call him names, like 'the destroyer of Judaism,' 'the nemesis.'"

"I think that's unfair. He is a great man, he can see far into the future. A great leader."

"I suppose. But don't forget that maybe two-thirds of the Jews in this country are Orthodox. The majority, to the east of us, come from Poland. They will never follow Löw."

Adolf shrugged. "That's their problem. But I think that any Jew who moves into a larger town, into a city, will follow him – the advantages will be so obvious for anyone with eyes to see. That does not mean that we must fully assimilate. We can still remain Jews, we must remain Jews, as you say. Or rather, Hungarians of Jewish religion. That's what we are now."

"I suppose..."

"Yes, we are. Look, in this town, and this was one of the most difficult towns, we are fully part of the community. Why, they have invited me to the town leadership meetings, so far as an observer, but it won't be long before I might get elected to some position. It is not that I personally crave such a thing, but it will be an important recognition of the Jewish presence here."

"You have actually attended such meetings?"

"Yes, I have. Twice now. It is most interesting, I tell you. Lots of people are there, tradesmen as well as long-coats."

"Long-coats?"

"Yes, the larger store owners, the dean parson, or whatever they call the most senior priest, the fiscal supervisor, the chief notary, the pharmacist, even papal chamberlain."

"And do you feel comfortable among those people?"

"Well, a couple of them seem to avoid me. That's their business. But others come over and talk with me, introduce me to others – on the whole they are friendly enough. Yes, I feel comfortable. I can talk with anybody. I must get a long coat."

"I don't think that I would like to be in such company. But then, there is no danger of them inviting me, so it's all right."

The conversation soon drifted to catching up on family members, and soon it was time to say goodbye.

In the evening Mor Wertheim and his wife came over and played *ferbli* for a while. Rozi thought of it as a silly card game, but Markus liked to play. After the guests left, the children played while the parents read books; summer was a good time for reading. Rozi hated the long winter nights, when it was just games, games and more games, since reading by the light of kerosene lamp wasn't so good for your eyes. But in the summer you could read until quite late. She loved the German romantic books, when Markus could get her one; now there were two unread books on the shelf, not to mention Berman's new Dickens. She felt rich.

Next morning, they watched as their neighbors hurried to church, dressed in their Sunday best. The Steiner family had a leisurely breakfast and then, toward eleven, they went down to the square to listen to the fire brigade's band. The children enjoyed that. They sat on low benches around the bandstand and watched the captain march in with his troop, resplendent with shining helmets, fancy uniforms with gold braiding, and all their brass instruments freshly polished – watching them was more fun than listening. But they played well – marches and the latest Johann Strauss waltzes; everybody applauded.

On the way back, they met David Rintl and his wife Roza – she was Mor Wertheim's sister, whom Markus knew from Zestmeadow. They exchanged a few words and told them about the fire brigade's band.

"But that's not real music," sneered Roza Rintl.

"I suppose not," replied Rozália. "But that's all we have here." Frankly, she had no idea what real music was.

"No, we do have better. Look, come with me. Just one corner." She held Rozália's hand; the others followed. One block away, they stopped in front of a large poster.

It announced that in three days' time, on Wednesday evening, at seven o'clock, there would be a concert held at the town hall, where the musicians of the Pozsony Orchestra would perform works by Haydn, Rossini, Weber and other notable composers. The famous young soprano Lujza Reindl and other singers with voices of great beauty were to join the orchestra's excellent musicians. The residents of Golden Morava were all invited to attend the concert, the entrance fee to which would be set at ten *krajcár*s per person.

"You will come, won't you?" asked Mrs. Rintl.

"I certainly won't," said Markus right away. "I'll be out of town."

"Yes, of course, but surely you will allow your wife to come?"

"Allow? Of course I allow, she does what she wants. But I don't know if she'll have the time…"

Rozália took the clue from her husband. "I am so busy, what with all the children, I could not leave a baby of two months with Leni. She is not experienced enough to handle her if there is a problem." Rozi had no intention of attending the concert of which she understood nothing, had no idea who those musicians were or what they did, what one was supposed to do at an event like that, what to say, how to behave, what to wear – no, she would not get herself into an embarrassing situation.

"Well, whatever you want, it's your loss." Mrs. Rintl was clearly annoyed. The Steiners were her third attempt to entice some acquaintances to accompany her to the concert – it seemed that these Jews here were totally ignorant about the finer things in life.

After they parted, Markus, Rozi and the children went home to lunch. They ate quickly, because Markus and Rozi had promised the children that they would go to the circus that afternoon and have a ride on the carousel. Once at the carousel all of the children chose their favorite seats. Herman, Peppi and Berman sat on horses; Sali, who was too young for the horse, sat in a beautiful landau with Leni and József. It was great fun.

Then they all went into the circus tent. There were acrobats there, two lions, and even a bear performing tricks. And there was a clown, too. "Mother, you missed it, it was so funny!" they shouted to Rozi as they ran out of the tent.

Then it was almost four in the afternoon, time for a walk along the promenade. Rozi put on her best dress, which was really her only nice dress. That bothered her a bit, but Markus often brought her something small when he came back from his trips, a new silk kerchief or a brooch. Not very expensive things, but enough to make her feel different from one week to the next, or so she hoped.

They walked the length of the promenade several times – the children running back and forth – meeting acquaintances. Markus tipped his hat, Rozália smiled and nodded, stopping to admire other people's children and vice versa – she enjoyed it so much. This was what she had missed the most when they used to live in that dusty little village.

At around five o'clock they entered the coffeehouse and chose a table on the terrace. They ordered coffee for the adults and chocolate for the children. This was the luxury that Rozi dreamed about; now they could afford it once or twice a month. Again, there were acquaintances there, people to greet, smile at. While the children amused themselves by looking at the menu and imagining all the delicious sweets they would order, Markus and Rozi went over to the Spitzers' table. The husband, Moritz, had just come back from a week spent in Losonc and he was full of excitement over the big town.

"You know, it's different there. It's almost like a city. There's a theater, and they perform almost every week. New plays, Hungarian plays. They're really very good. And there's a lending library."

"Oh, a lending library!" Rozi sighed. "That's what I miss most here. To be able to go there and ask for almost any book."

"Yes, they have every book, Hungarian and foreign. And they hold balls – I don't know if Jews go there, but it is nice to know that you could, I suppose…"

"I would love to go to a real ball."

Markus wondered if Rozi really would. What would she wear? Would she not worry about how to behave? How about the dances? Did she know how to dance a quadrille, or a waltz? He himself certainly had no idea.

"And of course, there are good schools. There's a gymnasium, so the smartest boys can go to school until age eighteen."

"That's what I would like for Berman." This time Markus sighed. "He is such a clever little boy, it would be a pity for him to become a merchant, like me, or a tradesman. I have dreams that he could go to a university, in Pozsony or Budapest…"

"Or Vienna," Rozi interposed.

"Yes, but Budapest is becoming an impressive city, I'm told," threw in Moritz.

"I've never been to any of those places. One of these days…" sighed Rozi.

"Don't worry, we'll get there before long. At least we should travel to Pozsony," Markus assured her with a grin.

"I know. Or if not Pozsony, to Zólyom. And if not Zólyom, then Léva." Rozi continued, good-naturedly, if somewhat ruefully. The Spitzers were not any richer than the Steiners; there was no need to pretend.

"And if not Léva, then at least to Perlep," Markus added and they all laughed.

"And you know," added Spitzer, "Losonc is full of Jewish leadership. In all walks of the business world, you find Jews. They're part of the city council. There are architects and doctors and lawyers, not only merchants. Of course most of the stores are Jewish-owned, but all the intellectual occupations are also full of Jews."

"I think there will be more and more of that here, too." Markus sounded sure of himself. "At least as far as the town council is concerned, we shall soon see Jewish members there, I'm certain of it."

"Well, of course, your cousin is getting to be very prominent, well respected." It was known that Adolf was becoming one of the leading citizens of Golden Morava. "I think this is exactly what Eötvös was trying to achieve when he, and Kossuth before him, wanted to make Magyars out of the immigrant Jews."

"Yes, to create this new 'middle class,' so we can be a truly European country."

"Exactly, and also a Magyar one, where the others remain a minority. So we are all Magyars now," he added. They all laughed at that, but at the same time they all felt a little proud of their new identity.

And the same subject came up later, when they continued their walk on the promenade, meeting and greeting acquaintances, stopping to talk to this family and that, admiring more children. Not that they knew most people; after all, the majority of the town's citizens, the more prominent people (for only the prominent and the Jews had developed the habit of promenading on Sunday afternoons) were in fact non-Jews. Hungarian and Slovak dignitaries greeted the Jews, if they knew them at all, politely and coolly. Markus and Rozália did not know any of them. But there were forty-seven Jewish families living in Golden Morava, and most of them were to be found on the promenade that warm summer evening.

One of the longer discussions concerned poetry. Why poetry? Because the conversant, young Nathan Ehrenfeld, was something of a poet himself, and in the Hungarian language, yet. He insisted on talking Hungarian to the Steiners, as to all of his acquaintances. This created no difficulty for Markus and the children, all of whom were perfectly trilingual in Hungarian, German and Slovak, but Rozi spoke Hungarian with a strong accent. Yet she understood it all, though she missed the finer points of the poetry quoted by Ehrenfeld.

He read a poem by Vörösmarty, quite lovely, and another by Arany. He insisted that Hungarian was a beautiful language, much nicer sounding than German; while Markus and Rozi were not convinced, they did not voice their disagreement. Who knows, the man might be right. In any case, there are no absolutes. One person likes the sound of Hungarian; the other likes German or Italian or French. But then Ehrenfeld talked about Jewish participation in Hungarian culture, literature, theater, painting and sculpture. He was quite enthusiastic on the subject. Markus and Rozi heard the man quietly, not knowing enough to agree or disagree, but young Berman listened raptly, his eyes shining. One would have thought he were twenty rather than a mere seven and a half.

Finally, seeking to stem young Ehrenfeld's fervor, Markus commented, "So we are all truly Magyars now."

"Yes, we are, and that's how it should be." Ehrenfeld nodded several times.

"But then," Rozália interposed, "what are we doing in this little remote corner of Hungary? Why are we not in Budapest, where all the great poets live?"

The comment surprised Ehrenfeld and Markus, too. The former assured them that that's where he hoped to move before long. On the way home, Markus questioned Rozi about Budapest.

"Is that your dream, really? Budapest?"

"No, of course not. You know that my dream has always been Vienna. I just didn't have the heart to tell him that, he was so keen on things Hungarian."

"I think that we have somebody in our family too who's just as keen," he said, pointing to young Berman, now racing his brothers and sisters back to the promenade's entrance.

It was time to go home, even though it was still quite warm. By late August there was usually a chill in the air, but not that year. As they walked home, Markus commented to Rozi that *Rosh Hashono* would be late that year – on September 26, still more than a month away.

Markus – 2001

I imagined that my great-grandfather's life was hard, but enjoyable. Living in Golden Morava was certainly a more sociable life than living in Perlep, after all. But I soon found out that difficult times were in store for the family. In the death registers of the Nyitra geneological center in Ivanka, Vladimir uncovered a number of significant facts about the Steiners of Golden Morava. He found that Hermina Steiner, daughter of Markus and Roza Steiner, died of cholera on February 19, 1873. She was three years old.

And he also found that in the year of 1878:

- Herman Steiner, son of kitchenware-salesman Markus Steiner and Roza Wasserman, of house no. 108, died of typhoid fever on January 9, at the age of nineteen years and eight months.

- Markus Steiner, salesman in Golden Morava, of house no. 108, died of tuberculosis on February 28, at the age of forty-four years.

*   *   *

Poor Rozi, poor family. Their eldest son dies at nineteen in January and the father dies a month later. I wondered whether they even told Markus about the death of his son, as by then he was already close to death himself. But they must have – Markus was most likely at home during his last month or two.

And so, at the age of fifteen, my grandfather, Bernát Steiner, became the man of the house. What did he do? How did these events affect his education? What livelihood remained for the family?

What about the girls? Leni turned twenty-two that February; she could have been married by that age. (Eventually, I learned that she actually did get married at age nineteen.) Even Peppi was seventeen. How would poor Rozi marry one or both of them off now?

Markus's Last Years

The Steiner family grew with the passing years. Markus's business never flourished, but by the winter of 1877 they were able to move to another apartment in a better part of town – on Plébániai Street, not far from Adolf's place. By then two more children were born to Markus and Rozi – Mathilde in 1873, and Ignácz in 1876. The Steiners were not without their share of sadness, though – little Hermina died at age three, the second child they had now lost.

The older children had by now grown into young men and women. Herman was working in his Uncle Samuel's butcher shop, and Berman was attending the gymnasium in Losonc. The Steiner's even celebrated their first wedding in 1875 – nineteen-year-old Leni, now quite grown up, married a young man by the name of Salomon Lustig. Rozi and Markus were overjoyed, and the whole family came to celebrate the wedding. The one cloud marring their happiness lay in parting from Leni, as the young couple were going to live in far-off Vienna.

And then life settled back into its normal routine. Markus returned to his cart, and Rozi had her hands full with the children. We find the family there one cold Friday in November of 1877, as usual awaiting Markus's arrival home.

Again, the family was worried about Father – when would he come? It was already four in the afternoon and getting quite dark; he should have been at home by then. True, their concerns weren't unusual, but that didn't make them any less worrisome.

This time it was little Mathilde who asked the usual question, "What will Father bring?" She was already five years old, and little Ignácz repeated the words after her. Nobody answered her, though inwardly they were all thinking "God, just let him come home. We don't want him to bring anything, just bring him home."

Two weeks earlier, when he came home, also late, he brought with him a story, one that upon reflection he regretted telling them.

"You know, I travel all around, sometimes as far as Nyitra, Léva, Zólyom, even Balassagyarmat and Vác, that is, Waitzen. That's where I was this week, at Vác, and I was hoping to meet a man there at the fair. He was there two or three times before. Very nice young man, his name is Aryeh. He is a ribbon seller–"

"What kind of a name is Aryeh?" Rozi interrupted. "It's a Yiddish name, isn't it?"

"Yes, Yiddish. Hebrew, really – *lion* in Hebrew. His family is from Galicia. They came from further north in Poland, and he himself is a very nice, honest man. His customers and suppliers all trust him. Trusted him, I should say."

"Why, did he do something bad?" Peppi asked.

"No, it's not that. He traveled from town to town, fair to fair, on a little two-wheeled cart drawn by one horse, just like me. His home was in Pásztó and it seems that he was at a fair in a small town in Northern Heves County. Apparently he had a girl there that he liked. She says she was his fiancée. She kept him there too long Friday afternoon, and he still had a few hours of driving his cart home to Pásztó, via Salgótarján. His fiancée, her name is Eszter Barna, wanted him to stay, but he told her that he couldn't. His widowed mother was waiting for him, her only child, for Friday night *Kiddush*. She was lighting three candles, preparing the braided *challa*, putting out water for washing his hands – he was his mother's light, hope, everything. He had to drive his cart home, and he left, but as I said, it was already getting dark."

Rozália glanced apprehensively at Peppi, who returned her look. Unfortunately Markus didn't notice the exchange, or he might have stopped his story right there. "Well, apparently two highwaymen attacked him in the dark, demanded his money. He wouldn't give it to them, so they hit him on the head with a club and split his head with an axe."

The women screamed and reached for each other. Markus finished his sad story.

"His poor mother waited and waited. It took several days before she was told why her son had not returned home, would never return. It took even longer for the fiancée to learn that she would never marry her Aryeh, the ribbon seller."

Rozi started to cry, quickly followed by Peppi and Sali. Mathilde and Ignácz didn't quite understand what was going on, but they joined in. "So now you can see why we are so worried about you when you come home late on Fridays!" Rozi exclaimed between her sobs. "So many things could happen. Did you have to go as far as Waitzen? Isn't that near Budapest?"

"Near enough. I sometimes think that I could go to Budapest one day, but there would not be enough time to get there and back in a week. In five days, really."

"Less than five days. I want you to be here by noon on Fridays."

"Well, maybe not noon, but early afternoon."

"Very early, especially in the winter. And you shouldn't be out so much in the cold. I'm not sure that you're so healthy – you've been coughing lately."

"Just a cold, everybody catches it. Everybody coughs."

But it was true that Markus coughed a lot, especially when on his cart. At home, he tried to suppress it, or if he had to cough, he went to the outhouse.

So on this Friday, two weeks later, the family waited tensely for Markus to come home. At length, once it was already quite dark, they heard the cart pulling up. By then there was no question of going to the *shul*; it was so late that the candles had already burned down. Markus quickly washed and changed, and the family sat down to the *Shabbes* meal.

Like the week earlier, Peppi questioned him about his friend Aryeh. She was deeply affected, thinking about the poor fiancée of the young ribbon seller.

"As I told you, he was a nice young man, red haired, from an Orthodox family. His father came from Lvov, that is, Lemberg, We had some arguments with him, but goodhearted arguments, about Orthodox and Neolog. He just did not believe in 'this Neolog nonsense,' as he put it. I told him that we were properly religious here, observe all the *mitzves*, well, as many as we can. But he just smiled and said, 'You know, that's like what the *goyim* do. You've made yourself a religion for the brain, not for the soul.' I didn't understand what he meant. I told him that we were planning to build a beautiful, new synagogue here, and he said that if his family lived here, they would have for themselves and others a little *shul* in somebody's house and continue going there – they wouldn't even come into our synagogue. The same for our school – they have their *cheder*. That's where he went and that's where he would send his sons, if he had some. But now, he's not going to have any sons," Markus finished sadly.

They ate their meal in silence for a while, thinking about poor Aryeh. "Who knows," Markus added. "Perhaps it's better for him. Who can tell what kind of life awaited him, what kind of family, or sickness, perhaps he might have contacted some awful disease, or…" Markus was thinking about his coughing, though he wouldn't mention it out loud. But Rozi interrupted his train of thought. "It is certainly not better for his poor mother, sitting there at the *Shabbes* table, alone, waiting for her son to come home, and he never will…"

"Or his poor fiancée," added Peppi.

Markus coughed. "I'll be back in a moment." He stood up and went out, as if going to the outhouse. He felt a bad coughing fit coming.

The children may not have noticed anything, but Rozi did. This was not the first time Markus had gone out suddenly after a bit of coughing. She worried. Next week, he might not have to travel so far. If he could stay in town on Monday or come back early on Friday, she would take him to see the doctor.

Rozí – 1877

"Rozália Wasserman?"

"Yes, that was my maiden name. Why? Who…"

"I am sorry for not addressing you by your married name. Fact is, I know that you were Rozália Steiner, but then, perhaps, you married again, and I don't know the name of your second husband. It doesn't matter now. I would like to talk with you about your husband, Markus Steiner."

"But who are you? And where are we?"

"It might be better if we didn't go into that. Let's just say that I wanted to write a book about your husband Markus Steiner and at least some of his descendants – and yours too, of course. I know a lot about his life, but I would like to find out more about his death. Well, about his last few months."

"He died on February twenty-eighth, in 1878. By the way, I never married again."

"Ahh… I see. Markus must have been ill for a few months before he passed away."

"Not so many months. In November, he was still traveling on that cart of his, but he coughed a lot. So I took him to the doctor, and he told us that he had tuberculosis. I had been afraid of that, but somehow I had thought that it was just my imagination."

"So what did the doctor order for him? Medications?"

"There were no medications, other than hot milk. He could not take it for long. No, the main thing was to stay in bed – not just for a few days or weeks, but permanently."

"You mean give up his trade?"

"Yes, exactly that. It was a big shock to us, because that's how he made his living. We had no other breadwinner. No, that's not true – Herman was already working at my brother Samuel's butcher shop, but only as a journeyman. He didn't earn much money. When he heard what had happened he told us that he was going to give us all his earnings. He was saving the money for some better clothes, so he could meet girls, but now he gave us all he'd saved."

"So in November Markus took to bed, and did that help?"

"No, the coughing got worse. By mid-December I caught him trying to hide handkerchiefs with blood in them. It got worse almost every day. No, there were days when it was better, two days in December when he hardly coughed at all. We all thought that maybe, just maybe, he would recover. But then…"

"Then it got worse again?"

"Much worse. By late December – I remember because the neighbors were celebrating their Christmas – he became so weak from all the coughing that we knew that he was going to die."

"Awful. Did the doctor not have any cure at all?"

"Well, he said that perhaps if we could send Markus to a bath, that might help. There were some famous baths around our part of the country, in Pöstyén, Szliacs, or a little farther, in Tátrafüred or Parád. If we could send him there, perhaps… But he did not sound too hopeful."

"So you didn't send him…"

"We didn't have the money. Maybe I could have asked one of my brothers. They had not done badly, but they were not rich men. Or Markus's cousin Adolf. But I knew that those baths would not do much good. Other people had gone there and none had come back. Why, later the doctors stopped sending people to the baths, people with tuberculosis, and they sent them to the mountains instead. But in those days, they did not send them to the mountains. Not that we had the money for that, either…"

"You only had the money that Herman gave you."

"Yes, and the little that we had saved up for rainy days. Well, these were rainy days, indeed. Snowy days. It was a cold winter. I did not let Markus go out at all, not even to the outhouse. He did everything inside the room. I sent the children out of the room."

"And then, what happened?"

"Oh, don't even ask. The worst thing happened. I don't want to think about it."

"I understand. Your husband died."

"No, it's not just that. Late December, Herman came down with some illness. He had headaches and diarrhea, and then he developed a fever that rose higher every day. He was living at Samuel's, so Samuel sent for the doctor. Herman was diagnosed with typhoid fever. He stayed in bed and got some medication, but it didn't help. He got sicker and sicker every day. He had a skin rash and he was shaking and confused. We were there every day, all of us, but we didn't tell Markus. He was in enough bad shape without having to worry about his son."

"And then…?"

"Then one day, on January ninth, Herman had a sudden sharp pain in his tummy. He shouted and sat up and vomited. I was there and ran for the doctor, and he rushed back with me, but by the time we got there he was gone… My poor Herman was gone…"

"I'm so sorry. It must have been a terrible time… And you didn't tell your husband?"

"We thought about it, but we had to tell him. After all, we had to go to the funeral. He would realize that we were all gone. And there was the *shiva* – even if we did it at Samuel's, he would see that we were not at home much of the time. And the black clothes? He wasn't a fool. Or perhaps he would think that the black clothes were for him? We had to tell him."

"How did he take it?"

"You can imagine. He collapsed. He shouted at God, 'Lord, why him? Why take a nineteen-year-old, beautiful young man? Why not me, who is old and sick?' He cried and cried, and he insisted on coming to the funeral. It was a bitterly cold winter day, and we all said that he couldn't come. But he started to get dressed, he put on warm clothes and he came – there was nothing we could do to stop him. He said that it wouldn't make any difference, anyway."

"And did it?"

"Well, you know what happened to him. But not right away. He came to the funeral, then went home. We made the clean room very warm and he lay there, for before this he had slept in the kitchen. And during the *shiva* he hardly coughed at all, as if the walk in the cold had helped him."

"Many people came, I suppose?"

"Oh, of course, everybody came. And Berman came back from school. It took us two days to send him word and two more before he could get there."

"He didn't know that Herman was sick either?"

"Well, he did. He was home for Christmas break, and Herman took to his bed the last week in December. But we didn't know how serious it was, so he went back to school on January second. Of course he knew about his father's condition."

Bernát at the *Shiva*

They buried Herman on the tenth, a Thursday, and by next Monday, when Bernát arrived, they had had time to get over their initial grief. This was somewhat of a shock to Bernát. Other than his parents, Herman was the most important person in his life, his big brother, and suddenly he was gone – dead. Bernát had cried on the journey home, and he cried still more when hugging his father, lying in bed, and his mother and siblings. But toward the end of the *shiva* the family had begun to recover, and after a while they started talking about everyday matters again.

The whole family had come in for the *shiva*. Leni, married in Vienna, had come for the week. And Rozi's brothers were all there. David had come in for the *shiva* and was staying at Samuel's for the duration. Mózes had had to go back to Szelezsény right after the funeral but he had come twice to the *shiva*.

They asked him about his school. Bernát was attending a gymnasium, a high school for boys ages eleven to eighteen. He had started late but had done very well; now, at fifteen, he was in grade six. His birthday was in December so he was one of the youngest in his class, but despite this he was one of the best students.

Uncle Samuel wanted to know all about the school. "We have eight subjects," Bernát told him. "Magyar, mathematics, Latin, German, history, geography, physics and drawing."

"Nothing practical?"

Bernát looked at him in surprise. "Practical?"

"Yes, like carpentry, or bricklaying, crafts…"

"But mathematics is practical. And physics is practical."

"For instance, what are you learning now in physics?"

"Right now, the behavior of gases under pressure."

"And that's practical? How about mathematics?"

"Analytical geometry."

"But not how to keep books for a plant or a store? Now that would be practical. Once you finish this school, you matri… What do you call it?"

"Matriculate."

"What qualifications will you have in your hand for a job? That you know what gases do under pressure? Your teacher is full of gases. Who will want you for that?"

Bernát's face turned red; he didn't really know how to answer his uncle. But his other uncle, David, stepped in to help him.

"Come, Samu, leave the kid alone. He will have plenty of job opportunities. For one thing, he learns in Hungarian, right?" said David, turning to Bernát.

"Yes, Uncle David."

"So there will be all the jobs open for him at the county hall and the town hall and all the other administrative places. Why, he can get a job at the parliament in Budapest."

"Parliament? Ha! Why, do they need somebody who knows about gases?"

"No, but they do need people who know how to write proper Hungarian. And then, for the gases, for physics, he may want to continue his studies and go a university. Become an engineer, how about that?"

Nobody sneered at that idea; being an engineer was the secret dream of every boy. Samuel's two older boys nodded their agreement.

"Would you like to be an engineer, Berman?" David asked him.

"No, Uncle David, I would prefer to be a writer. Or perhaps a lawyer."

"Hey, a lawyer. I like that. I know a Jewish lawyer. He is one of the smartest people I've ever met, and he makes good money."

Samuel interposed. "How much does it cost to put a boy through university, until he becomes a lawyer?"

Everybody wore a long face. Nobody knew. Samuel continued: "Look, I know that Berman here is a smart boy, but he doesn't have that kind of money. Nobody in our family does. And you know," he added quietly, with a glance at Markus sleeping on the bed, "he may need to work soon. Even now, I feel that he should earn some money for his poor mother. That's what Herman did before…"

But they were all against him, most vocal among them Rozi. She did not talk loudly so as not to wake her husband, but she insisted in a strong whisper: "Berman must study. He is the brains in the family. We shall manage somehow. Peppi will work. There are jobs for respectable young women. I can go out and work, too. Or I can sew. We will manage. And Markus may get better."

Nobody answered.

After a while, David took the matter up again, this time speaking more generally. "You know, education is that magic thing that we've been waiting for all these years. It's what gives the Jews entry into a country's cultural life. Educated people are all equals. Isn't that so, Berman? Bernát?" He corrected himself.

"Yes, Uncle David, I have seen that. Teachers, doctors, I think even lawyers talk to each other as equals, Jews and Christians."

"And become friends?"

"Yes, friends."

"Do you have Christian friends at school?"

"I have a few."

"So there, you see? The way to assimilation."

Markus was now awake, and after a brief coughing spell, he commented on David's words. "You know, assimilation can be a good thing. But it can be bad, too. Bernát, you must watch your step. Don't assimilate too fast, or too far. For instance, if you were a fully assimilated Hungarian, then what would you consider a Moravian Jew?"

"What would I consider him? A Moravian Jew."

"A foreigner?"

Bernát thought. "Yes, a foreigner."

"So you see? Yet he may be a lot closer to you than your Hungarian friend, who will leave you when you are in trouble. And if you are part of the ruling classes, if such a thing could ever happen, you would look down on most Jews, especially the Jews from Galicia, as primitive, backward people, would you not?"

Bernát did not answer his father.

"Yet they are excellent people. I know many. It's not true that they are opportunistic, or crafty, or dishonest, at least not more than anybody else – certainly not more than the Hungarians or Slovaks I know. Maybe smarter, but that is no reason to despise them. So don't let your education make you forget who you are."

Markus coughed again, turning to the wall so people would not see the blood on his handkerchief.

A Very Dark Day

Five weeks later, on a particularly dark Tuesday in February, they all knew that the end was near for poor Markus. By then Bernát and Leni had gone back and only Rozi and the other five children remained at home with Markus. Rozi was beginning to lean more and more on Peppi, while József and Sali, knowing how great the strain was on Rozi, made sure to look after the two youngest ones.

An organ grinder came, but nobody ran out to listen; they closed the window so he wouldn't bother them. Later they opened it again, and when the rag-and-bone man came, shouting his trade "old-clo!," they called him in. Markus was asleep – he slept a lot these days – and Rozi negotiated the sale of his great coat. They asked the man if he would be interested in buying a picture they had had on the wall for a long time, a landscape, but the man declined. "What does he know?" Rozi commented after she closed the door. Not that she thought the picture had any real value.

"Mother, we might have to sell other things, perhaps some of the furniture? Should I inquire about it?" Peppi offered. Rozi pretended that she had not heard. Then, after a while, she turned to her. "The cart. We still have not sold the cart. The axle is rusting out there."

"It's wood, Mother. It cannot rust." Somehow Peppi knew about such things.

"So then it's rotting."

"It's in the shed," Peppi offered.

"Even so. Let's put an ad in the paper. Peppi, you can go down there tomorrow morning."

"Yes, Mother."

The horse was no longer a problem. They fed her for two weeks after Markus took to his bed, all the time debating the worth of the animal versus the cost of oats, but then the poor thing took pity on them and died. That wasn't much of a help, as they had to pay the gypsies to take the carcass away.

The mailman knocked, bringing a letter from David at Kis Herestény. He had written to inquire after Markus's health, wishing him and the entire family well. He himself, Rebeka, and the three girls were well, thank God, although he had some liver problem – nothing new about that. Good old David, he was the children's favorite uncle.

"Peppi, Sali, go to the well. Take both pails with you. But dress warmly!"

After they were gone, Rozi ordered József to go out and bring in more firewood. That was almost the only luxury that they allowed themselves in those days. They wanted to keep the kitchen warm for Markus.

When the girls came back, Rozi told them to sit down and take care of the mending. Peppi mentioned that her friend Teréz's mother had just gotten a new sewing machine.

"Yes, that would be nice. They could have bought one for us, too," Rozi sighed.

In the evening, after dinner, a few of Markus's friends came over for a visit. They talked with him, when he was awake, and smoked a little. Once or twice they arranged a makeshift table so that he could play a little *ferbli* while lying in bed. He did not join them in smoking a pipe; that was strictly forbidden him. He did not cough so much now, he was just thin and pale and terribly weak. He could not get up without assistance, and there was usually no need for him to get up anyway.

As his friends were leaving, one said quietly to Rozália, "Rozi, you'd better be prepared. I think it's just a few days now." She nodded. She knew.

"You should know," the other friend added, "there's a new *Chevra Kadisha* in town now. They will be able to help, when the time comes, with all the arrangements. There was no need for you and your brothers to do everything yourselves when poor Herman died."

"Really? I didn't know."

"Yes, it will make things a little easier for you. And there is nothing to pay, you know."

"So who maintains it?"

"The community does. One day, when you will be rich, you will give them a nice donation."

Rozi managed a weak smile at that. After they were gone, she wondered how she was able to talk so factually about such matters.

Bernát's Future

"Grandfather, it is I again, Andris."

"Yes, Andriskám. What would you like to know?"

"Those bad days, when your father died, less than two months after Herman."

"Yes, those were awful days. I must say that I had my share of awful days in my life."

"True, but surely good days, too."

"You are right, good days, too. Some very good days."

"I shall ask you about such days, soon. But now, tell me about your father's death."

"The principal called me in. He had just received this telegram about my father having passed away. Told me to leave immediately. He was quite sympathetic for such a serious, strict man. He said that he hoped I would be back soon."

"So you traveled immediately to Golden Morava?"

"Yes, they delayed the funeral by one day, so I could be there. We buried Father on the coldest day of the year. The gravediggers had to use pickaxes to loosen the ground. We could hardly fill the hole, it was so hard and frozen. Then we all went home and sat *shiva*."

"And then you went back to school?"

"No, no, I didn't. Here is what happened: During the *shiva*, Uncle Samu called me over, told me that he wanted to have a serious talk, let's go out. So we dressed up warmly and went for a walk. As I recall, this is what he told me: 'Berman, listen to me. The last time we were talking about education, during poor Herman's *shiva*, I was only kidding you. Well, not quite, there was something in what I said, but don't worry about it. I know that education has its value – in the long run it can make you a more successful, wealthier man. But you must understand what the situation is right now. Your mother has no income whatsoever. She has already sold many of her belongings; most of your poor father's clothes are already gone. Even while he was lying in bed he had very little left. Soon, the family will be penniless. Now of course your relatives won't let your family starve. But you must understand that we are not wealthy men ourselves – we work hard for our living. Up until recently, Herman was in my shop. He did a good job and I paid him well, I think. I am willing to take you in for the same job. That way, there will at least be bread on the table.'

"He must have seen my face, perhaps I started to cry a little, because he put a hand on my shoulders and tried to ease my mind. 'Look, this arrangement won't have to be permanent. As your mother said, she can do some sewing. Peppi is seventeen now. She can find some good work, perhaps looking after small children somewhere. Maybe we'll find her a husband soon. And who knows, your mother is still a good-looking woman, maybe she will marry again. I know you can't even think of such a thing now, but with time passing, that would be the best thing for her. Then she would be well looked after, the children, too. So what I am saying is that after a year or two, things may be better and you may continue your education. But you must understand, again, that you are the oldest man in the family. They all depend on you.'

"That's what my uncle told me, and I had no words for a counterargument; there were none. He told me to discuss it later with my mother and family, and let him know the next day. I did as was told."

"So what did your mother say?"

"She hugged me and cried, but she knew that there was no other solution. Leni was also there. She said that maybe she and Salomon could send some money at times, but it wouldn't be easy for them. They already had a small son Moritz, two years old, so she had to stay at home. She was trying to earn some money by raising and selling poultry – they liked geese in Vienna – but things were tight. And as for Peppi, we did not want her to go out and work as a maid, earning little more than her keep. Mother said that she would sew, but she had no sewing machine and was not likely to acquire one soon. So we agreed that at least for the current school year, I would work at Uncle Samu's, and then we would see about the following year."

"And, as it turned out…?"

"As it turned out, I worked for Uncle Samu for quite a few years. A few years later Peppi moved in with Leni in Vienna, so she was no problem for Mother. In fact, Mother later decided to move to Vienna as well because she had additional grandchildren there – by 1883 Peppi already had two babies, and later more. Mother took all the smaller children with her, but I did not want to go with them. By that time I had other ideas."

"What ideas? Why not move to Vienna?"

"Andriskám, Vienna had always been my mother's dream city. But not for me. I always thought that the center of the world was Pest. Budapest. I was brought up on Hungarian books. Novels, poetry, Hungarian ideas. The words of Kossuth, Petőfi, Wesselényi, Deák Ferenc. The poetry of Arany János,

Vörösmarty. That's where beauty lay, wisdom, pride. Yes, I was proud, I became a consciously proud Hungarian patriot. The Kaiser and all that he represented in Vienna, that was, perhaps, a necessary and temporary burden on our nation. How could I go there and admire Franz Josef and his court, when they looked down on us, they despised our Hungarian nation?"

"But Golden Morava…"

"It was just a small town, but it was a Hungarian one. Well, not quite, there were lots of Slovaks there, too. But I was hoping to move into larger and larger towns, maybe cities, perhaps even Budapest…"

"Well, eventually you got there."

"Got there. Hmm. Yes, I did, but that was something else, not at all what I was hoping for. I'll tell you about that later."

"Please do, Grandfather."

Vienna – 2004

Vienna? Why Vienna? How did I find out that my great-grandmother and her daughters ended up living in the city of her dreams?

When I began researching my family's history, my friend Peter Hidas, a history professor and specialist in Hungarian genealogy, suggested that I get in touch with a researcher in Budapest, Judit B., who he said was very competent and resourceful. First Judit, and then later Dr. A.S.H., owner of a Budapest geneological research firm, were invaluable in unearthing my family's history.

One of the most significant things Judit found was the marriage certificate of my grandfather's second marriage – to my grandmother, Ilona Bauer. That certificate gave us a number of important pieces of information, as I'll relate later. But one of the most interesting facts recorded in it was that by that time, in 1897, both of Bernát Steiner's parents were dead, his father having died in Golden Morava – that I knew already – and his mother in Vienna. Very interesting. Vienna…why there? The best guess I could make at that point was that she married again, married a Viennese man, and moved there. True, she could have died there for many other reasons – she could have gone there to see the change of the guards, or the emperor himself, for all I knew, and gotten a heart attack. Or just visited friends. But that did not sound like a likely proposition. I also knew by that time that a death certificate of her late husband was taken out about five years after his death; Vladimir suggested that this was likely done to facilitate remarriage. It was taken out by a Wasserman, probably one of Rozália's brothers.

But no, our speculations all turned out to be incorrect. Dr. A.S.H. hired a fellow researcher in Vienna, who searched the archives there and found a document attesting to the death of Rosa Steiner (yes, under that name – she had apparently not remarried) of tuberculosis, on May 4, 1889. She had been buried in the Zentralfriedhof, Vienna's largest cemetery. The document, though in horrible handwriting, was nevertheless quite revealing. Dr. A.S.H. interpreted and translated it for me, and while I did not quite want to believe his conclusions (I think he had his own doubts at that point, too), in the end he turned out to be 100 percent correct. I enclose a copy of the document here.

K. K. Bezirksgericht Währing.

Todfalls-Aufnahme.

Vor- und Zuname des Erblassers

Charakter oder Beschäftigung

Alter *57 Jahre*

Religion *mosaisch*

Ob ledig, verheiratet oder verwitwet

Wohnung *Wien X. ...strasse 4*

Sterbetag und Sterbeort *...am 4/5. 1889 in Währing israel. Spital*

Nachgelassene Ehegatt

Name, Charakter und Aufenthalt der großjährigen Kinder und der großjährigen Enkel bereits verstorbener Kinder.

Name, Alter, Charakter und Aufenthalt der minderjährigen Kinder und der minderjährigen Enkel bereits verstorbener Kinder, ob für sie ein gesetzlicher Vertreter bereits einschreite, oder wer hierzu vorgeschlagen werde.

Name, Alter, Charakter und Aufenthalt der übrigen nächsten Verwandten.

The document, once deciphered, stated that the testator Rosa Steiner née Wasserman, from Golden Morava, Hungary, was fifty-seven years old and her religion was "Mosaic." She had lived in the Tenth District of Vienna, at Laanestrasse 4, and had died on May 4, 1889, in the Jewish Hospital of Währing.

Now comes the interesting part: "Description and residences of adult children and grandchildren born of deceased parents." Then appears the following list:

1. Helena Lustig, Tenth District, Laanestrasse 4, age thirty-three years. (It had taken us a very long time to decide that the first word was indeed Helena, for it looked like Salomon. In two other places in the document this name appeared but with one extra letter. Apparently it truly was Salomon, and the two shorter ones were Helena. What a strange writing system, where such different names are written almost the same way!)

2. Josephine Krieger, (some occupation), age twenty-seven, Second District of Vienna, ker...gasse (illegible) 3.

3. Berman Steiner, (some occupation), age twenty-five, Golden Morava, Hungary.

Incidentally, on the left side there was a brief reference to a Julie Steiner of Budapest. I have no idea who this person might be; of course the reading of the word *Julie* is questionable.

Then, under the next heading, "Description and residence of underage children and grandchildren," we have the following:

1. Josef Steiner, twenty-two years old...and then some strange comment about, apparently, Bosnia! The researcher seems to think that it says that he was born there, but that is clearly impossible. We know that he was born in Fekete Kelecsény, the village close to Perlep. Besides, this particular document deals with current residences, not birth places, so perhaps József was living in Bosnia at the time. Working as a junior in some kind of business?

2. Then follow two youngsters: Mathilde Steiner, age sixteen, residing at the Second District of Vienna, Reinhardtstrasse 27 (Why? Was she living at some school for girls there?)

3. Ignaz Steiner, thirteen, staying with his sister Helena Lustig, Tenth District, Laanestrasse 4. The son of Markus Steiner, who had died twelve years earlier in Golden Morava, Bars County, Hungary.

We haven't yet finished with the document, but here I'd like to mention the insight of a wise woman, my wife. She told me that I was living in the twenty-first century and looking at the nineteenth from the viewpoint of the present.

"School for girls? At age sixteen? Don't be silly. These were not rich people. Do you know what a sixteen-year-old girl did? She was finished with her schooling at fourteen. Then they sent her to work. She was obviously living with a family as a maid, or more likely looking after the small children, doing household chores. That would have been a reasonable thing for a young girl to do, until they could find her a husband.

"And as for József – a junior in some business? At age twenty-two? Come now. They conscripted him into the army and sent him to a unit stationed in Bosnia, which was part of the Austro-Hungarian Empire."

Yes, of course, she must be right.

Well, then, back to the document: These children were placed under the guardianship of their sister Helena's husband, Salomon Lustig, in Vienna, Tenth District, Laanestrasse 4, who had accepted the guardianship over the three children.

But why would a twenty-two-year-old boy, probably in the army, require guardianship? One could argue with some of the interpretations, but overall, we seemed to be on the right track.

Let's run through the list of the Steiner children once more. There were ten of them. Juda died as an infant in 1866. Hermina lived only three years, dying in 1873. Herman died at age nineteen, in 1878. That should have left seven children, but there is no mention here of Sali, who was born in 1864 and should have been twenty-four by the time her mother died. We must assume that Sali herself died before this event. So there remained Leni, Peppi, and Berman, József, Mathilde and Ignácz.

Chana – 2005

After deciphering Rozália's death certificate, my next step was to search the old birth, marriage and death records of the Vienna Jewish community on the Mormon microfilms. I did find the marriage record of Peppi Steiner to Boruch Krieger, though not that of her older sister Leni to Salomon Lustig – not even in the Golden Morava area or anywhere near. (That information was given to me later, by a very kind Magistrate Eckstein of the Israelitische Kultusgemeinde of Vienna.) I also found the birth records of numerous children from the two girls. Leni had at least four children: Ludwig, Moritz, Oscar and Camila. Peppi had more: Max, Yetti, Mitzi, Rosina, Richard, Oscar, Kamila, Julius and Herman. (Actually, I did not see Yetti's and Mitzi's names on the microfilm; I learned about them only later.)

But I found no marriage record for József or Ignácz, nor birth records of any children born to them. What became of Mathilde would have been even more difficult to figure out. One cannot read through every single item in the registers; one relies on the indices. Well, marriage registrations were indexed by the groom's name, but not by the bride's. The result? It is just about impossible to find out whom Mathilde may have married. Births, too, would be indexed by the father's name. So, unfortunately, to this day I do not know what happened to these three siblings of my grandfather and their offspring.

I posted the information that I did have on the Jewish Family Tree on the Internet, and that's where Chana Mills found me (though she claims that it was I who found her; we still argue the point). It turns out that her father was Alfred Lustig, Ludwig's son. Furthermore, her mother was Hildegard Schulz, the daughter of Kamila Krieger. They were second cousins to each other and to me.

Chana is a delightful person. She lives in Be'er Sheva and works at the university there. Her husband, David Mills, was a scientist and worked also at Ben Gurion University; unfortunately, he passed away in 2008. They have two lovely children. Chana also has one living brother, Miki; another brother passed away some years ago. We have gotten to know Chana's family well and consider them a valuable extension of our family.

We were fortunate to become aquainted with Chana's uncle Walter, my second cousin, before he passed away. His brother Eric died a few years before. Eric's wife Liesel was much younger than her husband and she is full of life. She knows many of the missing pieces of family data. Through this branch of the family I also got to know additional family members, and there are still many more to get acquainted with.

Chana, Walter and Liesel helped me fill in the gaps in the family tree, providing an almost complete picture of the descendants of Leni and Peppi Steiner, some sixty-seven people, of whom many perished in the Holocaust. The ones who survived did so in Switzerland, Holland, France (Eric actually served in the French Foreign Legion in North Africa) and Israel.

Chana also told me of a relative whom she had visited in Australia. Apparently she is the granddaughter of Julia Wasserman. I have tentatively added her to the family tree as the fifth child of Herman and Pepi Wasserman, a sister to David, Mózes, Samuel and Rozália, but she could have been a generation younger, perhaps the daughter of one of Rozália's brothers.

And I still hope to discover one day what happened to the families of József, Mathilde and Ignácz. I have no idea how many of them survived the Holocaust, or what other cousins I may still have.

In 2005 my wife and I visited the gravesite of my great-grandmother, Rozália Steiner, in the Zentralfriedhof in Vienna. There is no monument left there, but in one corner of the cemetery there is a huge heap of hundreds of old stones, most of them broken. At least we placed a stone on the site, a pebble we brought there from Israel.

Fanni ~ 2001

What did I know about my grandfather's whereabouts in those critical years after the premature death of his father?

I only knew two facts. That in 1889, when his mother died, he was the only child of Rozália listed as living not in Vienna (or Bosnia, where József may have served), but in Golden Morava, back in Hungary. And that three years earlier, Samuel Wasserman, butcher, died in the nearby town of Szelezsény. His death was reported not by one of his children (of which he had six; we have even seen the monument on the gravesite of one of them, Muki Wasserman), but by his nephew, Bernát Steiner. He must have lived with his uncle, perhaps worked there in the butcher shop.

And I could make one guess, so far unsupported: knowing that my grandfather managed to enter the demanding judicial system of Hungary, and there to rise to the position of director of the district court, he was likely to have had some formal education at some point. My researchers tried to locate the school records, for who knows where that high school may have been (there wasn't one in Golden Morava), but so far, to no avail. Perhaps he was self-educated?

I have already mentioned that Vladimir, my researcher in Slovakia, visited Banska Bystrica, the regional administrative center. There, among other things, he found that Bernát Steiner, then age twenty-eight, married Franciszka Tauszek, age sixteen, whose parents were Lipót Tauszek and Amália Klein. The couple was married on June 16, 1891, in Zólyom. This was very exciting news for me: up to this point I had not known the name of Grandfather's first wife, the mother of Rózsám.

Vladimir also found a death record of Jacob Tauszek, younger brother of Franciszka. The baby was born when Franciszka was ten years old, but died after four days. Unfortunately, by the time Fanni married, she was familiar with the death of small children.

My grandfather Bernát was also familiar with death. Not only had he lost siblings, but by the time he married Fanni he had lost both of his parents.

What else did I know of Fanni? I knew that she died when Rózsám was quite young. When exactly? My grandfather married again and had a child, Erzsébet, who was born on May 1, 1898. So the second marriage must have taken place not later than the summer of 1897. Fanni's third child Gyula was born in March 1896 and died in August of the same year. It is therefore certain that poor Fanni must have died sometime between March 1896 (perhaps in childbirth) and March 1897.

And there is one more thing that I know about Fanni. I know what she looked like. Among Rózsám's pictures that I have, there is a photo of Fanni. Here it is:

FANNI TAUSSIG

Bernát and Fanní

Andriskám, you wanted to know about the good days, the good years of my life. Well, let me talk to you about those years in Zólyom. Well, Zólyom and Rima-Sobota. You know, those were the very best years.

No, I should not say that. I had many good years, very good years. After all, when your father was born, what could be better than that? And when you were born? And all the years I spent with my Ilona, they were good years, for I loved Ilona. I really did. She was a very good wife, very suitable wife. I was lucky to find her. Why, we spent forty-three years together, and never had a serious problem between us. Never an argument. Never…

Well, we had a few little arguments, but everybody does. In the end, we always managed to come to some kind of agreement. She was a very rational person. She was a good partner for me. She really was. And I loved her. Your grandmother. I did love her.

Yes, but Fanni was different. *Her* I loved in a different way. I don't know if I want to talk about that. It still hurts. It hurts very much.

But it was so good, so beautiful, while it lasted. What a memory! Yes, Fanni. My little Fanni. My sweet, dear little Fanni. How I loved her. And how she loved me.

I shall tell you anyway. It is good to talk about her. It hurts, but it is also good.

It all started when I finally got a job at the Zólyom district court. No, I should go back a bit. You see, when my father died, I was only fifteen. I think I told you, my brother died a month before, and suddenly I was the oldest boy in the family. Somebody had to work, to make a living, so I couldn't continue my education. Before that, I went to a gymnasium. I did not live at home, but that cost money and anyway, my uncles told me that I must support my family. My uncle Samu offered me a job in his butcher shop, and that's what I did for quite a few years, I worked there. He did not want to train me as an apprentice, he said I did not have the build for a butcher; instead, I delivered things for customers and especially looked after the books. What books? Mainly, who owed what. People did not pay for everything they bought. It was all written up in a book and they paid at the end of the month, or when they could.

Soon it was noticed that I was good at that sort of thing. I wrote nicely and I was good with figures. So a couple of other store owners also asked my uncle if I could help out sometimes, and before long I was the main assistant of the notary of the town. Meanwhile, I read a lot and kept up with my studies, even if they did not lead to formal matriculation. But I visited my old Hungarian language and literature teacher once, we had a long talk, and he assured me that in his view I was as fully qualified for any administrative work as any matriculated high school graduate.

Then, in 1886, when I was twenty-three, my uncle Samu died. I slept in his house, so I was the first one to find him dead. I reported his death at the town hall and then I had to get messages to all his children and look after the funeral arrangements. I was very sad. My cousins were all working in other towns by then and nobody wanted to continue the butcher shop, so it was closed. I could have stayed there and worked at other places, but by that time Adolf, my poor father's cousin, had started an important financial institution in Golden Morava, a savings and loan, and he offered me a job there as a clerk. So I moved back there, stayed at that town for four more years. My mother and the smaller children left for Vienna, I told you about it, but I stayed. My ambitions were different. I was hoping to get a job at the government, ideally a pensioned position – with such a job I could marry. I thought, perhaps I could find a position at one of the district courts, in Nyitra or Zólyom. I wrote some letters asking for such a job. My handwriting was quite good. Many people commented on how nice and elegant my script was. And of course I was careful not to make any mistakes.

And so, in 1890 – the year after my poor mother died in Vienna – I got a position as clerk at the district court of Zólyom. No, it was not that easy, because in those days they were not used to the idea of a Jewish man working in government offices. Jews were merchants – that was the profession, if you can call it that, which was expected of them. Three times they advertised for clerks and twice they rejected me. I went to a lawyer, the only Jewish one I knew in Golden Morava, and asked his advice. His name was Lefkovics. I asked him if it was right that they should reject me without even trying to find out if I could do the job.

"Tell me your name again," he asked.

"Bernát Steiner."

"Well, Mr. Steiner, so long as you are Mr. Steiner, you will not work at the district court in Zólyom, or any other court in Hungary."

That shocked me. "What do you mean?"

"Just what I said. Your name is wrong. They never had a Steiner in their courts and never will."

"Because it is a Jewish name?"

He looked at me with a sad expression, as if I were somewhat retarded. "Why, what did you think? You thought it was the name of Hungarian nobles?"

"No, of course not," I stammered. "But why should a Jew not work in the court?"

"Because they are not used to the idea. A Jew should sell clothes."

"Well, what about you? You are a lawyer and your name is Lefkovics. It is not exactly an ancient Hungarian name."

He grinned. "Oh, but I was smarter. I got my qualification in Vienna. I came here with my diploma and experience. They could not refuse my entry to the court and now they are used to me."

"But look, no matter what the past may be, I am fully qualified for the job. Is there not something that I could do to get them to change their minds?"

"Such as what?"

"Such as sue them, take them to their own court, or some higher court that would force them…" I stopped because he was roaring with laughter.

"No?" I asked after a while.

"No, indeed, my friend. They would chase you out of the town and the county if you tried such a stupid thing. Don't even dream of it." He shook his head for a long time.

I sat there saying nothing. Finally he spoke. "But look, I told you what to do, so why don't you just do it?"

"You did?"

"Yes! I told you that your name was wrong. Change it, and you will get a job next time."

"Change it to what?" I was slow that day.

"I don't care. Change it to Szatmari or Salgo or Simonbogyei, for all I care. Pick a map, find a town. Or a trade. Change it to Sebesz, or Satoros, or Seregely. That's a bird. Change it simply to Sos. But write it with two os, like Soos, they will like it better that way."

"But… But…"

"But what?" He took out his watch and looked at it with feigned concern.

"But then they will not know that I am Jewish?"

"They will not care. Most of them don't really mind it, only they wouldn't dare to go to their superior officer and report that they have just hired a Steiner.

But if they were to hire a Szekszardi, nobody would care. If his boss asked whether the man might be perchance Jewish, he could simply say that he did not know. I don't think he would even be asked that question." Lefkovics stood up and so did I; the interview was clearly over.

I walked the streets for an hour. I just hated what he had said, but I couldn't think of anything better. It would have been so good to have a good lawyer prepare a suit against them, to make it a famous case that was reported in all the newspapers, and to win. But he had said that it just could not be done, and I suppose that he was right, he knew his business.

Change my name. But my father's name was Steiner, and so was my grandfather's, who had just passed away four years before, and my great-grandfather's. And now I was supposed to change it? Deny my Jewishness? Give victory to the anti-Semites, who organized the pogroms against us in 1883 with the Tiszaeszlár blood libel? No and no and no. I despised the man. I walked the streets and finally I said to myself, "No, I will not change it. I am Bernát Steiner and I will get a job in the courts as Bernát Steiner."

You say, Andriska, that I did change my name, after all. Yes, I did, but not then. It was nearly ten years later, at your grandmother's insistence. Maybe I should not have done so even then, but you see, by that time, Jews were Hungaricizing their names all over the place. Where I lived, all of my friends were changing their names. And Ilona was ambitious. She wanted me to advance in the court. Well, anyway, that's another story. But back then, in 1890, I remained Bernát Steiner, and eventually, through friends of friends in Zólyom, I got to know somebody at the district court, an intelligent man named Komjáthy, who became almost a friend. He agreed that there should not be prejudices like this, and after a while, when there was another opening, he did succeed in securing me an interview with the man responsible for hiring. Apparently, that man liked me, so I became a district court clerk. The first Jewish one, at least in Zólyom. It was not a pensioned position, not yet, but it was a start.

The salary was better than what I made at the savings and loan, so I could afford to rent a nice room in Zólyom. It was in the apartment of a very nice family named Taussig. Mr. Taussig was in the clothes business, but he did not have his own store. He was a salesman, like my father, who traveled from place to place buying and selling clothes. Apparently, he was more successful than my father, because they had a very nice home, four rooms, the smallest one of which was still of a good size. That was the one that I rented for the next year.

I liked Mr. Taussig, Lipót Taussig, a very pleasant man, although I did not see much of him. He traveled, like most salesmen, and usually returned home only Friday afternoon. His wife, Amália, was a simple woman, not like my mother at all, but still a very good person. They accepted me like a member of their family. They did not have a son, only one daughter, Fanni. Wrong, there was once a son, when Fanni was about ten years old, but he died after a few days.

I had all my meals with the Taussigs and spent much of my free time with them. They liked me, and I am sure that what developed there was one of those rare instances, when everybody has the same idea, an idea so obvious that it hardly needs to be stated. The only problem was, if you want to call it a problem, that Fanni was so young; she was not yet sixteen when I moved there. But what a lovely young girl, beautiful, pretty, well developed, sweet.

Mrs. Taussig often suggested that Franciszka and I (her proper name was Franciszka), that we go for a walk, when the weather was nice. We liked to walk down past the castle, all the way around, where there were not so many people, walked for two or three hours and I don't know if it was I or Franciszka who initiated our holding hands, but we always did. I kissed her when she had her sixteenth birthday and every day thereafter.

I think it was her eyes that bedeviled me more than anything else. The way she looked at me. There was so much love in those eyes, so much admiration, I could not think of anything else. I just cannot tell you how much I loved Fanni. Fanni, Fanni, Fanni, I kept saying to myself when we were not together. And yet I think that she loved me even more. You see, I did have other things to do. The work at the court was interesting. I was learning about the entire legal system, so really, my thoughts must have been on things other than Franciszka at times. But she had nothing else to do. Of course she helped her mother around the house, and eventually she had to work building up her trousseau. Because of course when she was seventeen, I approached Mr. Taussig and asked him for the hand of his daughter in marriage. He embraced me and told me how happy he was for both of us. It was really just a formality. Fanni's face radiated happiness, probably mine, too.

Her dowry was just enough so we could afford to rent a little apartment of our own. We bought on the market a heavy wooden table for the kitchen and two stools, and the Taussigs had some extra furniture that they let us have, a large cupboard and a table with four chairs for our meals. They also wanted to give us Fanni's bed, so we would only have to buy a second one for me and perhaps a little night table in between. But there I disagreed. You know, that was the only argument that I ever recall between my in-laws and myself.

"Now what is wrong with that bed that Fanni has used since she was six?" Mrs. Taussig, Amália, wanted to know.

"Nothing is wrong, but I have other ideas."

"Other ideas? What ideas?"

I was a little embarrassed. I got this idea from one of my colleagues at work. It was difficult to say it, but it had to be said. "These days, they have a new kind of bed."

They looked at each other in surprise. "What kind of bed?" Lipót demanded.

"Well, it is a larger bed. It is large enough for two. So there is no need for a second one. Or for a table in between." I felt that my face was all red, and so was Fanni's.

Amália and Lipót again looked at each other, and all at once both burst out laughing. "New ideas, eh? Oh ho ho. Modern world for you. Well, I don't mind, but make sure it is not so large that there is no room left for a little bed at the foot of the big one. You may just need such a thing before long." He kept laughing. Fanni and I grinned as expected, but we were very uncomfortable. It does not matter.

So we used some of the dowry to buy such a larger bed; it could not be found on the second-hand market. It was just large enough for us.

And my Uncle David sent us an almost new sewing machine. Fanni was very happy with that. She was not so busy with the housework, now she could sew some dresses for herself and she even tried a shirt for me. It did not fit very well, but I wore it on occasion, not to disappoint her.

We married in June of that year, 1891, in Zólyom, and moved into our new apartment. No, it was not new, only for us. It was a run-down two-story building, two blocks from her parents' place. The walls could not have been painted since they were built. I asked the landlord to repaint but he was not interested, unless I paid for it. How could I? So the old paint peeled and we were happy. I worked. Fanni cooked and cleaned and washed and ironed and mended my socks and sewed clothes and a shirt. And she read. Oh, she read a lot. I brought her books that I borrowed, sometimes even bought, and she read them all and enjoyed them. Her taste in reading was indiscriminate – she was not choosy. She best liked romantic novels, particularly books by Mór Jókai. She also liked German novels, but she preferred shorter ones, for she was not so proficient in German. In those days children were taught primarily in Hungarian, if you can believe that. Sometimes I could find a German or French book in Hungarian translation, a Theodore Fontane or a Gustave Flaubert, though I remember that she did not like those very much. I brought her a magazine or two. She liked *A Hét* – that means "The Week." It was published by József Kiss, you know, the famous Jewish poet.

Fanni had only two friends, classmates, but they both got married about the same time as she did, even a little earlier, and moved away from the town. Once or twice they came to visit her. They gossiped about other girls and then, in the evening, Fanni told me all those stories. They were not very exciting stories, but I always listened politely. Still, she was alone a great deal, had time to read, especially in that first year. Of course, she visited her mother almost every day, or Amália came over to our place. But by the fall we knew that she was not going to be alone much longer. My Fanni was expecting! Happiness, excitement, fear intermingled in our minds and souls. In our words, too, although we did not talk much about fear, we – Amália and I – constantly reassured Fanni about the excellent midwives in Zólyom, for she had heard some horrors stories. But it was true, there were one or two really good midwives, so she need not have been too concerned.

RÓZSA AS A BABY

Next May the baby was born, a little girl, Rózsika. Sweet little Rózsika. Oh, we loved her so! She was beautiful, too, everybody said so. Fanni's face was radiant. I was happy for her and for myself. Amália and Lipót were also excited – they came over to see Rózsika whenever they could. While they could, while we still lived in Zólyom.

For not very long after Rózsika was born, we had to move to Rima-Sobota. Komjáthy, my friend, talked to me about an opening at the law court there, told me to write and apply for the job. I was reluctant at first, because I knew that Rima-Sobota was one of those towns where they had not welcomed Jews until recently. But now there were quite a few Jews living there, seventy or eighty families, so I thought, why not try? I asked Fanni's opinion.

I caught her in a good mood. Rózsika was blossoming, she ate well. (We bought milk from a neighboring woman. Fanni did not have enough, so she soon stopped trying to feed Rózsika.) Fanni was reading a good book. She was happy and she said cheerfully, "Sure, Berci, why not?" Come to think of it, she did not call me Berci, at least when there were just the two of us. She had another name for me. It was Ilona who always called me Berci. Does not matter.

So I wrote a letter to the people in Rima-Sobota and they asked me to come over and see them. That was difficult, for I could not just take a day off from work. I could ask my boss to give me a day off, but he would not have liked it if I told him the reason. Fanni suggested that I lie, think of some excuse, but of course I could not do that. I even had some harsh words for her. She cried. Strangely enough, Komjáthy himself said that I could send a message of being ill. I had some harsh words for him, too. He did not cry, but he was surprised. I think our friendship was not quite the same after that.

But then, quite unexpectedly, I was sent over to the Rima-Sobota court with some urgent documents that had to be hand delivered, so my problem was solved. I visited with Mr. Felszeghy, the assistant director, and the following week I received a letter from him, offering the job. It was the same job I had at the Zólyom district court, clerk, but it paid more and it opened up some real prospects for advancement. Most important, the job offered a government pension; they made certain that I understood its importance.

I understood and eventually Fanni understood it, too, but she was not happy about it. "But what about my parents?" she asked again and again.

"Look, you can visit them as often as you like," I reassured her. "It is not so far, only about 120 kilometers by train. You have to transfer at Fülek to the Miskolcz train, but that will take you almost directly to Rima-Sobota."

"*Almost* directly?"

"Well, yes, almost. At Feled, you transfer again, but from there it's only two stops. Half an hour more. The whole trip takes four hours, five at the most. It depends on the connections. And it only costs six forints, coming and going."

"But that would be difficult with Rózsika."

"So perhaps it would be easier if your parents were to visit us."

She had tears in her eyes. "Every week?"

Poor Fanni, she was such a child. "Well, not quite every week, but as often as they like. We shall ask them."

And we did ask them. They were also very unhappy about the suggestion, but gradually, they came to understand that it was the right career move for me. They promised to come over to Rima-Sobota every other weekend. And they did, too, though not that often. It took them almost four hours to come Saturday evenings, four and a half hours going back Sunday afternoons. So after the first month, we reluctantly agreed that once a month would be enough for their visit; they were not that young any more. Fanni cooked a lovely Saturday dinner and Sunday lunch for them.

In Rima-Sobota we rented an apartment on Szíjjártó Street. It was somewhat larger than the one in Zólyom, but still in an old building. There, Fanni was much busier then before, what with the child, and, for some reason, everything was more difficult for her. Of course, her mother was not there to help. And when a woman is pregnant, she cannot be as fast and agile as otherwise. For by the time Rózsika was about five months old, my Fanni was expecting again. So her mother forbade her to prepare the lunches for them – she always brought plenty of food with her. Eventually, by the summer, Jenő was born.

Jenő. Cute little boy. We all loved him. Rózsika played with him when he was a few months old. It was more difficult now for Fanni, and I tentatively mentioned that maybe we should hire a servant girl. We could afford it now, almost. But there was no room in the apartment. Fanni kept protesting that she could do everything herself, but frankly, it was not seemly for someone in her position to be "her own servant," as they put it. Who were these "they"? The ladies who lived in the same building, Mrs. Haas, Mrs. Neumann, Mrs. Wald. They each tried to help, but they sure had sharp tongues.

I was promoted at the court, got a little more salary. We hired our first servant girl, Annuska, a very simple peasant girl from a nearby Slovak village. She learned, slowly, how to do things around the house, how to clean and cook. It was a great help. After that, we were never without help.

So, you see, Andriskám, those first two years were very happy ones. But they came to an end. Our little Jenő caught an intestinal infection. We took him to a doctor that somebody recommended. He prescribed an emetic, which only made matters worse. The poor little boy then developed a fever, could not hold his food, and by next morning was in obvious pain. Fanni became hysterical. She cried "Do something! Do something!" So we left Rózsika in charge of Annuska, took Jenő and ran all the way to the railway station and caught the 7:22 train to Feled and then another to Fülek and then the one to Zólyom. You see, there Fanni knew a doctor, her family doctor, whom she trusted. We arrived just before noon. A hansom cab took us to the Taussigs' place. Amália ran down and came with us to the doctor.

Jenő died in the doctor's office. There was nothing that he could do to save him. Poor little boy. Poor Fanni. Poor all of us. At least Rózsika was too small to understand.

We buried Jenő right there in Zólyom. He was only nine months old.

The family sat *shiva* in Zólyom. I could not, I had to rush back to my work. They were not that understanding toward Jews in those days; come to think of it, they were not understanding later, either. Annuska cried and cried when I told her about Jenő.

After that, somehow, it never was the same. My work was very demanding, or I took it too seriously, I don't know, but I spent less time at home than before. Fanni went for long walks in the park with Rózsika. She sat on the bench and read while the little girl played. In the evening, she smiled at me and kissed me and loved me, but not quite the same way as before. It was as if she was not quite there. Her thoughts were probably always with little Jenő.

This was in 1894, in the spring. Somehow, it is even sadder when children die in the spring, when hope is in the air. Everybody looks forward to renewal – everybody but you and your family. I know about that. Yes, I know a lot about that. My sister Hermina died in the spring, too. And Erzsébet... I don't want to talk about Erzsébet now.

I did not go to the synagogue very often, as a rule, but in those days I got into the habit of attending the services whenever I could. I cannot tell you why. It started, of course, with saying *Kaddish* for little Jenő. But I got to know some interesting people there. Before, the only Jews I knew were merchants of various kinds – with stores, without stores, wholesalers, maybe agents. Now I met some who were doctors, newspaper writers, bankers, lawyers, even a poet. At the court, I was still the only Jew, except of course that there were quite a few among the lawyers who came to argue their cases. It was nice to talk about serious matters with intelligent Jewish people. There were always plenty of things to talk about. Mainly, the situation of the Jews in this new, modern world. I was in the justice system – technically, only a clerk, but day by day I had more responsibilities – some thought that I was really running my department – and they respected that. But, looking at the situation from the viewpoint of "we Jews here," it was a constant uphill fight to achieve everything that we were capable of achieving. There was so much agitation against us. The priests gave sermons at the churches, urging the faithful to reject the advances of the Jews, who were Christ-killers. The Slovaks resented us because we spoke Hungarian. Somehow they were convinced that their advancement was inhibited by our own. And the aristocrats and nobles were losing their lands because they were incompetent managers. They were forced to enter the various professions and civil service; they did not like that Jews were ahead of them in most walks of modern life. That is why, for many years, I remained the only Jew at the law court in Rima-Sobota.

But life was not too bad then. The salary I had was enough for our daily needs and we could even put a little aside. We could also afford little luxuries. Fanni suggested one day that I go to the barber, not only for my regular haircut, but also for getting a daily shave. I was at first shocked by the idea. "But that costs a lot of money!"

"No, it does not. Just a few krajcárs a day. We could easily afford it."

And indeed we could. I was used to shaving myself, had a good razor and an excellent leather strap, but I must admit, it was more comfortable when the barber did it. He did not nick my skin as often as I did, and it is a nice feeling, when they pack your face in hot towels before and after the shave. Also, you meet with other people at the barber, more or less the same people every day, you get to know them, learn new things about the life of the town… Yes, it was the beginning of a new world.

A Day in Rima-Sobota

"Bernát! We were just looking for you!" The call came from two lawyers of Bernát's acquaintance, Dr. József Morgenbesser and Dr. Moritz Hoselitz. The two men were waiting for the morning's session to start; it had been delayed by half an hour because the judge was late. Bernát was also due to be present at the session with documents and the lawyers were eager to ask him about a new judge who had just been promoted; they wanted to have some inside information that would come very useful in presenting cases later. Bernát would not give them anything that was not public knowledge and they did not expect any confidential information from him, but there was no harm in trying.

Bernát, on the other hand, welcomed the opportunity to talk with learned lawyers. There was one matter that he always wanted to discuss with legal experts, a matter that had, over the years, become almost an idée fixe with him: the Tiszaeszlár blood libel and subsequent trial and pogroms. How could such a thing happen in a modern, democratic country such as Hungary was supposed to be, in the late nineteenth century? Why was the legal profession not better equipped to quash such horrible accusations – that Jews murdered a fourteen-year-old girl to use her blood in the *matzo* during the 1882 *Pesach* festival? And once the case was brilliantly defeated by the non-Jewish Karoly Eötvös, why were the people who submitted phony evidence not arrested and tried? They had also managed to force a fourteen-year-old Jewish boy to give false testimony against his father and others; how could the legal profession let such people go free?

"You are quite right, Mr. Steiner," Morgenbesser assured him, "but in a case like this it is always better to let non-Jews stand up for us. We are grateful for Baron Eötvös and his brilliant defense; how could we have asked him, once the case was won, to go after the perpetrators?"

"But they not only remained free, they were allowed to form an anti-Semitic party!"

"It's a free country," commented Hoselitz with a smirk. "Or so they say."

Bernát insisted: "If those local people, and the priest and the deputy Istoczy, were arrested and tried, well, it wouldn't have stopped the Pozsony pogroms in time, but it might have stopped the pogroms that took place the following year, and who knows, even in the future there might be pogroms. If people knew that by spreading false rumors, they would end up in jail, perhaps they would think twice…"

Hoselitz waved that aside. "There were always accusations and rumors and there will always be. But they'll be small, local affairs. You don't have to be concerned about an organized, nationwide anti-Semitic movement. Those days are over."

Bernát did not seem convinced. "Do you think that only the Germans and Slovaks are able to organize pogroms, not the Hungarians? I would like to believe that, but I am not as certain as I once was, not after Tiszaeszlár. And now they have the national anti-Semitic party – look how many people join it happily. My problem is that I consider myself Hungarian…"

"Why, so do we all," Morgenbesser assured him with a happy smile.

Hoselitz added, "And rightly so. Young man, do you realize that, with all its faults that you mention, this is the best place in the world? Tell me, where did Jews have opportunities like we have in Hungary? Opportunities for learning, for business, for finance, for culture, growth—"

"And where in the world," cut in Morgenbesser, "could you expect to see Jews take over a backward land and make a wonderful, modern country out of it? Soon this place will be more advanced than Austria or France, maybe even Germany. It will be all the Jews' doing. You must appreciate that, and if there are some problems along the way, we must always look toward the future."

"I know, perhaps I am impatient. I would like to make this country perfect, if possible. Well, I don't mean me personally, but all of us should do our best to make sure that it functions smoothly and effectively. For that, there must be justice, fairness, equality. I know those are big words, but isn't that what the judicial system is all about?"

The two lawyers thought for a minute. Hoselitz spoke: "Young man, you are putting us in a difficult situation. Are you suggesting that just because we are lawyers and also Jews, it would be our duty to defend the cause of Hungarian Jewry consistently, wherever it's in danger of being attacked? That would be a very great responsibility."

"One that would make private practice just about impossible for us," added Morgenbesser. "Surely we are allowed to earn a living?"

"Yes, of course. But if we don't defend ourselves, who will? Always Baron Eötvös? What would happen if an individual Jew brought a case against any anti-Semite who besmirched the name of the Jews, any false accusation, any disparagement, let alone any physical attack?"

"An individual Jew? Which Jew? Maybe yourself?"

"Maybe."

Morgenbesser was shaking his head. "And then, you would expect me and my learned friend to come to your help and present your case in court with a brilliance equaling that of Baron Eötvös. Well, I am sure that Dr. Hoselitz could do it, and I would like to think that perhaps I would also be up to the task, but tell me, who would pay for our time and effort? You?"

Bernát's face reddened. "Well, it depends. Of course, I could not afford a long case…"

"Of course not. Neither could anybody, any individual. These cases could drag on for months, years. You want the entire Hungarian Jewish community to set up a defense fund and to initiate such cases. Well, perhaps you should start a drive to build a major organization…"

Hoselitz chipped in: "You could even start a political party for the defense of minorities, how about it? It would be the right thing to do; after all, an anti-Semitic political party has been in existence for nearly twenty years. "

Bernát felt defeated. "No, politics are not for me. I am no organizer. I just don't like to be insulted. I want to stand up for my rights, but if you say that I cannot, really…"

They both tried to reassure him. "Yes, you should stand up for your rights," Hoselitz affirmed. "But not for the rights of everybody, for every single Jew of the country. It would be nice if somebody would do that, some organization, but you can't do it as an individual."

"Don't even dream of it," added Morgenbesser. "You have to be pragmatic. And remember, as my learned friend said, this is the best place in the world!"

"It may be, but pragmatism is one word I have always hated," admitted Bernát. "But I think that you're both right. Well, the judge has arrived. Shall we?" He let the two lawyers precede him into the courtroom.

Gyula – 1896

Oh, Andriskám, you remember me telling you that after Jenő's death things weren't the same? Fanni was just not happy. She was so attached to that little boy. Why, so was I, but it wasn't the same thing. She sighed a lot, and she hardly ever smiled. She took good care of Rózsika, she and Annuska together, but it pained me to see Fanni not being her happy, smiling self. So I decided that I had to cheer her up.

I tried everything. I took her to musical evenings, to performances of the local amateur theater company, to visiting groups – nothing helped. And then I suggested that maybe it would be time to have another baby, perhaps another little boy.

"No, I don't want it." She wouldn't explain, she just shook her head. I tried to argue with her, but she became hysterical and ran out of the room.

I waited a few weeks and tried again. The same reaction, the same hysterics. I didn't understand it. The next time her parents came over, I went over to Amália when Fanni was out of the room and asked her about it. "Amália (she insisted that I call her that way), don't you think that Fanni and I should have another baby? Wouldn't that be good for her?"

She looked quite concerned and whispered with her eye on the kitchen door, "Wait, not yet. Not yet."

I was puzzled. "But why?"

And she whispered again, "She worries. She thinks that another boy would also die."

I did not understand. I mean, of course he could die, many young children did, but what made her especially worried? I asked Amália.

"There is some superstition. A black cat or something like that. Annuska told her that she must wait for a long time yet."

"Annuska? But what does she know? She is just the maid, and a silly maid at that."

"Yes, but Fanni thinks that Annuska has some understanding of the hidden powers. But Berci, swear that you don't talk about this to Fanni. Don't tell her what I've just told you."

"But then, how can I try to talk her out of such nonsense?"

"Be patient with her, sooner or later she will tire of the superstition."

I wanted to argue with her, but just then Fanni came into the room and we did not get another chance.

In any case, I mentioned another little boy many times, during the next two years, but I didn't stress the argument. Eventually, in 1895, when I raised the subject once more, Fanni smiled and said, "If you really want it, let's try."

I was a little surprised. I kissed her, held her hands, and asked, "Are you no longer afraid?"

She had such beautiful eyes. I could see in them that she was afraid.

"It doesn't matter. Let us have another baby."

* * *

Gyula was born in March of 1896, on the thirteenth. It was a Friday. Annuska told her to hold back, begged her to make sure that the baby would not be born on such a horrible day, but of course she could not hold it; when it was due, it had to be born. Fanni cried and cried. She kissed her baby, loved him, fed him, but could not look at him without crying.

"He will not live," she assured me again and again. Annuska stood there with tears in her eyes and nodded.

"Stop that nonsense!" I was really angry with Annuska for telling such stupid, idiotic things to my wife. "This is all superstition, old wives' tales. If a child is healthy, well fed, well clothed, he will live, regardless of what day he was born. Gyula is a very healthy little boy and he will live."

But Fanni shook her head and cried. She cried a lot in those days and hardly ate at all during the next few weeks. I had to order her, in the strongest terms, to eat, if only for the baby's sake. So she ate a little, all the wrong things, and had very little milk.

Things got so bad that we had to get a wet nurse, a woman whose own child had died a few days before. The woman came five or six times every day. She fed Gyula, but her mood was not the best, either. The three of them sat there crying all day.

When Gyula was three weeks old, Fanni started to have all kinds of stomach problems. I told her that she had to eat better. But then, later that week, she complained that her belly really hurt, badly, on the lower right side. I took her to a doctor, who prescribed some medication for her. Next day the pain was worse. We went back to the doctor, who did not like it. He shook his head and told me to take her to the hospital, there was a hospital in town. I took Fanni there. She was crying because of the pain and because it was Friday again, April 10. They put her in a bed. I waited outside. Soon I heard her screaming. They would not let me enter the room, but a doctor came out after a few minutes and informed me that Fanni had died of acute appendicitis.

My Fanni. Dead.

There are no words…

But what can I tell you? I sent a telegram to Fanni's parents. They arrived by the next day. We buried Fanni and sat *shiva*, at least during the evenings, because I got only one day off work. I don't need to tell you how much Amália and Lipót cried. Rózsika, fortunately, did not understand – or perhaps she would have, but we did not tell her what happened. She asked for her mother. We told her that she had to go away for a while. And then, at the end of the *shiva*, when Amália and Lipót went back to Zólyom, they took Rózsika with them. They told her that her mother was ill, she would stay with them for a while. But Gyula stayed with me, or rather with Annuska and the wet nurse, who seemed to be good for him.

Before they left, Fanni's parents insisted that I start looking for a new wife as soon as possible, for the children's sake. The words meant almost nothing to me. I could not think of taking such a step, yet deep down I knew that I would have to do so. Eventually. It would not be me, marrying another woman, it would be someone else, some person into whom I might eventually change in some incomprehensible manner. But I did not think about such things.

I don't know if it was the loss of his mother, or that the food did not agree with him when they started weaning him, but Gyula took a turn for the worse. He cried a lot and lost weight. I took him to a doctor. To make a long story short, he died when he was just five months old, in August.

BAUER

ILONA BAUER

Békés – 2000

I was learning a lot about my grandfather's marriage to his first wife, but what about my grandmother? My father's mother? Did I know anything about her?

Well, I have already mentioned that she sat by the window and read novels, usually foreign novels, in the original language – she did not trust translations. Or she just looked out the window. She went to the washroom laboriously, using crutches.

And we had heard that her father (or some relative – perhaps grandfather, perhaps uncle) was an important man in Szeged, which was then the second largest city in Hungary. He was the head of the Jewish community, chief rabbi or something like that. Well, that made some sense: if her education was such that she was fluent in a number of languages, at a literary level, she must have come from a family of some distinction. We first thought that she had been born in Szeged, but that assumption had to be rejected when we received my father's birth record, stating that his mother was born in Békés.

So after our trip to Slovakia, my wife and I drove to Békés, which is in southern Hungary, to see my grandmother's birthplace and to try and find out something about her and her family.

The Great Hungarian Plain is flat enough, just like the Canadian prairies, but still interesting, with lots of small villages and creeks, some woods, and even a few hillocks; it was not a boring drive. By eleven in the morning we were in the Békés town hall, where we met the mayor, Mr. István Pataki, as well as Mrs. Apáti-Nagy, the keeper of vital records. Earlier, I had written to them about our upcoming visit, explaining that I was searching for information about the Bauer family.

They showed us records of Eszter Bauer, who died in 1891, and Paula Bauer, who married Vilmos Klein in 1902. They both lived in the same house in Békés, so clearly they were related. Almost certainly they were aunt and niece. Paula came from Gyoma (as did at least two other Bauer girls, according to the National Archives data that we had looked up the day before). We asked Mrs. Apáti-Nagy to call her colleague in Gyoma and ask her to look up records relating to the Bauers.

As a courtesy, they took us to see Mrs. Imre Weinberger, née Rózsa Geller. She is a Holocaust survivor, perhaps the only Jewish person left in Békés, where she lives with her very non-Jewish-looking (though technically Jewish) daughter and her family. Her entire first family was murdered in Auschwitz. She did not remember the Bauers. They had thought that she remembered the name as Bayer, but it was actually Bleier that she recalled, as indeed there had been many Bleiers as well as Bleuers in the town.

Afterwards, we visited the cemetery with the mayor and Mrs. Apáti-Nagy. It was in rather good condition, containing about three hundred graves, most of the stones still standing. We found many Bleiers, some Bleuers. But we also found two Bauer women, widows of other Jewish residents of Békés.

The mayor invited us to lunch. We thanked him but declined the invitation, explaining to him that we were pressed for time as we had to make an extra trip to Gyoma.

I gave a donation of twenty-five thousand forints to the city, as a prize for the upcoming music competition, in memory of my grandmother. Since then, I have received several letters and publications, announcing the winners of the competition and referring to the prize.

Then we drove to Gyomaendrőd – the towns of Gyoma and Endrőd merged, I think fairly recently. We visited the keeper of vital records. She had looked up, as requested, the birth and marriage records for Bauer between 1895 (the beginning of state record keeping) and 1910, but had found nothing at all. We consoled ourselves with the thought that the most relevant information would likely be in the pre-1895 rabbinical records, on the Mormon microfilms.

But back to Eszter and Paula Bauer. Was there any useful information about them in the town records? Information that might point to some relation to my grandmother, Ilona Bauer? I thought that Paula might have been her sister and Eszter, her aunt. Perhaps they all came from Gyoma (despite that Békés birth data) and lived with their aunt for some reason. We discovered that Eszter Bauer was the widow of Mor Rozner; her death, in 1899 at the age of fifty-four, was reported by her son, Ignác Rozner, merchant. Her father was Farkas Bauer, merchant, and her mother, Fani Veitner; both were from Gyoma.

Their son, Ignác, apparently married a Berta Bauer, also from Gyoma. Strange – perhaps a cousin?

Throughout our search I was still puzzled by the distance between Rima-Sobota, in northern Hungary, and Békés, in the south. The distance was nearly two hundred kilometers "as the crow flies" – but back then the crow had a much greater advantage over a man, or in this case a woman, than it has today, when we fly too. Our ancestors did not, and to travel two hundred kilometers – there was no full train service to Békés then – would have taken several days.

Those two towns were effectively farther apart than our two home towns today, Toronto and Haifa.

So once again, how did those two people meet? How did they manage to hear about each other?

I was not satisfied.

Mormon Records – 2000

The National Archives, located in Budapest, have lots of old records on microfilm; we spent a few hours studying them. It soon became obvious that the microfilms were prepared by the Mormon church, in Salt Lake City, and were just as easily accessible from our Toronto home as from the Budapest archive. So the next phase of the research was moved to Canada.

There we found many interesting things, and while at first we were disappointed about not having found other things, this still moved us forward. Let me tell you.

Paula Bauer was not born in Gyoma, but in Kallo, not far from Budapest. Her father was Elias Bauer, shopkeeper; her mother, Roza Fleiszig. Paula married Vilmos Klein, who was born... But I need not go into all that, as in the end most of that data proved irrelevant to my search. The one possibly significant conclusion that I reached: that Elias Bauer and Eszter Bauer, Mrs. Rozner, were almost certainly brother and sister.

There was the main rabbinical record – births, marriages, deaths. We also found such records recorded on a smaller scale in the congregational archives: the main book was probably that of the Neolog congregation, while the Orthodox community had a smaller one. But what did not appear in either was a birth record for Ilona Bauer, in 1867, the year of her birth according to my father's civil birth register (and also her gravestone in Budapest).

Indeed, there were no Bauer births registered in Békés at all, except an Elinora Bauer born in 1860. Her father was listed as Zsigmond Bauer; her mother, Roza Fellner. Clearly, these were not the people I was looking for. But then, where were they? The most likely explanation was that when Grandmother referred to her birthplace as Békés, she meant the county Békés rather than the town. The largest settlement in that county was its capital, Békéscsaba. So our next step was to look up the Mormon records for that town, as well as all surrounding towns and settlements. Indeed, in Békéscsaba, we did find many Bauers. Some of the more interesting or remarkable finds included two Sigmund Bauers, both ragmen. One was married to Kati Kóhn and had three children; the other, over the same period, was married to Gondi Kóhn, with six children. Clearly these were not the same two men or the same two women, but perhaps they were sisters. There were two other Zsigmond Bauers as well, but not related to me, I concluded fairly early. There were many Rozália Bauers, variously denoted as Rozi, Rosi, Rosa, Roza, Sali, Zali. The same person was even registered under many of these names, say on the birth registers of subsequent children. Ignác Rozner's parents, on their marriage register, now appeared as Mor Rozner and Nettie Bauer, not Eszter, but Nettie seems to be just one of the possible variants of that name. The parents of Mor and Nettie are also given. In the case of Nettie, they are Bernhard Bauer and Fani Veisz.

I was also searching for the marriage record of Bernát Steiner and Ilona Bauer. Surely they married in Békés. Would she travel up to Rima-Sobota to wed? It would be more proper for him to travel down south to her home. But I found no such marriage record. Nor did I find any marriage registration of my grandparents in Rima-Sobota.

Perhaps they married neither in the one place, nor in the other, but halfway in between? Specifically, in Budapest? Maybe that would have made some sense.

One marriage record that did interest me was that of Zsigmond Bauer and Roza Fellner, he from Szeged, she from Arad (a town now in Romania). We had found this record earlier as the parents of Elinora Bauer. Maybe this Elinora had a younger sister Ilona, not noted on the Békés birth register? There was also a Zsigmond Bauer whose parents were listed as Herman Bauer, born in Szeged, and Rosalia Leiznik from Arad. The Szeged connection… Was this the famous man from there? Unlikely, but worth pursuing.

Then there were at least two Bauer girls born in Békés, even though the local register never showed them: Hanni and Sali.

But no Ilona Bauer! Not born in 1867, not in any other year.

Next, we checked the birth, marriage, and death registers for the city of Szeged – maybe there was a reference to Ilona Bauer there. Surprisingly, there were very few Bauers born there during the relevant time period, though we did find quite a number of death records, including one Markfi Armin Bauer, retired Jewish community administrator. Who knows, maybe this was the sought ancestor? He died in 1874, at the age of seventy-four; no information was given about his birth place. Earlier, we had found a Zsigmond whose father was noted as Herman Bauer – well, Armin was a Hungaricised version of Herman.

At this point, I had to admit to being a little bit stuck. Elinora could have been Ilona's older sister, but where was Ilona? She hadn't been born in the town of Békés, nor in Békés County – where had she been born?

A small detail about Elinora bothered me: her Hebrew name, according to the birth register, was given as Leah. I knew that my grandmother's Hebrew name was Leah. If Elinora was unrelated to us, then this posed no problem.

But if she were an older sister, then the only possibility would be that she died before Ilona was born and was given the same Hebrew name. Would they do that? I wasn't sure.

* * *

I went to see my rabbi in Toronto.

"Rabbi, I would like to ask you something."

"Sure, go ahead."

"I would like to put you in a hypothetical situation. Pretend that you are the rabbi in a small town. We are talking about nineteenth-century Hungary, when only the rabbis, not the state, kept vital records. Well, one day, a young woman comes to you and has a request. She says, 'Rabbi, I'm getting married.' You say, of course, 'That's great, *mazel tov*. And who is the lucky man?' She says, 'A *shadchen* has found me a good match. It is very far from here, up in the north, in Rima-Sobota.' So you say something about pity that she will be moving away, but wishing her lots of luck and happiness. She replies, 'Thank you. I would like to ask you to issue me a certificate about my birth. I was born here, so it's in your register. The Rima-Sobota rabbi will need it.' You say, 'Sure, I'll look it up and write it for you.' So far, so good."

The Toronto rabbi was listening with a smile; he was very curious to find out where I was heading. I continued.

"But then, the young woman seems to be in some difficulty. She is embarrassed, doesn't quite know how to say the next thing. You try to encourage her, ask her, 'Is there anything else?' Finally she says, 'Yes, there is. You see, the young man is now thirty-four years old. He has just lost his first wife, who was twenty-two.' 'Very sad,' you say, and she says 'Yes, and the *shadchen* told him that I was thirty.' 'And…?' 'And he wasn't too happy with that, but he finally agreed to meet me. We met and we liked each other and decided to marry.' 'So then everything is well,' you say. And she comes out with it. 'But you see, I am not thirty years old at all. I am thirty-seven!' Well, you are a little shocked."

The rabbi was not shocked; he laughed. So I went on.

"So this is what the young – well, perhaps not so young woman asks you: 'Rabbi, could you write up that certificate showing that I was born in 1867, not 1860?' And you say – well, that is my question. What *do* you say to her?"

The rabbi seemed to enjoy the conundrum. He thought for a while. "I see the problem," he finally said. "But why? Is this a real situation?"

"Perhaps. You know that I am currently working on a book about my ancestors on my father's side. There is a possibility that what I have just said did happen to my grandmother. I am not yet sure, but what would you have done if faced with such a request?"

The rabbi thought some more and finally offered this: "I would certainly have sympathized with the young woman's problem. She was thirty-seven and still not married. Hillel did encourage the use of a 'white lie' in a good cause. Nevertheless, to issue an actual document, stating false data, data that could be checked by interested authorities at any time, no, I don't think that I would go that far. I just could not do that. But it is possible that other rabbis would do it, quite possible. Interesting question, certainly."

Elinora – 2001

When I first hired Judit B. to research my family's history, I told her that the most important thing was to find the marriage registry of my grandparents. I had not found it in Rima-Sobota or in Békés. My suspicion was that the marriage might have taken place in Budapest; I did indeed check some Mormon films for the capital, but they did not have a full set for Budapest. I asked Judit to try to locate that record and let me know all the vital data, especially those of the bride, as well as the names of witnesses and whatever else may be available. I gave her the only possible two years for the date of the marriage: 1896 or 1897. I gave her the name of the bride, Ilona Bauer, and her birth date, 1867, perhaps 1866.

In addition, I asked Judit to try to find many other pieces of information: When exactly did the family move from Rima-Sobota to Budapest – presumably after the partition of Hungary after the lost war in 1920, when two-thirds of the country was annexed to the surrounding nations. Rima-Sobota itself became part of the new country of Czechoslovakia. What did they do? What did grandfather do, when in Budapest – did he get a similar job at the law court as before? How did the family live? Where did the family live?

I also wished for some information about my father. He was born in 1901, and in 1919, just before high school matriculation, he became very active in the new Communist movement. After the defeat of the "reds" and the brutal return of the "whites," my father was consequently banned from completing his high school education anywhere in the country. Yet he must have completed it, because he went to university and became a lawyer.

Those were my initial questions; I eagerly awaited her response.

About one month later, Judit found a Budapest residence register, according to which in 1928 (the earliest relevant year for which such information is available), Bernát Steiner (?), retired law court director, and his son, then articling lawyer, lived at 30 Rákóczi Boulevard, in the Seventh District. Later, Judit also found a 1930 voters registration list for the same house, where they were listed as Bernát Székely, retired law court director and Dr. László Székely, lawyer. No mention was made of Bernát's wife, my grandmother; perhaps she was already an invalid, unable to go to the voting station and thus not qualified for inclusion on the list. Neither was there a mention about a maid living on the premises; either they could not afford one or the maid could not read and write, thus disqualified, again, as a voter.

To my recollection, Rákóczi Boulevard was more upscale than Garay Street, where the family lived later, but I was not certain of this. In any case, it is possible that in later years they needed a larger apartment, when the newly widowed daughter Rózsám came back to live with her parents; perhaps the Rákóczi Boulevard apartment was too small to accommodate her.

Next month, Judit found more exciting information.

She went to the National Széchényi Library in Budapest and looked at the death announcements in the local newspapers of more then a century ago. There, she found the report announcing the demise of Mr. Zsigmond Bauer, after brief suffering, on August 31, 1899, in Losonc. He had died in the sixty-eighth year of his life and fortieth year of his marriage, and the death had been reported by his wife, Roza née Fellner, his daughter Ilona, and Ilona's husband, Bernát Steiner.

From this, Judit concluded that if the Elinora Bauer whose birth record I had found had a mother named Roza Fellner, then Elinora must be Ilona.

Bull's eye! Elinora's mother was definitely Roza Fellner, so we had the right family.

Judit's identification of Elinora with Ilona was still not absolute, in my view, as there could have been an older daughter, who died young, and a subsequent girl who was given the same Hebrew name. But I had begun to discount that possibility.

After Judit had found out what she could in Budapest she made some further assumptions which opened up new venues of investigation. The major assumption she made was that the marriage of my grandparents took place in Losonc. In vain had I searched for some such document in Rima-Sobota or Békés, or even in Budapest. Finding the records could be difficult, as the Jewish community data was kept in Budapest, but only birth records and a partial set of death records were available – no marriage records at all. Neither is such information available in Slovakia. However, starting from 1895 state records were kept, so such information could be acquired from the Slovak authorities.

And she suggested that we should try to find out the occupation of Zsigmond Bauer from the newspaper, *Losonci Hirlap*; there might be relevant information there about this and other family data. Of course I authorized Judit to continue her search in the suggested directions.

Markussohn Herman Bauer – 2001

While Judit was researching in Budapest, I continued doing what I could in Toronto. I was interested in identifying the important ancestor that I had always heard of. He must have been known; he must have left some record of his life. Was there a rabbi named Bauer in Szeged? As far as I could determine, there was never such a person. The most famous chief rabbi of Szeged was Lipót Löw – well, perhaps one of his daughters married a man named Bauer. Yes, that made a lot of sense, and a friend managed to secure for me a book describing the descendants of certain famous Jews in Hungary, including Rabbi Löw. He had many children, five or six daughters, but none married any Bauer.

All right, how about this ancestor's writings? I found a book in the Toronto Public Library, a recent reprint of an old book by József Szinnyei, indexing and summarizing the works of all significant Hungarian writers. There, I found an interesting reference to a Markussohn (Markfy) Herman Bauer, the administrator of the Szeged Jewish community, born in 1801 in Hluboka, Nyitra County. I thought it might be worthwhile to note some of the information available about him. He became a teacher and taught at the Jewish school in Mako, where the Szeged community subsequently elected him as administrator. There he was very influential in the task of Hungaricizing the Jewish population. He retired in 1862 and died in 1874. Among his works: *A lelek halhatatlansagarol: Ket fuzet Mendelssohn Phaedonjeanak nyoman* (1836); *Fromme Anschichten* (1837); *Unnepelyes beszed a szegedi izraelita egyhaznak felszentelesekor* (1843); *Gyaszhang t. Palffy Janos ur, Szeged varosa tanacsnoka gyaszunnepelyere; A zsoltarokbol forditva* (1844); *Reden gehalten bei dem am 11, Elul 5604* [August 20, 1844] *gefuerten Leichenbegangnisse des hochwurdigen Arader Oberrabiner Aaron Chorim; Selomoh hasonlatai: Salamon peldabeszedei magyar es heber szoveggel* (1844); *Das For-und Nachwort der durch ihre k. maj. Franz Joseph I, und Elisabeth fur Allerhochst ihre Anwesenheit zu Szegedin* (1857); *Kereskedes es aruisme: Nemet kifejezesekkel, kulonos tekintettel as ausztriai birodalomra* (1853); and an unfinished Hebrew-Hungarian dictionary. Clearly, he was fluent in at least three languages and probably more.

Was this the man I was looking for? If so, his son Zsigmond would be my great-grandfather, and his granddaughter Ilona/Elinora, my grandmother. I could see here some explanation for her liberal education and language skills.

Judit mentioned that she had found some of her information in a work about the Szeged Jewish community written by Emanuel Löw, the son of Rabbi Lipót Löw. In that work, Emanuel Löw states that between 1862 and 1865 (but according to my information, between 1834 and 1862), the administrator of the community was M. Herman *Brauer* – presumably Bauer. She wondered if this might be the man I was looking for. In my reply, I told her about a Zsigmond Bauer that I had found, whose father was Herman. Perhaps this chain was the right one?

Right away, Judit assumed that Zsigmond Bauer was indeed the son of Markfy Herman Bauer. I wrote to her, pointing out a difficulty with that assumption. According to the marriage register of Zsigmond Bauer and Roza Fellner, his father was born in Szeged, not Hluboka in Nyitra County. That could be a simple mistake. But the key data could be ascertained by checking the name of Markfy Herman's wife. Zsigmond's mother was called Rozália Leiznick. If Markfy Herman's wife was called so, then he was the one.

Well, only three days later, Judit sent me the following message:

> I have worked for three hours today in the archives, checking the Szeged vital records. I found this: on May 14, 1873, in Szeged, Jakab Reichenbach, resident of Vagujhely, age 24, son of Jakab and Katalin, married Franciska Bauer, age 22, daughter of *Markfi Herman Bauer* and *Roza Leipnik*.

There it was. Markfi Herman's wife was indeed Roza Leipnik (or Leiznik; it is hard to read these old handwritten documents correctly.)

Judit had lots of additional information about other members of this family. Markfy Herman Bauer and Roza Leipnik apparently had ten children, most of them eventually marrying in Szeged. For the time being, this was of no import. The main thing was that the acknowledged intellectual had been identified as the grandfather of my grandmother. So that's where she had acquired her taste for books and her knowledge of languages – and probably also her snobbishness (though I think that she eventually outgrew that attitude, due to circumstances).

What about Ilona's father, Zsigmond Bauer? Was he also an intellectual? What did he do? Where did they live? Now it started to look as if the Bauer family might have lived in Losonc, for that's where Zsigmond died. That would explain a lot: Losonc was very close to Rima-Sobota so the mystery of how my grandparents met would be solved quite easily, the two-hundred-kilometer distance having melted away.

And Losonc had cropped up once before – in Vladimir's search for information on the death of Erzsébet, my father's older sister who died before he was born. He hadn't found any record of the death in Rima-Sobota, where they lived, but he had found one in Losonc. Here is what Vladimir's message said:

> Erzsébet Steiner died April 11, 1899, 3 p.m. in a steam mill in Losonc. The cause was convulsions. Her father, royal court clerk from Rima-Sobota, reported her death at the registrar's office in Losonc.

Poor little girl, dying of convulsions at eleven months. What convulsions? What could have caused them? But the more intriguing questions: Why in a steam mill? Why in Losonc? Perhaps they took her there, because there was a better doctor in Losonc? What about the steam mill? It must have been a warm place – April would still be chilly in the north – but could they not find any other lodging?

Zsigmond on His Father – 1860

"Mr. Zsigmond Bauer. How are you, sir?"

"How am I? I suppose I am all right, nothing hurts right now. But…what is this? Where are we?"

"Well, we are really nowhere. I am from the future and I would like to ask you some questions, if you don't mind."

"But who are you?"

"I am your great-grandson."

"Great-grandson? You mean Elino–"

"Yes, Ilona's grandson."

"Ah, Ilona's. That's good. I did manage to marry her off, finally, and so she had a grandson. Or more?"

"No, just one grandson and one granddaughter. But what interests me is not the future, your future, but the past, your early years. You see, I know that my grandmother, Ilona, was a highly cultured, well-educated woman, and I would like to find out something about her ancestry, particularly on your side, even more particularly about your own father. I think that he must have been a very interesting man and he must have exerted a major influence over Ilona, or am I wrong?"

"No, you are certainly correct, my father was someone special. He was the most knowledgeable man that I ever met, a valuable person."

"Tell me. Talk to me about him, and about your childhood, things you remember about your father."

"Well, he was a famous man, an important man in Szeged. I was born there, for he spent a lot of time in Szeged even before he received his appointment there."

"What appointment exactly? And what did he do before?"

"He taught in Mako. But he wrote many things, scholarly articles in several languages, and he got them published. So he was well known in Szeged and they often invited him to speak at special events. My mother usually went with him. Once, in 1831, they went for two months – that's when I was born."

"But he did not move there permanently until later?"

"When I was three years old he was appointed administrator of the Jewish community of Szeged. It was a big job, an important job. He held it till the end, till he had to retire because of his health."

"Yes, I know. But what was the job, really? The Hungarian term, *jegyző*, sounds like 'notary'. What did he have to note?"

"Notary? No, a lot more than that. Sure, he was responsible for maintaining the vital records and such, but that was just a small part of the job. He had to keep the community well in hand, collect the taxes, pay all employees, make sure the synagogue and the schools and the cemetery and everything else was well looked after..."

"Was he really managing all of those institutions?!"

"Not in person, of course. He had other people handling the school and the cemetery and all that. But he had overall responsibility. He hired those people and paid them, I believe even fired one or two. And he hired the rabbis."

"He did?"

"Yes, indeed. Now I don't mean that it was always he who decided which rabbi to hire. The community itself had a lot of say in that."

"So I would imagine. Surely a *kehila*, a group of people having their own synagogue, would have a leadership who would decide on such things?"

"Yes, but it was not enough to decide on a person. He had to be invited and looked after while he was there, and the salary had to be negotiated and all the terms – why, the community even provided a house for its more important rabbis. Who do you think arranged that? It was my father."

"Yet, with all that responsibility, he still found time to write?"

"Yes, he did. He wrote about the immortality of the soul, he created a Hebrew-Hungarian dictionary, he wrote about Solomon's parables in Hungarian and Hebrew, about commerce and merchandise – he wrote that for me, when I went into business and did not know the proper German expressions, he knew everything – and he wrote eulogies for famous rabbis and city dignitaries, a welcoming speech for the emperor and the empress, when they visited Szeged, oh, and so many other things. Important things."

"Ah, so you went into business. Then you did not follow your father into the more exalted strata?"

"No, those things were not for me. I suppose I inherited my nature more from my mother. She was a very practical person."

"Why, your father had to be practical to manage the entire Szeged community?"

"Yes, of course, but that was a different practicality. I never had to hire Rabbi Löw. I would not know how to start."

"Ah, tell me about that."

"I remember it quite well, because that was the last time my father attempted to make a community man out of me. I must have been nineteen or twenty. Rabbi Löw was quite famous by then. He had just been released from prison…"

"Prison?"

"Yes, because he participated in the 1848 revolutionary army as chaplain and also made a number of patriotic speeches. They imprisoned him in 1849 and had just released him back to his post in Pápa. He was chief rabbi there in those days. But our community wanted to bring him to Szeged. The idea was to invite him for a week or two, to lead the service and to talk to the community leaders, get to know the place and to like it so much that we could come to some agreement. So my father was asked by the community to travel to Pápa and talk to Rabbi Löw by person, rather than write a letter to him."

"I see. And he went?"

"He went, but he took me with him. He wanted to train me in the niceties of fine negotiations, in diplomacy, you could say. We thought that it would take a lot of convincing to get Rabbi Löw to come, even for a visit."

"But why? Was Szeged not the largest Jewish community outside of Pest and Pozsony?"

CHIEF RABBI
LIPÓT LÖW

"Yes, it was, but Pápa was also significant and they had given a free hand to Rabbi Löw. He was concerned that he would not be so unrestricted in Szeged. It did take a lot of convincing by my father to make the rabbi accept the invitation. I am afraid that I was no help at all. I sensed right away that this was a great man – how could I talk with him and argue with him? So I just stood there quietly, I think it was then that my father realized that some business, or a job at some enterprise, would be better for me than the world of higher learning."

"And Rabbi Löw?"

"Oh, my father got him to come for a week. And once he came, he loved Szeged and after some heavy negotiations, he decided to stay with us."

"Was that a good thing? How did he and your father get along?"

"Very well."

"Indeed? No problems at all?"

"Well, sure, they had their clashes. The rabbi was too liberal for my father, sometimes. Mind you, he did not entirely accept the German type of Reform movement. He wouldn't keep the Sabbath on Sunday, or seat men and women together, or allow people into the synagogue without a hat, no. But he advocated using the Hungarian language all the way through, even in service, which my father did not like. So they argued about that a lot."

"And who won?"

"Oh, the rabbi won all the time. He had convinced the entire *kehila* leadership of the merits of his approach. So after a while my father stopped arguing; he was afraid of losing his position."

"He had a good job."

"Good? It was one of the best jobs in the country. Why, his salary was three hundred forints a year! Not many people earned that. We could afford a large apartment and two maids and a cook, and lots of clothes. We always had fine food on the table. You didn't play with something like that."

"So what you are saying is that the rabbi and your father were not such great friends, after all?"

"But you are wrong there. They were friends all the way, despite the arguments. They enjoyed arguing with each other, and they argued in Hungarian and in Yiddish and German and French and Italian and Czech, even in Latin and Greek. When they were at it, we usually gathered in the next room and listened, peeked in. It was great fun."

"Who was this 'we'?"

"Oh, all the children. There were ten of us, thanks to the Lord, five boys and five girls. All survived – that was a rare thing in those days. My father was something of a doctor, too, not trained, but he knew what to do and what not to do. I wish I knew all that much later."

"And back to Rabbi Löw. How is it possible that such an innovator got to be accepted by a major Jewish community, that nobody opposed his views?"

"Who said nobody opposed? They opposed it strongly enough. He became the father of the Neolog movement in Hungary. But the Orthodox opposed him enough to leave the *kehila* and start a new *shul*. Later they built a synagogue for themselves. Don't forget, in the south of Hungary, the majority was still Orthodox. Actually, there were some harsh words. Some of the Orthodox called him the 'destroyer of Israel.'"

"And how about you, I mean your family? You said that your father did not agree to all the modernization – was he Orthodox? Were you?"

"Hmm. My father was not really Orthodox. He would have been what they called 'status quo ante,' but he didn't have a choice; his livelihood depended on him belonging to the *kehila*. As far as I was concerned, I did not take things so seriously. Neolog was good enough for me. Later in life, in Losonc, we belonged to an Orthodox community. There it was expected of one. But as I say, I never took religion very seriously."

"And what was the reason for this? Would you say that all this Neolog and status-quo business was what turned you away from religion? That if your family had remained Orthodox, you would have remained a religious man yourself?"

"Maybe, I'm not sure. For me, this was never very important."

"Are you sure? Not even in times of trouble? Like, as you say, later in life, when you lost someone, or maybe two persons, who were close to you? Didn't you miss then that tie to the community, or rather, to God?"

"There were some difficult times. Maybe I did miss God then, maybe I regretted having lost that thing that my father always had with Him, that personal contact, if you can call it that. But that happened only later in my life…"

"I would like to talk to you about this 'later in life,' about what you did and where you lived and so on. But perhaps not now, maybe later."

"Sure, why not?"

The Steam Mill and Andor – 2001

Two days after confirming that Markfi Herman Bauer was indeed Ilona's grandfather, Judit sent me another e-mail, a message that answered many of my perplexities. She had spent two more days in the library, studying the *Losonci Hirlap* – nothing there – and the *Losonc and Neighborhood* weekly newspaper for the last decade of the nineteenth century. A rich mother lode indeed! Let me relate to you what she found:

1. May 9, 1897: Andor Bauer, employee of the Miskolc steam mill and son of Zsigmond Bauer, officer of the Losonc steam mill, committed suicide on Thursday, May 6, apparently as the result of momentary mental disturbance. He was buried on May 7.

2. June 6, 1897: Ilona, the daughter of Zsigmond Bauer, steam mill officer, became engaged a few days ago to Bernát Steiner, Rima-Sobota law court officer.

3. July 4, 1897: Miss Ilona Bauer and Mr. Bernát Steiner are to be married on July 4, at 10 a.m. The matrimony is to be sanctified also by the clergy at 4 p.m. on the same day at the Losonc Synagogue.

4. May 21, 1899: Dead: Erzsébet Steiner, infant of eleven months, of convulsions.

5. September 3, 1899: Zsigmond Bauer, the manager of the Losonc steam mill, has passed away in the sixty-eighth year of his life, after brief suffering. The death was also reported in an obituary by the steam mills of the Borsod-Miskolc Steam Mill Inc.

*   *   *

Exciting, isn't it?

Miskolc is a larger town, a city really, eighty kilometers from Rima-Sobota and about one hundred from Losonc. It was the capital of Borsod County. Judit told me that the Borsod-Miskolc Steam Mill Inc. owned the Losonc steam mill (along with the Miskolc, Hatvan, Csany and Szeg steam mills). She promised to send me photocopies of all the newspapers; they arrived soon after.

Well, so there it was. Erzsébet died at the steam mill because her grandfather was an officer there, perhaps the manager of the mill. They took her to Losonc to see the grandparents, or maybe to visit a doctor that they trusted in that town, the hometown of her mother. Ilona had then been married for less than two years; she would have known few doctors in Rima-Sobota. When the baby got seriously sick she would have wanted to rush her to her own doctor in the nearby town.

Incidentally, when the newspapers arrived, it became clear that Zsigmond Bauer and his family actually lived *at the steam mill*. This surprised me a little. My image of the steam mill was that of a small building, something on the order of a Dutch windmill, powered by a steam engine. Then I received a drawing of the Miskolc steam mill. It turned out to be a huge factory, consisting of dozens of buildings, most of them six stories high and very wide. The plant even had direct freight railway access – the whole operation was comparable to a steel mill (why would they call *that* a mill?). I also thought that the farmers brought in their grain in bags, had them milled and took the bags of flour home, less perhaps a small portion in lieu of the fee. Not at all. It turned out that this was not a farmer-and-buggy operation: the steam mill bought grain from all over the county and sold the flour throughout Europe.

This explained why Erzsébet had died at the steam mill. She had simply been brought to her grandparents' home when she took ill, and she died there. That Zsigmond Bauer did indeed live at the steam mill was later confirmed when Judit found his death register.

So the location of Erzsébet's death was explained – but now there was Andor! So my grandmother did have a brother! A brother of whom I had never heard before, who died by his own hand a month before the engagement, two months before the wedding!

What was behind all of this? The more I learned, the more conundrums I encountered. Surely, this was not a normal, everyday situation?

Andor worked at a steam mill owned by the parent company of his father's employer. Was there something wrong at his work? Perhaps some irregularity? There could be many reasons for the young man's suicide; unhappy love was not an infrequent cause in those days. Such suicides were almost encouraged by the German romantic tradition, exemplified by *The Sorrows of Young Werther*, that popular book by Goethe, where the protagonist kills himself due to unhappy love. Is that what happened to Andor? It could have.

There are so many other possibilities. Homosexuality? Not out of the question.

While I speculated, Judit found the marriage record of Zsigmond Bauer (written as *Sigmund*, the German form) on May 22, 1859. The groom, twenty-eight years old, was described as a bookkeeper. He had been born in Szeged and was living in Békés, and was the son of Herman M. Bauer, administrator, and Rozi Leipnik, residents of Szeged. The bride was listed as Rozi Fellner (I told you that almost every girl was Rozi!), age nineteen, born in Arad, the daughter of Moricz Fellner and Juli Weisz, residents of Békéscsaba. The wedding actually took place in Békéscsaba; the witnesses were Moricz Fellner and Herman Bauer.

Further information: Rozi's father, Moricz Fellner was also a bookkeeper. He died in Békéscsaba on September 9, 1860, of fever. And in 1863, three years after Elinora's birth, Jakab was born to Zsigmond and Rozi prematurely; he died in Békéscsaba after three days.

It seemed from this that Zsigmond and Rozi had already left Békés by 1863, or that they traveled to Rozi's parents (mother, really) – perhaps the baby was born prematurely as the result of the trip.

All this set me wondering about the Bauer family's travels: how did they get from Szeged to Békés, from Békés to Békéscsaba – well, that's almost next door – and from there, directly or indirectly, up north to Losonc. How, and especially, when? I asked Judit to try to get me some information on this. She found an 1894 copy of the *Losonc and Neighborhood* weekly that reported on a charity ball of the Jewish community; among those present was Mrs. Zsigmond Bauer. This meant that they lived in Losonc for at least three years before Ilona's marriage, probably longer. Listed among the girls at the ball was also Ilka Bauer – so she called herself Ilka in those days. (I suppose that a twenty-seven-year-old girl would qualify, how about one at thirty-four?)

Alongside researching about Zsigmond's family, Judit also tried to find more information on his father, Herman Markfy (Markussohn) Bauer, and specifically his parentage. We knew that he had been born in Hluboka, in Nyitra County in northern Hungary (now Slovakia). That is a suburb of the town Szenice. There she found records of two men named Markus Bauer, each married and with children (one with a boy and two girls; one with two boys and a girl). Their occupations were noted as impoverished, thus they paid no taxes. Were they really that poor? Who knows? One of them may have been our Markfi Herman Bauer's father. And there were quite a few other Bauers in that town and in the surrounding area.

I soon received more information from Judit about Herman's family. She discovered that in 1847 Markfi Herman Bauer, administrator of the Szeged Jewish community, lived with his wife, five sons and five daughters, and earned three hundred forints per year. She commented that this was an unusually high salary, rivaled only by that of certain doctors – the usual salary being in the range of eighty to one hundred fifty forints.

Judit also found the marriage registers of four of Zsigmond's sisters in Szeged. Interestingly, one married a Leipnik, the other a man whose mother was Leipnik. Judit also found a Vilmos Bauer in Szeged, who died at age twenty-four in 1863 – probably one of Zsigmond's brothers. Vilmos was a medical student. Meanwhile, I found that a Lorincz Markfi Bauer wrote many scholarly articles after the incapacitation of Herman Markfy Bauer (who died of something like Alzheimer's in 1874); this Lorincz was almost certainly another son of Herman. If so, we were lacking the names of only three of Zsigmond's siblings.

*   *   *

I next visited my friend Dr. Peter Hidas. He has an extensive library, which includes a collections of books about the Hungarian Jews of the nineteenth century. He even has a number of items about Losonc of that period, as his ancestors also lived in that town. There, I found a volume of postcards of Losonc from the nineteenth century. One postcard gives us a beautiful aerial view of the Losonc steam mill (an imaginary viewpoint, I assume, as they had neither airplanes nor very advanced cameras in those days). It was a very large complex, with several tall buildings, some connected with bridges; railway lines running between the structures; and a nice residential building clearly visible, beautifully landscaped, with a fountain.

98. Parný mlyn, Lučenec (Kármán , Losoncz, 1910)
A gőzmalom
The steam mill

Both Zsigmond and Andor worked in steam mills... It seemed probable to me that Andor had gotten his job through Zsigmond's contacts – though how did Zsigmond have connections with the Miskolc mill? Judit then discovered that the Deutsch family sold the Losonc mill to the Borsod-Miskolc Steam Mill Inc. only in 1897. Interesting... If Zsigmond managed to get a job for his son at the sister company, that had to have happened early during that fateful year of 1897, as the two companies were unrelated before. Of course, business connections may have existed between them long before that – Zsigmond was surely in a position to know the important people in the business.

Judit offered her own suggestion regarding Zsigmond and Andor's somewhat similar positions in two related steam mills. She thought that rather than Zsigmond getting the job for his son after the acquisition of the Losonc mill, the son might have been working there for some time, and it may have been his suggestion that resulted in the Losonc acquisition. Possible. And if so, what are the implications to Andor's suicide so soon after the transaction?

We were far from solving the mystery of Andor's suicide, but in the meantime Judit succeeded in obtaining the actual marriage register for my grandparents, as well as the death register of my great-grandfather. Until then, we had had to rely on newspaper announcements. The death register confirmed that Zsigmond Bauer lived, and died, on the premises of the Losonc steam mill, as I mentioned above. And it gave the cause of his death as Bright's disease, which today is known as nephritis, a kidney disorder.

The marriage register was more exciting. The most important detail: Ilona Bauer was born, according to the marriage registration, on July 28, 1867. And what does the Békés birth register say? According to it Elinora Bauer, Hebrew name Leah (same as my grandmother's), was born on *the same day*, July 28, 1860! That was enough proof for me: Elinora was indeed Ilona. The poor woman had to lie about her age in order to be able to get married at thirty-seven.

Another interesting detail on my grandparents' marriage register was the names of the witnesses: Dávid Kóhn, plant director, and Béla Albrecht, retired colonel, of Losonc. Retired colonel! This Jewish family must have been truly assimilated to have been so accepted into the leading strata of the town that they would have an obviously non-Jewish retired colonel witnessing their daughter's marriage.

And finally – but no less interesting – the marriage register listed the parents of the young couple. On the bride's side, they are, of course, Zsigmond Bauer and Roza Bauer, née Fellner. Zsigmond is noted as manager of the Losonc steam mill. As for the groom's parents, they are, or rather were, Markus Steiner, of Golden Morava, deceased, and Roza Steiner, née Wasserman, of *Vienna*, deceased!

I've already told you about Rozália's move to Vienna so this won't be a shock to you, but at that point it was a big surprise for me. For a while, I thought that Bernát's mother Rozália had remarried, perhaps in 1881, and moved to Vienna. She was not likely to have moved to Vienna on her own. Was her new husband from Vienna? If so, how did they meet? Or did they only move some time later? And did she take all, or most, of the children with her? She must have taken at least the younger ones.

At this point Judit became busy with other things and I engaged Dr. A.S.H., owner of a Budapest genealogical research firm, to continue the search. It was he who found Rozália's death certificate, which clarified that she had not remarried and which gave us all the information about her children, as I wrote about above.

While Dr. A.S.H.'s firm was searching for this information, they came up with a number of smaller, but still significant items, among them the Zólyom–Losonc–Rima-Sobota railway timetables for 1891 and 1895. I needed those to understand how Bernát and Fanni were able to rush to Zólyom with sick little Jenő and, later, how Bernát and Ilona traveled between Losonc and Rima-Sobota…

In addition, the firm managed to locate the gravesite of my great-grandfather, Zsigmond Bauer, in Losonc – an impressive tomb; they sent me a photo of it. Also, upon my request, they looked at the Miskolc-area newspapers for 1896, to see if they could find anything of importance about the death of Andor. They found two news items in the same newspaper, in consecutive issues four days apart. The first announced the death of Andor Bauer, by his own hand, using a gun, due to money troubles. The second was a strongly worded correction, attesting that the young man had no financial difficulties, rather he had a chronic mental disease, and that he took his own life because he believed that his disease was progressively taking over. There was also an allusion to some unfair treatment by his superiors at work. Incidentally, they also found that Andor was thirty-two years old at the time of his death, and that he was born in Arad, the same town where his mother had been born.

The Bauer Family – 1875

"Mr. Zsigmond Bauer, we talked a while ago about your father, of blessed memory."

"Yes, I remember."

"Can we talk some more? This time about yourself and your family?"

"Sure, if you like."

"Tell me, please, about your work."

"Well, as I said before, I was not cut out for intellectual studies. That was for my father and for my brother Lorincz. But I was good with figures, and so I studied under a bookkeeper, and before long I did some bookkeeping myself, for small firms that my father knew through the synagogue. Later, I got better and better jobs, first in Békés, then in Békéscsaba, where my wife's mother used to live, then she moved back to Arad and got me a good job there. Andor was born in Arad – but soon after that, my father got me a better job in Szeged. That's where both children grew up. Then I had other jobs, more important ones. Eventually I got a really big job at the Losonc steam mill, where I was responsible for all financial affairs. That meant running the company, all but the most mechanical aspects – for that we had an engineer."

"And you did that for some years?"

"For quite a few years, yes. It was a fine job, a good mill. I think that I ran all the business aspects quite well."

"And you actually lived on the premises…"

"I had a nice, large apartment on the second floor of the office building. We had six rooms, one for me and Rozi, one for Eli… Ilona, one for Andor, a salon, a dining room and a hall. We also had indoor plumbing. And a big kitchen. There was also a maid's room – we had two maids."

"Would you say that you were among the wealthiest people in the Losonc Jewish community?"

"Well, I was certainly well off. But there were some that had more money. After all, I had a big job, but it was a salaried position, while Dávid Kóhn, for example, had his own factory, and so did a few others."

"But you had good relations with the, shall we say, leaders, of the community?"

"Good relations? Excellent relations! They were all my friends. Why, Dávid Kóhn was even one of the witnesses at Ilona's wedding."

"I know, along with Colonel Béla Albrecht."

"Ah, so you know that. Yes, I was quite pleased about that. Good man, Albrecht. We had some financial transactions together at one time."

"Nice, aboveboard transactions?"

"Now why would you be asking me that question?"

"Oh, I don't know. I'm curious, that's all."

"Well, I'll tell you that I never had an illegal transaction during my career. I knew the law and made sure that whatever dealing I had, it was always within the permissible limit. Nobody ever accused Zsigmond Bauer of anything illegal."

"All right, I believe you. Now let's talk about Andor."

"Andor."

"Yes, your son."

"I know very well that he is my son."

"Was – he died before you."

"So?"

"Tell me, he also worked at a steam mill, the one in Miskolc. Did you get him that job?"

"There was nothing wrong about helping your own son to get a good job. He worked hard there – he earned his salary and more."

"I am not suggesting that there was anything wrong. But you managed to find that job for him."

"Yes, I knew plenty of people in the business. I knew the managing director of the Miskolc mill – actually they owned several mills. I taught Andor everything about bookkeeping. He had a good head, perhaps not as good as his father, but he could handle the job all right. So they said that they would try, and they did, and it all worked out all right."

"At least for a while."

"What do you mean?"

"Well, the end, of course…"

"That had nothing to do with the job."

"But what *did* it have to do with?"

"I'd rather not talk about that."

"What if I were to ask Ilona? Would she tell me?"

"I don't know. Maybe. That's her business."

Elinora Still Unmarried – 1897

"Good morning, Grandmother."

"Who is talking?"

"Your grandson, Andris."

"Andriskám. Is it really you?"

"Yes, it is, Grandmother. But I am not quite the way you remember me."

"Why?"

"Much time has gone by. I am here from the future, talking with you only in my mind. You see, this is the year 2002."

"Two thousand two?! Then I must be long dead!"

"Yes, I am afraid so. If you were still alive, you would be…"

"One hundred thirty-five years old."

"Yes, or maybe even more."

"What do you mean?"

"We'll talk about that in a moment. You see, the reason I need to talk to you is that I'm writing a book about my family. About my ancestors, on my father's side."

"Our side."

"Yes. Grandmother, will you talk to me about yourself? About your life, especially the early years? Until your marriage?"

"Andriskám, I shall gladly tell you anything you need to know."

"Good, thank you. But Grandmother, I would like to ask for more. I would like you to tell me everything as it really was."

"What do you mean? Why would I lie to you?"

"Because you had to lie all your life and perhaps you got into the habit a little bit."

"???"

"Yes, you see, I had to do an awful lot of research. I had to look up the birth registers and all relevant records. I know about that little bit of, shall we say, adjustment that you had to make before your marriage to Grandfather. Exactly seven years. I know about that."

Silence.

"Grandmother?"

"I don't know what to say."

"Don't be embarrassed. I fully understand that you had to do that in order to get married. It must have been difficult to pretend all your life, making sure that Grandfather would never find out about it. I know the kind of man he was – straightforward. He could not abide with the smallest bit of dishonesty."

"He was like that. But I did not really consider myself dishonest. I loved him and tried to keep him happy."

"What would he have done if he had found out...?"

"I don't know. He would have left the house, perhaps. Or he would have kicked me out. I am sure that I would never have seen him again."

"Yes, that's what I thought. Tell me about it. Tell me about your life."

* * *

I was born as Elinora Bauer, on July 28, 1860, in Békés. My father was Zsigmond Bauer. He was a bookkeeper. My mother was born as Roza Fellner. She was born in Arad, which was later attached to Romania. Her parents were from there, but they moved to Békéscsaba by the time Roza was to be married. My father was living in Békés at the time – those towns were quite close – so they got to know each other and got married.

My mother gave birth to a boy when I was about three, Jakab, but he died after a few days. Two years later, another boy was born, Andor. We lived in Arad at the time. But soon after that, we moved to Szeged.

ILONA AND ANDOR BAUER

My Fellner grandmother did not play an important part in my life after we moved away from Arad. My grandfather died in the same year I was born. I saw grandmother from time to time, a nice lady, but there was nothing special about her. Later she moved to Budapest, and so did her other children, my uncle Manó and my aunt Berta.

The person who was special was my paternal grandfather, Markfy Herman Bauer. He was the head of the Jewish community in Szeged, a very large community. He was in total charge of everything there. He hired and fired rabbis. You may have heard of Rabbi Lipót Löw – it was my grandfather who hired him for Szeged.

But more importantly, he was an extremely well-educated man. He read everything. He knew all the important languages as well as his mother tongue, which was German. And he wrote scholarly articles, about all kinds of subjects – theology, etymology, a dictionary, commerce, politics, and so on. I was fortunate in that when I was still quite small, six or seven, my parents were able to move back to Szeged and throughout my formative years I lived in my grandparents' house. In a sense, it was he who brought me up. He taught me everything. I never went to school. There was never any point. I always knew so much more than any teacher, it would have been a waste of time.

That is not to say that I had been totally uninfluenced by my parents. My mother was always there, looking after me and my little brother. She and her mother-in-law, my grandmother, when we lived in Arad, got along very well and ran the household together. Then, in Szeged, my father was not so close to us, perhaps because of his father. But later, when I was growing up, when my grandfather was no longer with us, I did have long talks with Father. He had always felt that, somehow, he did not measure up to the family standard. That was not true. He may not have known as many languages as Grandfather or I did – we both read and wrote and spoke fluently in eight languages – but he did know German and French and, of course, Hungarian, and he was so good at arithmetic and business knowledge. He did indeed help some of his brothers and his brothers-in-law with business problems later in life.

Unfortunately, my education at Grandfather's hand came to an early end. By the time I was twelve, he started to forget things and behave differently. He slowed down and gradually became incompetent. Indeed, he had to be looked after like a baby in a year or so, and before my fourteenth birthday we laid him in his final resting place.

After that, I was forced to continue my education without any help. I read ferociously. There was a very good library in Szeged and I may have read every book they had there, certainly all foreign books, for there was no important foreign literature that I allowed myself to miss. Of course I read it all in the original language. I have always considered translations as abominations, butchery of the author's noble work. The one language that Grandfather did not teach me, Russian, gave me the most trouble, but eventually I mastered it – there were too many great Russian novels; they deserved my thorough familiarity with their language.

I read and read, but I did not do much else. Oh, I did go to the society events, of course, balls and concerts – but music never meant very much to me. My parents bought me a baby grand piano and I hated it. So did they. It was a mistake to have bought it. They never insisted that I should learn to play. But it was expected of me to attend many an afternoon at somebody's house, where, say, the daughter of the house was singing Schubert songs, while perhaps a famous pianist accompanied her and later played Chopin or Beethoven, when the girl rested. Frankly, I detested those events, but as I say, I had to go. Mother insisted and also Grandmother. How would I meet eligible young men otherwise, they demanded to know. I dreamed of a truly eligible young man, intelligent, well-read, sensitive, caring, perhaps even my intellectual superior – somebody like Grandfather must have been in his youth – but I did not find him at the afternoon teas and I did not find him at the balls, nor on the promenade or at the theater – yes, we had theater, too – and after a while I was beginning to wonder, where was I going to find this young man.

As you can expect, I was not the only one wondering. My mother started to worry. In Szeged, there were college students. There was kind of a college – really, a branch of the Kolozsvár university – and some of the students were Jewish. My mother invited a few of them to our house, but nothing came of it. I did not think much of any of them. Then there was the flood, in 1879. For two years, there were no social events, no culture, nothing but survival, until the city got rebuilt. By then I was twenty-one, a good age to marry. But I was too choosy. If they spoke no languages other than German and Hungarian, if they did not know at least the most important poems of Musset and Goethe, Shelley and Byron by heart, if they had not read all the novels of Hugo and Stendhal, and the newest works of Tolstoy, at least in translation, I despised them and made no secret of my views.

When I was twenty-three, we moved to a smaller town. My father had been offered a good job there, but the move certainly did not contribute to my marriage prospects. Gradually, the subject of the conversation turned to my future more and more. It started coming up at least a couple times a week, which nearly drove me out of my mind. I suppose that if my grandfather had still been alive, I could have stayed with him, but he was long gone by then, and my grandmother was old and sick – both my grandmothers, really – so I had no choice but to live with my parents.

Eventually, I had come to realize also that while as a young girl I may have been cute, I was certainly not beautiful. Pretty, perhaps, intelligent-looking, but that was unimportant. Sometimes I wondered if I was ugly. Looking at old pictures, now I know that I was not – indeed I was quite charming, but in those days I did not particularly enjoy looking in the mirror. Then I thought that I was plain, later even a little on the heavy side. I did not see anything particularly attractive or desirable in my features.

I suppose that earlier I was just not sufficiently interested in young men to lower my standards, but of course it was a mistake. Now I knew that I had two choices: get married to somebody my intellectual inferior, or try to find a job, a series of jobs as a governess to insufferable children. Perhaps save enough money to be able to live in poverty after my jobs were over. No, obviously, I had to get married.

But we were living in a small town. My mother engaged a marriage broker, more than one, at least three, over the years. She recommended various young men for me. Now I longed for the college students that I had met earlier. These men that came to meet with us were just stupid. Well, I suppose "stupid" is not quite correct. They knew certain things; they were typically salesmen, merchants – they must have known their business, their merchandise, their customers – but frankly, I was just not interested in those things. I knew that I must not be so choosy, and my parents reminded me of my promise to them, that I would accept anybody reasonably intelligent, but did that mean that I had to give myself to the first village idiot that came along? Yes, I know that I am exaggerating, but that is how I felt. And I am grateful to my parents that they did not insist, did not force me into an unsatisfactory marriage.

In a way, both my parents were a little intimidated by me. I was so much better educated than either of them. Strange, I looked down on both of them a little, yet when I came to meet the young businessmen who had jobs similar to those of my father's, I came to realize how clever, how knowledgeable *he* was. Why, I could talk to father about anything. If I mentioned a book by Dostoyevsky, or perhaps Dickens, that he had not known, on my recommendation he would get hold of a Hungarian or German translation and read it, then we could talk about it. He was not uneducated by any means. My mother also liked to read poetry, even if usually in translation. My little brother? He was not the smartest of children. Frankly, I never paid much attention to him. He went to an ordinary high school, not a gymnasium, and after that, my father taught him the intricacies of bookkeeping.

Other than the failed matchmaking attempts, nothing much happened during the next ten years. Where we lived, access to good books was somewhat limited. There was a public library, but it was not very well stocked. Sometimes I had to travel to Szeged or even Budapest, to visit libraries and bookstores. At other times, we ordered books by mail.

Then, in 1892 – or was it 1893? – my father got a big job up north, in Losonc. He was to be the head of all financial and administrative operations at a large steam mill. He was very pleased – we all were. Also, Losonc was not an insignificant town. It had many cultural events and well-to-do Jewish people, and we thought that perhaps there would be somebody suitable for me there.

But there was a little problem. By the time we moved there, I was already thirty-two years old. Not quite the young girl that most eligible men were looking for.

My father made a most important decision. We shall move to Losonc and I shall arrive there as a young woman of twenty-five!

We were all shocked. My mother smiled and said yes. YES! My little brother said nothing, he smirked. And I walked out of the room, slammed the door as if deeply insulted. But I knew that Father was right – we had to pretend, or I would never marry.

It was not easy. For one thing, how would I refer to Andor? In the Hungarian language I could say "sibling," but I could not say "brother" – there is no such word. Well, there is, but it is not commonly used. Only "older brother" or "younger brother." From then on, he was no longer "younger brother," but "older brother." That was difficult for me and for him, too – of course he now had to call me his "younger sister." I was afraid that he would let me down, but he did not; I suppose my father had threatened him with the most severe punishments.

So there I was in Losonc, living in a nice apartment in the steam mill (I would have preferred to live in a more elegant part of the town, but I was told not to complain). I helped Mother around the apartment, just to learn how to run a household, how to manage the maids. We went to the theater, we went to balls, we walked on the promenade, but still no husband for me. Of course, twenty-five was already a bit old, and if they knew… And then again, I was not beautiful, perhaps not even so pretty anymore.

But then! Four or five years after our move to Losonc, when we had already given up all hope, a marriage broker came to us, all excited, with great news. Not far from Losonc, in a somewhat smaller town called Rima-Sobota, a young Jewish man was suddenly widowed. He had a small daughter and needed a mother for the child. I made a grimace, so now not only shall I have an under-wear hawker for a husband, but his child to boot. No, no, the marriage broker assured me. This man is not a merchant, he *is* an intellectual, just what I had been looking for. An intellectual? I pricked up my ears. What are you talking about?

Well, it turned out that the young man in question was working as a clerk at the law court in Rima-Sobota. He was well educated, his prospects at the court for promotion were excellent, he was well respected and even loved, he was sensitive, kind, and most important of all, he had a pensioned position. That meant that we would be well looked after all our lives, while he works and when he retires.

This sounded very good. My mother was enthusiastic. Sure, get the young man here as soon as possible. How old would he be? Just right for the young lady, she says, thirty-four years old. She had a smile on her face, a smile or a smirk, I was not sure. She may have suspected something; after all, she was in the business of knowing young and not so young women, but it did not matter.

A man of thirty-four. I was thirty-seven, but called myself thirty. Well, it could work.

The marriage broker seemed to read my mind, for she added, "Try to make yourself look as young as possible. You see," she explained, "Mr. Steiner (that was the young man's name) has just lost his wife. And she was twenty-two when she died! They had been married five years; they had three children, but only the oldest lived, a little girl now four and a half. So he may find it hard to think of marriage with a thirty-year-old woman, after burying a wife of twenty-two. But then, he does need a wife." There were other women around, younger ones, but she had thought of me right away – we should grab this opportunity…

Of course we did. We asked the woman to arrange for the young man to come and visit us the following Sunday. This was not the first time a prospective suitor was invited to chocolate and pastry on a Sunday, we had a well-rehearsed routine, but this time I made a special point of prettying myself to the utmost and to be pleasant and charming, intelligent but not overbearingly so. Father and Mother were there, too, and of course the marriage broker, to smooth things if some difficulty arose. My little brother – no, older brother – came in briefly, to say hello. He was quite a good-looking young man by then, thirty-two years old. He too was unmarried, nobody knew why, but I think he had loved a girl once, hopelessly, for a long time, perhaps he still loved her.

So Bernát Steiner arrived with the marriage broker.

Bernát Is Introduced to Ilona – 1897

Bernát kissed the hands of both ladies. They asked him to sit by the round dining room table, they all sat around. He looked at them shyly, while they all smiled with encouragement.

"Well, Mr. Steiner, I am told that you work at the court," started Zsigmond.

"Yes, sir. Well, the law court. I am not trying to be pedantic, but there is a court, a district court, and a law court in Rima-Sobota."

"Ah. The law court. I suppose that is the highest of them all?"

"Yes, sir, the highest."

"And what do you do there, may I ask?"

"Well, my title is clerk, but essentially I do everything. All administrative work. The judges are not very good at administration. All judgments must be recorded, copied, sent to Budapest, sent to the litigants and to the accused, if it's a criminal case, and to all lawyers. Then summonses need to be sent out, sessions scheduled, witnesses called and paid, judges' vacations to be arranged, all salaries to be paid…"

"So you are busy, I can see that. And may I ask, who is your superior officer? One of the judges?"

"No, it is the deputy administrative director."

"Do you like him? Do you get along well with him?"

"Yes, he is the one who hired me five years ago, Mr. Felszeghy. A very good man. It is not easy to get a job like that for a Jew, but he seems to have no prejudices at all."

"And who is on overall charge?"

"That would be Dr. Hertzstuber. The law court director."

Zsigmond nodded. "Yes, I have met the man. Friend of a friend."

Rozália took over the questioning. She spoke in German. "Tell me, Mr. Steiner, I hear you have a small child?"

"Yes, Madam, a little girl, Rózsika. She is not yet five. A very sweet girl," Bernát responded, also in German.

"Is she at home now, with the maid?"

"No, ma'am. After my wife died, I sent the maid away and Rózsika stays with her grandparents. My poor wife's parents, for my own parents are both dead. Fanni's parents live in Zólyom."

"Very sad about your wife. How many years had you been married be-fore…?"

"Five years. She was very young when we married, only seventeen."

Ilona observed this exchange with a bemused expression, how her parents were interviewing this young man, prospective husband to her, as if to find out if he were suitable for the job. You would think that they were not at all desperate for such a son-in-law. For of course she knew that there was nothing they would have wanted more than this man, Bernát Steiner, to marry their daughter. And how did she feel about him? She asked herself and was surprise by her own thought: *I would love to jump into his lap and hug him.* He was such a sweet man, just as he said his daughter was.

It was time for her to speak; up to then, Bernát had hardly looked at her, as was seemly. Yet she wanted him to look at her. She thought that she looked very pretty. She wore a deep blue moiré dress with a pleated bodice, the long straight skirt reaching down to her ankles. She had chosen this dress because it emphasized her narrow waist – well, perhaps no longer so narrow, but made narrow by the corset. She had a white *fichu* decorating her neckline. She wore two delicate long earrings with small sapphires. She did not want to overdo the jewelry, not to frighten the young man away with her desire for luxury. Neither did she really have such desires; normally it was her mother who reminded her to wear this piece of jewelry or that. Her mother, in turn, was dressed in a very subdued manner, in a black silk dress enhanced by a flowered cashmere shawl, her gray hair put in a neat bun held firmly by two silver-handled hair pins. She also wore only a wedding band and a thick, long gold necklace with a clock pendant.

Let *me* interview him, too, she thought. "Mr. Steiner, is there a cultural life in Rima-Sobota?"

"Well, yes, miss, though perhaps not as lively as here in Losonc. But we do have an amateur theater group and from time to time visiting theater compa-nies perform. And there are concerts, and we have a good public library, lots of good books."

"Foreign books, too?"

"Yes, Miss Ilona. Many foreign books. Do you speak foreign languages?'

"A few, yes." She hid a smile. "How about you?"

"Not really. I learned French and Greek and Latin at school, but I would not really claim to be fluent in any of them." He did not mention Slovak; up there everybody spoke Slovak.

"Do you go to the theater?"

"When they have something interesting, we used to go."

"But perhaps you read plays, in book form?"

"I do, Miss Ilona, sometimes."

"Call me Ilka, everybody does."

"Yes, Miss Ilka."

"What do you think of Schiller's plays?" Ilona noticed the angry looks on her parents' faces, but she persisted. "Or have you read them?"

"Not all four that I know of, but I have read two of them. I really liked *Kabale und Liebe*, and when *Don Carlos* reached our library, I think about two years ago, I read that, too. Very exciting work, I would like to see it performed."

"Oh, but it was performed here last year. You could have come over…"

Bernát shook his head sadly. "Not last year, miss. That was about the time when I lost my wife."

"Oh, of course. I'm sorry."

The marriage broker put in a word. "Mr. Steiner has a well-stocked library of his own. Not perhaps as large as yours, Mr. Bauer, but then he is quite a bit younger. I am sure that the collection will grow with time."

As if it were Zsigmond who had built their library and not his daughter.

Zsigmond took up the questioning again. "How is the religious life in Rima-Sobota? Is there a nice Neolog synagogue? I can see that you are not Orthodox, or are you?" Bernát shook his head. Once he took off his hat, he was not even wearing a *kappedli*. "But you do go sometimes, do you?"

"Actually, sir, there is a very nice Neolog synagogue. There is an Orthodox one also, but I almost never go there. I attend the Neolog services, but not as often as I should. I don't go every Saturday, only on the more important holidays, perhaps six or eight times a year."

Zsigmond smiled. "Well, that's more than I do. I go only on *Rosh Hashono* and *Yom Kippur*, I'm afraid."

The maid served hot chocolate, *kugelhof* and pastry with whipped cream. They all ate and the conversation became a little easier. Zsigmond asked Bernát about various Jewish people in Rima-Sobota, business people who attended the synagogue. Zsigmond knew many of them by person. He made a mental note to talk to them, discreetly, about Steiner – not that he needed much checking. Zsigmond was a good judge of people; he knew that he was facing a decent, honest, straightforward man. But still, you can never tell…

The door opened and a young man came in. He was introduced to Bernát as Andor, Ilka's older brother. They shook hands and then Andor quickly excused himself. "Father, Mother, I am due to meet some friends. I just came in to say hello."

"Won't you have a chocolate with us? Or some pastry?" his mother asked.

"No, thank you, I would love to, but I must…" He left the second half of the sentence unspecified. As Bernát was to find on two subsequent visits, Andor was always a little vague. After some more polite comments, he left.

Bernát sensed that it was time for him, too, to take his leave. He thanked his hosts politely. Zsigmond told him, "Listen, your boss's boss, Dr. Hertzstuber. As I said, we have a common friend. If you like, I can put in a good word for you – it may help speed your promotion."

Bernát did not know how to respond to this. "Well, thank you, but I don't think there is any need…"

"You never know. Somebody might just sneak in ahead of you. It never hurts to have connections."

It would not have been polite to reject such an offer out of hand, but Bernát bristled at the suggestion. He did not want a connection. He worked hard and well, and he was sure that his work was being noticed and appreciated. Still, he nodded, whether in agreement or simply taking his leave. He kissed the hands of the ladies and left with the marriage broker.

They were only a few minutes away from the apartment when the marriage broker asked Bernát excitedly, "What did you think? How did you like the young lady?" She pointedly did not say "girl" so as not to provoke a negative response.

"Very nice, pleasant."

"Just nice? Pleasant? Surely she is more than that. Would you not consider her something special?"

Bernát thought. "Yes, you could call her special, I suppose. Very intelligent. Certainly more intelligent than most other young women that I have met."

"I would say that she is the smartest young woman that I have ever encountered. She has the education and the brains. But she also inherited lots of practical good sense from her father."

Bernát nodded. He didn't know if this was a positive thing, but after all, why not?

"And she is very pretty," the woman continued, "and charming. The sort of woman who adds a layer of sophistication to the career of any man. Don't pretend, Mr. Steiner, that you will advance fast on the basis of your merits alone. You do need connections, like Mr. Bauer suggested, and you do need a clever and charming and elegant wife. A loving wife," she added quickly; she knew her customers.

Bernát did not reply. He needed time to think; yet when pressed by the marriage broker, he admitted that he liked Miss Bauer, thought highly of her and even of her family (with some reservations), and was quite willing to meet them, meet her, again.

Ilona – 1897

Yes, we liked Bernát right away, all of us, even Andor. Clearly, he was a nice, intelligent, honest, kind, lovable man. He needed a woman's touch – his clothes were very proper, but perhaps a bit unfashionable. I liked the shape of his moustache, but his coat lapel had gone out of style some years before. We did not think that he felt quite at ease in society, or even spent much time at events; his poor wife must have been a very simple soul. I made up my mind that I would like to be his second wife.

Of course, there were many questions. First, there was the little girl; would I like her? Would she like me? Would her grandparents like me? If they did not, they would influence the girl against me, which could be disastrous.

Then, the question of the lie. The big lie about my age. I could continue to pretend, my whole family could, but what if somebody made a mistake one day? And a practical matter: the local rabbi, if we were to marry, might insist on some document from Békés, showing that I was born a proper Jewish girl. I was, of course, but *when*? And not only the rabbi, now it was worse than that. In the last two years, the state had also been insisting on keeping vital records; you had to register every wedding at city hall, something like a second wedding, with all the documents, again! What if the document would also specify the year when I was born? Surely that would be the end of the affair.

And, of course, all this on the assumption that Bernát Steiner liked me, that he would want to see me again and again, that he would want to marry me. We had a long way to go yet. But I decided, then and there, that I would do my utmost to bring this thing to a satisfactory conclusion. For there was no doubt that it would be satisfactory to all parties concerned. I would be married, my future would be assured; Bernát would have a good wife in all respects, or almost all (for I was not sure that when it came to that most important aspect of the marriage, the intimate man-woman relations, I would be able to behave as he would expect me. His first wife probably did, but I thought that I might not have that something within me; only time would tell). And the little girl would have a good mother – at least I would make the most serious effort to assure that.

Well, Bernát came to visit again. My parents left us alone in the room for half an hour. He talked more easily. I encouraged him to call me Ilka, no need to insist on "miss." I called him Bernát and made up my mind that when we married, I would call him Berci.

On the third visit, we talked a lot about his daughter, Rózsika. I told him that I would very much like to meet the little girl. That was difficult, because she was then living with her grandparents in Zólyom. We were thinking about ways to arrange a meeting, but pretty soon it became obvious that such a subject was much more sensitive than we both realized at first; after all, it presupposed a certain relation between the two of us. How would Bernát introduce me to his former in-laws? As his fiancée? I was nothing of the sort – yet. So I quickly changed the subject, but hoped secretly that soon our relationship might become more defined.

And defined it became. Of course, the marriage broker was there in the background. She would not let either party forget the object of these visits – not that we were likely to forget. So on the fourth visit, when we were alone, Bernát stood up and asked me, "Ilka, if you have no objection, I would like to ask your father for your hand in marriage." It did not come out easily from his mouth or heart; he blushed. But I had known the proposal was coming and I was ready for it. Right away, I stood too, went over to him, held his hands, looked into his eyes, smiled, and bravely kissed him. He kissed me back too – he was a good kisser. We both smiled and he took a box out of his pocket. The ring. He had bought it the previous day. I was pleased about that; I would not have liked to receive the ring of his poor dead wife; let her daughter inherit that.

So I opened the door; my parents were sitting just outside, as if waiting for some development (which, of course, they were). I called them in and as they came in beaming, Bernát stood and made his formal proposal to my father. He hugged him, my mother did too. It was done. Next day Father sent the money to the marriage broker.

But, as I said before, that was just the beginning of our difficulties.

*   *   *

I have not yet mentioned the dowry. Of course, the dowry plays an important part in any marriage. My dowry was quite sizable; that was, I assume, one of the first things that the marriage broker told Bernát and to any other potential suitor.

The dowry did not exist.

Oh, it had existed at one time. It was deposited in a very solid bank account. But I was not married, the years went by, and from time to time there was need for money, so my father borrowed from the dowry, fully intending to replace it soon. Eventually, the account was depleted.

Don't worry, my father assured me when the situation with Bernát started to look promising, he was going to replace the entire amount within two weeks or so. And you know, by the time I got married – for of course I did, eventually – the amount was indeed replaced, or most of it. Bernát never quite understood why it was only three-quarters of what was promised him, but he wasn't greedy; it was more money than he had ever had. He was told that later the missing quarter would be turned over, which never happened. As I say, for Bernát a contract was a contract, but he was not going to sue his own father-in-law, so he ended up in quite a bit of confusion over this.

But, I wondered, how could my father rebuild a large portion of that account within a few months? He must have sold something, some important investment that he held; he did not discuss such matters with me or, indeed, with my mother. I think that he did discuss them with Andor.

About a year earlier, Andor had started working in Miskolc, also at a steam mill. My father knew everybody in the business, so he used his connections to secure a good job in the financial area of the large Miskolc mill. Later that year, due to some favorable reports prepared by Andor in Miskolc, it was decided that the Miskolc mill, which owned several other steam mills in the northeastern part of the country, would acquire the Losonc mill, where my father worked. That was very advantageous for everyone concerned. I was not familiar with all the arrangements – obviously it was none of my business – but I could not help overhearing Father and Andor discussing many of the details. Lots of moneys were involved; the arrangements took place just a couple of months before my engagement.

Then something horrible happened. One day, my father received a telegram from Miskolc. It said, "Regret to inform Andor committed suicide stop. Come quickly for funeral arrangements stop. Schoenfeld." Moritz Schoenfeld was Andor's boss in the accounting department.

We were devastated. We got on the train right away to Miskolc – it was a long ride because of the necessary transfer and waiting at the stations. We arrived there the next day and went to a hotel. Father wanted to go to the mill alone. He talked to Schoenfeld. I don't know what was said, but he came back very angry and worried. He slammed the newspaper down on the table.

> **Young Man Commits Suicide**. Sensational suicide happened just as the paper was going to the press. Andor Bauer, young and highly talented officer of the steam mill, committed suicide tonight at five thirty. He shot himself in the head and died immediately. He committed this act due to financial difficulties.

We looked at each other and did not know what to say. Father went out again to send telegrams, I think for money, lots of money. Then he went to see the rabbi.

The rabbi would not bury Andor in the cemetery proper, because of his suicide. It took Father another day before he managed to arrange everything. He assured the rabbi that this was no suicide; Andor was sick, mentally imbalanced. He showed the rabbi the article that was to appear in the paper the next day, explaining about poor Andor's health.

The article that appeared had this to say:

> **The Suicide of Andor Bauer**. On Thursday afternoon around six o'clock Andor Bauer, young steam mill officer, spilled his life that he had just barely begun to know, with a foolish revolver bullet. The public opinion, this insatiable moloch, is trying to solve, in different versions, that sphynx-like riddle the freshly covered grave now hides forever. With irresponsible thoughtlessness rumors take wing everywhere, implying that monetary difficulties prompted him to commit his horrible act. The respect for the dead commands us to repudiate this untrue report and to state that he committed his fatal act in a state of mental disorder stemming from his excessive neurotic illness. This great illness had tortured him through many long years; despite which fact he was an exemplary, conscientious and dutiful officer who worked from early in the morning till late in the evening, if only to forget his grave and incurable disease. Lately he developed the mistaken belief that the paralysis was progressively taking hold, and his fear of this, to which we may add the excessive strictness of his superiors and the injustices to which he was subjected – put the revolver into his hand. This is the truth, the pure fact. Let peace – for which his tired body had longed for so long – hover over his grave!

We buried poor Andor in Miskolc.

We did not talk about it on the way back. Not one word about Andor, or anything else. Just sat in the train quietly, each of us deep in his or her own thoughts. I was thinking, Andor never suffered any mental disorder that I had ever seen or heard of. No, of course Father had to manipulate the newspaper announcement for the rabbi to bury Andor properly. I think that he paid big money there, very big money. But surely the burial was not the only reason. Bernát! Would Bernát have married me, if he knew of some financial irregularity in the family? What was it, anyway? Cards? Horses? Something about the books in the office? Perhaps a combination of those things? Whatever it was, it had to be denied! Also, of course, if it was something about the office, my father himself might have been involved, or at least such a rumor could develop – his own job could have been jeopardized! Then there was the public opinion in Losonc; we could not really live there with whispers and innuendos. And those would, again, get back to Bernát. As it turned out, the marriage was saved, Father's job was saved, but the rumors could not be stemmed; I think Father's early death was a result of those.

Later, much later, I tried to talk to Father about the reason, what really happened, why did Andor do it. He would say nothing. I prodded. My speculations may have been mistaken. It could have been something simple, something personal, like an unhappy love affair. I did not think so; I would have heard of it, known something of the situation. Then perhaps something unnatural about him? Or his physical health? Or was it really the business? Something to do with the company buyout? Something about money? My dowry? Had somebody lost a lot of money somewhere, on something? Did Andor gamble? Did Father gamble? Did he cover up for Father? Did he die for Father? Did he die for me?

I think Father knew, but he would not say a word.

Mother and I never talked about it. I suppose that she must also have been asking Father; I suppose that he would not tell her anything, either.

The most important consideration was Bernát. Andor killed himself in May, on the sixth. We were supposed to get engaged a week later and get married by early June. What should we do now?

Of course Bernát kept asking about Andor. He really wanted to know why Andor would kill himself. He knew that the mental illness was just a necessary ruse, to provide for a proper burial. I kept hinting about some girl, even though I knew of no such girl at all. I feared that the real reason was worse, something that Bernát must never find out. He never did; neither did I. If Father knew, he took his secret to the grave. A very early grave, for after this it was downhill for him. He died only two years later…

My parents were concerned that Bernát would change his mind. On the last day of the *shiva*, we asked him to come over to our place and meet with the Losonc rabbi, who would conduct the service. Ostensibly, the object of the meeting was to get the rabbi's "official" view as to what was to be done in a case like this. But the rabbi knew that my parents were desperate to marry me off, as I was no longer so young. He thought that I was already thirty years old. If he only knew! So he gave his opinion, to the effect that the living always come before the dead. My mother assured us that this was what Andor would have wanted, for us to go ahead with the engagement, with the wedding. So eventually it was decided to arrange a very quiet engagement on May 31, just for family and two or three friends, and then hold a proper though not too ostentatious wedding on the fourth of July.

I was worried about our little lie. What if the rabbi asked for a birth certificate? Or the city authorities? We would have to send away for one to Békés, and the result could be disastrous. But Father assured me. "Don't worry," he said. "The matter is well in hand." And so it was. The rabbi did not ask for any document. The city did, and Father handed them some paper. They looked at it and were satisfied. I asked him afterwards what it was, and he told me not to worry about it, it was all right.

The wedding, then. Bernát came over on Friday. We went to the city hall and arranged the appropriate steps. They said that we were now formally married, but of course we were not; we had not yet had the synagogue ceremony. That came on the Sunday. There were over a hundred guests there. I had a lovely white wedding gown, full of lace and frills, but my mother was dressed all in black, unusual for such an occasion; everyone knew why. Bernát wore formal wear; Father helped him order it at his own tailor. After the service, they were all invited to our place for some food. There was, of course, not to be any dancing. I did not mind; I hated gypsy music and the only other kind available, "salon music," was so boring. Bernát detested dancing, in any case.

And then, it was time to move to Rima-Sobota. A cart was already hired for the trunks, portmanteau, suitcases, boxes containing my quite sizable trousseau and many, many books, more than half of the library that we had in Losonc. Also, quite a bit of furniture that I was to take with me. We rode in an elegant carriage hired by Father as his last gesture. Earlier, before Andor, there was some talk of his hiring for us, or perhaps even buying for himself, one of those new automobiles, but such extravagance was now out of place. Our tearful good-byes had more to do with Andor than with my departure, for I was not going far; we knew that we should see each other every few weeks.

Well, let me stop my story right here. We were married, we loved each other and we lived happily ever after. Actually, we didn't, but that's neither here nor there.

Planning to Get Married – 1897

"Grandfather, you were kind enough to talk about your first marriage before, how you married Fanni and what happened after."

"Yes, they were good years at first, but afterwards, unfortunately…"

"I know. But then, next year, you married Ilona. If you don't mind, I would like to ask you to talk about that. After all, she was my grandmother."

"Ilona. Of course, I shall talk about her. She was a good wife to me. We were married for forty-three years."

"Tell me about her."

"Well, after poor Fanni died, I had a big problem with Rózsika. For a while, Lipót and Amália took her – you know, her grandparents. They were devastated by Fanni's death. So was I. But they were older – perhaps it was even more difficult for them, I don't know. In any case, it was good for them to have Rózsika around. But that was clearly not a permanent solution."

"No, I suppose you wanted her with you."

"I did, of course. And a child cannot be left permanently with her grandparents. What if they get sick, or worse? As it were, Amália and Lipót were not the healthiest people even then. So I had to find a new wife."

"How did you feel about that?"

"Feel? Feeling did not come into it. This was something that I had to do. It was my duty."

"Yes, but a wife is not something like a servant. There is a certain personal relationship between husband and wife, and you loved Fanni so much, you told me."

"I know. But I thought that such things would eventually evolve by the nature of the things. I married Fanni on my own, because we fell in love, but remember that most people marry somebody chosen for them by their parents, yet they usually end up loving each other."

"So you thought that after a while you and your next wife would love each other the same way as you and Fanni loved…?"

"The same way? No, that would have been impossible. I knew that. I was a realist. But I thought that if I found a good woman, then there would be a good household with enough love for everybody, even if not the kind of love that Fanni and I had."

"And did it work out that way? No, I am getting ahead of myself. You were going to tell me about how you found Ilona."

"A marriage broker found her for me. She came to me from Losonc. She had heard about my tragedy and said that I must get married again. I knew that. And she knew of a wonderful girl in Losonc, just ideal for me."

"What else did she say about her?"

"That she was not as young as my Fanni was, she was already thirty, and she explained the reason for her not marrying earlier."

"What was the reason?"

"That she was too choosy. That her grandfather was the famous Markfy Herman Bauer, of Szeged, that she got most of her education from that man, that she set her sights too high and could not find anybody her intellectual equal."

"Whew. What did you think of that?"

"I thought that it would be nice to live with an intelligent woman, but what if she was too intelligent, well above my level, and would look down on me?"

"That's what I thought. But you decided to go and visit them anyway, make your own judgment about the young lady."

"Exactly. I went and I liked what I saw. She was very intelligent, but also nice, kind and beautiful. What more should a man want? I thought that if this girl, this woman would marry me, I would be a very lucky man."

"Intellectual superiority notwithstanding? Or you were sure that your intellect and education were at par with hers?"

"Hmm. Education, perhaps not. Except that, like me, she never went to formal schools. She learned everything from her grandfather and later, from books she read. Mostly novels. Novels, plays, poetry. There were many areas where I was better educated."

"Not languages or literature, for sure."

"No, but arithmetic – though she certainly picked up a good knowledge of numbers from her father – and geometry, perhaps geography. I knew as much history as she did. And of course, I knew a lot about law, the judicial system which is somewhat complicated, and she only had vague ideas about that."

"Ah, yes, life experience."

"Come to think of that, I knew about butchery, too."

"Butchery?"

"Yes, after high school, I worked for some years at my uncle Samuel's butchery in Szelezsény. But don't take me seriously, I'm being flippant. I would never brag about a thing like that."

"Did you then have to brag about your mastery of this subject or that, sometimes?"

"No, never. Ilona never flaunted her knowledge, her sophistication. In practical things we were equals, and life is really a series of practical things. When would we get involved in an intellectual competition?"

"So you were never afraid of her, intimidated by her?"

"Well, truth to be told, I was, at first. I certainly tried to avoid discussing books and poetry, the intricacies of the French and Italian languages and such matters. But there was no need. We had so many practical things to talk about."

"When she first moved in with you, after the wedding, I suppose there would have been hundreds of things to discuss, about the domestic arrangements."

"Yes, about the furniture and the daily routine. About servants, because at that time I had no servants at all. She wanted to hire two or three, I wanted just one. But we ended up with a maid and a cook. That was a suitable arrangement."

"You could afford two servants?"

"Yes, because it was not only my salary. She brought a sizable dowry with her. We put that in the bank and used the interest, which was enough for additional things. Not only for a cook, but we soon moved to a large house."

"Of course, you needed the room, for Rózsika and then for expected other children."

"Ye-e-es. More or less. You see, one of the first things we decided, soon after the wedding, was that much as Ilona would like to see Rózsika, we were not going to bring her home for a little while yet. Not until we got used to each other, so as to create a harmonious, pleasant home for her."

"You were worried about how she would like her new stepmother?"

"It was more complicated than that. Once we decided that we should marry, Ilona had an idea…"

Ilona's Idea – 1897

They were sitting in the salon, just the two of them. Bernát was wondering if it might be appropriate to try to get hold of Ilona's hand, but decided against it. This was soon after she and her family had accepted his proposal.

"Tell me about Rózsika," Ilka asked him.

"Rózsika. A sweet, smiling little girl. She is so loving, so warm-hearted. She has dark hair, like yours, but very curly. There is always a smile on her face."

"I suppose it was horrible when she found out that her mother…"

"You know, she never actually found out about that. At first, we kept her in the maid's room, who told her not to come into the bedroom because there was a contagious illness that she might catch. Then, when the grandparents arrived, they hugged her and kissed her, but still would not let her into the bedroom, and suddenly we decided that it would be better for her not to be told about her mother's death. She was too little, only four years old."

Ilona was speechless at first. Then thoughts rushed through her mind. "And then she has never been told? To this day?"

"No, never. When she asks about coming home, they tell her that she has to wait until her mother gets better. To tell you the truth, I did not much like this. I prefer to tell the truth, no matter how difficult. But her grandparents thought that the child should be spared the painful truth until she gets a little bigger."

"I think they were right about that."

"You do?"

"Yes, why harm a little girl? There is plenty of time to learn about something like that. Perhaps even now she should not be told."

"But she must be told now. Surely she should come home and live with us."

"Yes, of course. She shall live with us as soon as possible."

"But then, she will see that her mother is no longer there, that there is a new wife, a stepmother."

"Must she?"

"What do you mean?"

"She was four years old when they took her away from home. About a year has gone by. Do you think she still remembers exactly what her mother looked like? I think not."

It was time for Bernát to be dumbfounded. "Do you think… Are you proposing…"

"Why not tell her that her mother has now recovered, she is healthy again, let her come home and I will hug her and kiss her and she will think that I am her real mother?"

Bernát had never heard a more shocking suggestion. He stood up and walked around the room, speechless.

Ilka saw that she might have made a mistake. She could not take it back, but hastened to improve it. "Look, Berci (I may call you Berci, may I?), think of the little girl, think of Rózsika. Why hurt her, why cause her so much pain? She's been spared the pain until now, why ruin the whole effort just because of us? It's not fair to her. Let her be happy."

Bernát came back to the table, but still stood. "But that would be a lie! How can we let her live year after year in a lie, in a situation that is just not true?"

"Because it will be good for her. She will have a loving mother, not a step-mother. She will be happy, and so shall all of us be."

"And when would you tell her? Never?"

"No, not never. Sooner or later she should be told, when she is big enough and strong enough to take it. We would have to judge her strength year by year, and we should know when the time was ripe for the truth."

Bernát shook his head with doubt. He did not want to reject the sugges-tion outright, even though every part of his mind objected to it. Yet who knew, perhaps there was some merit in what Ilona was saying. She saw that she could strengthen her position.

"Look, Berci, I have an idea. Let us travel to Zólyom and meet the grand-parents, but not yet Rózsika. Could you arrange that?"

"Yes, I suppose I could. But why?"

"Let's ask their opinion. Maybe they will see it the same way as I do."

"I doubt it. What you are saying is that they should pretend that you are their Fanni. How could they agree to that?"

"If it was in the interest of Rózsika, they might. Their Fanni, God rest her soul, is gone for a year now. But Rózsika is around, she is important for them. I think that I can explain this to the two old people. Are they old, by the way?"

"Not that old, but they are not healthy. I don't know. I could arrange it. I can write a letter explaining that I am planning to remarry and my bride would very much like to meet them, but not yet Rózsika. That we wanted to discuss with them what to tell Rózsika and when to tell her. Ask them to meet in Zólyom, at a friend's house, have someone look after the little girl for a few hours. And specially ask them not to say anything at all to Rózsika. Yes, I could do that."

"Do it, Berci, please. Do write that letter."

And so it was. Bernát wrote the letter and it was arranged that they would meet at the apartment of the Kleins, Armin and Kati, friends of the Taussigs. But the Kleins considerately left the room after the introductions.

Ilka wore a very simple forest-green wool dress, with a belt made of the same material around her narrow waist and a small white collar she had crocheted. She was sweet and charming. Bernát introduced her to the Taussigs. They tried to be more than polite, they said that they were very pleased that Bernát had finally found a suitable young lady for a wife. "Young lady," not "girl." Doesn't matter.

They asked her about her family. She told them, wiping a tear from her eyes, about the recent death of her brother, an event that nobody understood. She also explained that they had thought of postponing the engagement and the wedding, but the rabbi had insisted that it should not be postponed, that the living always came before the dead.

Then Ilka said, "The most important thing in this marriage will be the well-being of Rózsika. Her and any other children that may come." She glanced at Bernát, who said nothing, so she continued. "We discussed what to tell Rózsika. The idea came up – it was my idea – that she may not remember Fanni so well by now. What if we tried to spare her the shock, the sadness, by telling her that her mother is well and healthy again, she can come home, and then I would play the role of Fanni?"

They were both shocked, as she expected them to be. So she continued. "I know that I could never replace your daughter, I would not even try. But I think that Rózsika would be happier this way. Oh, she would have to be told the truth eventually, but much, much later, I think, when she is big and can better cope with the sad facts."

It was Lipót who spoke first. "But look, my dear, how could this be? I mean, I appreciate that you would be doing it for Rózsika, but even if she believed that you were her mother, you don't look like Fanni, her clothes would not fit you, and your name is not Fanni. Would you want Bernát to call you Fanni?"

Ilka answered thoughtfully. "She knows that her mother's name was Fanni?"

"Of course she does," answered Amália now, forcefully. "She is a clever little girl, she asks questions."

"But tell me, does she also know that Fanni stands for Franciszka?"

Lipót and Amália looked at each other. "No, probably not," he answered.

Now Ilona looked at Bernát. "Berci, how would it be, then, if you actually called me 'Fanni,' just for a little while, and then we explained to Rózsika that 'Fanni' is a diminutive form of 'Ilona,' and from now on it would be more proper to call people by their real names."

"Like Berci?" asked Amália sharply.

"Touché. I would have to give that up, at least for a while." Ilona smiled; she had an engaging smile.

But Lipót was not comfortable with the idea; neither of them were. "How could 'Fanni' be a form of 'Ilona'? Surely that is unlikely. And what about people who know you? Who come to visit? What would they say when Bernát calls you 'Fanni'? Would that not be ridiculous?"

"Or worse, macabre?" added Amália.

"Yes, I thought that you might use that word," Ilka responded. "That is the worst thing that you could say about the idea. Look, we don't have to do it. You could simply tell Rózsika that her mother has died and that her father is now marrying another woman and she will have a stepmother. Would that be better for her?"

Amália and Lipót looked at each other again; there was a long period of quiet in the room.

Bernát broke the silence. "If you agreed to the deception, I could manage to call Ilka 'Fanni,' just for a few weeks, then use her proper name more and more often, so Rózsika would slowly get used to the new name." He stopped, looked at the older people, then added, "I must admit that it would be painful, a constant reminder of Fanni. Perhaps it would not be an auspicious start to our marriage?" Now he looked in Ilka's direction.

Ilka nodded. "Yes, I have thought of that. You would always remember her, when it would be in my interest to make you forget Fanni as fast as possible, to not bring her memory back constantly by using her name. Still, don't you think that the little girl's happiness should come first?"

The Taussigs were won over. They looked at each other; Amália wiped her eyes. "Well, my darling, if you don't mind, perhaps we should do it that way, the way you are suggesting. Lipót?"

"Yes, I could see that it would be best for Rózsika. If you don't mind." And then, looking at his ex-son-in-law, "And you too, Bernát."

"No, we can both do it. It will take some will power, on both of our parts, but we shall manage."

Ilka added, "But give us some weeks at first, a chance for the two of us to get used to each other. Then Rózsika will come home and we shall each play our parts."

They all nodded. Ilka spoke again, "I have another idea. We have been talking about perhaps moving to a larger apartment or even a house in Rima-Sobota. But now I think that we should delay that for a while. Let Rózsika come home to the place that she remembers, and then, some time later, we can all get excited about moving."

They all loved that. Amália went over to Ilona and hugged her. "If we had to lose our daughter, at least it is good to know that our granddaughter will have a good mother."

"And you will come over often to see Rózsika and us?" Ilona asked them.

"We shall. And then we should behave as if you were our own daughter. If only for Rózsika's benefit."

"And I shall be proud."

Bernát was now beaming, proud of the wisdom of his new bride.

SZÉKELY

LÁSZLÓ SZÉKELY

Erzsébet and László – 1899–1902

"So Ilona and I visited Fanni's parents in Zólyom. But not right after my proposal, in late April, because early in May something happened."

"Oh, and what was that, Grandfather?"

"Something horrible. Ilona's younger brother Andor, whom I had only met a few times, died. He committed suicide at the place where he worked, in Miskolc."

"Why did he do that? Do you know?"

"No, I did not know it then and I have never found out. Ilona did not know either."

"Still, you might have guessed something…"

"If I had to guess, I would have said that it was a question of unhappy love. You see, in those days many young people did that, committed suicide over being rejected by the girl of their dreams. Or vice versa, girls also killed themselves. It all came from those romantic German novels. Very stupid books, in my view. If you are unhappy, you just have to bear it."

"You had your share of unhappiness in your life."

"I certainly did. Not perhaps unhappiness in love, but many other kinds. I lost so many people that I loved dearly, my father and mother and two brothers and a sister and two wives and several children…"

"Yes, I know. But life goes on, right?"

"It does. And often, in the long run, things right themselves, to some degree. I could never get back my Fanni, but Ilonka was such a good wife for me."

"Ilonka?"

"Yes, I preferred to call her Ilonka. Ilka was, somehow, too artificial, and Ilona, too formal. She did not mind; she liked Ilonka, even if it was a little country. It came into fashion just about that time."

"Well, tell me about the wedding and those first days and months and years."

"All right. The wedding was very nice, almost too nice, considering the recent tragedy. There were many people attending, more than a hundred. Practically all of the leading Jewish men of Losonc were there with their wives, and quite a few non-Jewish people, too, friends of my new father-in-law. About fifteen people came over from Rima-Sobota, a few friends and colleagues from the court. It was a very dignified ceremony stressing our being part of the Hungarian establishment. The rabbi made a special point of mentioning Zsigmond's important position at the mill and mine at the law court, emphasizing how far we had all come and what a great contribution we were making to the Hungarian economy, industry, legal system, and of course, the arts and sciences. He quoted directly from a speech made the previous year by Chief Rabbi Kóhn, at the opening of the Israelite Hungarian Literary Society in Budapest. I remember that part of the speech well – I even asked the rabbi to write it down for me. It went like this:

"During these last thousand years, filled with adversity, together with the Hungarian nation, Hungarian Israel cheered, cried and bled, and learned to love, like his mother, this holy land which has nurtured him for a thousand years and gathered in her lap the ashes of his fathers, even before she had recognized him as her own beloved child. We, whose happy millennium of the fatherland has brought the legal recognition of our religion, not only feel ourselves as Hungarians, but now we know that we are such; for us the word 'Israelite' is, even within our religious life, only an adjective to the word 'Hungarian,' the meaning of which, within the context of faith, is Israelite, or let us say proudly, Jewish Hungarian."

"That's what he said? Truly?"

"Yes, I memorized it."

"Neolog rabbi?"

"Yes, he was. Why?"

"Let me put it this way. This is your story, so we shall keep my own opinion out of it."

"I think I know what you mean, Andriska, you are thinking about what happened a half century later. But in those days we were all so optimistic. We believed that we were now fully accepted into this nation, that we finally had a home, after two thousand years of wandering…"

"Well, what about a real homeland for the Jews? In the ancient country of Palestine? Did nobody talk about that idea?"

"Oh, you mean the Zionists. Yes, there were some, but nobody took them seriously. People just laughed at their ideas. They said that those were silly dreams, while in reality we have finally achieved all those dreams right here, in this lovely country. And we were indeed welcomed as brothers, it was not an illusion. We became enthusiastic Hungarians, ready to do our utmost for this country, to help make it the best, most advanced, most cultured, wealthiest, happiest land in Europe. There was hardly any opposition to that idea. Most people accepted us as Hungarians of the Israelite religion."

"Most people? Perhaps those that you knew, the intellectual circle."

"Maybe. True, I did not know that many peasants and industrial workers. Or aristocrats, for that matter."

"No, and given the option, they all turned against you. But let us leave that for now. We are still talking about a happier era, the one just before the turn of the century. You got married and were, again, quite happy."

"Yes, I was. We both were. We had a few weeks to ourselves before Rózsika came home. We got to know each other well, and that was good."

"Was Ilona everything you hoped for?"

"Depends what you mean. She was not like Fanni. Why would she be? Fanni became a woman beside me, which was a different thing. Ilona was already thirty years old. And her personality was also quite unlike Fanni's. One had to accept that. But she was kind and considerate. We hired a maid and a cook; we put most of the new furniture in the bedroom for the time being, to make as little change in the apartment as possible for Rózsika's return."

"And it was all smooth, I mean your relation with Ilona? No arguments? No misunderstandings? No differences of opinion, difficulties due to different upbringing?"

"You mean that she came from a higher class, that I would not know how to behave?"

"Well, perhaps not higher class, but more well-to-do, more used to the ways of sophisticated society…"

"I knew how to behave, thank you. Well, there were many small things – she would place the knives and forks in a certain way that was not the way Fanni used to do, many such, shall we say, surprises – but it did not matter. She was sometimes quite annoyed with the apartment. We had no indoor plumbing; she was used to having running water in the bathroom and the kitchen. Why, we did not even have a bathroom. She kept telling me how much I should enjoy when we finally moved to a nicer place. That depended on Rózsika. So after about three weeks I wrote to the Taussigs, told them to prepare her, tell her the story about her mother having recovered, and then I traveled to Zólyom and brought her home."

"How did it go? Tell me."

"It was difficult at first. When we got home, Rózsika ran into the room. There was Ilonka waiting with open arms, and Rózsika stopped, stood there, would not go to her. Ilonka asked her to come closer. She held onto me and when Ilonka reached for her, she hid behind me. I scolded her. What a way to greet your mother. Ilonka took the trouble to use Fanni's perfume; she even altered one of Fanni's dresses that would not fit her, to wait for Rózsika in a familiar appearance. But no, the girl hid and would not go to her, then started crying. Then, of course, Ilonka cried, too, and finally I got Rózsika to go there and look at her. Asked her to put her hand on Mother's face, which she reluctantly did. Then Ilonka stroked her and kissed her. It took a while, but in the end they were mother and daughter. I think Ilonka's efforts paid off."

"And after that…?"

"After that everything went well. We were worried that the maid and the cook, who knew about the deception, would prattle. So when we moved from the apartment to a sizable house we bought, with Ilonka's dowry, we fired both of them and hired new ones who did not know that we were just married. It was always Ilonka who thought of these things."

"And what did you think of them? Of the deception and the necessary measures?"

"What did I think? In retrospect I always had to agree with Ilonka. She was right, this was the best way."

"You say 'in retrospect.' Why? Did you have any doubts at the time?"

"Well, 'doubts' is not the right word. To tell you the absolute truth, I hated deception. I hated untruth. I had this idea all my life that one must not lie, ever. The truth must always be respected, no matter how unpleasant. And there were still more lies to come; once you start, there is no stopping, it's like a slippery slope. Consider: if the Taussigs were to be Ilonka's parents, then who were the Bauers? They came to visit, we visited them. The solution was, they were to become my own parents. As it happens, both of my real parents were dead by then. It became more and more complicated and I must admit that I hated it. But Ilonka assured me that she felt exactly the same way, except that this was a special situation which required special action on our part. So I suppose that she was right."

"Did you ever wonder how things would have worked out if the truth was told to Rózsika?"

"I did wonder. Sometimes I thought that she was young, she would have overcome the shock and everything would have been normal anyway. But Ilonka worried that Rózsika would hate her as a stepmother, and perhaps it would have been so."

"So after the first difficulties you lived happily in your new house. Was it a nice house?"

"Very nice. It was on Jánosi Street, a nice area of town. It had two stories, with a dumbwaiter for sending up food from the kitchen. But not everything worked properly, the dumbwaiter was broken – they did not tell us this when they sold the house – and the roof also needed to be repaired. I sued the man who sold the house to us."

"Did you win?"

"No, he had better lawyers. I lost and had to pay the legal expenses. I appealed, all the way up to the law court, where I worked. The judges there knew me, but still agreed with the other party. It was very disappointing."

"Did Ilona agree with your suing that man?"

"Ilonka? She was not involved in any way. Besides, she had other concerns. The household, Rózsika, and then, the approaching birth."

"Ah, approaching birth. Tell me about that."

"That? Two years after the marriage, Erzsébet was born."

"Good name, Erzsébet. Was she a nice little girl?"

ERZSÉBET STEINER

"Beautiful little girl. We all loved her. But there was a problem. Ilonka loved her, perhaps, too much. She never let her out of her hands. She would not let the maid bathe the child, or feed her, when she was weaned, and she worried when Rózsika wanted to play with her. Rózsika was a little clumsy, perhaps, but she would have handled her sister with extra care. But Ilonka did not trust her, and tried to keep everybody away from Erzsébet."

"And I suppose Rózsika resented that."

"Yes, she was seven years old by then, went to school and was quite mature for her age. She complained that her schoolmates had little brothers and sisters, and they were allowed to play with them. But Ilonka would not listen."

"And so…?"

"And so nothing. It was all right, for almost a year. But then, one day, Erzsébet became sick with the measles. Many other children had it, too, so we were not concerned, not unduly so, except of course Ilonka, she worried too much. Then, after a week, Erzsébet seemed to be better. But then, one day, she started to have mild convulsions. They did not go away, so we called for the doctor. He said that it has to do with teething, it will stop in a day – but it didn't. We called him again, he examined the baby thoroughly, said that it might have been something she ate, did she have constipation? She did, so he gave her a laxative. But the convulsions got worse. Ilonka started to become hysterical, and so did Rózsika. So I went and called another doctor that somebody recommended. He was younger and more respectable. He shook his head and told us to give Erzsébet a hot bath and afterwards keep her warm. He would come again the next day. The bath helped, but by next day the convulsions had gotten worse. Ilonka's hysterics also got worse. She said that these doctors didn't know a thing, she knew the best physician who treated her whenever she was ill in Losonc, we must take Erzsike there immediately. I was reluctant, because I remembered the time when we took Jenő to Zólyom, although that trip was a little longer. But Ilonka insisted – what could I do? It was already late in the morning, I ran down and caught a hansom cab. We rushed – oh, my God, again! – to catch the 7:22 train – it would have taken us three hours with the two transfers. But we missed the train, it pulled out of the station just as we approached. I asked about the next train. It would leave at 10:59, but it was the slow train, with the transfers taking more than four hours to Losonc. Only twenty-six kilometers! The hansom cab would not take us there, but the driver's brother had a cart with two horses. I hired him – not very comfortable, but fast. He got us there by ten o'clock, directly to her parents' place, in the steam mill. As soon as we got there, her father rushed to the doctor. But the convulsions were really bad by then. To make a long story short, by the time the doctor came, Erzsike was dead. It was awful."

"I am sorry."

"Yes, we were all very sad. For me it was the third. Gyula was just a small baby, but Jenő was not that much younger then Erzsébet when he died. And of course I did lose siblings, older ones, too. But then, so did Ilonka."

"And how did Rózsika take it?"

"She was devastated. She was not with us, we left her with the maids, but of course I had to travel back to Rima-Sobota. Ilona stayed with her parents. You know, the whole thing was very similar to little Jenő's death a few years earlier. Except that we had Jenő buried in Zólyom, but Erzsébet was buried in Rima-Sobota. It was more proper. We did not take Rózsika to the funeral, of course, but she knew all about it. Very sad."

"And I suppose it took a long time for all of you to recover, especially for Ilona?"

"Yes, a long time. But Rózsika started insisting that she wanted another sister, or a brother. And she kept saying that if we had another child, she would take care of her. Or him. As if Ilonka were at fault somehow. I sensed that this was the beginning of a changed relationship between them, a new one that was not quite good."

"So what did Ilona say?"

"Eventually, she agreed that we should have another child. And the worst of it all was, that she started to believe what Rózsika was implying, that she was a bad mother, that she did not know how to raise a child. So she said, all right, Rózsika shall raise the next child. And you know, that's how it was done."

"You must be joking."

"I am not joking. I don't mean completely raised by her, but almost. It was a boy, László, Lacika. He was born a year and a half after Erzsébet's death, a nice little boy, and of course Ilonka nursed him. In the new house, Lacika had his own room. When he was six months old, we started to feed him by spoon, and Ilonka allowed Rózsika do that. She was very good at it, and she changed him and bathed him, a real little mother she was. Of course by that time Rózsika was ten years old. László was born in November of 1901. I have not told you that we had crossed into the new century."

"I gathered that. Did that have any special significance?"

"Only that we were so full of hope. This would be the century of full enlightenment, equality, freedom, peace, the century of the mind, the spirit, humanity was about to elevate itself to a higher plateau. We were proud of being humans, proud of being Hungarians…"

"And proud of being Jews?"

"That, too, I suppose. The matter was not even discussed so much. It had lost some of its importance. It was just the religion, as the rabbi said, an adjective to Hungarian."

"You really believed that."

"Absolutely. The few nasty comments that one heard were obviously uttered by primitive people stuck in the nineteenth century, which we had by then put firmly behind us. People of intelligence, people who mattered fully understood that we were all equal, distinguished only by our mind, our behavior and primarily by our honor."

"Were you perhaps a little naïve?"

"At that time, no. I know that things did not work out that way, but the world changed later. Listen, I see that you don't believe me, but it was all so new, beautiful, modern. We became human beings, fully accepted, appreciated, and respected. We were somebodies, finally, after all those dark centuries. You could not just ignore all that."

At the Club – 1904

As a man married to the daughter of Zsigmond Bauer, as the owner of a sizable house on Jánosi Street, Bernát Székely was highly respected and invited to join the local Jewish club. Ilona liked the idea and insisted that Bernát accept the invitation. He liked the atmosphere, even though the main occupation at the club, playing cards, held no special interest for him. But there was always talk, discussion, argument, presentations, poetry – there Bernát was in his element.

One day he sought out his old friends, well, acquaintances really, Dr. Marosi and Dr. Harsányi; they used to be known by their old German names, Morgenbesser and Hoselitz.

For a while, they talked about the recent problems with the aristocracy and the gentry, who increasingly complained that now, when finally they became willing to earn their keep and join the civil service, they had found all the good position already occupied by more competent Jews. Obviously they did not quite use those terms. There were many jokes told about the typical aristocrats; good laughs could be made at their expense. No doubt the aristocrats and the gentry were laughing at their clubs over the Jewish jokes.

"I have come across a poem by József Kiss." Bernát changed the subject. Kiss, formerly Klein, was the greatest Hungarian poet of the age. They were all proud of him. "A poem about the grave of his mother. '*Far from here, long ago, a grave was dug at the edge of the yard....*' And according to the note, that faraway place is right here, in Rima-Sobota."

"Really? I never heard that he used to live here." Harsányi was surprised.

"I am not sure that he lived here – we could ask him. But his mother certainly did. So I went out to the cemetery and found the grave. There is no monument, no stone, no marker at all. I had to check the book in the office to locate it."

"But why would there be no stone?" Marosi wondered.

"Because poets are hungry beggars," Harsányi assured him. "That's how it has always been and shall always be. How could he afford a nice gravestone?"

Dr. Adolf Lichtenstein, the county chief medical officer, sauntered over and heard the last few words. "What cannot a poet afford?"

Bernát explained about the grave of József Kiss's mother. Dr. Lichtenstein became quite excited. "But look, if he could not afford it, surely we could."

Marosi looked at him with surprise. "I suppose, but…"

"Look. It would be a great honor for the town and especially for the Jewish citizens. Let us erect a beautiful monument. Then the poet will come for the unveiling. It will be an event of national importance."

The others looked at each other, nodded, but were not sure about the cost of the project.

"Wait here," Lichtenstein asked them, "I'll bring over one or two people."

He was away for three or four minutes only and came back with Dr. Samu Veres, the principal of the gymnasium; György Lőrinczy, a writer and the county's chief educational officer; and Dr. Aladár Kármán, the head of the county hospital. He explained the idea to them and slowly it became clear to everyone that if enough participants could be found, the cost of the monument would be quite reasonable for each contributor. It would indeed be a great honor.

Before long, the matter was discussed by everybody in the club. Dr. Lichtenstein started a contributors' sheet and signatures were collected; nobody wanted to be left out. It was mentioned that the names of the contributors would be shown at the back of the monument, in discreet, smaller letters.

Bernát was asked to look after the collection and administration of the funds, once the costs were known. Dr. Veres and Dr. Harsányi volunteered to visit a stone carver, the best in the county, to get ideas about the design and the cost, and come back with a proposal. Dr. Lichtenstein would visit all the other wealthy men who were not present at the club that night.

Bernát made a suggestion. "Should we not bring this matter to the attention of the person most involved, namely the poet, József Kiss?" They all agreed and asked him to try to find out the address. Mr. Lőrinczy would write the letter to the poet.

A week later, Dr. Lichtenstein proudly reported that he had close to a hundred contributors signed up – not bad for a town with about two hundred Jewish families. The design was presented and approved; the cost was quite acceptable. But a few days later a letter arrived from József Kiss.

The poet thanked the Jewish residents of Rima-Sobota for their kind initiative. He really appreciated it, on behalf of his poor mother. Nevertheless, he asked them not to proceed with the erection of the monument. That was his responsibility and he was going to erect an appropriate stone himself.

There was great disappointment everywhere. The news of the undertaking had already been reported in the newspapers; now it had to be retracted. Great pity, everybody said. Still, the poet will surely come here for the unveiling of his own stone.

Yes, but there was no unveiling. József Kiss never erected the stone on his mother's grave.

Ilona and Rózsika – 1907

"So you became full Hungarians."

"No question about that. Our children couldn't even understand that there could be any alternative, that when I was born, my father still thought of himself as German. Of course we were Hungarian. I even had my name changed to Székely."

"Oh, yes, tell me about that."

"Well, it was Ilonka's idea. Such a change had been suggested to me before, perhaps ten years earlier, but I did not consider it seriously then. But now the situation was different. Nobody was forcing it on me, yet it was the trend. Everybody was Hungaricizing their names. Somehow it was the correct thing to do, an affirmation of one's belonging to that nation. A clear severance with the past. After all, why should we wear German names? Our fathers did, but only for three or four generations. It was forced onto them; before that they had Hebrew names. We were no longer Germans. There was as little reason to use their names as there was reason to wear the clothing of the Polish nobles of the sixteenth, seventeenth centuries that some of the Orthodox Polish Jews still wore in those days."

"All right. Back to László and Rózsika, then. So things worked out well? He remained a healthy boy and she looked after him?"

"Yes, she looked after him very well."

"And how was the relationship between her and Ilona?"

"Hard to say. They were mother and daughter, no question about that. When Rózsika's grandparents came over from Zólyom, they no longer called Ilonka "Fanni"; gradually that name was forgotten. But Ilonka's real parents from Losonc – well, her mother, for her father passed away in 1899, not much time after poor Erzsébet – she came to visit often. And we had to maintain the lie that she was my mother. But this became harder and harder, for her name was Mrs. Bauer, and Rózsika was likely to come across some document showing Ilonka with her maiden name as Bauer. Indeed, there were a few instances where fast thinking was needed to explain such anomalies. So gradually we reached the conclusion that Rózsika would have to be told the truth."

Rózsa as a Young Girl – 1908

"Hi, Rózsám."

"Who…?"

"It is me."

"Andriska?"

"Yes."

"Andriska! Where are you? Where am I?"

"Rózsám, this is not real life. You are only in my imagination right now. But don't worry, real life is coming. We shall all be together again before long."

"So I am dead?"

"Yes, I am afraid so. If you were still alive, you would be exactly one hundred ten years old now. Well, next month."

"And you? Are you alive?"

"Yes, thank God, I still am. I am sixty-eight now. Zsuzsika is also alive, and so is our mother, though she no longer recognizes us."

"That is sad. Then it is better to be dead."

"Perhaps. But I am trying to reconstruct the past, to the best of my ability. I would like to talk with you, ask you questions about the olden days, questions that I should have asked when we were together. There were so many opportunities, but I never thought of asking you about your youth, your parents, your life as a young girl, and so on. I know that this is not the same thing, but let me ask those questions now, anyway."

"You want to know about my youth?"

"Yes, if you could talk to me about those days. About your life in Rima-Sobota. Your relationship with my father and your own father and mother. Stepmother, really."

"Yes, she wasn't actually my mother. Sure, I can tell you a few things. Where shall we start?"

"Start where you began to look after your little brother."

"Lacika. Sweet little boy. I was convinced that Mother, as I knew her then, did not know how to care for babies. I had friends, they had little brothers and sisters. I saw what their mothers did – it was not right to overprotect a baby. Always wrapped in swaddling clothes, never letting anybody come near them. I wanted to play with Erzsébet, but she would not let me. Then the baby became ill and died. We cried so much. So after that, I told her to have another baby and I'd look after her or him. And you know what, she started to believe me. Before Lacika was born, I already thought of him, or her, as 'my baby.' I awaited the birth with great excitement. I knew how babies were born: delivered by the stork. So, on the day when the baby would be born, my best friend and I, both nine and a half, waited all day in the back yard, watching the sky, looking for the stork. All day we waited and late in the afternoon the maid came running out, shouting 'Rózsika! Rózsika! The baby is born! It's a boy. Come quickly.' We were surprised and very disappointed. How could the baby be born, when we were certain that no stork came anywhere near the house all day."

"These days children are not so naïve."

"No, it was a more innocent time. But he was born, a very beautiful little boy. After a week or so Mother let me touch him and play with him, if I washed my hands, of course, and when he was weaned, I helped feed him. When Mother saw how good I was at it, she let me take care of feeding him completely, then bathing, too, everything. So by the time Lacika was one year old, I was really his mother. I did everything. And Mother, Ilona, preferred it that way. She could go back to her books and saw us just once or twice a day."

"And your father?"

"Oh, he liked children. He spent more time with us than Mother, but he did not really know how to talk to children. He was always so serious. He would not joke and he would not say that he loved us, or anything like it. But we knew that he did love us. He was a good man."

"And about your mother, again. What did you call her, by the way?"

"I called her *Anyuska*, little mother. Just as I called Father *Apuska*."

"So tell me, you believed that she was your real mother?"

"I did. I did for a long time. Too long, if you ask me."

"Why too long?"

"Because I was stupid. She was obviously not my mother – there were so many things telling me that."

"Were people telling you that?"

"No, nobody would, even though many people did know. I think that all the friends of my parents knew the truth. But they would not say anything. There were, perhaps, a few strange remarks, about 'your poor mother' – why poor, I would ask, and they would change the topic – or 'your grandparents, I mean the other ones,' and so on. I was puzzled about my grandparents. I saw my grandmother often, she came over from Losonc; grandfather died two years after I came home. But there were the other grandparents, in Zólyom. I asked them if they were the parents of Father or Mother, and they would just smile and would not say. I asked Father that question and he said that it was very complicated and he would explain when I was bigger. Mother, Ilona, said the same thing. And once the maid made a comment, something like 'Grandmother – ha!' Mother heard it and she was fired the same day."

"So did you start suspecting something?"

"No, I was so credulous. I could have hit myself afterwards. The main thing was that Ilona could not possibly be my mother – she was an entirely different type. Later I found a picture of my real mother. She was much more similar to me."

"So tell me, what happened? How did you come to find out the truth?"

"Ah, how I found out the truth. It was dramatic. Ilona often visited the cemetery. She looked after the grave of Erzsébet, made sure there were always fresh flowers there. Sometimes she took me too. After seeing to the flowers, we visited a few other graves, friends of hers that had passed away over the years. Well, on this occasion, she asked me to come, and having nothing better to do, I would have gone willingly, except for that black cat."

"What black cat?"

"A black cat had run across the road in front of me earlier, and I thought that perhaps I should not go anywhere that day."

"Were you superstitious?"

"I was and I am, to this day."

"But how old were you then?"

"Sixteen. Ilona insisted, so I agreed. We walked to the cemetery. It was not far, and the weather was nice. We bought flowers, as usual, but she asked me to buy an extra bunch. 'Why? For whom?' I asked. 'You'll see.' The cemetery was on the side of a little hill, at the edge of the Christian cemetery. Not very large, as Jews had not yet been living there for a very long time. So we went to Erzsébet's grave, arranged the flowers and plants, stood there quietly for a while. We went to two other gravesites, and I was wondering about the extra bunch of flowers. Then Ilona took my hand and we walked over to another grave in the older part of the cemetery. There was a stone marker on it that said 'Mrs. Bernát Steiner, née Franciszka Taussig.' And she told me, 'Here lies your mother.'"

"How awful. What did you say? What did you feel?"

"How could I say anything? I was shocked. I looked at her, did not understand anything. She held my hand tighter, tried to hug me. I suddenly screamed, yanked my hand away. She said, 'That was your real mother, but I brought you up and I have always thought of you as my real daughter.' And I screamed and screamed. Suddenly I understood the whole thing. The trick, the deception. Her part in it, my father's part, the grandparents' part – everybody was conspiring against me for so many years. I ran away."

"Where?"

"I don't know. I ran and ran, then when I got tired, I sat down somewhere and cried. People came by and asked me what was wrong. I did not answer, jumped up and ran further. When I could reason a little, I tried to think where to go, but no ideas came to my mind. I could have gone to one of my friends, but then I would have to tell her everything, and I could not do that."

"Why not?"

"What, to let them know of my humiliation?"

"But they meant well. They did the whole, shall we say, performance, for your benefit."

"Performance? Perhaps burlesque. Tragicomedy. I thought, how much they all must have laughed at my naïveté, my parents, or whatever I can call them now, their friends, the maids, perhaps my teachers also knew, perhaps my classmates knew. I imagined that the whole world knew, all but me, and they were all laughing behind my back."

"So what did you do then?"

"At first, there seemed to be no other solution: I had to kill myself. It was the only way. I started to plan the best way of doing that. Jumping under a coming train was most simple, although I could drink something awful, something like rat poison or lye. Scullery maids sometimes drank lye when their soldier left them in trouble. I imagined how sorry everybody would feel for me, how much they would regret the way they had treated me, how much Ilona – no longer my mother! – should be punished by all, mainly by Father. Then Father started to appear in my mind in a little more sympathetic role, as if he were not really active in the deception, only a reluctant participant (actually, I think that this was the way it actually happened). I started to feel sorry for him, having lost Erzsébet and much earlier, two little children. Now he would be losing me, too. And then I thought of little Lacika, about six years old then. How much the sweet little boy needed me. How could I punish him by disappearing, when he was certainly not guilty? And I kept thinking of Lacika, and I cried and cried, but this was a different crying – I was sorry for him, not desperate for myself. And it was a happier crying, because I knew that the worst did not have to happen; I could still be around him. It was Lacika who saved me in the end."

"So you decided to go home."

"I decided to go home, continue to care for Lacika, but speak to nobody at all, nobody at home. So I arrived home. The door was open. There was a great commotion – everybody was looking for me. When they saw me they shouted, 'Rózsika is back! She is all right, she is found!' as if they had found me. That made me feel a little better, but I did not speak to them. My father hugged me and tried to talk to me, ask me where I had been. I would not answer, would not say a word. Ilona stood there, looking at me, but she did not try to touch me or speak. She saw in my eyes what I thought of her."

"And then?"

"They insisted that I eat, which I refused, without saying a word. I went to the kitchen and, while everybody watched, prepared dinner for Lacika. He was already six years old. He was to go to school that fall, but I still made his dinner. My own meal was left on the kitchen table. I did not touch it, except for the raisins."

"What raisins?"

"I always took my cake apart, picked all the raisins and gave them to Lacika. He loved raisins, so all my raisins went to him. But on that day he would not eat much, only the raisins, because the maid had already given him something to eat. Still, I stayed with him until it was quite late, then went to bed. Father and Ilona also came to say goodnight, which I ignored. Later, though, I thought of sneaking out to the kitchen, for I was awfully hungry, but decided against it – somebody might catch me at that. It would have destroyed the whole act."

"Ah, the act. So you considered the whole thing an act?"

"Well, not quite an act, but yes, a performance to make them understand what I thought of the whole thing, the trickery, the deception."

"But you did not consider at all that they might have done it for your own good?"

"That's what they kept saying afterwards. For weeks, Ilona tried to make me speak to her, repeating that I was too little to cope with my mother's death, that it was for my benefit, so I would not be an orphan with a stepmother, how much she loved me and all. I remember the words, but they went by me. I never for a moment considered that they could be true."

"Never?"

"Well, maybe later, much later, I allowed in my own mind that they might have meant well, but it was wrong, so wrong! To cheat me, to deceive me, to make a fool out of me!"

"So when did you start talking to them again?"

"To Father, I talked after about a week. He kept asking me about school and one day I showed him my report card, which was better than usual, for I thought I should show them that I was worth something. He was pleased and talked about that, not about the other thing, so with *him*, things gradually got better, almost normal."

"But with your…with Ilona?"

"I did not speak with her for at least half a year, and even after that, very coldly, just as much as necessary. You see, the more I thought about it, the more I believed that she was the architect of the deception. Even today I am convinced of that. So I hated her more and more. Let me tell you what I did."

"Tell me."

"I thought more and more about my real mother. Franciszka Taussig. Of course, Fanni! I remembered that my Zólyom grandparents were called Taussig, while the Losonc grandparents were Bauer. Of course. How stupid I had been not to have figured that out myself. But what was my real mother like? So one day I asked my father that question and he said that there was a photograph of her and he would find it for me. He must have mentioned it to Ilona, because the next day she came to my room with a box of photographs and took out one, saying, 'This is a picture of your mother. Fanni. She was very lovely.' She gave me the picture. Of course I did not answer, but I watched her as she went out and then followed her quietly, to see where she put the box. Then I looked at my mother's photo for a long time. I saw where I resembled her. She was not that much older in the picture than I was at that time. I looked at it and cried a little."

"And then?"

"And then I stole the whole box, took it into my room and went through its contents picture by picture. I knew what I was looking for. First, I hoped to find a wedding photo of my real parents; there weren't any. But then, I did find three wedding photographs of my father and Ilona. Those I carefully hid under my pillow and put the box back where I had found it. Later that day, when I had an opportunity, I cut those three photos to tiny fragments with scissors and went down to the street and threw them into a garbage bin."

"Strong action. Were there any repercussions?"

"There sure were. Ilona thought of checking the box the very next day; she came screaming to my room demanding the pictures back. I shrugged, said nothing at all. She searched my room from top to bottom, screamed and cried. Later that day, of course, she complained to my father. He came to me, asked about the picture. By that time we were on speaking terms, but I would say nothing to him on that day. Later, I heard him trying to calm Ilona, telling her that the photographer must have the negatives, they should be able to order new prints from him."

"And did they?"

"They tried, but the photographer had moved his studio to Budapest. They wrote to him, but apparently he did not keep the old negatives."

"So those wedding pictures were lost forever?"

"They were. I did not care. For me, the only wife that my father had was my mother, Fanni Taussig."

"But Ilona was the mother of Lacika, whom you loved."

"That's beside the point. Or at least it was beside the point at the time."

"Did Ilona grieve for those lost pictures?"

"She did. The tables were almost turned after that. It was almost as if the insulted party were her, not me. She told me that she would never forgive me for that, and she never did."

"And your father?"

"He was also angry. I suppose he was less sentimental – a wedding picture may have meant less to him, for he did forgive me after a while."

"Would you say that he was a good man? Good and fair?"

"Yes, and honest. Straightforward, and he expected everybody to be like him. He did not understand dishonesty and could not tolerate it."

Bernát and the Law – 1908

"All rise!"

Everyone stood; the judge looked at them sternly and sat down.

"You may be seated."

The judge shuffled his papers, then looked out at the hushed crowd. At length, he spoke. "This is the decision of the appeal brought by plaintiff Bernát Székely against defendant Elemér Ágostoni in the case regarding the distribution of proceeds from the sale of jointly owned property. The lower court has rejected Mr. Székely's claim and ordered him to pay all expenses. He appealed to the district court, which upon thorough consideration of the merits of his claim, has also rejected them. Mr. Székely has now appealed to this law court, asking it to review the findings of the district court and reverse its decisions."

There was not a sound in the room as they waited for the final decision.

"This law court has examined all relevant documents and has listened to the claims and counterclaims made by the advocates representing the parties in this case. Upon full consideration of all facts, this court has decided that Mr. Székely's case lacks sufficient merit to justify the reversion of the earlier decision. Mr. Székely is hereby ordered to pay for all court expenses, including all expenses of Mr. Ágostoni. Case dismissed."

And that was that. Bernát was sad and bitter, but not entirely surprised. This was not the first suit that he had brought and lost. There was no question in his mind about the merits of his case; indeed, he had been simply cheated out of his share of profits from the venture. But he did see that the other party had a better lawyer, a man who was good at twisting the facts until almost the opposite was proven. Still, an intelligent judge should have seen through such machination.

Why did he not hire the best lawyer himself? Because he could not afford his fees. But now, in retrospect, it was the wrong decision. He had to pay the fees of the best lawyer anyway, except that the best lawyer represented his opponent.

He went home. Ilona could see right away that he had lost. "I need not ask, I suppose."

Bernát shook his head.

Ilona persisted. "Court costs and lawyers' fees, too?"

"Yes."

"Was it a question of who had the better lawyer?"

"Definitely. If I could have a lawyer like Korányi, I would have won, no question."

"Berci, you should not have sued that man in the first place."

"Not sued him? But he was cheating me out of my dues!"

"Yes, but it would have been a relatively small loss. Now it has become a big loss."

"And what about justice? Do we live in a civilized society, or in the jungle?"

"Yes, but in the long run you always lose. Look, during the last few years you have advanced so nicely in the court. You have a respectable position and a much larger salary than you had before. You've had four increases during the last ten years. But all that extra money goes to lawyers and courts. Whatever extra the court pays you, you give it straight back."

"But Ilonka, are you suggesting that from now on I should allow any man to treat me like dirt? If somebody wants my money or my possessions, tell them to come straight into the house and help themselves to whatever they desired?"

"You exaggerate. We are not talking about criminal cases and you know that. But for civil suits, it always comes down to judges' opinions."

"Not all judges are so shortsighted. I always hope that this time I'll get an intelligent, straight-thinking judge."

"One who is beyond reproach, beyond corruptibility?"

"What are you suggesting? That they would accept a bribe from my opponent?"

"Who knows? Maybe they do."

"How can you say such a thing? This is a civilized country, not the east."

"Well, then why do they reject your cases?"

"Because the other lawyer is better."

"Or because they are anti-Semitic?"

"The judges? I don't think so. Well, some might be, but not today's judge."

"So it is just a question of who has the better lawyer. Well, then, hire the best one yourself."

"Yes, that's what I will do the next time."

"But Berci, let there not be a next time. Stop litigation. Let us live quietly, normally. You don't always have to sue somebody. Yes, yes, I know. Then anybody can walk into your house. Nonsense!"

"Ilonkám, it goes deeper than that," Bernát responded sadly. "It is really a question of justice. I think that justice is the most important thing in human society. Justice must be preserved at all cost."

"And it is your duty to preserve justice?"

"Yes, to the extent that I can. I must be just – we all must be – and then, when I find unjust behavior, I have a right to go after it, try to defeat it. Whether or not I succeed, that is immaterial. And I repeat, justice must start at home. We must be just and fair, and that means, among other things, that we must never be untruthful. Never lie."

"Why do you say that?" Ilona's voice was quite sharp. "Do you imply that I lie?"

"Not at all. Don't get excited. I just want to make sure that this household is permeated with a desire to tell the truth always, without any exception."

"Well, we did have that one exception, about Rózsika. We did that together, jointly."

"Yes, and look at the trouble it has caused us in the end. I regret that I ever agreed to that one. I regret it very much."

"I still think it was the right decision. But that was the only time that I was involved in any deception, you know that. I have never told a lie in my life, other than that. Surely you must know that."

Bernát did not disagree. After a while, he turned to her again. "You know, Ilonka, I could have represented myself better. I would have been a good lawyer."

"Perhaps. But you are not. It is too late for that."

"Yes, but it is not too late to have a good lawyer in the family."

"Do you mean…?"

"Yes, of course. Lacika will be a lawyer, and the best one."

Ilona shrugged. "I don't mind, if that's what he wants to be. I was hoping that he would become a literary man, a writer, a poet, but sure, if he wanted to become a lawyer, at least there will be more money in that. Less intelligence, less feelings, less sympathy for the wounded, the unfortunate, the unloved, but more money."

"I don't think that lawyers must be unfeeling, uncaring or especially unintelligent. He can be all those things that you wanted him to be, and he can know his literature, poets and writers, but he will also know the law. That will help him to do all the good things for the unfortunate, the poor, the unloved."

Ilona did not argue. László would be what he wanted to be; only time would tell.

✣

Rózsa as a Young Girl, Continued – 1909

"So tell me, Rózsám, did you continue living together with your stepmother on such frosty terms?'

"No, Andriska, it was not like that. I told you that we did not speak, or at least I did not speak with her, for at least half a year. She did sometimes speak to me, issuing orders."

"Which you ignored, I suppose."

"No, I could not. My father told me, more than once, that in the house, her word was paramount. Whether I liked her or not, I could not ignore her orders. They were mainly forbidding orders. For instance, 'In the salon, you will find a new carpet. It is very expensive, and you must not step on it. Do you understand? Never step on it.' So I did not step on it, at least not when anyone could see me."

"It could not have been a very healthy situation, the constant tension between you and your stepmother."

"No, but it did get better after a while. Something happened."

"What happened?"

"Something very interesting. I had developed the habit of rummaging through old letters and papers, hoping to find more things about my real mother and perhaps myself. I found a letter written by Rozália Bauer, Ilona's mother. She wrote to her own mother about little Elinora – several times she used her Hebrew name, Leah – about how nicely she was coming along. She wrote this letter in 1861, when the little girl was one year old. That was strange, I had never heard of an older sister of Ilona's. So I asked Father about such an older sister. He assured me that there was never such a person; she did have a brother, Jakab, who died when he was a few days old, and another brother, Andor, who died when he was thirty-two. Never a sister."

"So what did you think?"

"I knew that Ilona's Hebrew name was Leah. I started to suspect something. I read all letters feverishly, her own letters, those that were written to her by her parents, by relatives. Soon I found that when she was about my age, she started to call herself Ilona; until then she was Elinora. There was no question, it was the same person. And she was born in 1860, not 1867, as she claimed!"

"Quite a discovery. Did you run to your father with it?"

"First I wanted to do that, I was so excited. But then I thought, let's wait, think it over. Finally, I went to Ilona, started to talk with her. She was quite pleased that I talked, until she found out what I had to say to her."

"Well, tell me, how did the conversation go?"

"I remember it so well. My life changed from that day on."

Confrontation – 1909

Rózsa entered the room without knocking. Ilona looked up.

"I want to talk to you about something."

"Rózsika, of course, Sit down."

"No, I prefer to stand. I have found something."

Ilona looked at her, puzzled. "What have you found?"

"Some papers. Showing that you lied about your age. That you are seven years older than what you said."

Ilona paled. "What nonsense is this? Where did you get such a stupid idea?"

"It is not nonsense. It is not stupid. I found a letter that your mother wrote to your grandmother, when you were one year old. She called you Elinora, but it was about you. She wrote it in 1861. And another letter a few months later. And again, in 1862."

Ilona looked at her, her face frozen. Finally, she stated firmly, "I had an older sister called Elinora. She died before I was born."

"No, you did not have. I looked at all the letters. You were called both Elinora and Ilona when you were sixteen, seventeen. Even the Hebrew name is the same. I have saved and hidden all the letters. I can prove that you lied."

Rózsa had never seen Ilona like this. She slowly crumbled. Her self-confidence, perhaps her most prominent character, disappeared. It was as if Rózsa were facing a different person, a much older person. Of course, she thought, she is not forty-four years old, like she claimed, but fifty-one. Very big difference.

She just looked at Ilona, saying nothing, waiting. Finally, Ilona broke the silence. "What shall you do? Tell Father?"

This was Rózsa's moment of victory. She savored it. "Maybe."

"Don't tell him."

"Why not?"

"Because that would be the end of everything."

"Everything?"

"Our marriage. Our happiness. This house. Lacika's happiness. Lacika's future."

"Why? Why would it cause trouble for Lacika?"

"Because Berci would divorce me, and I would take Lacika with me. And he would no longer have the opportunities, good life, good education. He would no longer have a big sister who always looked after him."

Rózsa's victory was suddenly less secure. But she fought back. "Why would you take Lacika? If Father kicked you out, surely he would get to keep his son."

"No, he would not. The mothers always get the small children. In any case, if it came to litigation about that, I could afford the better lawyers. I still have lots of money on my name. Your father always loses his lawsuits."

Rózsa knew that this was indeed the case. She did not know what to say next.

Ilona said it instead. A measure of her self-confidence was returning. "Rózsika, let us be friends. I always loved you. I only wanted to do what was good for you. Don't be angry about that deception. I thought it was for your own good. Let us be friends. Don't tell your father. I will always be on your side. I will always help you with whatever you want to do, let you raise Lacika. You don't have to do anything around the house that you don't want to. Is it a deal?"

Rózsa looked at her, not knowing how to get more out of her. Finally, she nodded.

"Good." Ilona grabbed the opportunity. "Give me your hand." She took Rózsa's hand, shook it and then hugged and kissed her daughter, like in the old days.

"Let us have some tea. I want to talk to you more. All right?"

Rózsa nodded. This was a new experience for her, being treated like an equal, like an adult. Ilona rung for the maid, asked for tea. They sat down.

"Look, Rózsika, try to understand what I went through. I was already thirty-seven when somebody introduced your father to me. He needed a wife badly; he was recently widowed, with a small daughter. And I needed a husband, for my parents were no longer that healthy. What would I do if, God forbid, they were both to disappear from my life? What is a single woman? Nothing. There would have been some money, perhaps, from my father, but not enough to last me for a lifetime. In any case, a woman cannot live alone, you know that. If a woman does not marry, she is nobody. You do know that, don't you?"

Rózsa nodded her head. What a revelation! What an experience! Ilona continued.

"So I decided that instead of being three years older than your father, I would be four years younger. I was really good-looking then, so nobody could tell. This would be good for your father and good for me. And also good for the little girl who was at the time staying with her grandparents. I swore that I would be a good mother to her. I did not want to be a stepmother, I wanted to be a real mother. I tried my best." She was crying a little. She wiped her eyes with her lace handkerchief.

"Tell me, did I do wrong? Should I have told your father the truth about my age? He surely would not have married me. Or should I have told you about your real mother having died? Would that have been better?"

That was a difficult one for Rózsa, for there were two questions made into one. She really did not know how to answer. Finally, she thought of the right comeback. "Apuska always says that the truth must always be told, no matter how unpleasant."

"Yes, he does. Yet he agreed that it would be best not to tell you about your mother. There are always exceptions to every rule."

Rózsa had nothing to say now. She sipped her tea and thought that she had accomplished her task. Ilona was not her mother, nor was she her commander any more. And Ilona? Ilona thought that her life might be more difficult from now on, but perhaps she was safe, after all. She had another thought.

"Let us live to make sure that they are happy. Bernát and Lacika. Those two men. I will do everything I can to keep them happy, and I am sure that you will too. Let us not cause either one any unhappiness, okay?"

Rózsa nodded. She was sure that this was her main purpose in life: to keep her father and her brother happy. Perhaps another one too, later.

Ilona stood up and kissed Rózsa. "Rózsikám, I would like to ask you just one thing. Please call me Anyuska, like before. So I won't have to cry in my bed every night. Will you do that, my dear?"

Rózsa was saddened, yet cheered by this. She kissed Ilona back. "Yes, Anyuska, I will."

ILONA BAUER, AGE 55

Rózsa as a Young Woman – 1916

"So, Rózsám, from that time on you and Ilona lived together happily, as friends?"

"Yes, we did. She did not demand anything from me and I tried to be nice to her. Father noticed this, did not understand the change. I don't know if he asked Anyuska for an explanation, he never asked me. But he was certainly very pleased, much happier than before. And I think that Lacika also noticed and he was happier, too."

"And so the years went by…"

"Yes, but not there."

"How do you mean not there?"

"I mean that I did not stay in Rima-Sobota for quite as long as my parents."

"No? Why not? Where did you go?"

"Let me tell you about that. It all started with Lujza Blaha."

"Who?"

"Don't tell me you have never heard of her! She was the greatest singer and actress of all times, the 'nightingale of the nation.' The greatest! Even after she died, everybody knew that there would never be another like her. That's what she was called, officially, the Nightingale of the Nation. You have not heard of her, really? How could that be?"

"Maybe I have heard of her. Was there not a square named after her, right in the middle of Budapest?"

"Of course there was. And at least two streets. She was famous in Budapest and everywhere else, but she was most famous in Rima-Sobota. You see, she was born there! She was originally called Lujza Reindl. Later she Hungaricized it to Kölesi, then married a conductor named János Blaha. That's how she got her name, even though she divorced him later. I saw her twice. The first time was when she came to accept a gift from the grateful population of her hometown. She was over fifty by then, but she looked like thirty. Beautiful, she was, and her voice! She sang two songs on that occasion. We were all enchanted."

"And the second time?"

"We all went up to Budapest to see her in *The Red Purse*. She played Zsófi Török, the wife of the judge. She was just lovely!"

"When was she born?"

"I think around 1850. She was forty years older than me, but I never managed to look as beautiful as she was even then. Yet I tried to make myself beautiful, for her sake. We all did. We had a club at school, the Lujza Blaha Club, and most girls were members. We all wanted to be like her, actresses and singers."

"But I suppose that few if any of you did succeed."

"Well, now, it depends how you look at it. It is true that the others gave up the idea after they finished school, but I did not. I was quite serious in that I would become an actress and singer. I even got permission from my parents to take singing lessons. My father was not so keen at first, but Anyuska talked him into it. Of course, she would do anything for me. So I learned how to sing properly."

"And then?"

"So one day – I was already twenty years old, so I was not afraid to speak up at the table – well, I announced, right in the middle of dinner, that I wanted to be an actress and singer. Father almost choked over his dumpling."

"He did not like the idea?"

"Like it?! When he could speak again, he told me that it was out of the question. A nice Jewish girl would never become one of those – he would not say what, but we all knew what word he swallowed. He did not consider actresses reputable. Inevitably, I mentioned the name of Lujza Blaha, and he asked me how many times she'd been married. Two or three, I said. Three or four, he replied. And what happened to her husbands? Did they die? No, she divorced them. What does that make her? He asked but did not answer his question; neither did anyone else."

"And so…?"

"Well, nothing happened for a year or so, but I did not give up the idea. I talked to Anyuska about it – yes, I now called her Anyuska. That's what I called her all my life, at least all her life. I told her that I was serious about this and I expected her to talk Father into letting me make my own decisions. She promised that she would try, and after a long, long time, when I dared to raise the subject again, she indeed supported me. So did Lacika – he was twelve years old by then – he made a comment. Father looked at him with a serious frown and told him quite brusquely to shut up. It was unusual for Father to be that strict with Lacika."

"But you were getting closer to having your idea accepted?"

"I thought that Father would come around, but when I mentioned it for a third time, a few months later, he said outright, 'No daughter of mine will ever be an actress. I don't want to hear about such a thing ever again.' End of discussion."

"What did you do then?"

"Then I decided that I would go to Budapest and become an actress."

"Really?"

"Yes, and I asked Anyuska to help and keep it a secret, which of course she did. She helped me get together an appropriate wardrobe. She also wrote some letters to distant relatives in Budapest, asking them to let me stay with them for a few weeks, until I found my own lodgings and the right acting position."

"And then you just left?"

"Yes. I wrote a letter to Apuska, asking him to forgive me and promising to be good. I kissed Lacika goodbye. I also kissed Anyuska and had a hansom cab take me to the train station. I bought my ticket and rode alone to Budapest. That was the first time in my life that I was alone on a train. Quite exciting."

"So you arrived in Budapest. What did you do then?"

"I had another cab take me to those relatives. They welcomed me very warmly. But I told them that I did not expect to stay with them for long. And I did not."

"Did you find an acting job right away?"

RÓZSA SZÉKELY, AGE 23

"Well, not quite. It was not easy. The war started soon after I arrived in Budapest and that caused all kinds of confusion. But I did have money – Anyuska gave me a lot. So after about three weeks I found an appropriate room and moved there. As for a job, that was more difficult. To start with, I had written a letter before I left to Lujza Blaha. I was hoping that she would help me, but apparently she never got that letter, I don't know why. So I went there, to her place, but they would not let me in to see her. I wrote another letter; she did not answer. I went to see her again, but then she was away at her house in Gödöllő. The empress also had a house there – they might have been in each other's company. Next time I went, she was away, entertaining the troops. I went once more, and then she was at her villa in Balatonfüred. I never managed to see her."

"And was that the only way to get an acting job?"

"No, I tried many other connections. Lots of promises, but nothing ever panned out. I even went to see the minister of defense."

"You're joking. Why the minister of defense?"

"Because he was from Rima-Sobota. Do you know who he was?"

"No, how would I know?"

"He was Samu Hazay, a Jew from Rima-Sobota. We were all very proud of him. I knew his family. Of course he converted. He could not very well be the minister of defense as a Jew, but it was only for form's sake."

"Or so he said."

"No, really. There were many Jews who converted, well, not so many, but I knew quite a few."

"Was that a good thing?"

"I don't know. Anyway, I went to see the minister. He did receive me and we talked about some members of his family. I asked him to find me an acting job and he said that if he heard about something, he would let me know. It was he who recommended a cabaret. He was apologetic, said that he knew that might not be what I was looking for, but because of the war and everything, that's all that he could think of at the moment. I went to see the owner, and he asked me to sing for him. I did and he liked what he heard, so he offered me a singing spot every night. I thought that I would not get the job, because he made some lewd suggestions, which I rejected, of course, quite indignantly. I almost walked out, but he apologized and asked me to take the job. So I did, and it was all right."

"You became a cabaret singer."

"Yes. Later, I was asked to join another place. It was better, more dignified, and the pay was also a little more. That's what I did throughout the war. I sang patriotic songs, because of the war, and love songs, even some folk songs. I really liked the Palóc folksongs – then I dressed up in Palóc clothes, that was a great success. I even went to Balassagyarmat to study their customs."

"A real folklorist you must have been. And those patriotic songs – did people really want to hear them in a cabaret?"

"Yes, they did. You see, most of our customers were Jews. And they were really patriotic. Jewish soldiers came in, on leave from the army; there were many even from Rima-Sobota. Yes, they were proudly Magyars. They wanted those songs. I sang one to commemorate the death of one Jewish boy whom I knew in Rima-Sobota."

"Interesting. And when the war ended, I suppose that the songs changed, too."

"Yes, but my life changed, too. I'll tell you why."

"Please do. But not now, Rózsám. Soon."

The First World War – 1917

"Grandfather, I would like to talk with you again. I need to ask you more questions."

"Go ahead, Andriska, What is it that you would like to know?"

"Now about the world war and its aftermath. You know that later we called it the First World War, for there was a second…"

"Oh, yes, I remember. Much worse than the first."

"Much, much worse. But let's talk about that first one. What were you doing during that war, you and the family?"

"By the beginning of the war, I was assistant director of the law court. Our life did not change so much. Of course I was nearly fifty-two by the time the war started, so I was too old for army service, and Lacika was too young. But many people, many friends went to the war, joined the army, sons of our best friends. Two or three lost their lives."

"Of course, it was not like the second war. Jews were not forced into slave labor units, used as cannon fodder."

"What nonsense. Jews participated in the war, just like anyone else. Why, I knew many, many Jews who were soldiers, or whose sons were soldiers, fighting bravely, killed on the fronts."

"Decorated, too?"

"Decorated plenty. And promoted. There were hundreds of Jewish officers, throughout the army. Even generals. Why, the minister of defense was a Jew, from Rima-Sobota."

"Yes, I've heard about him. Pity that you were too old, you probably would have made a good general."

"General? No, I don't think so. I never liked to give orders. But I would have been a very good field soldier. Yes, I regretted that I was not allowed to join the army. I was a good Hungarian and wanted to defend our land."

"Yet as things turned out, your daily existence continued as if nothing was changed?"

"I would not say that. For one thing, there was always some military activity going on. Marching units of soldiers, companies and regiments. This was not new, of course, for soldiers, hussars, gendarmes were always there, from my childhood. But now it was a daily affair, several times a day, and on three occasions army officers were billeted at our house, as in every large house. They did not cause much trouble."

"You just lodged them and fed them."

"Yes, except that food was not as easy to come by as before the war. We had to send the maids to line up for groceries and such, and there was a coupon system. There were difficulties. There were deprivations."

"You still had two maids?"

"We had three – rather, two maids and a cook. But when the war started, one left to look after her mother, because her brother had been conscripted, and we did not replace her. Somehow it did not seem appropriate. Besides, with Rózsika gone, there was less need for service around the house."

"Oh, yes, she had gone up to Budapest."

"Let's not talk about that. I was not pleased about that."

"All right. So as the war progressed…?"

"The director of the law court retired and I took over the position. That was a great responsibility. Although the court was not as active as before. Somehow, in a war, people are less inclined to litigate and also there are fewer crimes. Maybe the criminals were all called up. Many of the lawyers were also in the army."

"Was László nowhere near the minimum military age?"

"He was old enough to become one of the cadets – that was kind of a pre-military service, where they learned all about the soldiering without actually being one."

"Was he looking forward to being a soldier when he would reach – what – his eighteenth year?"

"No, he was not. In that respect, he was quite different from me. He hated the military, he hated the army. He hated everything that was German-style, and our army was modeled on the Austrian-German tradition."

"He was never in the Boy Scouts?"

"Yes, but that was not a German model, it was English."

"And he was not a patriotic Hungarian?"

"But he was, of course he was. He loved everything Hungarian: the people, the achievement of the land, its literature, its architecture, its art, its democracy, its liberalism, its enlightenment. He thought that Hungary was the best country in the world. But he expected it to become still better, much better. There was, he thought, so much room for improvement."

"A sixteen-, seventeen-year-old boy thought such things?"

"Yes, indeed. He was extremely well educated. I don't mean formally, though of course he did very well in school – at least in all humanistic subjects, he was not as strong in physics and algebra. But his mother also educated him at home. He read ferociously. He probably read everything that was written by anybody that counted in the whole world. Writers, philosophers, poets, dramatists, essayists…"

"So what did he want to improve about the country?"

"He insisted that the Enlightenment was not yet complete. He thought that wars should be outlawed, that all nations should be united, that all production should be under a worldwide collective control. He had many such ideas. In my opinion, most of them were impractical at the least and potentially quite dangerous. But where it concerned justice, universal justice, he had my support."

"If he wanted to internationalize the world, then he could not have been much of a Hungarian patriot. I mean, you are either a proud member of one nation, or of the entire human race, not both."

"Why not? There can still be nations within the international community of men and women – at least that's how he looked at it. After all, Hungary was part of the Austro-Hungarian Empire, so why could it not be part of something larger, at least of a united Europe, later the whole world? He was indeed proudly Hungarian, as I said. He thought that the poetry of Vörösmarty, of Arany, Petőfi were superior to anything that the West had produced. But that did not mean the rejection of the West, rather the education of the people in the Western countries."

"And being a Jew, how did that influence his thinking? Did that color his views at all?"

"Of course. He thought that the Jews were the best Magyars."

"Real Magyars?"

"Yes, after all, they came into this country with the Magyars a thousand years ago. You must have heard of the Kabars. They were a large Jewish tribe that shared the duties and rights of the other Magyar tribes when they occupied this land. Ever since that time, the Jews made some of the most important contributions to the nation and have been at the forefront of building it and flourishing it and making it the great success that is had become by our time. That's what László said, many times."

"And he expected the rest of the nation to be grateful to the Jews, appreciate our contribution and love us dearly?"

"He did and he did not. You see, he became a member of the Jewish Boy Scout group, and the new Zionists heavily influenced them. There, nobody was talking about getting rewards for good behavior from the Hungarian nation. They were training the young men to be tough, so as to hit back when attacked, to make sure that we, as Jews, could defend ourselves. I did not agree with that approach, but in retrospect they did have a good argument."

László in the Jewish Boy Scouts

They were marching and singing. This was the first time they had marched with this new song in the town. Previously it was always in the countryside. There were arguments and counter-arguments about the song. Zionism had actually been temporarily banned. And the Zionists finally convinced the rest of the young ones that they must be brave, they must not worry about the reactions of the others. Let them worry, let them think twice before making an anti-Semitic remark, before hurting another Jew.

They marched and they sang. László sang loudest, even though his voice was far from musical. He had tin ears; he could never appreciate music. Usually only his sister sang in his family. But with the scouts he raised his voice strongly, calling for courage and revenge.

LÁSZLÓ SZÉKELY,
AGE 16

Raise your arms to the sky, the man, the brave,
Looking into the future without any fear.
Let the camp roar, scream, howl,
The great oath song of the young titans.

Let the sky hear our words.
Let it see how, in our eyes,
The desires, the passions burn.

Here we swear with oath, with oath,
Loyalty to the tears and the blood.
Loyalty to the tears and an oath to the blood,
That for millennia has been shed in vain.
That wherever fate might drive and throw us,
We shall revenge all the misery.
That wherever fate might chase and throw us,
We shall revenge all the misery!

The people on the street did not like it. And László and the others could not have cared less.

Later, though, after the terror, Jewish boy scouts were forced to change the text slightly. After Horthy, they still sang the song, but at the end, it was "we shall shake off all the misery." It was not considered smart to sing about revenge.

Aftermath – 1920

"So, Grandfather, you and László disagreed about how a Jew should relate to the non-Jewish Hungarians?"

"Perhaps for a while, but later, he accepted my views that the Hungarian nation would appreciate our contribution and reward us for it in a suitable manner."

"That's what you thought?"

"It was naïve, of course, I know, and László also knew that later. We learned. Yes, we learned."

"Later. But during the war, you were still enthusiastically Magyar, full of idealism."

"Yes, and László wanted to reform the nation, its administration. For he considered the government to be anti-democratic – worse really, socially oppressive. He said that the nation deserved better leadership."

"Did he actually propose to do anything about that? About changing the leadership?"

"Well, at first, when he was just a gymnasium student, it was all talk. But then things started to happen."

"What things? Tell me."

"By 1918 it became obvious that the Austro-Hungarian Empire and its allies were going to lose the war. That embittered many people, but others saw it as an opportunity to kick out the Austrians and at the same time create a modern, democratic, liberal nation. László was among those. So when the empire collapsed in October, a new government was formed, an independent Hungarian government, very socialist, with lots of Jews involved. László, of course, supported this government enthusiastically."

"And you?"

"I was more ambivalent. I worried about the socialist aspect. A year earlier there was a socialist revolution in Russia, and it had begun to sound as though a terrorist clique were taking over there. I wondered if there might be a connection to this new Hungarian government. But László did not see it that way. He wrote articles, made some speeches at school in favor of the government, as it was moving further and further to the left. I did not like it."

"Why?"

"I had been around, I knew that the situation could easily change, as it did indeed, later. But first, in March, the Károlyi government was replaced by a

Soviet republic, headed by a Jew, Béla Kún, a detestable man. I was shocked to find that László even supported this Kún government; they repelled me. We had many discussions. We disagreed all the time. Just about the entire nation turned against Kún, after he established something called a 'red terror.' Soon, by August, they were forced to escape and then Romanian troops invaded the country."

"What did László have to say to all this?"

"By then he was totally confused and did not say much. The Allies forced the Romanians to leave and another temporary government was formed that repudiated all laws brought by the Károlyi and Kún governments. Then Admiral Miklós Horthy organized a counterrevolution, assembled an army, instituted a 'white terror' in which they murdered many, many Jews – it was really a pogrom of the worst kind. Then he was elected regent."

"Doesn't sound good, at least not for the Jews and revolutionaries. What about László then?"

"He was called in to the police, interviewed at length, interrogated so roughly that at one point he feared for his life. He thought that if he didn't get killed, he would be imprisoned for a long time. He probably would have been, but my name still carried weight around Rima-Sobota. So I suppose that we should have been happy that instead of imprisonment, he was 'only' expelled from all the high schools of the country. And just before matriculation."

"And then?"

"Then came the Treaty of Trianon, one of the most awful turningpoints of my life. In June of that year, 1920, the Allies forced a partitioning onto the country. What that meant was that the areas where the majority of the population was Slovak, they gave to the new Czechoslovakia. The southern Slavic territories they gave to Yugoslavia, also a new country. The entire Erdély they gave to Romania. Some other parts they gave to Austria, Italy, the Ukraine, Poland. So what was left, as Hungary, was about a quarter of the original land."

"Yes, I know. That was a horrible blow to the Hungarians. How did it affect you and your family?"

"Try to imagine: I spoke Slovak, but Ilonka and László did not. That was just the beginning. I was a senior employee of the Ministry of Justice. The *Hungarian* Ministry of Justice, not the Slovak one, if there was such a thing. Perhaps there was; perhaps they would continue the court system the same way as the Hungarians did, who knew? But even if they did, would they keep the same employees? The same director? Unlikely."

"Yes."

"And then, there was the question of the pension. One of the most important aspects of my position was the government pension. I was already fifty-seven, so before long I would be retiring and collecting my pension. But not from the Czechoslovak government: they did not owe me any pension."

"Bad. Very bad. So what could you do about that?"

"Only one thing was possible: to sell our house, for a fraction of what it was worth, pack up and move to Budapest."

"And that's what you did."

"Exactly. We arrived in Budapest and moved directly to a hotel. Our furniture was sent directly to a storage facility."

Bernát Visits the Ministry – 1920

Ilona and László arrived back at the hotel almost at the same time. He kissed his mother's hand and helped her with her coat. He hung both coats in the closet, put his hat on the shelf, washed his hands, and sat down in the salon.

"Should we order tea?" Ilona asked.

"Yes, of course." He rang the bell. The bellboy came running. They ordered tea and some pastry.

Neither appeared very cheerful. "So what happened at the school?" Ilona asked László.

"They kicked me out. I went to the principal's office with that nice letter of recommendation, and his secretary looked up some papers, told me that I was not wanted in that school or any school and ordered me out. It was humiliating."

"Poor boy. And then?"

"Then I went to another gymnasium, but my self-assurance was probably weaker than before, for it took them even less time to tell me the same. I did not want to try a third."

Ilona sighed. "Berci will have to do something through his connections at the ministry. You must get your matriculation and continue with university."

"Anyuska, I could always go abroad."

"I hope it won't come to that. Pity. What a pity."

"I know. I am sorry, Anyuska."

"Well, you could not have known. But it always pays to be careful."

To change the subject, László asked his mother, "And how was your day?"

"Don't ask. Terrible."

"Why? What happened?"

"Nothing happened. I went shopping."

"So? Did you buy anything?"

"How could I? That's just the thing. Everything is so expensive, I could not afford to buy even a pair of gloves. You know what our money is worth? Nothing. Nothing at all."

"Yes, the inflation."

"We knew about the inflation, the value of our house also inflated, we sold it at grossly inflated prices. But even during the last few weeks, something like 90 percent of that money has eroded. What shall we do?"

László had no answer. Finances were never among his favorite subjects.

"Perhaps when your father gets his new job, his salary will be commensurate with these new high prices."

"I hope so, Anyuska."

The waiter knocked and entered with a tray of tea and sweets. When he left – László gave him a painfully high tip – László continued the conversation. "Maybe I should get a job, at least for a while."

"Out of the question! You must continue with your education. That is the one, that is the only important thing in my life."

"Yes, but—"

"No 'but' about it. Ask your father, he will tell you the same thing."

Just then, Bernát entered the room. László stood, shook hands with his father – he had developed that habit during the last year – and helped him with his coat and hat. Bernát washed his hands and sat down. Ilona poured him tea. They both looked at him expectantly.

Bernát sat quietly and said nothing.

"Well, Berci, so what did they say at the ministry?"

"I had to wait more than an hour. Then I got to see the deputy of the Department of Employment. He was very cordial, offered me a cigar. Then he asked me if I was aware that we were not the only refugees from the lost territories. I told him that of course I was aware. But he said that there were four hundred thousand such refugees, and the country was broke; there was no way to feed them or clothe them. So I said we were not looking for charity, only an appropriate position, similar to what I had in Rima-Sobota. Ha, he answered, and where are we going to find such a position for you, you and all the others in similar positions from three-quarters of Greater Hungary? So right away I had to tell him that I would settle for something similar; it didn't have to be identical. Something quite a bit lower level? he asked. Well, not that much lower, of course – but you see that all this already put me into a very weak position. Then he told me that the unemployment was tremendous, the country was not only broke, but impoverished because of the displacements, because of the loss of its most important mineral resources, and most of all, because of the inflation, the like of which no one had seen before."

"Yes, I was telling Lacika about that. I could not afford to buy a pair of gloves."

"Gloves? Soon we shall not be able to afford a loaf of bread."

"Berci!"

"Well, in the end, he offered me a position as a clerk, with no pay at all for the first three months."

They both stared at him. "What did you do?" asked Ilona.

"I stood up, said 'Thank you for your time,' and walked out."

"And so…"

"So I have no position. No employment, no salary. Nothing." And he started to cry. László had never seen his father cry.

"Oh, Berci." Ilona went over to him, put her arms around him. Then she started crying too.

Between sobs, he spoke again. "And you know what? After I left in a huff, I had to go back for my hat. And I heard the deputy telling his secretary something about the dirty Jew who would take the bread of good Hungarians away. As I entered, both men became quiet. I took my hat from the rack and left again."

László and Ilona just stared at him. What could they say?

After a few minutes they became calmer. "You know what I think?" Bernát told them. "I think that they no longer need us."

"What do you mean?" Ilonka stared at him.

"I mean that when they invited us into this country, when they offered us citizenship with no distinction, they needed us because there were too many Slovaks, Romanians, Croats, Serbs, Rutenians in the country. They were afraid that those people would get together and take over, so the Hungarians would be an oppressed minority. They needed more Hungarians, and we were it. But now that those territories are all cut away, what is left is pure Hungarians, so they no longer need us."

"But Berci, we are Hungarians! Are we not?"

"Tell them," he said bitterly. They just sat and thought about that, about the new world facing them.

Bernát turned to László. "And how did your day go?"

Ilona stopped her son from answering. "Let's discuss such matters tomorrow. Today we shall relax, have a nice supper here at the hotel…"

"And tomorrow we move out into an apartment." Bernát finished her sentence.

"Yes, into a very small apartment. Without any quarters for maids."

"We shall not have maids?" László was most shocked of all. Both of his parents shook their heads. No maids.

Ilona had never cleaned an apartment, never cooked a lunch before. A thought struck her. "Berci! What about your pension?"

Bernát started to cry again. "It's all gone. I will get it. It will be toy money. Not enough for a tip to the janitor."

Ilona suppressed a shriek. Bernát knew that the pension had been one of the most important assets that he had brought to the marriage. The other was her dowry. Now both had dissolved like a spoonful of sugar in a pitcher of water.

They sat there in silence for a while, sighing.

Another knock on the door. Rózsa entered. They had written to her two days earlier about having arrived in Budapest. She kissed everyone and apologized for not having received the letter until that morning. "So how do you like the city now?" she asked cheerfully.

There was no answer, but László tried to indicate with his eyes to her that the subject was sensitive, to be avoided. She did not seem to understand the message. "Why, don't you like it now?"

Her father answered. "Rózsika, I have no job."

"No job?!"

"No, nothing. No job, no money, what we got for the house is worth nothing at all."

"And I cannot afford to buy anything," Ilona added.

László pitched in. "So tomorrow we are moving to a very small apartment, with no maids' quarters. We shall have no maid at all."

Rózsa sat down. "Is it really that bad? No reserves at all?"

"Plenty of reserves," Bernát assure her bitterly. "Worth not even the paper they are written on."

He stood up, walked to the window, looked out. László used the opportunity to whisper to his sister, "And they will not accept me into any school at all."

It was Rózsa's turn to start crying. After a while she thought of something. "I have a little money saved, good money, I can give it to you."

"Out of the question!" Bernát said vehemently. "What would your husband say?"

"He need not know about it."

"Yes, he would. We don't want any secrets, any subterfuge in the family."

Rózsa did not answer, she knew that a way would be found to help them. Ilona's principles were not on the level of her husband's.

She changed the subject. "You know, I could hardly get here. There was a demonstration in the street."

"What kind of demonstration?" László asked.

"You will not like this. A demonstration against the Jews."

"What?!" they all asked in unison.

"Yes, they carried signs, saying that the Jews are to be blamed for all the miseries of the country."

"But why? Upon what consideration?" Bernát was shocked.

"Who knows? The revolutions, I think they blame those on the Jews."

"And without the revolutions, would not the Allies have taken away three-quarters of the country?" Bernát argued.

"Go, Apuska, tell them that. No, don't, I would not like you to go among them; you would start an argument and they would beat you up. I know you. One young Jew started to argue and they kicked him and beat him. Told him to go back to Palestine, where he belonged. As if he were not a Hungarian, like themselves."

She turned to her brother. "Lacikám, please be very careful. You were involved with the revolution. I have heard of arrests and internments. There are some armed groups, they're called White Terrorists. They attack everybody even remotely associated with the Béla Kún thing."

László knew about that group. "And what about Horthy?"

"Yes, I know about him, he took over the country. They now call him Regent. He rules instead of the king. Not good for the Jews."

"All this is enough cause for suicide," Ilona cried. "Why don't we just put an end to the whole thing?"

"Now, Ilonka! I won't hear such stupid talk." Bernát was quite angry.

"Well, is there any other solution?"

László stood up, unusually strong. "Don't worry, Mother. We shall manage."

Bernát nodded his confirmation. "Our ancestors faced worst situation than this. They survived, and so shall we."

*　*　*

And so they did. They found a small apartment on Rákóczi Boulevard, not far from the hotel and the Eastern Railway Station. László helped his mother with the chores. Bernát visited all the important people he knew in the city, including Baron Samu Hazay – no longer minister of defense – and they put him in touch with some businessmen. Eventually, one offered him a job as office manager, far below in importance and responsibility to the court job, but it put bread on the table. Enough bread – with a little help from Rózsa – to enroll László in a private school that was authorized to issue matriculation to qualified boys. And then he was enrolled in the university. Just ahead of the enactment of that first of a series of anti-Jewish laws in Hungary. This first one regulated the number of the Jews to be accepted in universities to only 12 percent of all students; normally, over 30 percent would have been Jewish.

Rózsa as a Married Woman – 1919

"Rózsám, tell me now about those years, during the war and afterwards, all the way to 1933. I believe that was an important, even fateful year for you."

"It was, indeed. Sure, I'll tell you about that time. But you're talking about a whole chunk of my life, a good twenty years. I went up to Budapest at the beginning of the world war."

"Yes, but you have already told me about starting your career as a singer in a cabaret."

"I don't know if I would call it a career. Not much, anyway. I never managed to become a real actress, as Lujza Blaha did."

"Not many people did. But you told me you switched to a nicer cabaret at some point?"

"Yes, I managed to move to a fancier place. I became better at singing and performing. I was certainly in demand. Many people came in just to hear me sing."

"Any important people among them?"

"Yes, many. I mentioned to you the minister of defense, Baron Samu Hazay. He came once or twice. And others, military men, and from the government. Businessmen, too."

"Did they come only for your singing, or were they trying to get to know you personally?"

"What do you mean, personally?"

"Well, you know, you were a very attractive young woman. I've seen your photos."

"Well, I was not available for the entertainment of men, if that's what you mean."

"No, I certainly did not mean disrespect. I am sorry. But you did speak to some of the more important customers."

"I did speak to them occasionally, of course. I spoke to Baron Hazay and quite a few other important people. I also spoke to people from the art world. And among them, I spoke to a Mr. Andor Szemere."

"Ah, tell me about him."

"He was a very handsome man, quite a bit older than me – he was almost forty years old already…"

"And you?"

"I was twenty-seven. But he was more than handsome. He had a deeply soulful face, full of intelligence and sadness. A very lovely face. Of course, the sadness had something to do with the fact that he had lost his wife not long before."

"What happened to her?"

"Oh, she had tuberculosis. And they had a daughter, he told me. She was twelve years old, very nice girl, very artistic. Art meant a lot to Andor Szemere."

"Was he an artist, then?"

"No, not at all. He was a salesman. He traveled a lot, and that was a big problem, for the little girl was left alone. Sometimes she was sent over to Andor's parents, but she did not like that very much. After a while, it became clear that he was looking for a wife, for a mother to his daughter."

"Just like you father did."

"Interesting that you should say that. I told him the same thing, and how important it was to be a good stepmother. Of course, it would not be the same situation. This girl was twelve, not four, like I was, and she would not be fooled into believing that her mother lived, only changed her form."

"Of course. But did the matter of marriage come up, naturally?"

"When he learned I was Jewish, just like he was, he invited me out to have coffee with him in the afternoon, in a lovely pastry shop, all very proper. We did that several times, then one day his daughter joined us. I liked her, though she was very shy. But apparently Andor was pleased with the way I talked to the little girl – her name was Lenke. For soon after that he asked me if I would be willing to marry him."

"When was this?"

"Right after the end of the war. In 1919."

"And did you accept right away?"

"I did not want to say yes right away, told him I would like to think about it, but I accepted two days later. There was no question in my mind, I really wanted to marry Andor. I liked him and I wanted so much to be a good stepmother."

"Was that perhaps the most important aspect of the marriage?"

"Yes, how did you know? It was so important for me to be a good step-mother."

"Why, was your own stepmother not good to you?"

"No, that was totally different. She was good, after that event I told you about, but she had to be good."

"And before?"

"I don't remember."

"You don't remember?"

"She was a different person then, and so was I."

"Well, all right. So what did you do to Lenke, after you married her father?"

"I loved her so much! Maybe too much."

"Why do you say 'too much'?"

"I think sometimes she did not want to be loved so much. She rebelled, she refused to eat. She was always so thin!"

"Did you cook her favorite food?"

"I tried, but she did not have a favorite food. Somehow, in that family, food never mattered very much. I think that her real mother was an awful cook, and she got used to uninteresting food."

"Maybe you sewed her clothes?"

"Ah, her clothes."

Lenke – 1922

"Lenke, we have not talked for some time. Quite a few years, in fact."

"Andris?"

"Yes, it is me. But you see, this is different. Jutka and I used to visit you in Zurich, take you to a restaurant, it was always very pleasant. But now some time has gone by. You would be ninety-six years old, but unfortunately you did not make it. So this is kind of a posthumous conversation."

"Posthumous on my part?"

"Yes. I hope you don't mind."

"Mind? So you are telling me that I am dead."

"Yes, but look, everybody has to die sometime. All I am doing is recalling your person, your spirit, as it were, from my memory, asking you about things that I did not think of asking when we met some years ago."

Sigh. "Sure, so go ahead and ask me. What would you like to know?"

"First of all, may I call you Neckó? Like Rózsám called you?"

"Neckó. Yes, they called me that when I was a child. My father called me Neckó. Later I was just Lenke, and when I came out of Hungary, went to Paris, I became Madeleine."

"Yes, even though your Hungarian name wasn't Magda."

"Didn't matter. I was comfortable with Madeleine."

"But I wanted to ask you about those days when your mother died, when your father married my aunt."

"Rózsika. Yes, I remember those days clearly."

"How did you react to your new stepmother?"

"I did not think much of her. I thought her ordinary. Her thinking was conventional, quite limited. She had no feel for the arts at all."

"Despite the fact that she was a singer."

"I don't think she was much of a singer."

"No, probably not. But she told me, many times, that she loved you."

"I suppose she did. But I did not love her."

"Why not?"

"Because she was not an interesting person."

"Like your real mother was?"

"No, not at all. She was not interesting, either. She was boring. I did not see much of her, anyway. She was always sick."

"So then what do you mean by being interesting?"

"My father was interesting. So was my brother. So was my husband."

"Ah, all men. You did not care for women?"

"Perhaps. My father raised me to like the out-of-the-ordinary, the unconventional. He took me to galleries, taught me to appreciate the best, the exciting, original thinking. And look at my husband's work. He certainly did not imitate anybody. He was one of the greatest inventors of new forms, one of the greatest artists of the twentieth century."

"Yes, he is being recognized more and more. So are you."

"Really? Nice to hear. But I am afraid that my work was influenced too much. By my husband, by Dubuffet."

"Maybe. But back to Rózsám. Rózsika. There was something about the clothes she sewed for you?"

"Sewed? No, she bought it. She bought me a coat."

"A coat? What kind of a coat?"

"A very fancy coat. A fussy, frilly, ornate coat, totally tasteless. Ridiculous."

"I see."

"No, you don't. The point was, we did not have much money. I wore my old coat, even though it was far too small for me by then. I asked her if she could let it out. She smiled and said 'Just leave it to me.' Apparently, she had a little money hidden somewhere, just enough for such a coat. And she went out and bought that thing for me. I was shocked. I ran into my room and cried."

"Did you tell her what you though of it?"

"Not in so many words, but I think she knew. I never wore that coat."

"It could not be taken back?"

"Back? There was no such thing then."

"So you had troubles with your stepmother."

"Not too many troubles. I tried to avoid her as much as possible."

"And be with your father instead?"

"He was not around much. He traveled a lot."

"So what did you do?"

"I drew. All the time I drew. I became quite good at it."

"Yes, I heard about that story with the queen."

"Yes, that."

"But tell me in your own words."

"I don't like to talk about such things, it was such a long time ago."

"Still, try."

"I drew a picture that my teacher sent in my name as a gift to Queen Zita. They did not want to believe at the palace that it was done by a child. They investigated, and when they found out that it was indeed by a twelve year old, she sent me a present, a valuable necklace. I had it for quite a while."

"And then you started painting in oil?"

"Yes, I was fortunate that I had two excellent teachers, István Réti and Adolf Fényes. They helped me a lot, and by the time I was sixteen, I found a collector who was willing to help me with my studies, so I did not have to worry about money…"

Rózsám ~ 1933

"So Lenke was a difficult child."

"But she was a lovely child. I really loved her, even when my own son was born."

"Yes, tell me about him."

"I married Andor in 1919 and Gyurika was born in 1921…"

"His name was György?"

RÓZSA, AGE 40

GYÖRGY, AGE 8, AND ANDOR SZEMERE

"Yes, of course. He was a beautiful little boy, and we all loved him very much, Andor and me, and also Lenke. But he arrived at such an unfortunate time."

"Unfortunate? Why?"

"During the previous year, my parents and Lacika moved up to Budapest, when Rima-Sobota was given to the Slovaks. But Apuska didn't get a job at the ministry, and their money just melted away in the inflation. So for a while I had to support them a little, until Apuska found a very low-level job at a private firm. He thought of simply retiring, but his pension was worth nothing at all. We did not have that much money either. Andor's job, as salesman, paid less and less – we could barely afford to buy food and coal in the winter. There was no money left for clothes."

"It must have been difficult."

"It was. And then, in 1921, Andor lost his job. He was simply fired."

"So what did you do?"

"We just about starved. That winter we had no coal, no wood. We went over to my parents' place in cold days – they had some fuel. They had to buy coal, because Anyuska suffered horribly from rheumatism the previous winter, when they could not afford fuel. I think that was the cause of her troubles later. So now they bought coal and wood before food."

"But they had more money than you did, by then?"

"Well, as I said, my father had a job, not very good, but they could buy coal and a little food, too. Simple food. But the whole situation was awful. And so, that was the year when Gyurika was born. We were very happy, but so worried. What should we do with this little boy, and no money at all?"

"And what did you do?"

"I told you, we almost starved. We took Gyurika to my parents' place and I fed him there. But then a miracle occurred."

"Miracle? What was that?"

"You know that Neckó was in the way of becoming an artist. She drew a picture of the last queen of the country and the queen gave her a nice present in recognition."

"Yes, I know that."

"Well, after that, she started to paint. She took lessons from famous painters. And in 1922 they brought her to the attention of a rich collector, who undertook to finance her studies and pay her a nice stipend. So suddenly she had lots of money, at least more than we had seen in quite a while. And she gave most of it to us, so that we could buy food and coal, even some clothes for the baby and all."

"That was really nice of her. How old was Neckó – Lenke – then?"

"She was sixteen. So we no longer needed to freeze and starve. For several years she helped us, until Andor found another job. It was not really a job – he started his own company. He had a small information bureau. He helped people find out anything they needed to know. That provided us with a good living for some years."

"And that must have been a relief for your parents, too, your not crowding their space. I suppose that they had a rather small apartment."

"Quite small. Yes, and they were happier, too, because the next year Laci was accepted to the law school, so it looked like finally he would make it – he would be the lawyer that Apuska always wanted to be, and there would be some more money in the family, too."

"So let's jump ahead a few years, or did anything exciting happen during, say, 1923 to 1929?"

"Exciting? Of course, many exciting things happened. Gyurika learned to walk, and to talk, he grew into a handsome little boy. Andor was very proud of him. We all were. Neckó loved him. She prospered, had many exhibits. Even in Rome, her name was mentioned among the important artists. Andor did quite well at his company. So things went all right. Laci graduated and found a lawyer who accepted him for articling. He did that for a year. Eventually he opened up a tiny little office, had a few clients."

"But then…?"

"Why do you say 'but then'?"

"Well, didn't things start to change in around 1930?"

"Yes, they did. They suddenly took a turn for the worse."

"Tell me."

"First, Lenke decided that as an artist, if she wanted international recognition, she must live in the West. So one day, she just packed up and moved to Paris."

"I suppose that was hard on Andor."

"On Andor and on Gyurika and also on me. It was not the money – by then we did not take any money from her – but we all loved her."

LENKE AND ZOLTÁN

"And did she succeed in Paris?"

"Within two months, she found a man there that she liked. He liked her too. He became her permanent boyfriend – later they married, too. His name was Zoltán Kemény, and as she put it, he was a greater artist than she was. So all the attention was on his work."

"He was also from Hungary, then?"

"Yes, of course, and also Jewish. They were quite happy together. But that came later. In 1930 she left, and about the same time Anyuska began to suffer from pain all over her body. Apuska took her to many doctors, but eventually they all agreed that she had rheumatoid arthritis, and nothing much could be done about it. They suggested expensive baths, in Hungary and abroad, but they also said that such baths would not do so much in the long run. Anyway, Apuska could not afford those."

"How old was she, then?"

"Well, that's the thing. She told all the doctors that she was sixty-three when it started, but she was really seventy. Only she knew and I did. She couldn't say so to any doctor, and in any case it would not have served any purpose."

"So then…?"

"So by 1932 she was practically a cripple, sitting in a chair and walking, when she had to, with crutches. And in that year…oh, it was horrible."

"What, about your mother?"

"No, about my husband. One morning I woke up and found Andor lying beside me, covered in blood, dead."

"Dead?! What happened?"

"Apparently, he died of nose bleeding. He slept and didn't notice, and neither did I."

"What did you do?"

"I screamed, and Gyurika came in, and he saw his father, and he screamed too, and then neighbors knocked on the door – you cannot imagine how horrible it was."

"And afterwards…?"

"Afterwards? We buried Andor and lived as before. We had a little money saved by then. Just as well, because of course we could not count on Neckó sending us money from Paris. I think Andor actually sent her money before he died. Our money lasted for about a year."

"And then?"

"Then it was time to move back with my parents."

"Did they have enough space? For you and Gyuri?"

"Well, it was crowded. But at least Laci was no longer living at home; he had a small apartment of his own by then. That was about the time that he met Mimi."

"Tell me about that."

"He met her at the law students' ball. I don't know why he went there, he was no longer a student, and why she went there, well, I suppose to meet somebody like Laci. Somebody introduced them and they started to see each other. Her name was Hermine Schlesinger, but she didn't like the name Hermine, wanted to be called Mimi."

LÁSZLÓ, AGE 30

"That was in 1932?"

"Yes, in the spring."

"I want to know more about that, because after all we are talking about my parents. But first, your moving back to *your* parents…"

"Well, as I said, space was very tight and they had been thinking about moving to a larger place, but they still did not have much money. So I found this apartment on Garay Street. It was not a very nice area or a very nice building, either, but the apartment was more spacious than the one on Rákóczi Boulevard. It was on the main floor – that was essential for Anyuska. It faced the street – only two front apartments faced the street; the rest, the courtyard. And most important, it had an indoor toilet and a bathroom."

"The Rákóczi Boulevard apartment did not have that?"

"No, you had to go out to the corridor. Everybody, on all floors, could see you going there. And Anyuska was already walking with a cane, later with crutches."

"And so this Garay Street apartment…"

"Only the two main-floor front apartments had en-suite toilets and bathrooms. It even had a gas boiler for making hot water for bathing. A real luxury in those days."

"It was?"

"I mean for the circumstances. After all, we had an indoor bathroom with hot water, and a toilet, in our house in Rima-Sobota. But that was different – we had been well-to-do then, now we were poor."

"So you moved there and you had your own room?"

"Yes, a very nice room for me and Gyurika, even though our room faced the courtyard. The salon and my parents' bedroom faced the street."

"And what kind of street was that?"

"Well, not the nicest. Across the street, on the other side, there was some kind of a metalwork factory or plant, I'm not sure. All I knew was that on metal beams, little pulleys ran back and forth all day."

"Interesting, I suppose."

"Boring. But Anyuska watched them."

"Why?"

"I am not sure. As she became increasingly immobile, she sat in an arm-chair by the window and read. I brought her books from the public library and she read. Then, after a while, she must have tired of reading. She would drop her book into her lap and stare out the window, watching those pulleys scurry back and forth."

"She must have been very unhappy."

"Yes, but she did not complain. She married Apuska because of his pension – well, among other reasons. But she might have been afraid that if she complained about that, about that pension having turned out a sham, I might say something about that not being the only sham that was brought to the marriage. Of course I would not have. Never."

"Because you loved her by then?"

"Yes, I did. And also because saying such a thing would not only have destroyed her, but would also have killed my father."

"So you just watched her sitting there and felt sorry for her."

"Yes, the way she sat there, my heart ached for her. She looked like some-body I once saw, a photograph of a painting, I think an American painting, an old woman sitting in a rocking chair, just as Anyuska sat, even though her chair didn't rock…"

"Yes, I know the painting you mean. And what else happened then? About my parents?"

"They got married just about the time when we moved to Garay Street."

"Was everybody pleased about that?"

"In our family, yes. You see, she came from a good background. Her family also originated in Moravia, then they lived in Óbuda for quite a few generations. They were less cultured than we were. Her father was a businessman, a real estate broker, but quite successful. And Mimi liked books and she liked music, something that was almost totally unknown in our family. She looked a little like Neckó, small and slim – they would have liked each other. Oh, and most important, in the same year, Neckó and Zoltán also married."

"In Paris?"

"Yes, in Paris. Pity that I could not possibly attend the wedding. But I went to Laci's wedding, even though my parents didn't."

"They didn't?! Why not?"

"Well, Anyuska couldn't go anywhere, of course, except for a few painful steps with her crutches. She encouraged Apuska to go, but he wouldn't go without her. Of course he might also have been bothered by the fact that we could not contribute anything at all to the cost of the wedding. It was a very big, fancy affair, in the Dohány Street synagogue, with a big dinner afterwards."

"Were there lots of people?"

LÁSZLÓ AND MIMI SZÉKELY, AT THEIR WEDDING

"Lots and lots: 150 or 200. You see, they had a large family. Mimi had a sister and four brothers. Also, both of her parents had lots of siblings. Aunts, cousins, friends. It was a very nice wedding."

"And were they also happy with Mimi's marrying Laci?"

"I am not sure. I had a feeling that they were hoping for somebody richer. They knew that Laci was an extremely handsome, highly cultured young man, loving literature, the arts, everything that was fine. But he also had expensive tastes and up to then, he couldn't very well afford them. They may have worried that he would waste the sizable dowry on luxuries."

"What kind of expensive tastes?"

"Well, for instance, Laci had to have dried figs for his breakfast. That was very expensive in those days. And other exotic fruits. He liked to travel on autobuses, where the fare was double that of streetcars. He also used taxis. He liked to eat in restaurants, go to an espresso bar after dinner."

"That doesn't sound so extravagant to me."

"No, but he also joined the Lipótvárosi Casino – it wasn't really a casino, more like a very exclusive club for Jewish intellectuals. He did play cards there, though, mainly bridge, sometimes a little poker. He won sometimes, lost at other times. His in-laws did not like that; they were not used to such things. And of course he also supported us, his parents and me."

"But he earned good money as a lawyer?"

"So-so. His father-in-law brought him lots of business. They were always suing some customer who would not pay the commission. But I think that Laci was not as tough a lawyer as they would have liked. He should never have been a lawyer, if you ask me."

"What should he have been?"

"A poet, of course. A writer, a literary critic. A philosopher."

András – 1941

I suppose it is my turn now. I was born in 1934 and my first memories are of a pleasant life with my parents in a comfortable, ultramodern apartment, at 12 Gyöngyház Street. Kindergarten was fun; they had a little puppet theater, with performances on every child's birthday. I enjoyed books – I learned to read and write and count by age three (which record was easily surpassed later by at least one of my nephews). One memory that stands out was a two-week period, when my mother had a kidney operation. My father took me to lunch in a garden restaurant, my first such experience. I did not sleep at home then. I spent one week with my maternal grandparents and the next week with my father's parents. The difference was remarkable. At my mother's parents' I had a private room, I did what I wanted, nobody took much notice of me – they were always very busy. Then, at the other grandparents', I slept in a large bed between the two of them, two loving people, and during the day Rózsám was there. She always tried to prepare my favorite dishes – hot chocolate, and raspberry pudding, and all kinds of pastries. I loved it. But I had trouble understanding why they didn't have hot water running from the tap in the bathroom. Rózsám said that if I wanted to take a bath, they could make hot water in the boiler, but that wasn't the same thing as having hot water all the time, as we had at home and as my other grandparents had, too.

Friday nights we always had dinner at the Schlesingers, with their six children, six children-in-law, and eventually numerous grandchildren. I say eventually, because I was the oldest of the ten grandchildren, my mother being the first in the family to marry. The dinner started with *Kiddush*. Then we had cold jellied carp – I particularly liked the fish eggs, *ikra*; then a goose soup with semolina dumplings; then goose confit with roast potatoes and cucumber salad, followed by compote and cake. When I got older, my grandfather insisted on taking me with him to the *shul* on Friday evenings and holidays. The *shul* was a little Orthodox place near where they lived. His wife went to the large Neolog synagogue one street away.

The Székely grandfather never took me to any *shul*, even though he went to another Neolog synagogue in a less affluent part of the city. But we had lunch there every Sunday. The lunch consisted of chicken soup, wiener schnitzel with roast potatoes and cucumber salad – this kind of food was standard in that environment – then pastry. After lunch, Apu (I called my father by that name; Mother was Anyu) went home and took a two-hour nap, while we stayed to talk and play. But not Grandfather – he read or watched us benignly. Not Grandmother, either – she sat by the window, reading or just looking out, watching the pulleys run back and forth across the street (yes, they ran on Sundays, too).

ILONA BAUER, AGE 75

What did we play? Rózsám was the play leader. She arranged dominos and card games, and most exciting of all was building card houses and castles. We also had a game of flipping empty matchboxes that were half off the edge of the table; you flipped it with one finger, it flew up and landed on the table. You got one point if it landed on its front or back, five points if it landed on its side and twenty-five for ending up on the narrowest edge. Minus points for falling on the carpet.

And we read beautiful old picture books, lovely stories about bear families and cute devils and whatnot. Now I search for these books but can't find anywhere; nobody remembers them anymore.

Then, at around four thirty in the afternoon, we had coffee or, in my case, hot chocolate, and *kugelhof*, and by that time Apu usually joined us and then took us home.

But 1940, my sixth year, was different. During our Sunday visit, the last day in March, while we were playing games between lunch and coffee, there came a croaking sound from Grandmother's chair. Everybody jumped up. Her head lay fallen as she sat there. Anyu grabbed me and hustled me into the kitchen. She told me to stay there and not move until they would come for me. She ran back. I did not know what was going on; I worried. *Something must be wrong with Grandmother*, I thought to myself. *She might even be dead.* I had no experience in such things, but I was correct. Anyu went out and knocked on the door of the other large front apartment; they were the only people in the building with a telephone. She called home from there and woke Apu. *Come quickly, big trouble.* He came by taxi. Soon I was told that Anyu would be taking me home, for Grandmother had died.

That was half a year before my sister was born. Everybody commented on how sad it was, the poor woman didn't live to see her new granddaughter. There was no ultrasound detection of the gender of a fetus, but we all knew that it would be a girl.

Meanwhile, the mood in Hungary became increasingly militant. They were still smarting over the lost territories, and now, with the increasing strength of Nazi Germany, regaining those territories seemed to be a strong possibility. All they had to do was to support the German policies, particularly vicious anti-Semitism – something that was dear to the heart of most Hungarians, anyway. Indeed, in that year, 1940, they did manage to recover some large parts of the land from Czechoslovakia, the Ukraine, and later, Romania. This necessitated military preparedness. There was a general call-up.

And so, Apu was called up to forced labor. It was decreed in Hungary that Jews were not to be trusted as members of the regular army. This despite their heroism in the first world war. Yet they could not just be left out, to continue getting rich while the Hungarians suffered. The *Hungarians*, mind you – the Jews were totally confused by that. *What, are we something else? We're just as good Hungarians as everyone else.* But no, the Hungarian Christian leadership thought otherwise. So Jewish men were conscripted to forced labor, to do the most ugly, most unpleasant, most dangerous chores. Apu was to become a rankless soldier, not even a private. Yet in this call-up – unlike the second one, two years later – they were only sent to a work camp, to labor in a stone quarry.

LÁSZLÓ SZÉKELY, AGE 40

It was hard work, but they received quite humane treatment, were considered people, not chattel. And he was demobilized before the end of that year, 1940. Why? Perhaps the reason was that by that time he had entered his fortieth year.

A good thing, too. In his letters, he mentioned that he was worried that he would not be back by the time Zsuzsika was to be born. But he was freed, as it were, in November. Zsuzsi was duly born in December. She got a second name, too: her grandmother's. She was named Zsuzsanna Ilona; in Hebrew, Shoshanna Leah. The day of her birth was one of the few when Apu voluntarily visited a synagogue, to say thanks for his daughter. In his younger days, God meant nothing to him. Now, especially after his first forced labor service, his thoughts turned to God in a surprisingly intense way. But not to *halacha*, the formal Jewish law, as we shall see.

Our apartment on Gyöngyház Street was getting crowded. Apu's clientele had shown a modest increase, so it was time to move. They found a much larger apartment on Hollán Street, in the same general area as before. This was a somewhat older building, but very elegant, with lots of marble in the hallway, large rooms, and good service. We moved in early 1941.

I think that for some reason my parents did not take the political situation seriously enough. In retrospect, it was truly awful. There were an increasing number of regulations stripping the Jews of their most basic rights. As a child, I probably thought of these as normal, if I thought of them at all, but it is hard to understand how grownups could accept such rules in a once-democratic country. Among the first such laws, Jews were limited in their participation in industry and commerce to 12 percent, in intellectual activities to 6 percent, and in civil service to 0 percent. Later laws banned Jews from owning or running any private business, and buying or owning agricultural land. Worse, they were forbidden to employ a maid, or own a radio or bicycle – they had to take these items to a central depot and simply give them to the government. It is hard to imagine such laws today, but still worse was to come.

Hungary was aligned with Hitler's Germany; yet it was widely believed that Horthy, brutal as he had been against the Jews in the beginning, had by then moderated his views and would stand up for the Jews, if needed, against the might of Germany.

The war was progressing; the German army attacked the Soviet Union in mid-1941 and by 1942 they were making significant advances toward the heart of Russia. Hungary also declared war on the Soviet Union, which meant that its army was going to support the German war effort fully. My parents expected another call-up at any moment. Perhaps secretly they thought that having passed forty would disqualify Apu, but they talked about soon being apart for a long time.

In any case, Apu had nearly two years with his family in the new apartment. He enjoyed his new daughter, his son, and his wife. They were very much in love, especially in those days; I have the letters to prove it.

My last memory of my father was of him covering all of our linen window shades (even though there were also wooden shutters behind them) with dark paper, so light would not filter out to the street at night – it was punishable as treason. He also covered half of our living room chandelier lights with green cellophane foil, for the same purpose. Separate switches controlled each half of the chandelier, allowing us to turn on only the dimmed lights at air-raid time. These were great achievements by Apu, as he was totally untalented in mechanical and household chores; I am certain that he would not have known how to hold a screwdriver in his hands.

The call-up came in October; he went. First, he was stationed in a small town not far from Budapest; Anyu was allowed to visit him once. Then Apu wrote one short letter, asking her to bring certain things on her next visit, particularly sweets and bacon! Real, all-fat Hungarian bacon with paprika. He may have loved his God, but he was certainly not a religious man. Heading into the frigid Russian winter, he knew that having a large piece of bacon, whether to eat or barter, could save his life.

Anyu was told that she could come for a second visit, late in November, but when she and the other wives got there they found the men already in a freight train just leaving for the Ukraine and Russia. Unfortunately Apu's letter telling her not to come had not reached her in time.

Apu sent one letter from Russia in December, as they were approaching their destination – Voronezh, as it turned out – and a brief note in March, as he was walking back toward Kiev, after the Hungarian army was annihilated in January at the Don river. This note was written on the back of a medical document that he had obtained the previous October, attesting to various spots found on his lungs. The note was probably a vain last-minute attempt to avoid the call-up, though it possibly reflected a real condition – Apu was a heavy smoker. In any case, there was no longer any need for the document, and he had no other paper to write on.

After that, a notice came, and then a letter and a poem…

My Father's Letters

From the Camp, Just Before Leaving for the Russian Front

Musi, my dear angel, goodbye! Now, when it has become certain that we are starting out on that road from which return is a big question – and if there is a return, how and when is still unclear – I want to take leave once more from you, who are my everything. On Friday we are leaving for the front.

I consider my life finished. You know me, I have never had secrets from you. You know that I was strong, I am not worried about myself now. I want to return and I shall return to all of you, for my place is beside you. And if this parting is tearful, that is not for me but for you. I know that once you said I don't love anybody – I have loved, better than my life, you and our two dear children.

My balance: forty-one years. What was bad in those, I have forgotten. I only remember that I had so much happiness that others probably do not have in a life twice as long. If I return, my life will be a gift, only for you. If I don't return, accept the decision of God calmly.

My Musi, we have spent ten happy years together. Everything that was beautiful, that was good, I owe to you, and now, when preparing my balance, I know that I have not paid for it. I want to keep living only so that I should live for the three of you.

Take care of our children and tell them that their father loved them very, very much.

With hugs and kisses to all three of you,
Your father
Egreskáta, Nov. 24, 1942

From the Russian Front

My dear little mother, finally I have an opportunity to send you a sign of life. I am well, have had no illness and I hope that I shall not have any in the future, either. I am longing for you all, that is my only, but very big trouble.

I wish all the best, belatedly, for my father's birthday. A thousand kisses for him and also for Rózsi. Our Zsuzsika has become two years old. I think a lot about her, about Andris, I am sending kisses to them.

I don't know when you'll get news from me again, so I wish you now – with me – a happy new year, in my thought I shall be with you on our wedding anniversary, too.

We have got to be immeasurably distant from each other, yet every evening

I am with the three of you. If I close my eyes, I see you, I am with you. Think of me a lot, all of you, also, love and ask God to lead me back to you before long.

As soon as possible, I shall write, and when there will be postal service again and the possibility to send parcels, do send me some little things, particularly sweets.

Our friends are all well. I shall visit, if possible, the gravesite of Kalman.

Don't count on another letter or card from me soon, the opportunities for that are very rare – we have not yet reached our destination and are still on the road.

A thousand kisses for all of you – I live only for you.

Your father

Dec. 16.

Brief Hand-Delivered Note from the Russian Front

To Mrs. László Székely

9 Hollán Street, II. 3.

Budapest, V.

My dear little one, please pay two hundred pengős to the one delivering these lines to you. I have already received its value.

Dr. László Székely

March 23, 1943

My dear Musi, I still cannot write – we march and hope that it will lead toward home. I am thinking of the three of you all the time and only the knowledge that you are waiting for me gives me strength. A thousand kisses for you, Andris and Zsuzsi, together and one by one.

Your father

Official Notice from Kiev

To Mrs. László Székely

9 Hollán Street

Budapest V.

I respectfully inform you that Dr. László Székely, forced laborer (born Rima-Sobota, Nov. 13, 1901; mother's name: Ilona Bauer) died on April 14, 1943. Cause of death: typhoid fever.

With excellent respects,

Dr. [illegible]

Military doctor

109. Mobile military hospital

April 16, 1943

Letter from the Kiev Hospital,
Received a Week or Two After the Death Notice

My Musi! I have not seen you in four months, have heard no news about you. It is horrible to bear this!

I'll tell you briefly what has happened to me. If there is hell on earth, I have crossed it. I got to know all the horror of the winter and of human depravity – I shall not go into details. I was never in direct personal danger, but I was cold, I starved and I have even learned how to beg for alms.

We reached our destination after walking 180 km. There we stayed for three weeks. Then the great retreat started, and since then we have been marching westward, so far I have walked 750 km. We had no field mail service, nor do we have now. That's why I could not have written or received letters.

I have practically nothing left, I ate it all. The prices are fantastic and my appetite is excellent.

Now our only concern is, do we go home? For me – I feel – this is the last chance to get home. Lately, nostalgia has taken such a gigantic role in my mind that were they to keep me here, my nerves could not stand it.

I had seen the essence of this journey wonderfully clearly, when we parted, yet I was just as wonderfully blind regarding the details of it.

I wrote the attached poem to Andris, back when we were in the freight car. I think a lot of Zsuzsi, she must speak fluently by now. I love all of you very much.

I have lost my glasses and therefore I am spending a few days now at the Kiev hospital. I am healthy, I have no problems.

I have met here Sali Krausz. He is arranging for this letter to get home. Ernő Forgács is here, too. Tell his mother that he is healthy.

[Left half of the last page is missing.]

> *…is here, healthy*
> *…Karcsi Edinger. yester-*
> *…direction – on foot.*
> *…I fell behind*

> *…to write down this honestly*
> *…all of you, – always of that*
> *…I should be, if*
> *…involved in a report*
> *…– and all of you – are*

> *…any more; never forget*
> *…your… Pray for me.*

László's Poem to Andris

Letter to My Son

In a distant, in a strange land
With his tears shed, forgetting not
Every evening, every morning
Father thinks of you!

> *In Russia, in that strange land*
> *Sitting in a rolling freight car*
> *Sorrowfully, full of worry*
> *Father thinks of you!*

His eyes teary, his heart bleeding
He mutters and they can't hear him.
They will not ask why he grieves so –
Father thinks of you!

> *Oh where does his journey take him?*
> *Who would know that but God Himself*
> *Who in your ear whispers nightly:*
> *Father thinks of you!*

In Budapest, in the distance
Your little heart never forget!
Ask the Lord morning and evening
That back to you He should lead him,
Who lives for you, struggles for you,
Father, who loves you.

Informing Rózsám – 1944

A distant relative from my mother's side was dispatched to notify Rózsám. Her name was Bebu (Bella, really), and she had met Rózsám on one previous occasion.

She rang the bell. Rózsám answered.

"Mrs. Szemere? Good morning. You may remember me, we met when Zsuzsika was born. I am Bella, Bözsi's sister. You know, Laci Szamosi's wife, Bözsi?"

"Yes, of course I remember. Don't they call you Bebu?"

"Yes, that is my nickname."

Rózsám looked at her, an elegant woman dressed rather somberly, and a shiver ran through her body. Why was she here now?

Strange that Bebu would not speak. "Is there anything wrong?" Rózsám asked her then.

"Can we talk where we are not overheard?"

"Nobody hears us here, but if you would like to come in…"

"No, no, this will be fine. I am afraid that I have some bad news for you."

"Gyurika…?"

"No, Laci. Your brother."

Rózsám almost screamed. "He is dead!"

Bebu nodded.

Rózsám collapsed. Bebu squatted beside her, shook her, helped her to her feet.

"Maybe your father should not be told?"

Rózsám started to cry. Between her tears, she ushered Bebu to the kitchen, bade her to sit. She sat down, too, and the sobs shook her body. Bebu hugged her and tried to calm her. It took a long time before she could talk to her.

"Mimi got a card from a hospital in Kiev. He died there of typhoid fever."

More crying, more shaking of her body. Finally, Bebu could repeat her earlier suggestion. "Don't you think that your father should not be told? At least not yet?"

"He must not be told! Not now, not ever. It would kill him."

"Yes, that's what we thought. That's why they sent me, to tell only to you. Is he at home now?"

"Yes, he is in the salon reading the newspaper."

"He will not come out here, will he?"

"He might."

"Could you manage to just open the door and say that a friend of yours stopped by and you shall be with her for a little while? But don't let him see your face."

Rózsám just shook her head, sobbing.

"Please, try. Force yourself to tell him cheerfully, that you will be out for some minutes."

Finally, Rózsám did as she was told. She came back, and Bebu asked her, "Will you let me make a tea for you? For both of us?"

"No, I shall make it." She made tea for both of them.

They drank in silence for a while.

Then Rózsám asked, "Will everybody keep the secret?"

"Yes, Mimi and Andris and even little Zsuzsi."

"Andris! Zsuzsika!" And her tears started again. "Orphans! Little orphans! What will become of them?"

Bebu patted her hand. "Everybody will help them. They will be all right."

"And Mimi. A widow!"

"Yes, indeed." Bebu's eyes were not dry either.

"What will become of all of them?" she repeated her question.

"They will be all right. She has brothers and a sister, parents, lots of relatives. They will be looked after." Bebu wondered if this were true.

"How can I keep this from Apuska?"

"I seem to recall that you said, when we met, that you were an actress once. You will have to act, behave normally, and then you will cry in your bed at night."

But Rózsám cried right there. After a while, Bebu spoke. "Tell me, what about your son?"

Rózsám started sobbing again. "I got a letter from him last week. He was also on the Russian front, but he is heading home. Walking. But I don't know where he is now. I hope he's all right."

"I'm sure that he is. Strong, young man, surely?"

"Well, he is young. I don't know if he is that strong…"

"He will be all right." Bebu repeated her assurance; Rózsám needed it.

"You know, he was in Paris last year," Rózsám told Bebu. "He visited his sister. Neckó. He stayed with Neckó and Zoltán, her husband."

"And he came back?"

"Neckó did not want to let him come back, she knew what was happening here. But Gyuri was in love with a girl, a Hungarian aristocrat's daughter, and when she came back to Hungary, he wanted to follow her. Neckó begged him not to go, but he said that he would be all right. A soon as he got here, they took him to forced labor." More tears.

Bebu raised still another subject. "Tell me, what newspaper does your father read?"

"He reads the *Esti Kurir*. Why?"

"Because there will have to be an announcement. It will be in the *Magyar Nemzet* tomorrow. Make sure that he does not see it."

Rózsám nodded, cried a little more. Bebu stood up, hugged and kissed her one last time, and left.

The Jewish Building – 1944

"Rózsám, let us talk some more."

"Andriskám, of course. What should we talk about?"

"Those bad days, in 1944."

"Horrible days. One law after another against the Jews. First we could not have a radio. Or a bicycle, not that I wanted one. Or a maid. I had not had a maid in a long time, but Mimi had a maid, and now she had to send her away. Then it got worse."

"Tell me."

"We had to wear a yellow star on our coats when we went out."

"Yes, I remember that."

"Of course you do, you were already nine years old."

"Yes, I remember many of those things, but not as an adult. So tell me more."

"The Jews were rounded up in all smaller towns and villages, really everywhere in the country except Budapest. Not yet."

"So you were lucky to live in Budapest."

"If you can call that luck. Perhaps it would have been better if they just took me to Auschwitz, like they took so many others. I would never have come back; it would have been easier…"

"Don't say such things. Life is always better than death."

"No, not always. If I knew everything, if I knew what was coming, it would have been so much better to end it all sooner."

"Well, tell me what happened."

"You remember, Andriska, that in October of 1944, they brought in a new rule that said that Jews could only live in certain apartment buildings, Jewish buildings. Ours was not such a building, but yours was. So it was decided that we should move into your apartment. It was large enough – now that Lacikám was gone, and the maid was sent away, only Mimi lived there and the two of you. So we left all our furniture at Garay Street in the care of some friends and moved over to Hollán Street."

"As simple as that?"

"No, it was not so simple. Do you know why?"

"Why?"

"Because we all knew that the brass plate on the street, in front of the main gate, had been changed."

"Yes, I know, but do tell."

"It used to say 'Dr. László Székely, Lawyer.' But then it had to be changed, so the new brass plate said 'The Widow of Dr. László Székely.'"

"Yes."

"But we couldn't let Apuska see that plate! Well, in the end we hired the janitor to stand there and wash the signs and hide them with his body while we were moving in."

"Did that work?"

"Yes, it did."

"But what about later? When he would go out and come back alone?"

"We did not want him to go out alone. For one thing, he did not want to wear the yellow star, he found that too insulting. So we agreed that I should do all the shopping with Mimi and he would just stay in with the children."

"And he never did go out?"

"Only once."

"Once? Where? How?"

"I didn't know, I was busy with the laundry and Mimi went to her parents'. Apparently, Apuska wanted a newspaper and he decided to go without bothering me. He put on his overcoat with the yellow star on it, despite his hurt dignity, and went out."

"And did he notice that brass plate?"

"It was not that…"

Insulted – 1944

Bernát went down the stairs and wondered if the superintendent would be willing to operate the elevator for him when he came back. He went out to the street and turned left, toward St. István Boulevard; he remembered there being a newsstand there.

The boulevard was about two hundred meters from the house, so he got there in under ten minutes. He walked with a cane those days. He looked at the stores on Hollán Street; most of them were closed. They used to be owned by Jews. After they were evicted, Christians took them over and drove them to bankruptcy in a matter of weeks.

There were many posters on the walls. Most of them were issued by the ruling Arrow Cross Party; their logo, a green arrow-topped cross, was ubiquitous on posters, storefronts, and newspapers. The posters all seemed to warn the Jews against doing any activities that made living possible. No work, no possessions, no freedom to go anywhere. No maids, no radios, no living in most buildings.

He reached the boulevard and after some hesitation, turned right toward the Danube. It was just one block away and there was indeed a news kiosk there before the bridge. He reached it and asked for a *Magyar Nemzet*. He paid for it and started to walk back, away from the river.

Four youths came toward him, in ragtag clothing resembling some uniform. Each was wearing the hat – a hybrid of a hat and a cap – of the Arrow Cross. None of them could be more than eighteen. They were laughing loudly, and when they saw Bernát, they stopped and stared at him.

They were directly in front of him. He moved to the left, toward the wall, to pass them by, but they also moved in that direction, so he was forced to stop. They kept staring and said nothing.

Bernát didn't know what to do. Should he talk to them? Ask them to get out of his way?

But then one of the Arrow Cross youths – they called them Nyilas in Hungarian – spoke. "Where are you going, Jew?"

To talk to him like that! But he decided to reply politely. "I am going home."

"And where is that home? Palestine?"

"No, here on Hollán Street."

"Hollán Street is not your home, Jew. Do you know why not?"

Bernát did not answer.

"I'll tell you why not, Jew. Because Hollán Street is the home of Magyars. Good Magyars, not dirty, stinking Jews, like you."

Bernát's blood was boiling. He started to formulate an answer, but then another Nyilas spoke. "Ya, stinking Jew, get out of our land! This is the land of Hungarians, not Jews. We'll show you, we're gonna shoot you into the Danube."

And they all grinned. That was enough for him.

"Where did your ancestors come from?"

"What?" one asked, his face registering shock.

"I'll tell you where," Bernát continued. "Seventy percent of the Magyars have ancestors from the Slavic lands. Many of them have no Magyar ancestors at all. They are all Kuns, Palocz, Wallachs, Serbs, Slovaks, Rutenians, Germans. I am willing to bet that your ancestors were not Magyars at all."

"Dirty Jew!" one shouted at him.

"While my ancestors have been living in Hungary for three, four generations. Probably more than yours. And don't forget that there have been Jews living here for a thousand years and more. The Kabars came in with the original Magyars to the Carpathian basin in the year 897. They were a Jewish tribe, the allies of the Magyar tribes. And we have been better Hungarians than you, ever since. What do you know of Hungarian culture? Did you study the language of the poets? Can you recite a poem by Vörösmarty? By Arany? Berzsenyi? Come, recite one. Any of you. Recite a poem."

They stared at him in disbelief. Then the youngest Nyilas – he could not have been more than fifteen – raised his hand and slapped Bernát's cheek. He slapped him hard, and then he slapped his other cheek, too. Then he spat on him and they all laughed. They knocked him to the ground, roaring with laughter as he fell, and then walked away.

A man and a woman came over and helped him stand up. "Are you all right?" they asked him. "Is anything broken?"

He couldn't answer.

"Try walking," the man said, and helped him take a few steps. Bernát did manage to walk and registered half consciously that nothing was broken. They handed him his cane and he started to walk home. His newspaper was somewhere on the ground; nobody bothered to give it to him. He limped on.

When he got to the building, he saw the brass plates under the gate, but they did not register in his brain. Yet perhaps they did, for later he had a vision that bothered him. He kept thinking that somewhere he had seen a sign that said "The Widow of Dr. László Székely." But that came later, days later.

He rang for the superintendent, to take him up on the elevator. The man came and saw him with his yellow star, his dirty clothes and torn pants. He turned away and went back to his apartment. Bernát stood there; then he rang again. Nobody came.

He started to walk up the stairs. It was two flights, forty-six steps in all. He had to stop four times, but eventually he reached the apartment. He rang and Rózsám opened the door.

"Apuska! Where have you been?! I was so worried." He went in, but did not answer. Rózsám helped him with his coat, hung it up, put the stick in the corner and tried to remove some of the dirt from his clothes. Meanwhile, she kept badgering him with questions. "But where were you? Why did you go down alone? What happened to you?"

Finally, when he was sitting in an armchair, he managed to say a few words. "He slapped me."

"Who? Somebody slapped you? Who?"

"An insolent boy, a rascal. A Nyilas."

"A Nyilas slapped you?"

"I was trying to explain to him and the others that we belonged here at least as much as they did. He did not understand a word. He slapped me, twice. And then they knocked me down to the ground."

"Oh my God. But you did not break anything?"

"No, I did not. Otherwise I could not have walked back here alone."

"Oh, Apuska!" She hugged him and cried. "What should we do? What should I do? Do you want a tea? What would you like?"

"I don't want anything."

"Do change your clothes, and I'll see if I can fix them. I'll make a tea meanwhile. Not a real tea," she added apologetically. "A Planta tea. But it's very good."

"He slapped me."

"I know, Apuska. But it will be good for you if you change and then drink a tea."

Bernát was shaking his head. He said nothing more that day, but kept shaking his head.

The Ghetto – 1945

"Oh Rózsám, it must have been horrible. He was such a dignified man."

"That was one of the worst things that could have happened to him. Being slapped by a young brute like that. He never got over that day."

"Not that life was so pleasant otherwise?"

"Life was awful. Let me tell you about those days."

"Yes, and what happened afterwards. All the way, to the end."

"His end."

"Yes."

"All right. Well, I was worried that he might have seen that brass plate under the gate, but apparently he had been too upset to notice it. Yet later he made a few comments that made me wonder. Still, for a week or two nothing changed. And then you went away. You and Zsuzsika and Mimi, too."

"Yes, you remember that the Nyilas wanted to take Anyu away, along with all the young women, but she came back up for something she had forgotten and then she hid for some days and paid a lot of money to the superintendent to let her out. So my mother's brother Laci got us into a Red Cross orphanage. Anyu got a job there, and we stayed there for a few weeks. When that became dangerous, Laci procured some false documents for us and we hid as Christians for the duration of the war."

"He hid the entire Schlesinger family, but not us. Not Apuska or me."

"No, but you were in less danger than the others, because you were already not that young."

"Less danger? The old people from the next building in the ghetto were marched to the Danube and then shot into the icy water, one by one. Tens of thousands of people were shot into the Danube."

"Yes, I know that. The grandfather of Jutka, my wife, was shot into the Danube on December sixth. And they murdered six hundred thousand Hungarian Jews."

"It could have been more. They wanted to ship the entire ghetto to the death camps at Auschwitz and Birkenau and Bergen-Belsen and Mauthausen, but they ran out of time. That's why they marched so many people to the Danube."

"Then you were lucky not to be among those. You and your father."

"You call that luck? Perhaps it would have been better for both of us. And he did not live much longer, anyway."

"I know, Rózsám, but you did. Tell me, how did you get to the ghetto in the first place?"

"The building where we were, where you lived, was first just a Jewish building. Then it became one of the Swiss-protected apartment houses. Then that wasn't good enough, so Laci tried to get it Spanish protection, but by the time he managed that we were already taken into the ghetto. There we lived in a cramped apartment, thirty people in three small rooms. And we had very little food – at the end almost nothing. If you had lots of jewelry, you could still obtain some food, but I ran out of jewelry long before the end."

"How long were you in the ghetto?"

"Almost two months. From the end of November to January. We were liberated by mid-January, and before long we went back to our own apartment. But Apuska had to be carried – he was too weak to walk – and we still had no food."

"When we first managed to come and find you…"

"It was too late by then."

"Not that we had any food, either. Anyu managed to exchange all of Apu's clothes for three turnips. That's what we ate for weeks."

"We did not even have turnips. And meanwhile I worried about my Gyurika."

"Why, did you learn anything new about him?"

"Yes, somebody brought news that he had arrived back in Hungary, he was about to get out of the forced labor and he would be coming home soon."

"That must have been exciting."

"It was very exciting. But then he did not come."

"Do you know why?"

"No, I don't know. Some think that the Russians got him and shipped him back to Siberia. Others think that the Germans took him at the last minute. I waited and waited. Nothing. So from that time on I spent years looking for him."

"Where did you look for him?"

"Mainly by people who knew about such things."

"What things?"

"You know, things that are hidden from ordinary view. They can talk to those who are gone and who have a better view."

"What, you mean spiritualists?!"

"Women who can talk to the dead. There were many of us there – she could hardly accommodate all of us. Everybody was looking for somebody, a son, a husband. Sometimes a person came and talked to us, somebody who died alongside one of the missing ones. He could tell us a lot about our sons."

"A séance."

"Yes."

"And did you learn anything about Gyuri that way?"

"I did, but in the end none of it was true. He never came back."

"Rózsám, you still cry. Don't cry, now it is all right. Now you shall soon see him. All of them. Gyuri and Apu and Andor and everybody."

"May God grant me that."

"And your father, of course."

"Those last days were so sad. I knew they were the last days, that he was finished. We had nothing to eat but a little stale bread and chicory coffee. We had a little milk powder and also some saccharin for a while, so I could at least sweeten it, and I soaked the stale bread in the coffee. So-called coffee. Every time he asked for something to eat, I made a little chicory coffee and soaked bread, so that he could eat it. Then the bread ran out, so it was only chicory coffee…"

Epilogue – 2002

"Grandfather, I have learned many things about your life and I am writing it all down. This book will be mainly about you. Well, you and your family."

"You have got all of it? To the end?"

"All that I could get hold of. Not all the information is available, but most of it is. You had a good life, a fantastically good life."

"Good life? Why do you say that? Why was it so good?"

"Because you lived it as a man must live. Honestly, lovingly, dutifully, bravely, to the best of your abilities, and they were considerable."

"Don't you mean naïvely, pitifully, miserably, perhaps even ridiculously?"

"Of course not. How could you say such things?"

"Because I suspect that that is the truth."

"But why, Grandfather?"

"Because I was a naïve man. And everybody took advantage of me."

"No, don't say that. You were not naïve, only sincere, honest, and expected everyone else to be such. Just as the poet said…"

"I was not crafty, scheming. I trusted people, I trusted the nation, my fellow citizens, and they all took advantage of me."

"Well, some certainly did…"

"Everybody did. Almost everybody. They all lied to me, all cheated me."

"You exaggerate."

"Yes? Well, let me recount. Start with the family. Ilona and her parents cheated me, lied to me…"

"About her…"

"Yes, about her brother. I have no proof, but I am sure that when Andor killed himself, it was not because of a momentary mental confusion. He had a good reason, and nobody ever told me what that reason was. I could guess, there are two or three probabilities – they're all ugly."

"Well, I couldn't say. Maybe you're right. But so what?"

"Then, near the end, there was Laci. Your father. He died on the Russian front and nobody told me. Everybody lied to me."

"But it was so much better that way, Grandfather."

"Ah, so now you admit it. There, I knew it. Everybody lied to me, it was a conspiracy."

"Yes, it was."

"Now, the nation. They all lied to me. They promised me a pension when I was to retire, and they gave me toy money instead."

"True, but the circumstances were such that—"

"Circumstances? But they could provide good jobs to others, so they could at least house themselves decently and have enough clothes and food. Not to me. And when I say *me*, I mean *me, the Jew*. Not just Bernát Steiner. *The Jew*."

"That is quite true."

"And they said that they wanted me, *the Jew*, to be a true Hungarian, to become a Magyar. They needed more Magyars. So I did become one. I loved the country; I was the best Magyar there was. I improved the land, I built on it, I created industry and commerce and transportation. I built bridges and schools and places of culture. I subsidized the major poets and playwrights and composers. I was the greatest promoter of Hungarian culture abroad. I was proud to be a Hungarian and I gave up all idealistic longing for a Jewish state. Yet that would have saved me. No, I had to be a good Magyar, and when they no longer needed me, they threw me out and robbed me of my rights and my possessions and my life. I was faithful and loyal and I was punished for it. Am I right?"

"Yes, Grandfather. But I remain proud of you – you as Bernát Steiner, you as *the Jew* – very proud. And believe me, it was not in vain. The next generation has learned its lesson and knows what to do. We don't need them anymore. Goodbye now. I know that I shall see you again, in a different world, before long."

Selected Descendants of Moses Steiner

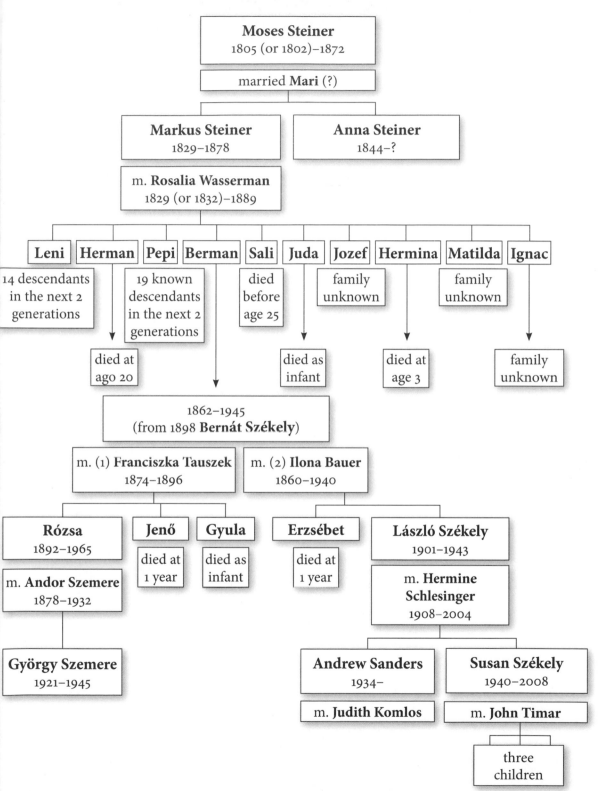

Glossary

B'ezras Hashem: with God's help

bar mitzva: the initiatory ceremony occurring when a Jewish boy reaches his thirteenth birthday, thereby becoming obligated in the commandments

bentch: recite the grace after meals

bima: synagogue platform, upon which the Torah scroll is placed during services

bris mila: circumcision ceremony

chazan: cantor

cheder: a small religious school for Jewish boys, focusing on Talmud study

Chevra Kadisha: religious burial society

chochem: smart aleck (lit., wise person)

daven: pray

El moleh rachamim: memorial service for the dead

goyim: gentiles

Gut Shabbes: May you have a good Sabbath (a traditional Sabbath greeting)

halacha: Jewish law

havdala: ceremony marking the end of the Sabbath

Kabbalas Shabbes: prayer service welcoming the Sabbath

Kaddish: prayer recited over the dead

kashrut: Jewish dietary laws

Kedusha: communal prayer recited at the conclusion of the *Amida*. The *Amida*, recited privately, functions as the climax of every prayer service.

kehila: community

Kiddush: blessing recited over wine at the start of Sabbath and holiday meals

Maariv: evening prayers

matzo, matzes: unleavened bread, traditionally eaten on the Passover holiday

mazel tov: a congratulatory expression (lit., good luck)

mechitza: divider separating the men and women during prayer services

Mincha: afternoon prayers

minyan: quorum of at least ten men, traditionally required for communal Jewish prayer

Mishebeirach: prayer for particular individuals or groups of people, particularly the sick

mitzves: commandments

mohel: one performing a circumcision

Mussaf: the additional prayer service, recited on the Sabbath and holidays

parve: the status of food that is neither dairy nor meat

Pesach: Passover

Rosh Hashono: Jewish New Year

Shabbes: the Sabbath

Shacharis: morning prayers

shadchen, shadchanim: matchmaker(s)

shamash: community servant, generally responsible for the synagogue's upkeep

Shavuos: Jewish holiday celebrating receiving the Torah, occurring in the springtime

sheitel: wig

"Shema Yisrael, Adonai Eloheinu, Adonai echad": "Hear O Israel, the Lord is our God, the Lord is one"; principle of faith recited thrice daily by traditional Jews

shiva: weeklong period of mourning

shochet: ritual slaughterer

shul: synagogue

treif: not kosher, according to Jewish dietary laws

Yom Kippur: Day of Atonement

yontef: holiday